THE WAR ETERNAL

DEATH'S BEATING HEART

ROB J. HAYES

FOR ALL THOSE WE'VE LOST
ALONG THE WAY

PROLOGUE

WE LIVE IN PROPHETIC TIMES. I AM SURE EVERY bard throughout history has said the same thing. Our age is different, more impactful. The destiny of our futures, and the legacy of our pasts hangs in the balance. Our heroes are mightier than all those who have come before. Our villains more devilish, sinister, destructive. The stakes are the highest they have ever been. The consequences more devastating.

What a pile of shit.

We are living in an apocalypse set in motion by my daughter. Sirileth brought one of our moons down on us. She killed thousands. But she saved the world. Yes, she also opened it to a new threat, but well… that is what the stories never tell you. There is no happy solution to every problem. There are actions, and there are consequences. Could Sirileth have done it another way? Maybe. But who is to say it would have turned out better? And who gets to decide what better means?

It was perhaps my fault. I will admit to that much, at least. I abandoned Sirileth when she needed me most. Left her, a young girl, to rule a queendom in my stead. To fight a war she never asked for. I ran away because I could not stop the momentum of my own reputation. The Corpse Queen could never die while I still lived, so I vanished. It was unfair of me. To heap such responsibility upon the shoulders of my daughter. My sister, Imiko, raised Sirileth as best she could in my stead, but Imiko was never one to take a firm hand. It was my fault. For not being there when I was needed. For not raising my daughter as I should have. And for shielding her from too much of the truth.

When someone started tearing open new scars in the reality of our world, Imiko came to find me. Of course Sirileth was the culprit. Forcing people into Source rejection so they would release a catastrophic combination of wild magics that ripped open holes in Ovaeris. If only I had understood at the time why my daughter was doing it, perhaps I could have found another way to… but no. Sirileth was always smarter than me. If she couldn't find another way then there was no other way to be found.

I chased my youngest daughter across half of Ovaeris, desperate to find her, to stop her. I thought she was planning to rip open the great rift above the Polasian desert. To allow the Maker, the being that birthed our gods, to flop through and devour our world. I didn't understand.

When I finally caught up with my daughter, it was too late. No. That is an excuse. I chose to take her side. I chose to believe in Sirileth. She assured me she was doing the right thing, and I trusted her. I had no idea, at the time, of what she was planning.

Sirileth ripped our twin moons apart, pulled Lursa down from her orbit and through the great rift. The Sourcery suppressing ore contained within the moon reset the rift, pushing the Maker back into its own realm. She saved us all. Then the moon crashed into Polasia and… well, I guess we still have to deal with the consequences of that.

I was not expecting Imiko to sacrifice herself. She swallowed an Impomancy Source and stepped into the reset rift. Her catastrophic breakdown redirected the giant portal to Sevorai, the Other World. The other half of our world. Two sides of the same coin, united at last. The first stable portal to Sevorai. And all it cost was my little sister's life. The price was too fucking high.

Judgement is a pedestal held up by the twin pillars of context and perspective. I needed to start at the end of my story to provide you with the perspective. But I must also go back to the start, because without everything that led up to it, without understanding the decisions we made and those that were made for us, you will not have the context needed to pass judgement.

As has been made abundantly clear, I am not qualified, nor unbiased enough to render a verdict myself. And so, I give you everything you need. Context. Perspective. The truth as I see it, as I lived through it. I leave you to form your own opinion.

Did Sirileth do the right thing? The just thing? The conscionable thing? And know this, understand this. There is a difference between being on the right side of morality, and the right side of history.

CHAPTER ONE

SHADOWY WINGS CARRIED ME THROUGH THE great rift into Sevorai. The Other World. Created by the Djinn, populated by the Rand with monsters and nightmares pulled straight from terran imagination. I had never been to Sevorai, not physically, only ever as a psychic projection of myself. I was not prepared for the experience.

In many ways Sevorai is a dim reflection of Ovaeris. Colours are less vibrant, the air is thinner and cooler, the sky is endlessly grey. The ground appears rocky and barren of life, though that is a lie. It is actually teeming, but the grass often mimics the rock around it, and the trees do not leaf or flower, but are skeletal things with bleached white claws for branches. Many have needles that are sharp as razors.

Look again, Eska, Ssserakis said in my head. After so long apart hearing my horror's voice in my head was like music. Discordant, screeching music, but music all the same.

We floated down to a rocky outcropping a few hundred paces from the rift. I staggered when we touched down, my feet unsteady and my body exhausted even with the strength my ancient horror was lending me. My wings faded as Ssserakis retreated inside my shadow and I immediately turned back to stare at the portal, back into Ovaeris. The rift fizzed at the edges like foam washing up on a beach. Beyond it, I saw only the swirling orange storm Sirileth had created when she crashed our moon onto our world. I could see nothing of my daughters.

They will be fine, Eska. Look down.

I did. I saw grey rock, brown grass, shapes wriggling through the foliage. There were tufts of something like orange moss clinging to the side of the cliff face below. Beyond that, on the stony ground, I saw small animals darting through the undergrowth nestling in the shade of the cliff. A river flowed in the vast canyon below, the waters dark and murky, the rapids white and crashing. Near the base of the cliff, the river fell into a fathomless crack that split the ground.

"What am I looking at, Ssserakis?" I asked.

You have been to my world before with your magic. What looks different?

"Just tell me." Ssserakis always did like to lead me to conclusions rather than point them out to me. I had not time for it. I was worried about my daughters back in Ovaeris.

My world is not as populated as yours, Eska. Yet it teems with insignificant life, too primitive to provide anything but scraps of fear.

It is a strange truth that sentient peoples fear differently than beasts and insects. Or perhaps we just fear more intensely. Whichever it is, I long ago learned that Ssserakis liked the taste of more complicated fear. But that was not what my horror was getting at. I had been to Sevorai before through use of Impomancy. It was a mostly barren place with pockets of life in large acropolises, across expansive plains, in jungles made of bone and caves made of glass. But close to the rift, it was thronging with foliage, undergrowth, minor beasts, insects, flies, snails, odd beetles with oversized horns. Everywhere I looked was life.

"Is it because of the portal?"

No. It was like this before you opened the way to your world. They are fleeing, Eska.

"Fleeing what?"

The Beating Heart of Sevorai.

"Norvet Meruun?"

I will show you.

My shadow twisted, wings bursting from my back again. Ssserakis gave them a single beat and then another and we lifted off. We had never been able to fly before, only glide, but something was different now. Perhaps it was because we were physically in Sevorai, but Ssserakis was more real, less insubstantial.

We flew swiftly along, climbing higher into the featureless sky. My body ached from the strain and my limbs dangled uselessly like a pup picked up by the scruff of its neck. Below, the world passed by in a dizzying blur of greys and browns. The occasional splash of a more vivid colour where beasts and monsters darted about. I saw a copse of creakers crawling between a forest of bone-white trees. They were moving towards the portal. Fleeing, as Ssserakis had said.

What has happened since we parted? How have our daughters grown so? Why are you so frail?

"You've been gone twenty years, Ssserakis." In truth, we had been separated for far longer than we were ever together. But there was a rightness to our reunion. Like I had found the missing part of myself. A friend once lost and now found, the presence both comforting and easy. But even that was too separate a distinction. We weren't friends. Ssserakis and I were closer than that. In each other we had found completeness. Two souls resonating as one. Stronger, more harmonious.

Is that a long time?

I laughed and the wind took my breath away. Ssserakis beat our wings a little harder, not understanding my sudden joy. Of course an immortal being with no body or age hadn't any concept of time.

"Twenty years is a very long time, Ssserakis. Especially for me." I was an old woman. I had only been alive for maybe forty years, but the Chronomancy had wreaked its terrible curse upon me. Back in the Pit, so long ago now, when I was fighting Josef I swallowed a Chronomancy Source. The rejection had hit hard and fast and in one minute I aged ten years. That was bad enough. But I had somehow absorbed some of the Chronomancy just as I had the Arcstorm and Geomancy. That innate Chronomancy continued to age me unnaturally fast. Alive for just forty years, but in the body of woman closer to seventy.

"Sirileth said she could feel you, Ssserakis. She's always known about you. What did you do to her?"

Ssserakis was silent for a while. I heard the leathery beat of our wings, watched the grey world zip by below. Saw a pack of khark hounds nipping at a yurthammer's legs. The yurthammer belched out steaming orange fire, but the pack split and nimbly dodged away before dashing back in to harry the monster some more. Then we were past them.

I spoke to her. When she was a part of you. I showed her my world.

Is there any wonder Sirileth turned out how she did? Before she was born, my horror tormented her with visions of a world formed of nightmares. I was supposed to keep her warm and safe. But I was never warm inside with Ssserakis possessing me. I could not protect her from myself.

Our daughter is stronger than you give her credit for, Eska. I did not break her, only showed her what she deserved to see. Sevorai is as much her world as Ovaeris. She is mine as much as yours.

I considered that. Ssserakis might not have had any hand in creating nor raising Sirileth, but it had been with me the entire time I carried her. As closely bonded as we were, maybe it did make Ssserakis a parent to Sirileth. Certainly, she never knew her father. I barely knew the man. I wondered if my horror had filled that void.

Such foolish concepts. Parents. The child is yours and the child is mine.

"She's not a child anymore."

Below us, a wide plain streaked with deep crevices stretched out for as far as I could see. Patches of pale shrubberies clung to the soil here and there, but the cracks in the ground were too common, like veins of fat in abban steak. I saw the start of a great skeleton. Small, at first, though perspective made that a lie. It was massive. A monstrous skull like that of a tiger but elongated and much much bigger. The skeleton stretched behind it like a serpent, winding along, ribs and bones buried half in the dirt and half reaching for the sky, all the flesh long since eaten away.

At places, the skeleton had fallen into the crevices, but it was so long and large I found myself staring down at it for minutes as we flew above. And then recognition dawned on me.

"Is that Hyrenaak?"

It was. There was a strange edge to Ssserakis' words. I think it might have been fear. It takes a lot to scare the living embodiment of fear.

"What happened?" I couldn't quite fathom it. Hyrenaak was as timeless as Ssserakis. One of the lords of Sevorai. Almost as old as the world, the giant serpent had never touched the ground. Now it was nothing but half buried bones.

The enemy happened. Norvet Meruun is more cunning than we believed. She infested a pack of terrablooms with her children and waited for Hyrenaak to feed on them. Once he had swallowed them, they erupted from the flesh and tore the serpent apart from the inside while he still flew. He thrashed and screamed, ripped chunks of himself free, but Norvet Meruun's children clung to his body and consumed him. I heard him crawling, screaming, begging, Eska. But there is no mercy in Norvet Meruun. Her children swarmed him, ate the scales from his back, the flesh from his guts, the eyes from his head. He took a long time to die.

We passed the tail of Hyrenaak, the Landless. A bony protrusion half buried in grey dirt, half erupting, the final spike at the end pointed towards the sky it had once ruled. We flew on, Ssserakis beating our wings harder, gaining more speed as if eager to be away from the sight of the dead serpent.

"Why?" I asked, still trying to comprehend it. "You said Hyrenaak took no part in your war against Norvet Meruun. Why would she kill him?"

Don't be a fool, Eska. It is what she does. Norvet Meruun consumes everything. She is the death of Sevorai given form. The beating heart and eventual end rolled into a mountain of pulsing flesh. Ssserakis fell silent for a few moments. I felt it brooding over its next words. *And she no longer fears me.*

We glided towards a waterfall that flowed upwards instead of down. The water somehow rushed up the side of a cliff and burst free in an azure spray before gathering into a roaring river and flowing down the mountainside.

Prepare yourself, Eska.

In the distant sky I saw hellions and wind thrashers swarming, buzzing through the air. The hellions, bat-like in appearance though each as large as one of those awful horse creatures, were carrying things in the claws of their back legs, though I could not make out what. The wind thrashers were more insectile, with six overlapping iridescent wings that beat against each other creating an awful buzzing sound that hurt the ears. They had squat bodies with no legs, but eight arms, some ending in claws, others in suckery tentacles, and others still with hands. They also had terran-like faces with goggling black eyes and mouths full of serrated teeth. I will remind you that all the inhabitants of the Other World were ripped straight out of the nightmares of terrans, pahht, and tahren.

As we touched down next to the top, or bottom, I suppose, of that waterfall, I stared into the valley beyond and finally understood the depth of what Ssserakis had been trying to show me. Norvet Meruun dominated the horizon.

Pallid flesh the colour of maggots with red veins running through them extended as far as I could see. It pulsed every ten seconds or so and I felt a heartbeat thrumming through the earth at my feet. My innate

Geomancy came alive and tried to convince me a quake was coming. The maggoty flesh rose out of the cracked ground, splitting it where the mountainous body of Norvet Meruun could no longer be contained even by solid rock. Gargantuan tentacles, each the length of the great chain of Ro'shan I had once climbed, flailed in the air, occasionally falling and lashing at the ground.

I looked to my left and saw only Norvet Meruun. To my right and she was all I could see there, too. She was everywhere. Plastered across the horizon, clinging to Sevorai like a pestilent tumour breaching the skin, roots sunk so deep they clung to bones of the world.

This is only the barest glimpse of her. She has already consumed half my world.

Creatures swarmed around her. The hellions and wind thrashers above, and others below. Some were her children, the Abominations slithering slowly along, searching for more to consume. I watched a smallish one, probably the size of large dog, split off from her flesh and start undulating its way forward like some pale, rubbery slug. A few minutes later, a huge Abomination the size of ten abbans, blobbed forwards and re-joined Norvet Meruun's flesh, becoming one with its mother once more. There were other land bound monsters too. I saw a pack of imps digging at the riverbank, slowly altering its course for some reason I could not fathom. Their skin writhed, little worms poking out of their flesh all along their arms and necks, waving, wriggling at the air like blades of grass in a breeze. Further back, a pack of ten ghouls, some small as a terran, others large as a house. They were dragging a dead yurthammer along by its thick, scaly tail. They deposited the dead creature near the line of pulsing flesh and backed away, yipping and cavorting, the smaller ones scaling the larger and leaping off their backs in apparent glee. Norvet Meruun pulsed again and the flesh touched the yurthammer and immediately began dragging on it, pulling it in and absorbing it into the disgusting mass.

There were other monsters too, large, and small. Some I couldn't even name, had never seen before in all my studies of the Other World. I saw a giant creature many times the size of an abban, with curved horns and a mouth that drooled an inky black fluid. It had those little worms infesting its back and skull, tails wriggling in the air. Then it reared onto its jointed hind legs and strained against a huge cart full of rock, pulling it away from the expanding border of hideous flesh.

"What happened?" I stepped closer without thinking, slowly ambling down the hill alongside the flowing river.

The Iron Legion happened.

"Of course it was that sceptic bastard."

When he took me from Sevorai, he upset the balance.

"What balance?"

The balance, Eska. Since our creation by the Rand, we lords of Sevorai maintained the balance. We positioned our territories around Norvet Meruun. We kept her small. Each of us carving off bits of her. Not letting her grow. Her fear was an exquisite thing I could have feasted on forever.

"You penned her in like an animal? Like cattle?"

No. We caged her like a memory too painful to bear. She is the Beating Heart, Eska. From the moment of our creation, we knew she would be the death of our world if we let her. Only through our combined efforts could we hold her back. We each took our places, built our territories, cultured our minions. I had the grandest city of all, you have seen it. My horror fell silent for a moment and I felt it brooding. *You have seen how it once was. How it should be.*

Hyrenaak took the sky, tearing apart any of Norvet Meruun's minions that dared to leave the ground. That is why she killed him first. Without his guardianship, the skies belong to her creatures now.

As if in answer, one of the wind thrashers buzzed closer, the racket of its wings beating against each other a persistent drone that crackled in my ears. It stared at me, two hands twisting around a barbed spear that appeared hewn from rock. I ignored the monster and paced on.

Kekran and his army of imps served a similar purpose on the ground. He could not stand against Norvet Meruun's tide of flesh, so hunted the minions she sent out past the lines of her territory.

I had met Kekran once. A strange creature almost terran in appearance, but a twisted version of my people with skin that seemed to swirl, eyes that glowed with malevolent red light, and limbs that didn't quite match his body, as though he had pulled them from another creature and grafted them onto himself. I was told he had fought Hyrenaak once, had lost an arm, but had taken an eye. That was enough to convince me that though Kekran might look terran, he was far stronger than any of my people.

"Is Kekran dead?" I asked as I walked on. Another wind thrasher flew closer, wings buzzing. I now had an audience of two. They darted about above me, watching, never staying still for more than a second or two.

Not quite. Norvet Meruun tore off an arm, both his legs, and half his torso away. He fled to recuperate. That Kekran could apparently survive being ripped to pieces was terrifying in its own right.

"What about the other lords of Sevorai?"

Ssserakis chuckled bitterly in my head and my shadow writhed beneath me. *Brakunus was supposed to hunt Norvet Meruun's minions just as Kekran did, but the ghoul is a coward and a fool. I should have taken him long ago. For all his failings, he would have made a powerful host. A pause. Not as powerful as you.*

"I don't need flattering, Ssserakis. The other lords."

Aire and Dialos. The one that is two that is many that is two that is one. Ssserakis laughed again. We call them the twins and they hate it. They have their own territory and try to keep Norvet Meruun at bay, but they are fated to fight each other for all their lives. Recently they have let that fate distract them from the greater task.

Lodoss wanders Sevorai and cares nothing for its problems. His torment is unending. He cannot die, and yet wishes for nothing but. As powerful as he is, he is useless.

Flowne has always taken her task the most seriously, but since the balance was disrupted she cannot hold back the tide. She blames me and has sworn to tear me apart if I approach her territory again.

"Could she do it?"

Ssserakis sulked for a few moments. *Yes. I am weak, Eska. I have been weak for too long. When the Iron Legion took me, the balance was disrupted. Norvet Meruun surged forward and took my territory, consumed, or enslaved my minions. By the time you sent me back, it was too late. My cities were destroyed, my minions gone or too mindless to fear anything. Norvet Meruun herself has grown so great she no longer fears me.*

"Slow down." I was still trying to grasp it all. The buzzing of the wind thrashers wasn't helping. We had an audience of five now, their wings creating such a drone my ears hurt. Each of them had those same worm-like extrusions poking out of arms and torso and head, waving in the air.

"You're saying you're too weak to fight Norvet Meruun because nothing fears you anymore?" I had long known my horror fed on fear, grew fat with it. But starved of fear, or when too much of the energy that terror provided was expended, Ssserakis grew small and weak and lethargic.

Yes. Watch.

My shadow shifted beneath my feet. A spike of inky black shot out, upwards, skewering one of the wind thrashers through the eye. It died immediately, its wings falling still, its arms going limp. Ssserakis withdrew my shadow and the monster dropped to the ground, twitching its final spasms. The worm-like extrusions embedded in its skin wriggled for a few more moments, then writhed free. And I sensed nothing. The other wind thrashers continued to watch. Wings buzzing, they flitted about above me.

They did not fear me. Always, through Ssserakis I had been able to sense the fear of those around me. The horror drank it in, fed on it. It often used me to scare others, providing it a hearty meal. But from these creatures there was nothing.

One of the gargantuan tentacles reached out from the main mass of Norvet Meruun, stretching the vast distance between us, towering above me. My wings burst from my back and Ssserakis beat them hard, pulling us back and up into the sky just as the tentacle fell, slamming onto the ground where I just stood, cracking rock and sending dust pluming up around it. The remaining wind thrashers darted easily out of the way and approached me once more, not attacking, just watching. The tentacle slowly withdrew, dragging along the ground, tearing a new furrow in the earth.

You feel it. There is no fear. I grow weak without it. There is nothing for me to feed on. Norvet Meruun no longer fears me. I could hear my horror growing panicky. It was not something I had ever felt from Ssserakis. It was an ancient horror, as old as Sevorai itself. But when faced with an implacable enemy, it didn't know what to do.

"Why don't they fear you?" I asked as we hung there in the sky, rising and falling to the steady beating of my wings.

Norvet Meruun has grown too large to care. Her body is sluggish to react but does so on instinct alone. She knows I cannot do any significant harm to her growing flesh, so does not care. Some of her minions follow her willingly. The ghouls are cowards and place their bets on the monster most likely to win. Others are enslaved.

"The worms infesting their skin."

Ssserakis made a sound in my head like a snort of disgust. *They are little more than puppets. The infestation controls them. They feel nothing. I can slaughter a hundred of them and still, they will not fear me!*

I stared down at the vastness of the enemy Ssserakis was fighting. It overwhelmed me. How could anyone hope to fight something so huge, so all encompassing? It stretched from horizon to horizon. Ssserakis said Norvet Meruun had already consumed half of Sevorai. Did that mean half the world was already covered in her pulsating flesh? I turned to stare back in the direction we had come, as though my failing eyes could pierce the distance and see the great rift. The first stable portal between our two worlds.

"Oh fuck!"

Yes. In connecting our two worlds, our daughter has

doomed Ovaeris along with Sevorai. Once Norvet Meruun has
consumed everything here, she will do the same to your world.

"What do we do?"

Fight! Swallow your Sources. We were always stronger
together. We'll carve her flesh apart and slaughter her minions. If
we hurt her enough, she will learn to fear me again.

It was all too overwhelming. To vast to comprehend.
Too big to fight. "I can't, Ssserakis. I'm old. Tired." I didn't
need my horror to whisper the next bit in my head, it was
a fear I had tormented myself with for a while now. "I'm
weak."

A wave of disgust poured over me. Ssserakis finally
realising the state of the body it had possessed.

You have let your body wither. Your magic rots within you.

I laughed bitterly as we hung there in the sky, wings
beating slowly. "Age will do that, yes."

Again, the sharp sense of disgust crashing against me.
This is not age. The Iron Legion was old, but he was strong. You
have ALLOWED yourself to become weak.

"I'm tired, Ssserakis. I have been tired for a long
time." I didn't say the next bit. I didn't need to. I was tired
and I was alone.

You're not alone anymore.

I couldn't help it. I couldn't fight. I was despair made
manifest. The inevitability of failure turned my limbs to
stone, weighing me down. Even my wings beat slower and
we glided down to the ground. I collapsed next to the top
of the waterfall, staring at the enemy stretching before me. I
knew we had no chance against it.

"I'm tired, Ssserakis," I said. The words came unstuck
and flowed from me. I finally admitted the truth to the only
creature in existence who could truly understand me. "I've

made so many mistakes. I'm tired of making mistakes."

The call of the void surged and dragged me out to sea with it. Trying was so hard. The effort too great. The inevitable failure, the consequences were too high. The horrible truth was in front of me. Just like Imiko, I wasn't strong enough to bear both the weight of the world and my conscience. Life was so much pain and it would be easier to not be. I was so fucking tired of being me, of making the same mistakes, fucking everything up. So much easier to just let it end.

Stop wallowing, Eskara! Listen to me. I know you. You are not tired of being you. You are stronger than that. You are not ground down by your mistakes, you are sturdier than that. You are tired of facing them alone. But you are not alone anymore. I am here. I am with you. We are each other's strength.

"What if we're each other's weakness?"

STOP IT! This self-indulgent whining is unlike you. It will not help my world or yours. It will not save your people. It will not save our daughters. Snap out of it and help me. Or shall I crush your heart in your chest, flee your carcass, and find someone who will. Perhaps I should have gone to our daughter after all.

"Don't you dare." As much as I loved Ssserakis, I would not inflict the torment of carrying it on another, especially not Sirileth. She might think she wanted the possession, but she didn't understand what it would cost her. The cold inside, the nightmares. The need to cause fear in others to feed it.

Then stand up. Swallow your Sources. Shed this useless notion of weakness. Together we will carve Norvet Meruun apart. We will make her fear us.

I stood unsteadily. My legs were weak, but the leaden feeling had passed. The wave of despair retreated, and the call of the void no longer drowned me. It was always this way. When it rose it seemed insurmountable, a towering monstrosity that I could never hope to fight. Despair and disgust and pain, and over it all the need to be free of it once and for all. But then, like the tide, it ebbed and left me feeling raw. Raw, but no longer beaten. Despite that, I didn't swallow my Sources. I didn't leap into battle as Ssserakis demanded. Instead, I turned back towards the great rift.

"Take us back, Ssserakis." I was unused to the horror inside my body. I had not yet regained enough control to summon my wings myself.

But the enemy—

Once, both long ago and perhaps not so distant, I would have done as Ssserakis wanted. I would have swallowed my magic and leapt into the midst of Norvet Meruun and dashed myself upon its insurmountable flesh. But I was older, weaker, and wiser. I knew we would lose.

"If we strike at it now, we'll die."

Ssserakis grumbled but didn't argue. My shadowy wings boiled out of my back and Ssserakis took us into the sky, flying swiftly towards the great rift.

"I need time, Ssserakis, to recover from… Well, a lot has happened recently."

I hung limp as my wings beat to a steady rhythm, carrying us above the Other World and its myriad greys. Such muted colours, but there were colours. Like a reflection of Ovaeris seen through a dusty mirror. I crossed my arms and bent my mind to the puzzle of how we could hope to defeat a creature such as Norvet Meruun. Then I realised how much I had missed being able to cross my arms.

I had gradually come to accept the little annoyances of having only one arm. There was no sense in grumbling

over something that was done and could not be undone. I
learned to cope, adapt. Less crossing of arms, more holding
my left shoulder, or thrusting my hand into a pocket. But
now I didn't have to adapt. Thanks to Ssserakis, I had a
second hand again. It was formed of shadow and skeletal
like all the flesh had been stripped from the bones. Each
finger ended in a sharp talon. Just like my wings, it was
Ssserakis' power, but my shadow. They were a part of me
and a part of the horror. Two beings from separate worlds
working as one to a common goal. Just like the Auguries,
those ancient prophecies that claimed I was the one who
would end the eternal war between the Rand and Djinn.

A plan was beginning to form in my mind. "We can't
kill Norvet Meruun alone, Ssserakis."

We cannot kill her, Eska.

"What?"

*She is the heart of Sevorai. As long as my world exists, so
will Norvet Meruun.*

"So what is this all for? How can we win?"

*There is no winning this fight. Only prolonging it. The
balance, Eska. It is about the balance. We need to cut her flesh so
it withers and dies, beat her back until she can be contained once
more. She must learn to fear me again.*

Our fucking stupid, mindless, arrogant, arsehole
gods! So enamoured with their petty squabbles, their
vaunted war eternal, they reproduced it here in Sevorai. A
war that can never be won but must be fought for the sake of
that world. Fucking Rand! Fucking Djinn! Idiots, all of them.

"We can't do it alone, Ssserakis," I said, staring at
my shadowy hand again. "You say Norvet Meruun covers
half of Sevorai, there is no way we can prune back that bush
alone. We need help. Allies. An army. Two armies. Five.

What happened to yours?"

She ate it. Ssserakis fell silent. I basked in the quiet beating of wings, the rush of cool air against my face.

You wish to rally your world against mine?

"Can you think of a better plan?"

No. Nor can I think of a worse one.

CHAPTER TWO

WE PASSED THROUGH THE GREAT RIFT BACK into Ovaeris and the heat hit me like a good right hook I hadn't seen coming. I gasped and struggled to draw another breath. The air was hot and dry and thick with sand. The storm raged all around like a hungry predator kept at bay only by the reality-bending presence of the rift.

We had seen a great many ghosts on the Sevorai side. They passed through the rift but seemed to have little purpose beyond that. They milled about the canyon in the Other World, listless. Their ethereal blue forms stark against the grey. There were ghosts on this side of the rift too, thousands of them, all trudging towards the portal. Queuing as if waiting for water from a well. It was bizarre, and for once I was certain that I was not the cause of these ghosts. They were not mine. They were Sirileth's, but my youngest daughter was no Necromancer.

Irad, the capital city of Polasia, was gone. Crushed,
I supposed. Or whatever happened when you dropped a
moon on a continent. I guess it didn't matter how they died,
only that Irad was gone and its entire population dead. All
thanks to my daughter. She saved our world by sacrificing
a city and everyone in it. In the grand scheme of things, it
was a small price to pay. But grander schemes are for the
immortals. We are terrans, and we look at things in small
ways because we are small. Hard to give a fuck about the
forest burning when you're a fly caught in a spider's web
and the eight-legged prick is bearing down on you.

*Ahh, this infernal light burns. I forgot how much I hate
your world.*

I smiled. "There was a time you said you'd stay here
for me."

*I was intoxicated on victory. How you can stand this light,
I don't know. It hurts.*

"Take us down. Pull back inside my shadow." I would
have to re-learn how to control my wings to spare Ssserakis
the pain.

Beware, Eska. Look.

We started gliding down quickly and I had to squint
to see what Ssserakis meant. When my eyes focused, I saw
a stand-off. On one side, my two daughters stood in front
of the ten survivors from the oasis. Between them and the
point where the great rift touched the ground was a ghoul
easily ten times the size of an abban. It was the largest living
creature I had ever seen save for Hyrenaak. Even from the
air, I could tell the ghoul was monstrous. It crouched on
all fours, legs bent and ready to spring at any moment. Its
flesh was the pale grey of ash, its hands and feet taloned
claws that tore great gouges in the sandy dirt beneath it.

Huge swathes of dirty cloth trailed from its head and arms
and torso. I still have no idea why they do it, but all ghouls
collect rags and clothes, wrapping the fabric around their
limbs and head, always covering their eyes.

That is no mere ghoul, Eska. That is Brakunus. Coward.
I heard the disdain in Ssserakis' words. There was more
history between the two of them than I could claim with
everybody I'd ever met. Immortals are a strange concept to
come to terms with.

We touched down a dozen paces from my daughters.
I stumbled, almost fell. My knees aching and unready for
the sudden shock of bearing my weight. Ssserakis pulled my
wings back, retracting into my shadow and settling atop my
head and shoulders like a black cloak.

"Eskara," Kento said. She used my full name so I
assumed she was displeased with me. "What is this thing?"

I paced over to join her and Sirileth in their defence of
the survivors. "A ghoul."

Kento shook her head. She hadn't taken her eyes off
Brakunus yet. "Ghouls are small," she said. "Terran sized."

"Uh, no. That's wrong," Sirileth said. Her arms were
held out in front of her, locked in place by the metal fused to
her skin. "I mean, they can be. But they can also be bigger.
Much bigger. I've been trying to explain to her, Mother.
Ghouls never stop growing. This one must be old."

Ssserakis chuckled in my head. *Our daughter is smart
but underestimates the enemy. Old is…*

"Quiet." I'd forgotten how hard it could be to think
with Ssserakis prattling on in my head. I felt the horror grow
still and sullen inside. It did not like being chastised.

Sirileth looked crestfallen for a moment, then her
brows pulled together in anger. "You don't get to scold me

like a child, Mother."

"I wasn't talking to you."

Sirileth glanced down at my shadowy arm and frowned. She was probably going for brooding, but she hit sulking. It's a fine line, to be fair.

"It's not *a* ghoul," I said. "It's *the* ghoul. The first and oldest. One of the lords of Sevorai."

"It's not enough you drop a moon on our world, now you unleash a plague of monsters, too," Kento said, her voice sharp enough to cut. But the accusation was not levelled at me.

"You keep blaming me, but I did what I had to do," Sirileth said, rushing through the words. "No one else would. Or, I mean, could. And…"

I walked away from my bickering daughters, approaching the giant ghoul. I felt the ground trembling under my feet. My innate Geomancy told me it was no earthquake. It was the ghoul growling, its belly resting on the earth. The noise was low enough I barely heard it, but I felt it. It resonated like a threat.

Do not let him intimidate you. We are stronger than him.

"Are we?" I wasn't so sure. I was old, tired, hungry, thirsty, kept standing only by the strength Ssserakis was lending me. My horror was not as strong as it claimed. It had been starved of fear for too long. We were both weak.

As I drew closer, the size of the ghoul daunted me. It was crouched on all fours like a dog trying to make itself small, and still, its head was twenty feet above me. Its arms and legs were thin — that's a comparative term — but they were corded with ropey muscle. I knew from many long years of sparring with Tamura that thin did not mean weak. Its eyes were covered by thick swathes of dirty cloth, but it

snuffed the air as I approached, and cracked lips drew back
from brown and yellow fangs. A string of saliva as big as
my head dropped from the monster's jowls to splash on the
ground, quickly swallowed by the parched earth. I was fairly
certain the damned thing was big enough to swallow me
whole if it tried, and it would likely ask for dessert. One of
its hands pawed at the ground, tearing great sandy furrows
in its black claws.

I stopped a dozen paces away, craned my neck to look
up at its face. The ground continued to tremble from the
monster's fierce growls. I was easily within striking distance
now. I knew with a damning certainty it could kill me before
I could respond.

"Brakunus," I said loudly. The growling stopped
immediately. The ghoul cocked its massive head to the side.
I reached for something else to say, found nothing. Up close,
the monster was huge. I could not understand how any
living thing could grow so large.

Brakunus lunged forward, his head thrusting at me
and coming to a stop just a hands breadth away. It filled my
view. I could see nothing but the grey face, its skin cracked
and blistered, almost terran but the proportions wrong in
every way. Its muzzle was slightly elongated, its nose too
flat, its ears were mere pits, and its hair was coarse, stringy,
and white as bone. And the smell. I wasn't sure if it was
the creature itself or the rags it wore, but the stench was
overpowering, like carrion left to rot for days. It was sweet
and sickly, and it took every bit of will I had not to gag. The
ghoul snuffed again, so powerfully my shadow cloak stirred
and I almost stumbled into the monster's maw.

"I know you," Brakunus bellowed, a harsh growl
slurring over the words. Probably not surprising considering

the creature wasn't made to speak terran. Honestly, I was quite surprised it could. I'd never heard of a ghoul speaking before. It's also worth noting that as bad as the general stench of the monster was, its breath was worse. I'm a little amazed I didn't keel over from infection just being in the path of that virulence.

ESKA! Ssserakis shouted my name in my head and I realised I had been standing still for some time, saying nothing. Awe is ever one of my failings.

"Why do you wear all that cloth over your head?" I asked. Well, it was probably more like shouted. The monster's head was right in front of me, close enough I could have reached out and touched it, though I couldn't imagine wanting to do such a horrid thing. But for some reason, perhaps its enormous size, I felt the need to shout at it to be heard.

Fool! How can you expect to dominate a creature when you begin by begging for answers.

Brakunus opened his mouth wide and his tongue slithered out from between his jaws. It was long and pink and spined like a cat's. It was also as big I was. It waved in front of me for a moment and I felt the overpowering need to turn and run.

STAND YOUR GROUND! Ssserakis' shout almost knocked me over it was so loud in my head.

"*If you wave that thing at me again, I will tear it off, Coward,*" I snarled. Well, I say *I*. The words certainly issued from my mouth, but they were not mine. Ssserakis spoke through me. I didn't know the horror could do that. To be honest, I was a little alarmed that it could usurp control from me like that, but I didn't have time to worry about it with an ancient ghoul the size of a mansion one lurch away from chewing on my corpse, queen or no.

The giant ghoul pulled back a few feet, snuffed the air. "Ssserakis?" Rancid breath blasted me in the face again.

I felt words not mine surging up and loosening my tongue. I clenched my jaw and clamped down on Ssserakis, wrenching control of my body back. Ssserakis raged inside, like a snake thrashing against my soul. Or possibly like a child destroying their room in anger, only the room was my mind. My horror did not like being cut off like that, but it had to learn all over again which one of us was in control. We needed time to adjust to each other again. Neither one of us was used to sharing a body anymore.

Brakunus was watching me. I think. Hard to tell with the cloth covering his face, but his giant head hovered nearby. I noticed his clawed hands still gouging the earth, as though he was eager to tear me to shreds.

And he can. Let me out, Eskara. The other lords of Sevorai are mine to deal with.

"Shut up!" I hissed, walling my horror away inside. Then I turned my attention to the overgrown ghoul. "Ssserakis is in here. But my name is Eskara Helsene."

Brakunus' lips pulled back, baring a host of discoloured fangs. I recognised the expression from the pahht. The ghoul was grinning. "Are you trapped in there, little horror?" The ghoul's voice was a mocking, fetid growl. "How weak you are. Would you like me to free you?"

Ssserakis' anger flared. It battered itself against my control like a wolf throwing itself against the bars of a cage. I winced, suddenly remembering another time when Ssserakis had gripped my heart, threatened to burst it inside my chest.

I would never do that to you. Not now.

"But you could."

Brakunus pulled back, rearing up on his hinds leg to tower over me. I ignored the fool and his posturing.

Let me out. Brakunus is a coward. They only respond to strength. I must show him I am dominant.

I staggered as Ssserakis half broke through the wall I had tried to cage it in. My shadow writhed beneath me like hail smashing into the still waters of a lake. My left arm, the shadowy one, moved.

"I will not let you assume control, Ssserakis. This is my body."

We had been apart for too long. Ssserakis always took hosts, I knew that, but in Sevorai it took only what it deemed to be minions. Disposable creatures, mindless beasts, those it could kill and flee at its whim. It controlled them: mind, body, and soul. I would not let that happen to me.

You cannot keep me locked up, Eskara. I will not hide inside you while my world is devoured.

"This is my body, Ssserakis."

Brakunus, it appeared, did not like being ignored. The ghoul crashed down on all fours, shaking the earth with the impact. Then it sucked in a deep breath and let it out in a bellowing roar that set my shadowy cloak flapping and nearly knocked me off my feet. It also stank like rotting sewage.

"ENOUGH!" I screamed at Brakunus.

"*I will deal with you in a moment, Coward.*" Ssserakis snarled through my voice.

My shadow surged, pulling away from me as though trying to detach. The world darkened, the light fading as Ssserakis exerted its pressure through me. Brakunus leapt back, looking around in a panic, head twitching one way then the other. I could taste the fear pouring off the ancient

ghoul and it was sweet as honey. New strength flooded me.
No, not me. Ssserakis.

We cannot show division before this creature. Let me out!

"Go!" I shouted at Brakunus, pointing towards the
rift with my shadow claw. "Fetch me a khark hound. I'm
hungry."

Brakunus backed away another step, still panicked by
the encroaching darkness. Then the ghoul turned and fled
through the rift back to Sevorai. That was for the best. We
needed to sort out our division before he returned.

"Mother?" That was Sirileth.

I didn't turn to look at her, but flung my hand out
behind me. "Stay back."

Ssserakis pulled its strength back from me and I
stumbled, almost collapsed. All my aches and pains flared
to life. The weariness from the fight less than a day ago,
defending Sirileth against Kento, then against the Maker.
Protecting all the survivors from the impact of Lursa and
the resulting storm that even now raged around us. It was
too much. I was too fucking tired for this. I hadn't slept in…
days. Hadn't eaten. I was thirsty enough my throat felt like
I'd been sucking on sand. I needed to rest, not fight with
my horror. You can't win a fight against yourself. No matter
which way the victory falls, you still lose. I dropped to my
knees in the dirt, the shock of pain making me cry out.

"We can't do this, Ssserakis," I rasped, tired and so
damned weary. "We can't be at odds."

*Then you cannot shut me out. I will not be locked inside
anymore, Eskara.*

"And you can't take control. It's my body, Ssserakis."

We sat in silence for a while, both of us brooding
over our differences. I will admit, I had imagined our

reunion. Twenty years had passed since Ssserakis and I were parted, but I had often imagined finding my horror. The joy of coming together once again, of finding that comfort of constant companionship. We'd had that for a moment, I suppose. But always in my dreams we would settle into the same easy reliance we once shared. Like two friends, long separated, but easy and comfortable no matter the time and distance spent apart. It's abban shit. People grow, they change. And those we once fit, those who once slotted into our worlds so easily, suddenly have sharp edges that grate away any chance of comfort and leave both parties wounded. Ancient horrors from another world also changed apparently. We no longer fit each other. All elbows and knees, awkwardness, too hot, too cold.

I sagged, released the hold I had on the horror and let it out. I found I missed the privacy I had once hated. I always feared being alone, but a decade away from all those I knew and loved, had taught me to value my solitude. I no longer had that. Ssserakis was in me, in my body and in my head, listening to my thoughts.

My shadow bubbled, stretched, rose up beside me into an amorphous blob that was mostly me shaped. Ssserakis and I sat beside each other in the dirt, neither knowing what to say to the other. The silence stretched thin. It couldn't last. One of us had to speak the truth.

You know I can't leave. Once Ssserakis possessed a host, only death could free it.

"I don't want you to leave." That was also true. As much as our reunion was awkward and painful, I still wanted it. I wanted my horror to stay. For us to be one again. I just didn't know how to make it happen with the new us.

I don't want to leave. The words were barely a whisper.

We sat side by side, staring at the rift that both connected and separated our two worlds. "Then we need to find a new way to coexist. To be together. A new balance."

Agreed. I will not be locked inside you anymore, Eska. I will not hide from your world. I must be allowed to be free.

I nodded. I had been a captive more than once. I knew the need for freedom. "My shadow then. It's yours. My hand and my wings need to be mine. I cannot have you controlling half of me. But you can do what you want in my shadow." It felt like we were parcelling up a house. I'd take the furniture but Ssserakis could have the pots and pans. Only it was all me. The house and everything inside it was me.

"And sometimes I need privacy. If I tell you to draw back, you do it."

My shadow rippled beside me. *"Agreed."* I realised Ssserakis was speaking out loud, through my shadow, its voice almost like my own but as if I hissed the words. *"And I extend the same demand to you."*

"What? What would you need privacy for? And how would that work?"

"Just agree, Eska. The details are insignificant."

"Alright. I agree." Compromise and capitulation are two very different things. I trusted Ssserakis. I had to show that trust. Trust is such a strange thing; it can never be proven through words, only actions. Yet, a single word can shatter a mountain of that proof.

"And I must be allowed to deal with the other lords of Sevorai. You can negotiate with the people of your world."

"Agreed."

And that was the new bargain we forged. It dawned on me, it had ever been bargains with Ssserakis and I. When we first met, I agreed to carry it back home to Sevorai, and in return it would not kill me. Yes, you don't need to remind me how shit a deal that was. But we had eventually grown past the terms set. I only hoped we could again.

I tried to explain it to my daughters. Sirileth was still angry, I think. She believed Ssserakis was her right, inherited from me. Things did not work that way though. She had explained to Kento about the horror while I was gone, and that saved me the awkwardness. Kento watched me warily. I do not think my eldest daughter liked the idea of me sharing my body with the living incarnation of terran fear. Well… fuck, it wasn't her problem. Not like she had to live with the horror. Perhaps she was starting to realise what sort of a monster her birth mother truly was. I should probably be amazed Kento turned out as hale as she did. She had two mothers: one a possessed mad woman who had brought entire empires to ruin to sate her lust for vengeance, and the other was a god. You play the hand you're dealt, even when it's rusty and fucking you sideways.

Brakunus returned, slinking back through the rift, a dead khark hound clutched in hand. A small pack of eight ghouls, most of them no larger than a terran, followed him. He dropped the dead hound on the ground before me and snuffed the air again.

See what can be accomplished when your minions are brought to heel.

"I thought Brakunus was a lord of Sevorai," I said.

Lords can be minions too, Eska. The timid will wear as many chains as you slip over their heads and thank you for the weight. I was not sure I agreed, but things were done differently in Sevorai. I had to let Ssserakis handle that world its own way.

My shadow congealed beside me and Ssserakis explained as much of the situation as it cared to Brakunus. The giant ghoul shifted back and forth as the two lords of Sevorai spoke. The smaller ghouls hung back, keeping low to the ground, wary of Brakunus' pacing. I turned to look at my daughters and the survivors of the oasis. It was oddly freeing to be able to look elsewhere while Ssserakis handled things.

The survivors cowered, hugging each other and staring fearfully at the ghouls. Ten of them. The pahht couple and their two children, a Polasian woman, another pahht couple with a terran child, and a mad terran man. However we were going to get out of this, we needed to take them with us. I had no doubt if we left them here, the ghouls would eat them.

Kento set about butchering the khark hound and spitting steaks of its flesh over a fire. It would not be a pleasant meal, but at least it was enough to feed us all. Sirileth stood close to me, listening in to the conversation between Ssserakis and Brakunus.

"You seek to raise an army against her?" Brakunus said once Ssserakis has finished explaining.

"Yes. The likes of which has never been seen."

The giant ghoul shifted, paws tearing at the earth. "You'll lose. Norvet Meruun will absorb your army. Better to run."

Ssserakis rippled my shadow and I felt the anger of my horror as a sharp stab passing through our connection. *"There is nowhere left to run."*

Brakunus snuffed the air and swung his head about. The orange dust storm Sirileth had created when she crashed Lursa down on top of us raged all around, lit by the occasional flash of lightning. "This world is vast. It is ripe."

"*NO!*" My shadow swelled, Ssserakis growing tall enough to match Brakunus, an inky black giant. Yes, you might see the shadow I cast being larger than I myself. Take from that what you will. "*This is not our world.*"

Brakunus slunk backwards, cowering, dragging his belly on the ground. The other ghouls did likewise, submitting before a more dominant creature. My shadow surged forward, still attached to me but moving independently, it chased Brakunus, towering over him.

"*I will scour this world for allies, Coward. I will bring them here and tear Norvet Meruun back to the pustule she is. You will stay and guard this rift and let nothing through. None of her minions can be allowed to cross into this world.*"

Brakunus whined, long and low. His paws tore at the ground, his head twisted away from Ssserakis like a dog expecting a beating.

"*Do you understand?*"

Brakunus' whine turned into a growl and the giant ghoul leapt forward, not at Ssserakis, but at me. Towering over me. Filling my vision. Claws reaching to tear me apart.

My shadow crashed into the ghoul, sending it tumbling away. The impact as Brakunus hit the earth, shook the ground. I instinctively steadied myself with my innate Geomancy. Brakunus rolled back to his feet, but Ssserakis was on him. A shadowy spear shot out and sank deep into one Brakunus' front paws, pinning him to the ground. The ghoul howled in pain. Ssserakis pushed forward, swelling to even greater size, threatening to engulf the ghoul. I felt how much it cost my horror. The power it was using to control my shadow like this was a wearying drain. I felt some of that energy coming from me. Always before, Ssserakis had provided me with strength, but now it was taking what little I had left to put on this show. I gave it willingly. I knew… we both knew, it couldn't last. This was an all-in gamble, a bluff. Our last bet on a shitty hand.

"*Do you understand, Coward?*" Ssserakis' voice echoed like thunder. My legs wobbled. I locked my knees. My vision dimmed.

Brakunus whined again, bowed his head. "Yes. Yes. I understand, Ssserakis. I will stay. Guard the rift." He tugged his paw, trying to free it from the shadowy stake pinning it to the ground. Ssserakis pushed forward a little more, driving the spear deeper. Brakunus flattened himself against the ground. Fear sweated through the ghoul's skin and Ssserakis drank it in, but my horror was burning that strength as quickly as it consumed it.

And then it was over. Ssserakis pulled its shadowy spear from the ghoul's paw and shrank back, returning to my side. Brakunus slunk away, cradling his injured paw, fleeing back toward the rift. He didn't pass through it though, just waited there.

I am sorry, Eska.

I turned away stiffly. My legs trembled and I knew I didn't have long before they gave up completely. My vision had tunnelled to a fine point. Kento. The fire. Warmth. I suddenly realised I felt cold.

"Mother?" Sirileth was beside me. I think she might have taken my hand, but her arms were still locked in place. It was for the best. I couldn't allow her to prove I was that weak. Not while Brakunus was still watching.

"*She needs rest.*"

"Mother?" Sirileth said again, ignoring Ssserakis.

Step after step, I staggered toward Kento and the fire.

It was maybe twenty paces, yet it felt like leagues. I saw
the worry on Kento's face. I shook my head at her, hoping
to convey the need for secrecy. When I arrived at the fire,
I forced myself to stand for a few moments. I wanted to
sink down into oblivion, but I couldn't. The ghoul was still
watching. Kento was talking, but I couldn't hear her. Sirileth
said something too. Then my horror was there, tiny where
before it had been towering.

"She needs to rest but cannot be seen to be weak."

I had just enough strength left use my innate
Geomancy to raise a small wall of rock from the ground. I
lowered myself to sitting, placed my back against the wall,
and was gone.

CHAPTER

THREE

THE HOST DIED. SSSERAKIS FELT THE MOMENT
her heart stopped, shocked into nothing by her own storm. It fled,
finally released from the meat and bones it had been possessing for
so long. So many hosts over so many years, but none had held it
as well as Eska. Most were driven insane by the extra presence in
their mind or surrendered their wills entirely and gave Ssserakis
complete control. It had once thought that was for the best, but
the union with Eska had proven beneficial in ways it had never
expected. There appeared to be more power in cooperation than
control.

   Ssserakis fled through the burning portal just moments
before it snapped shut. It left the painful light and noise of Ovaeris
behind. Sevorai welcomed it. The world no longer burned it just for
existing. Ssserakis was home. Finally home after so long. Time had
never seemed to matter much before, but Ovaeris warped things
made the worthless of note. One more reason to despise that world

of brightness and foolish creatures who thought themselves more important than they were.

It missed the host, Ssserakis realised. Only moments separated, but it missed Eska. She was dead. There was an emotion. It gnawed away at Ssserakis as if hunger, but emptier and hollow. A great void, a yawning abyss. Foolish. Terran emotions pressed upon it by prolonged contact with the host. They would fade. They had to fade. Ssserakis could not live with such emptiness. It needed to fill itself. It needed to feed.

Ssserakis took to the sky and flew. It heard a great roar that could only come from its fellow lord, Hyrenaak, the Landless. Ssserakis knew it would have to reacquaint itself with Hyrenaak and the others. They needed to know it was back. They needed to bow once more. But first, it needed strength.

A pack of goresnors milled about in a waving field of bluish blade grass. The goresnors fed endlessly, needing the energy to regrow their constantly rotting flesh. They were near mindless and would not provide the sentient fear that was most pleasing, but they would do for a quick meal. Ssserakis dove towards them, grew large, and made threatening moves. Mindless beasts were so easy to scare. The merest hint of a predator was all it took. The goresnors panicked and attempted to bolt, but Ssserakis surrounded them and penned them in. The wild, bestial panic grew and Ssserakis drank in the terror, feeling new strength embolden it.

The problem with mindless beasts was that it was so easy to overstimulate them. A sentient creature could be kept in a state of constant fear forever. Or at least as long as it lived. Subtle suggestions could bring out all manner of different types of terror or anxiety. But beasts only had the animal panic, and if it pressed too hard, the beast simply stopped. Catatonia, most often, but sometimes death. The goresnors provided a decent meal, but it was far from enough to sate Ssserakis' ravenous appetite. It needed more. Better quality fear. It needed to reclaim its acropolis. An entire empire of minions all kept in a state of constant fear. That was how Ssserakis would regain its true strength. Then, and only then, would it be ready to announce its return to the other lords of Sevorai.

Ssserakis roared into the sky and streaked towards its old territory. It would reclaim its city, relight the Evergloom at the heights of the towering spire, and summon its minions back to worship. It shrieked as it went, causing all those it passed over to look up and fear. Even the other horrors, young things, many of them barely even sentient, feared. It was as it should be. Ssserakis was the oldest of them, the most powerful. Ssserakis knew what it was like to live and rule and love. No! That last was a terran emotion. A leftover artefact of experiencing the host's feelings. She was dead. She could corrupt Ssserakis no further.

Ssserakis stopped shrieking, slowed to a halt and floated above a vast forest full of trees and ghouls and ghasts. She was dead. Somehow that didn't feel real. Never again would it taste her fear. Never again hear her voice or feel the raw power of her will. Never argue about which action to take. Nor feel the power of their combined might. She was gone. It felt… wrong.

The rest of the journey was a blur of silent landscape to Ssserakis. It barely even remembered moving. It stopped inspiring fear in all those beneath it but passed unnoticed.

Ssserakis arrived at its city just in time to see the towering spire fall, the embers of the Evergloom snuffed out for eternity. Norvet Meruun had come. She had grown so vast. She was consuming Ssserakis' acropolis. Its minions bowed and scraped before the mountainous flesh. They feared her and Ssserakis drank in that fear, but that it was aimed at the Beating Heart was an insult Ssserakis could not abide.

It dropped to the ground, streaking along between dark,

towering buildings. The minions that saw Ssserakis panicked,
recognising the return of their master. Their fear blossomed
all around, lighting up the city. Finally, Ssserakis came to the
crashing tide of Norvet Meruun's flesh. She surged onwards,
pulsing, growing, flattening, absorbing. Ssserakis screamed,
made itself whole, and sliced into the flesh, tearing bits of Norvet
Meruun away, projecting an icy shadow into her, and showing her
images of her own bulbous skin rotting, liquifying, sluicing away,
burning to nothing. It had always worked before. She had always
feared it before and that fear had made Ssserakis strong. But it felt
nothing from her. No terror. No fear. No panic. Nothing. Nothing.
Nothing.

Norvet Meruun pulsed, her flesh pushing outwards,
growing, closing in on Ssserakis from all sides. She couldn't kill
it, couldn't absorb it. Ssserakis had no body to lose. But no matter
how much it sliced at her, cut bits of her away, she surged on.
There was too much of her to curtail. Ssserakis' city fell, crumbled,
was absorbed by the irresistible tide of flesh.

Ssserakis knew with certainty it was too late. It had been
gone too long. The balance was destroyed and Norvet Meruun was
unleashed. And Ssserakis was no longer strong enough to stop
it. Without the host, without Eskara, it was not strong enough.
Sevorai was dying.

I don't know how long I slept. It was dark when I
woke. I imagined Lokar would be up there somewhere,
staring down at us. Cracked open and split apart by the
sudden absence of his lover. Was he searching for her,
watching our world for any hints of his twin moon? Of
course not. Our moons were not people, not alive. We
ascribed them that because it is romantic. Lokar chasing
Lursa across the sky, catching her, gathering her up in his

arms, holding her so tight they ground together becoming one over time. Well, if Sirileth had proven anything it's that our moons were just rock. Or, moon, I suppose. Could we still call Lursa a moon now she had crashed into our world? I don't know. Either way, I couldn't see Lokar with the sky shrouded in such a daunting blanket of clouds.

Ssserakis was the first to realise I was awake. *I'm sorry for draining you, Eska. I had no choice. We had to...* My horror trailed off. It could already feel I understood and had forgiven it. I knew what was at stake.

I was slow to come awake and still felt as though I hadn't slept. My eyes were gritty and heavy, and just opening them was a monumental strain of effort. But I smelled food and my stomach growled. How long had it been since I had eaten?

My daughters and the other survivors sat around the fire. Some were chewing on khark hound, tough and stringy though it was, others were waiting for another steak to finish cooking. I watched Kento form a Sourceblade and carve a mouthful of cooked steak, then hold it up to Sirileth. My younger daughter glared at my older one.

"This is embarrassing, sister," Sirileth said. "I shouldn't have to... I mean, if you'd just give me my Sources back, I could fix my arms and feed myself. You are being..."

Kento pushed the steak into Sirileth's face and she had no choice but to open her mouth for it. "Stop complaining, sister. You're not getting your Sources back until I'm certain you won't use them to bring down our other moon."

Sirileth chewed stubbornly, frowning. "I couldn't if I wanted," she said around the mouthful of steak. "The staff is gone."

Kento carved off another slice of steak and waved it in front of Sirileth until she quickly swallowed and opened her mouth again. I saw my elder daughter smile though. I could have watched them for an age, but my stomach decided to give another grumble, louder this time, and Kento glanced my way, saw that I was awake.

She fussed over me then. Handed me a small clay cup she had procured from somewhere. It was full of earthy-tasting water that reminded me of the Pit. It was the best water I'd ever tasted, or at least my dehydration convinced me so. Then I was given steak to worry at and chewed it down as quickly as I could. I ached everywhere and even with Ssserakis drinking in the fear of the other survivors, we were both still weak. I noticed Kento was careful not to touch my shadow. Not the cloak Ssserakis draped over my head and shoulders, nor the claw. She pulled away whenever it came close. Sirileth, on the other hand, was ignoring Ssserakis. She didn't so much as glance at my hand and whenever my horror spoke out loud, she didn't respond.

"We can't stay here," Kento said once I was fed and watered and feeling a little more alive again. "This storm is not stopping. If anything, it's getting worse. Only the rift is keeping it from scouring the flesh from our bones."

The rift was doing more than that. It was drawing in ghosts, too. They flocked from all around in their tens and hundreds, all drifting slowly towards the portal and passing through into Sevorai, though I could not fathom why.

"We should head to Dharhna," Sirileth said. "It's the closest city. I mean, now that Irad is gone."

"It's still days away," Kento said. "Weeks maybe on foot. Through the storm. We'll never make it. What's through the portal, Eska?"

"Sevorai."

"The Underworld?" This came from the Polasian man who had survived. I never learned his name.

"The Other World," I corrected him. Though now I thought about it, Underworld also fit. Sirileth had only recently revealed that Sevorai and Ovaeris were one world, but also two. Like two sides of a coin. Now connected by a stable portal.

"Could we travel through it?" Kento asked. "Find another rift? Open another portal beyond the reach of the storm?"

"This is the only stable portal between the two worlds," I said. "I could maybe tear open a temporary one at the sight of a scar, but I don't know where or how to find one."

"Dharhna," Sirileth said, not looking at me or Kento. "I mean, there's a scar in Dharhna."

Kento glared at her sister. "How do you know?"

"I know where all the scars are, sister. Or, um, most of them, I think."

"Because you created them by killing people?" That was how scars were created. They were places where wild magics had been unleashed when someone with more than one Source in their stomach broke down in rejection. It thinned the barrier between worlds. They were a smaller versions of the great rift.

"I didn't create all of them," Sirileth said. She clenched her hands into fists and I knew she wanted to touch her braid of hair like she always did when nervous, but she still couldn't move her arms. "Some the Rand and Djinn created when they clashed. Others when people broke down naturally. I mean, when Sourcerers rejected their magic on their own. There are scars all over our world, sister. I created only a handful of them. But I know where they all are. I think. Most of them, anyway. I studied them."

"And there's one in Dharhna?" I asked.

Sirileth looked up at me, hesitated a moment, then looked away. "Yes." I knew that hesitation. She was lying about something.

"Can we use the scar in Dharhna from within Sevorai to create a temporary portal between the two worlds?"

Sirileth nodded. "I believe so. I mean, now the two worlds are connected by the great rift, that connection is permanent. What happens in one affects the other."

"Wonderful, so now all we need to do is figure out a way of navigating the Other World to where Dharhna is."

Kento refilled my empty cup with water she pulled from the ground and handed it to me, still careful not to touch my shadow. "I don't understand."

"It's really quite simple, sister," Sirileth said. "If you think about our two worlds as one, two sides of the same." She leaned forward towards the ground with one hand, winced in pain, and almost fell over. Then she sighed wearily. "Please give me back my Sources."

"No."

Sirileth glared at Kento. "Fine. Draw a circle in the dirt." I did it quickly before a larger argument could start between my two daughters. "Thank you, Mother. Place a stone in the centre, then another stone a small distance away. This circle is both Ovaeris and Sevorai. The stone in the centre is us, the other stone is Dharhna, but they only exist in Ovaeris. If we cross through the portal to the Other World. Remove the centre stone please, Mother. Then make

the trip through the Other World to the approximate location
of Dharhna, we can use the scar in Ovaeris to open a portal
between the two worlds and pass through into Dharhna."
She nodded firmly. "I think."

Kento stared at the circle again and shook her head.
"That's still weeks of travel on foot. I don't know much
about the Underworld…"

"The Other World," I corrected her.

"But I know it's dangerous and we don't have weeks
to waste." She thumped a fist against the earth. I guessed she
was thinking of her daughter, Esem. My granddaughter. She
was most likely in the safest place in the world, protected by
her other grandmother who just so happened to be a god.
But still, we worry about our children when they are not
around. Especially when the world has just been subjected to
something of an apocalypse.

"We can use portals within Sevorai," I said. "Leapfrog
large distances. It will cut down travel time significantly.
Weeks of travel in a day or two."

Kento frowned. She was considering it, her resistance
cracking. She clearly didn't like the idea of travelling
through the Other World, but her need to get back to her
daughter was a powerful drive. "How will we know when
we reach Dharhna?"

My shadow rippled and grew beside me into
something vaguely child shaped. *The ghouls can help.*

"I wish you wouldn't do that, Eskara," Kento said,
pulling away.

"It's not me." Part of me wished I could pull Ssserakis
back. Its presence was causing the wound between Kento
and me to tear open. But I couldn't smother my horror, I had
promised not to.

Ssserakis chuckled. *"Ghouls always could sense both worlds. They can travel freely between them."*

In all my studies of the Other World, I had never heard of this. I considered myself to be the authority on the denizens of Sevorai. How fucking foolish I was to believe I knew anything but the barest sliver.

"They are not the only creatures who can do it. The eight-legged things. You call them spiders. The ones that vanish."

"Phase spiders?" Kento asked.

"Yes. Mindless insects. But they can travel between our two worlds as easily as walking."

I could see Sirileth working things out in her head, the way her eyes went distant, her mouth slack. I wondered if I looked so foolish when I was puzzling things out.

You do.

We all knew that phase spiders could vanish and reappear, but I don't think anyone had ever considered they might be moving between worlds. "Their venom," I said. "When they bite a person, the bitten limb just vanishes. Phases away leaving a gaping wound. It drags the body part to Sevorai? Does that mean hands and legs appear in your world, Ssserakis?"

Another chuckle. *"Yes."*

Kento shook her head. "Which doesn't help unless we want to appear in Dharhna one body part at a time. How can the ghouls help us?"

"It's how they breed. Or, I mean, reproduce. Not breed." Sirileth's darklight eyes were still distant, shining brightly as she worked over the puzzle. "Ghouls have no genitalia. There is no true distinction between male and female. No way to carry a baby to term. There may be a type of ghoul that reproduces via another method. A queen, like with ants. Unlikely. They're scavengers of the dead. Pack animals. They don't form large communities."

"Our daughter is smarter than you, Eska."

I didn't rise to Ssserakis' goading. Sirileth's burning gaze flicked to the horror for a moment, then away, ignoring it. "Then there are the reports of missing children. They occur everywhere. Babes vanished in the night with no sign of violence. Just gone. Sometimes with a smell of rotting corpses. We used to blame it on ghouls as a scary bedtime story, but in recent years the blame has fallen on another's shoulders." She looked at me. "The Corpse Queen. Breaking into houses and stealing children."

Fuck! So that's where that damned story came from. I was just the latest scapegoat for something that had been happening for thousands of years. Easier to blame the bogeywoman than reason out the truth, I suppose.

Sirileth gave me a brief sorry smile. "Ghouls take children. But not to eat. I mean, they could, I suppose. But I don't think so. They turn them. Make them ghouls."

A couple of the oasis survivors muttered curses, reached a hand to the sky as if the moons... sorry, moon, would protect them.

"Our daughter is correct. The ghouls are more sly than you ever gave them credit for, Eska."

"That's horrific," Kento said sharply. She turned a dark stare towards Brakunus and his pack. "We should kill them all."

"We need them, sister," Sirileth said.

Kento shook her head. "They take children."

"And would you sacrifice a world for that small measure of justice?"

Kento clenched her jaw hard, muscles writhing as she

ground her teeth. She stared so intently at the dirt beneath us I thought it would catch fire. Eventually, she raised her head, her rage mastered and nodded grimly.

"Good," Sirileth said. "Now give me back my Sources, sister. I cannot help like this. I mean, if we are to travel through Sevorai, you need me to be able to fight. Able to help. At least give me my Ingomancy Source and let me remove this metal from my arms."

Kento relented. She saw the sense of it. We were set on travelling through a world filled with nightmarish monsters. We would already be dragging a bunch of ragged survivors, including children, with us. We could not have a wounded Sirileth slowing us down.

Sirileth used Ingomancy, a Sourcery she was not attuned to, to peel the metal from her arms. Kento used Biomancy to help with the healing. The wounds would leave scars. Ugly burns streaked down my youngest daughter's arms, but that was the price she had paid for bringing down Lursa and cutting the Maker off from our world. I wondered if the scars on her conscience would be as bad. Guilt is such a strange drug, so easy to get addicted to, so necessary for sentient community. I hoped Sirileth's guilt was killing her inside because that, at least would make her terran. At the same time, I wished I could take her guilt from her, save her the pain.

Sirileth was bleeding from the eyes and nose, suffering from rejection, by the time she had finished removing the metal from her arms. She compressed it into a ball and slotted it away in the satchel at her hip, then she took a pinch of Spiceweed and retched up her Source. Kento snatched it away before Sirileth could recover. She didn't trust her sister with any Sources yet, not even ones that would kill her.

We waited the night out there, filling our stomachs with khark hound meat, drinking as much water as Kento could pull from deep underground. Ssserakis secured the help of one of the ghouls by threatening Brakunus. The huge ghoul backed down immediately and sent one of his pack along with us, a runt no bigger than the young pahht boy. The ghoul could not speak terran, but Brakunus assured us the little monster would lead us right.

The next morning, as the sun rose behind a sky of dust and baked the storm into a fierce amber maelstrom, we passed through the great rift into Sevorai. It was our only choice. That didn't mean it wasn't a bad choice. Thirteen of us entered the Other World and I knew... I knew not all of us would make it out again.

CHAPTER FOUR

THE OTHERS WERE NOT PREPARED FOR
Sevorai. How could they be? As far as I knew, I was the first
terran to have ever set physical foot in the Other World,
and that was only a day earlier. It was likely many of the
survivors had never heard of the place before. Certainly, they
kept calling it the Underworld instead of Sevorai. I stopped
correcting them early on. Ignorance is a strange force. The
harder you push against it, the more solid it becomes.

The pahht family held each other close, the man and
woman clutching their children as if they expected them to
wander off and never return. A valid fear given we had all
just learned how ghouls reproduce. I saw Sirileth watching
them, a wistful look on her face. I thought I understood it. It
was a childhood she'd never had. No father. A mother who
should have been more loving, more present.

The ghoul crept around us on all fours, snuffing at us,

the grimy cloth covering its face completely obscuring its eyes. When it noticed me watching, it pointed in a direction and I assumed that meant it knew the way. Either that or it was leading us to a particularly pungent corpse it wanted to sniff.

I popped my Portamancy Source in my mouth and opened a portal with a sound like tearing paper. I couldn't take us far. I didn't know the terrain, couldn't risk opening a portal into a cliff face or a lake or a pack of creakers. So, I opened the portal only as far as I could see, down into the canyon and across the flowing river. It would cut hours off our journey, but I knew it would take a long time and many portals to reach Dharhna. I was not so strong with the magic that I could transport us there in one day.

The ghoul, much to my surprise, leapt through the portal immediately, yipping and cavorting like a playful puppy on the other side. Kento was next, sourceblade in hand, ready for danger. Then the survivors went one at a time. It took far longer to herd them than I would have liked. Holding open portals was draining and the longer it took the fools to summon their courage and move, the fewer portals I would be able to open. And that meant it would take longer. I considered pushing them through with a swift kick up their dawdling arses.

Then it was just me and Sirileth on this side of the portal. Well, and Ssserakis, but my horror was resting inside of me. It still kept my shadow as a cloak about my shoulders, and my claw replaced my missing arm, but for the most part, Ssserakis was happy to hide and feed on the fear of the others.

"This isn't over yet, Mother." Sirileth turned her darklight stare on me, pinning me. Blindingly beautiful. It burned but I found it impossible to look away. "You know as well as I do, we can't pass through Sevorai unnoticed. I mean, things will find us. Won't they?"

I nodded. Ssserakis knew it, and I knew it. We were now in a world full of nightmares. And one thing I have long known about nightmares is they hunt you. Relentlessly.

"I need my Sources," Sirileth said.

I shrugged at her. "Kento has them. I can't order her to do anything."

"But you can convince her. I mean, she listens to you, Mother." She stared at me. So earnest. So innocent and so guilty all at the same time.

The next portal I opened was to a rocky ridge at the far side of the great canyon. The ghoul pointed the way, but I chose the location. It would provide a good line of sight, allow me to take us further with the next portal. I tore it open and we passed through in the same formation.

We spent the day like that, jumping from spot to spot across the grey landscape. We saw plenty of Other World monsters, but none took notice of us. And none dared to come close. That didn't stop the idiot survivors of the oasis pointing to them and calling them demons. Ignorance spreads like a disease. And, like an infection, often the only cure is to cut it out.

The portals drained me far faster than I had hoped. I have said I am not strong in that school of Sourcery. If you want me to burn things I can do it all day, but portals weary me. I needed a few minutes to rest between each one, and those times only increased as the day wore on. I say day, but it could have been night or anything in between. There is no sun, no moons, no celestial bodies of any kind in the Other World. There is only endless grey sky.

We stopped underneath a hanging tree. It was growing out of the side of a cliff, reaching out like a great hand to shelter the ledge we sat on. Bushy yellow leaves dangled from the branches and I spotted rusty orange fruit hanging higher up in its overlapping canopy. It was not a good vantage point, but it was shelter. I could already see where I would send our next portal; the top of a crumbling fort whose walls were blood red.

"Eskara, stop," Kento stepped before me, placed her hands on my shoulders and recoiled when my shadowy cloak shifted a little under her touch.

Our daughter is an Aspect. I can feel it. Just like that venomous one you used to invite into your bed.

"Silva," I said, looking down at my claw. "Her name was Silva. And as you are just as responsible for her death as I am. You should remember it, Ssserakis."

Kento was frowning at me. Worrying. I waved her away. "Best we get on with it." I dragged my feet to the edge of the canyon and stared down into its depths. My vision swam. I staggered. Kento pulled me back from the edge.

"Eska, stop. You need to rest. I can see the great rift in your eyes. When they're not flashing."

"Fuck!" A peculiar thing about Portamancy. When a Sourcerer is close to rejection, you can see everywhere they have recently been in their eyes. Almost like looking through portals. Kento was right, I had to stop, to rest. I needed to retch up my Source and sleep.

I took a pinch of Spiceweed and shoved it in my mouth. The taste was bitter and spicy and sweet and a dozen other things all at once. A moment later, I was on my hands and knees, vomiting up the contents of my stomach, my Portamancy Source only the first thing to hit the ground. It

was larger than I liked and hurt to swallow, and even more
to bring up.

The pahht man was arguing with his wife, holding
his children close. The argument was in pahht, so I had no
idea what was being said, but it looked quite animated. The
wife pointed above us, past the tree, to where a lone shack
sat atop the cliff face. The man sighed and raked a clawed
hand through the fur on his face. Sirileth watched them all
with that same wistful look. The young boy hid from her
darklight stare, but the girl stared back.

The pahht man pushed his two children behind him
and stepped forward to speak to me. I've never liked it when
people talk to me while I'm vomiting from spiceweed. It
always feels like they choose that moment for the advantage
it gives them.

"We canno sto here," the pahht man said in clipped
terran

I raised my head to tell him to fuck off, but my
stomach heaved and I dry-retched into the dirt instead.
Probably for the best.

"We don't have a choice," Kento said far more
diplomatically than I would have managed. "There is…
a limit to how many portals a person can open in a day."
Sometimes it's important to dumb down the truth for the
idiots listening.

The pahht man spat a word I didn't understand, but
I figured it was probably a well-earned insult. He glared at
me, then at Sirileth. "Shack worry. Smell monsters."

"This is the Other World," I managed to say, still
on my hands and knees. "There are fucking monsters
everywhere."

Sirileth took a step towards the man, held his angry

gaze. "You want to protect your family. I understand. I mean, I want to protect my family, too. I'd do anything to spare them this."

The pahht man nodded. "Yes."

Sirileth turned back to Kento. "Give me my Sources, sister. I can move us on, past this dangerous valley."

"You're not a Portamancer," I said. The retching had ceased and I scooped up my Source and put it back in its pouch.

"No, I'm not," Sirileth agreed. "But I know more about Portamancy than you do, Mother. And I would gladly suffer rejection for a few minutes to move us somewhere safer. Let me help, sister."

Kento was taller than Sirileth and looked down on her. "No. You caused this, Sirileth. I'm not going to risk giving you back your Sources." She turned away.

"Then you do it, sister. I mean, you're an Aspect. You can use all the schools of Sourcery. Use Portamancy. Get us out of here."

"Yes," the pahht man said quickly, moving to stand beside Sirileth. "Help ge out."

Kento stared at the ground and shook her head. "I can't."

"Help ge out," the pahht man repeated.

"She won't," Sirileth said. "And she won't let me help either."

Ssserakis chuckled in my mind. *Our daughter is masterful.* I thought it was just me, but my horror was seeing it too. Sirileth was playing the situation, playing the survivors. She had brought the moon down on top of us, had created this situation, killed tens of thousands. And yet, here she was using our peril to paint Kento as the villain and draw allies to herself. But to what end? I couldn't see it.

"Rest," Kento said. She looked exhausted. "I will protect you if any monsters attack."

We were not attacked, and a bloody good job it was, too. We were all exhausted. I was recovering from Source rejection. Honestly, I felt like for the past ten days I had been driving myself to the precipice of rejection every day. I had no idea how long a body could take such harsh treatment and what internal damage I might be doing to myself. Kento was flagging. I could see it in the way her limbs hung heavy when she wasn't paying attention, in the slight drag of her feet, and the way her eye blinks became slow, laborious things. Sirileth could fight with a blade or staff in hand, but she had none and no Sources with Kento hoarding them. I didn't trust the other survivors to do anything other than run around screaming and getting in the way. I've never understood why people scream at danger. If you're falling off a cliff, it's not like screaming at it is going to make gravity let you off its inexorable pull. If anything, the wailing will probably just piss it off and make it pull a bit harder. Ssserakis was our only other likely defender and my horror had not the strength to protect us.

We ate a few more strips of khark hound meat, our reserves already running low. We had not the time to preserve it properly so it would likely start spoiling soon. One of the survivors, the crazy terran man who kept muttering about the Maker, plucked an orange fruit from the tree we had been resting under. Before any of us could think of stopping him he had half devoured the juicy green flesh beneath the orange skin and was already reaching another of the low-hanging things.

Ssserakis chuckled. *You should leave that one behind. He*

is already dead.

I stalked towards the crazy fool and knocked the fruit from his hands, then gave him a solid shove with my shadowy claw. He stumbled away, spitting curses and seeds both. "What do you mean?" I asked Ssserakis.

Leave him here, before he becomes a danger.

"Why?"

Or better yet, bring him along. It will inspire delicious fear when he turns.

"Turns?"

When will you learn, Eska? Everything in my world is trying to kill you.

I trusted my horror, but I couldn't think of a way to leave the man behind. The others wouldn't accept it. And I already knew that trying to explain that the shadow monster possessing me had warned me the man would die, would not go down well. People: terran, pahht, garn, mur, all people act bloody weird around the idea of possession as if women haven't been carrying around parasites for eternity. Let me tell you, I much prefer being possessed to being pregnant.

We moved on quickly. I opened a portal to the strange fort with its bleeding walls. The ghoul leapt through, cavorting on the other side. I had to poke Kento to get her moving. My eldest daughter was asleep on her feet and startled.

We passed over a cracked plain in a half dozen portal jumps. It was that wide. The ground had formed into hundreds of pillars and pedestals, massive ravines running all around them. I stared over the edge, down into the depths of one of the ravines and saw darkness, black and complete. Then my eyesight shifted, colour draining away,

the gloom vanishing with it. Ssserakis' strange night sight.
The horror did not see colour, but darkness held no mystery
to it. Everything was shades of grey, just like the world it had
been born into. There was movement down at the bottom of
the ravine, shapes writhing against each other like maggots
in a fisherman's bucket.

"Geolids," I said, and knew it was true. I had seen
them once before. Nasty things. They do look a bit like
maggots, but with segmented bodies. They have hideous
maws on their front end that can chew through solid rock.
They also have faces on the joints of their many legs. Terran
faces. They are all frozen in rictus screams and chewed-
up rock dribbles from their open mouths. That rock paste
quickly solidifies as hard as… well, rock.

They are preparing the way for their master. She is close.

We moved on as quickly as I could force another
portal out.

I pushed myself a little too hard that day. How many
portals did I open? How far did we travel? I don't know.
But I called us to a halt when I started seeing that tree again.
Already I felt blood leaking from my nose, my stomach
clenching, limbs cramping. I was shaking as I shoved a
clump of spiceweed in my mouth and started retching.

"We can't stop here," Sirileth said. Her voice trembled
with fear but I didn't sense any from her.

"Bit late…" I brought up my Source. "For that."

I heard the other survivors talking. The pahht man
was loudest among them, arguing with his wife again.
He was clutching his young boy close to his side, but his
daughter had snuck away to stand close to Sirileth.

We were a few portals past the cracked plain. I had
deposited us on the banks of a large lake. The waters were

a muddy brown but whipped into a white-capped frenzy like rapids, except the water wasn't going anywhere. I didn't understand why, or how, but then we were in Sevorai and a lot of things in the Other World don't make sense.

"What's in the lake?" I asked after my stomach gave its final heave.

Water.

I could feel my horror's amusement and knew I'd get no better answer from it. The ghoul was pawing at the bank, yipping and howling, pointing across the lake.

"What is it saying?"

How should I know? I do not speak gibberish.

I had never thought about language and my horror before. What language did most of Sevorai speak? What language was natural to my horror?

You think in such simple terms, Eska. I can speak your language because you think and feel in those words. I know it because you know it. But communication does not always require words. Natural language. Ssserakis laughed. *My kind speaks in emotion. Fear. Anger. Love. Longing. It is beyond the limiting scope of your words.*

"Your kind? Horrors?"

That is what you name us. We are many, though none are as old as I. We feed off emotion. I was made to feed off fear, but there are others who seek to inspire anger and gorge themselves. Ilyeka feeds off lust. Creeps into the minds of their prey and stirs within them a passion they cannot ignore.

I thought about how many times I had lusted after a woman, a passion suddenly ignited inside so fierce I wanted to take a bite out of the object of my sudden affection. Had I been visited by Ssserakis' sibling?

You would know it. You would feel Ilyeka's touch in your

mind just as you are attuned to my own.

The ghoul was still yapping, pointing, frantic. Sirileth watched, one hand absently rubbing the frayed ends of her braided hair, the other near her mouth as she chewed on a fingernail. The young pahht girl stood beside my daughter, copying her pose as closely as she could.

"I think we're close," Sirileth said loudly.

The pahht man looked up from his argument with his wife, spotted his daughter, and rushed over, pulling her away from Sirileth.

"Two or three more portal jumps and we should be there. I mean, we should reach the approximate location of Dharhna back in our world."

The ghoul leapt up and down and pointed across the lake again. It seemed to be agreeing with my daughter. Not that I could have opened a single portal to get us there sooner. I scooped up my Portamancy Source and tucked it into the pouch. Sirileth watched me, eyes blazing.

"Then we wait here for a few hours, get some more sleep, and tomorrow... Or whatever passes for tomorrow here, we'll complete our journey."

The ghoul mewled and pawed at the ground again. It was agitated, didn't seem to like the idea of waiting at the lakeside.

My shadow rippled, extended beside me, and raised up from the ground into an inky, solid shape. *"You should listen to the ghoul. It is unwise to rest near water."*

The other survivors backed away from me as though a talking shadow was the worst thing they had to fear. I heard the Polasian woman say demon and Underworld and tried my best to ignore her. Fucking idiots.

"I can take us the rest of the way," Sirileth said. "I'm

good at coping with rejection. Sister, give me my Sources."

Kento had been standing, swaying, staring out over the waters, but I did not think she saw them thrashing. I don't think she saw anything. She absently reached for the pouch hanging at her belt and was halfway to handing it to her sister before she came around. She snatched the pouch back and glared at Sirileth. Then she sagged and almost collapsed. Sirileth hastened the last few steps between them and steadied Kento by the arm. She did not make a play for the Source pouch though.

"Sister, you can't keep at this. You need to rest."

Kento swayed, closed her eyes. I almost thought she wouldn't open them again. Then she stood a little straighter and pulled her arm away from Sirileth. "I'm fine. I can keep going."

"You need to rest," Sirileth repeated.

Kento shook her head. Not the controlled motion I was used to seeing from her, but wild and slow. "Not here. When we're out of the Other World."

"Then give me my Sources and let me help," Sirileth said, so earnest. "I'll get us to the right location. Then, as soon as Mother is rested, she can use the rift to take us back to Ovaeris."

I frowned. Something felt wrong about the statement, but I was also tired, not thinking clearly.

"I'm not going to kill us all with a couple of Sources, sister," Sirileth continued. "It's not like Sevorai even has a moon for me to bring down." She smiled, darklight eyes shining in the ever-present gloom.

Kento met her sister's gaze for a few seconds. Something broke in her then, the will to resist shattering against the iron edge of exhaustion. She handed over

Sirileth's pouch of Sources.

Sirileth took us the rest of the way in two portal jumps. She was bleeding from her nose and mouth and eyes by the time we were all through and quickly sucked on some spiceweed to throw up the Source before it killed her. We stood at the base of a great cliff face that rose hundreds of feet into the air. It was sheer, no handholds, barely even a crack I could see. It stretched out from one horizon to the other. A giant wall erected in the middle of nowhere. I had no idea what was on the other side.

I do. Flowne built this wall. My shadowy cloak twisted, forming into giant wings, and Ssserakis gave them a beat. My horror took us straight up until we crested the top of the wall. It did seem to stretch on forever in both directions and was easily a hundred feet thick at its slimmest.

"One of the lords of Sevorai built this?"

Flowne is a master of warping rock. She has hardened it so even the Geolids struggle to chew through it.

I paced across the wall to the other side. A strange noise reached my ears. A resonant thumping that trembled the air and shook the wall through my feet. I had a horrible feeling I knew what I would see on the other side.

Norvet Meruun was everywhere. Endless. A sea of pulsing flesh. She surged up against the wall, delayed by it but nothing more. Every beat of her heart saw her grow upwards, claiming another finger width of the wall like a rising tide. The horizon lit with her menacing red glow, the light racing along the folds of her flabby mass. Even with an army, I couldn't see how we would beat her back.

You do not chop down a forest in one swing.

"You almost sound like Tamura."

The Aspect was smart. I liked him.

"Also, forests don't normally fight back while you're cutting down trees."

Maybe not in your world.

We glided back down to the others. The ghoul was dancing on the spot, pawing at the ground. It seemed to think we had arrived in Dharhna. Or the approximate location at least. Kento was resting with her back against the cliff face. She was trying to keep her eyes open, but they kept drifting closed. My oldest daughter needed desperately to sleep. Sirileth paced nearby, rubbing at her braided hair. I noticed the pouch of Sources Kento had kept from her for so long was tucked into her belt.

The other survivors milled about in small packs. The crazy old terran man was rocking back and forth alone, clutching at his stomach.

He does not have long. You should kill him before he becomes a danger.

"I don't think the others would trust me if I did that." Besides, I was worried about what Kento and Sirileth might think of me. I wanted to be better in their eyes. I would not murder a man in front of them.

The pahht family was close to Kento. The young boy was asleep, curled up in the mother's lap. The man was standing watch, clawed hand scratching at the fur on his left arm. The girl only had eyes for Sirileth.

I heard a howl from above and knew the noise well. Hellions. They had talons that could slice metal and flesh, were nimble in flight, and could spit great wads of saliva that hardened like steel in moments. Dangerous creatures well suited to battle. I know because I had used them myself many times.

Sirileth looked up, smiled. Then she glanced at the

terran man clutching his stomach just as he slumped over. We were out of time. I ran over to Sirileth, grabbed her arm and turned her to face me. Her darklight stare blazed.

"Where is the scar?" I asked. "You said there was one here, that we could use it to cross worlds."

Sirileth smiled and shook her head sadly. "I'm sorry, Mother. There is no scar in Dharhna. I mean, not yet."

CHAPTER

FIVE

DECEPTION IS ONE OF THE FUNDAMENTAL
necessities of sentient existence. You only know that about
me which I choose to share and believe me when I tell you
there are things I have not shared. You know the truth only
as far as I have allowed you to see it, and I have hidden
things.

The masks we wear every day, those we allow others
to see are not the truth. They may be glimpses of it, but
even open books hide the pages that have come before, and
those that are yet unread. The thoughts that race through
our minds may not always be moral or just or fair, so we
hide them. It is a necessary deception to save others from
drowning in our madness.

I believe Sirileth lied to protect us. To protect me.
She knew what needed to be done. She knew that someone
needed to die. I think she was afraid I would take it upon

myself if I knew the truth. She always did think me better than I truly was.

"What are you saying, Sirileth? If there's no scar here, why did we come?" I felt like shaking some sense out of her. But she met my gaze, stood tall, and didn't flinch even as a chorus of howls sounded above. Hellions swooping down from the top of the cliff.

The survivors panicked. One of the Polasian men, a tall fellow with the grey veil of a slave across his mouth, ran. He was the first to die as a hellion crashed into him from above slamming him into the dirt with enough force to shatter bone. Then the monster leapt into the air, carrying the limp body away. Sirileth didn't break my stare the entire time.

"I have been studying these rifts for years, Mother. Hundreds of experimentations and calculations."

"Start making sense," I growled.

Kento staggered to her feet, using the wall for support. She formed a Sourceblade in her hands and took a ready stance just as another hellion swept down, skimming the surface of the wall. It made a grab for the pahht mother, Kento stumbled into its way, clumsily swinging her sword. The kinetic blade skittered across tough hide, knocked the hellion off course. It slammed into Kento, throwing her to the ground, then beat its wings, climbing back into the sky. Kento rolled over slowly, got her hands and knees beneath her, collapsed. The pahht girl rushed to Kento's side, flung my daughter's arm over her shoulder, started helping her up.

Five paces away, the crazy old terran man screamed and convulsed. White roots burst out of his skin, through his fingers, and out his chest. He lurched upright, his eyes gleaming red like they were lit with fire from the inside. The Polasian woman had been rushing over to check on him but skidded to a halt. He reached for her, claw-like branches snaking from his hands. She recoiled, fell backwards.

"Rifts cannot be created too close together, Mother," Sirileth said, her eyes blazing at me. "They interfere with each other. If we had tried to form a new minor rift too close to the great rift, its destination would have been drawn off here, to the Other World."

I was confused. Wasn't that what we wanted? A portal we could use to escape Sevorai. I shook my head at her, but my daughter barrelled on. "I mean, we needed the minor rift to be far enough away that any portal created here would be flexible enough to reach elsewhere. We also needed it to be behind the walls of Dharhna to protect us from the storm when we exit it."

I grabbed her arm in my shadowy claw. She didn't try to pull away.

"You trusted me with Lursa and the great rift, Mother."

"And you brought a second cataclysm to our world."

Sirileth winced. That accusation hurt her. Shame it was also fucking true. "Trust me now. I know what I am doing."

Another hellion swept down, howled, wheeled overhead, spat a gobbet of saliva at Kento. It hit her in the chest, splattered along the pahht girl's arm and face, solidified in seconds, bonding the two together. Kento staggered, fell, dragged the girl with her. The pahht man rushed over, started trying to pull his daughter away. The hardened saliva was too strong. The crazy terran tree man was lurching after the Polasian woman. Every moment that passed he looked less terran and more like a creaker wearing a man's skin as some macabre disguise.

"Ssserakis?"

I cannot help. The tree is too young to feel anything but hunger. The hellions are controlled. They feel nothing because they are but puppets.

I let go of Sirileth's arm. "What do we do?"

She shot me a sorry smile, tears dancing in her darklight eyes. "We need to kill someone."

Again, I had the dizzying thought that she had somehow planned all this. From dropping the moon on us all, to the storm, to Imiko's sacrifice, to meeting Brakunus, to travelling through the Other World to Dharhna. How could she have planned everything in such an exact manner? But, of course, she hadn't. She had expected Irad to be evacuated. She was certain Ssserakis would go to her not me. She had no way of knowing about Norvet Meruun or Brakunus. This wasn't planning, but adaptation to a spiralling situation. I recognised it because it was what I had so often done.

You are dancing to someone else's tune, Eskara. It is unlike you.

My horror wasn't wrong. Not entirely. It was unlike who I had been.

Who you need to be again.

Sirileth turned from me and strode over to Kento and the young pahht girl stuck together. She pulled the pahht man away from his daughter and fixed him with a darklight stare. I drifted behind to hear.

"Do you want to save your family?" Sirileth asked.

The pahht man frowned, nodded emphatically. "Yes. Help."

"I can't. Only you can do it." Sirileth reached into her

Source pouch and brought out three small Sources, each no larger than a pea. "Swallow these."

The pahht man stared at the Sources for a moment, then at Sirileth, aghast. A hellion swept down on us. Kento stood, dragging the pahht girl up with her, raised her hand. A kinetic barrier burst from her fingers, a flickering purple haze. The hellion smashed into it, knocking Kento down with a cry of pain, her shield vanishing in a puff of energy. The hellion bounded away, flapping huge, leathery wings to get back into the air. Kento struggled to rise again, but she was too exhausted. Days without sleep, everything that we had been through. It was too much for her.

"You will die," Sirileth said, relentless. "It will be painful. But I promise I will protect your family. I will get them home."

Sirileth and the pahht man stared at each other. The Polasian woman scrambled over to us, the tree man creaking after her, eyes gleaming red, skin stretched unnaturally and poked through with branches.

Perhaps I could have done something if I had known all the facts. Probably not. As damning as it was, Sirileth was right. This was the only way. Of course, she had engineered it to be the case.

The pahht man snarled, snatched the Sources from Sirileth's hand and shoved them into his mouth. He winced and growled as he swallowed. Sources are not easy to force down even to those of us who are used to it, but he managed. I was already backing away, pulling the Polasian woman with me. Sirileth grabbed the pahht woman and her boy and followed me. Kento was helped upright and staggered away with the pahht girl. It said a lot about how tired my oldest daughter was that she didn't even argue with Sirileth over what was happening.

Source rejection is quick when it starts. Especially for those who aren't Sourcerers. If he had swallowed a single Source he might have a minute. But he had swallowed three. He had seconds at best. I only hoped Sirileth knew what she was doing because we were too close to survive a large blast.

The pahht man gagged. Blood streamed from his eyes, matting his fur. He reached a clawed hand towards his family, snarled something in pahht, gagged again, spat crimson onto the rocky ground.

The boy broke away from his mother, tried to run for his father, but I caught him in my shadowy claw, dragged him back and turned him around. He didn't need to see his father die. The boy scratched and punched me. I weathered his assault.

The other survivors joined us, huddled together as hellions howled and swept down from above. One slammed into the dying man, claws driving into his shoulder, it tried to lift him away, but it couldn't. Already the man's legs had turned to metal, weighing him down. He snarled one more word to his family. Then he detonated.

It was more of an implosion, really. One moment the man was there, then a flash of white light and he was simply gone. Half the hellion that was trying to drag him away was gone too. In the man's place was a hole leading down into the earth. The air shimmered with vague glimpses of other places like mirages.

"Your turn, Mother," Sirileth said. She let go of the pahht woman who dropped to her knees, wailing out her grief in warbling shrieks.

I looked aghast at my youngest daughter. She stared back. "Swallow your Portamancy Source and tear us a portal back to Ovaeris."

She had created a new minor rift here and the barriers between worlds were thinner. I could get us out of here.

I shoved my Source into my mouth and swallowed hard. It was not so long since I had suffered my own rejection. I had not had time to recover yet. Swallowing that Source was tough, as though my body knew the strain it was already under and fought against me putting it through more. I swallowed, thumped my chest, forced it down.

Rejection started immediately. My body decided it had had enough of my shit and I was far too old to be putting it through the wringer like this. Cramps started in my stomach and I felt my limbs trembling. I didn't have long. A few minutes at most.

A hellion swooped down and Kento thrust a hand at it, releasing a kinetic blast. It hit the flying monster and set it veering off course. I looked up through bleeding eyes to see a host of winged shapes launching over the precipice above, diving towards us.

"Now, Mother," Sirileth prompted.

She will be the death of you if you are not careful.

I ignored my horror and drew on the Source in my stomach. I tore open a portal to Ovaeris. It burned at the edges, fire sparking and roaring. On the other side, I saw a sandy street, gloomy and all but abandoned. Dust and dirt whipped about along with a roaring wind that surged through the concourse. Buildings stood tall and square, windows shuttered against the storm. Dharhna. The ghoul had led us right. I glanced about for the monster, but it had already fled.

Kento was first through, the pahht girl with her, sobbing but supporting my daughter. I pushed the boy towards his mother and they went through next. The Polasian woman leapt through after, and then the pahht couple taking care of the terran child. Then it was just Sirileth and me in Sevorai.

"Thank you for trusting me, Mother," she said, smiling at me. She stepped forward and wrapped her arms around me. I felt torn in two, and not just because of the magic that was ripping me apart inside. My daughter was grateful for something I should have given without reservation. But at the same time, I was seeing the woman she was becoming and she scared me. Her ruthlessness, conviction, ability, and foresight. How could I see what she was capable of and not be both terrified and so very proud?

Sirileth backed up and stepped through the portal into Dharhna. The hellions screamed as they dove at me and I leapt through after her. I snapped the portal shut behind me.

The change was dramatic. Sevorai was strangely cool and humid, and though I hadn't noticed it before, far too quiet. It was an odd stillness that held that world in thrall and made everything sound muted and distant. Ovaeris, however, was all noise and light and friction.

Yes. It burns.

My horror hid inside me, as far from the light of my world as it could be. Yet Ssserakis still wrapped me in my shadow as a cloak. It protected me from much of the stinging abrasion as the storm gusted around us, whipping sand and dirt into our faces. The air was hot, despite the blasting wind, and dry as sun-baked rock. We huddled together in that empty street, trying to shield ourselves and each other from the worst of the storm. It raged all around us. All around Dharhna. I could see nothing of the larger city past its fury. I knew that Dharhna had large walls protecting it from the desert side, and a mountain at its back, and I guessed that was doing much to keep the city standing despite the storm Lursa's impact had created.

I squinted past the flying sand and saw shadows shifting behind some of the closed shutters. A figure stood to our left, inside the arch of a building's doorframe. Whoever they were, they were covered head to toe in dark robes, leaving only their eyes uncovered. They held a stout wooden stick in one hand, and I had the sudden impression we would not be receiving a warm welcome in Dharhna.

My stomach cramped again and I doubled over. Blood leaked from my eyes, running down the side of my nose and pooling at my lip.

You are dying, Eska. I cannot hold back the damage much longer.

I had almost forgotten how Ssserakis somehow shielded me from the effects of rejection. Perhaps 'shielding me' is the wrong term. Shared in the pain, lessening it as much as it could. I reached for my spiceweed pouch with a trembling hand, found it missing.

Sirileth clutched the pouch in her hand in a way that left me under no false impression that she was keeping it from me. "You have one more job yet, Mother. I mean. It has to be you."

The wind howled around us, spraying us all with stinging sand. Already I saw the Polasian woman and the pahht couple with the terran child slinking away. I hoped they found some safety in the beleaguered city.

Sirileth stepped close, loomed above me, gripped my shoulder. "Listen to me, Mother, you don't have long."

I trembled at her as furiously as I could. "I'm aware."

"You can get us home. I mean, you can open a portal from here to Yenheim." She squinted at me, shielding her face with one hand scarred by molten metal. And I realised, she was fucking serious.

I shook my head at my mad daughter. Yenheim was half a world away. A different continent. Weeks by sea, days by even the fastest flyer. There was an ocean, vast and cold and deadly between us. I could barely open a portal to the limits of my line of sight even when I wasn't minutes away from catastrophic rejection.

Her grip on my shoulder tightened. "Distance doesn't matter, Mother. All the rifts are connected. I mean, you can open a portal from any minor rift to its relevant place in Sevorai. Or you can open a portal from a minor rift to any other minor rift on Ovaeris. You just need to know where you are aiming for."

My stomach cramped. It felt like a ferret was trying to claw its way out of me. Blood ran from my nose and I spat it into the sandy dust at my feet.

Sirileth was relentless. "Do you know the cavern underneath Yenheim palace, in the depths? There is a single broken pillar, the rest still run with blue veins. A room off to one side is enchanted with Chronomancy so the contents don't feel the decay of age. Do you know it?"

I tried to speak, gagged on blood, could only nod. Of course I knew it. I had sex for the first time in that dingy cavern. Isen and I had created Kento in that damned hall.

"There is a rift in the centre of that cavern, Mother. I created it. You need to open a portal to it now."

I tried to concentrate but found I was in too much pain. My limbs trembled, ached, spasmed. My stomach was on fire. Blood streamed from my eyes and ears. I couldn't focus.

Then it all just stopped. The pain vanished. My limbs still trembled, but I couldn't feel them. I saw Sirileth speaking but couldn't hear the words. Even the howling of the wind was gone. I heard nothing but silence, the gentle swooshing of waves against a beach.

"*I cannot take your burden for long, Eska,*" Ssserakis said the words in my voice. With my mouth. The horror had pushed me down, assumed control again. No. Not quite that. Ssserakis hadn't pushed me down, but had risen beside me, taking some of the control and all the pain. It left me able to move my arms and think, but all my senses bar sight were gone. "*Hurry!*"

I pictured the great hall where Sirileth claimed to have created a minor rift. I remembered it well enough. A vast cavern. Two dozen behemothic pillars stretched from floor to ceiling, each one snaking with blue veins. One of the pillars had collapsed when I pulled Yenheim palace from the earth, its rubble lay strewn across the cavern floor. There had been imps living there once, their leavings still littered the place, but the little creatures themselves had long since fled or been wiped out. I knew that cavern. I could picture it. I could see its location. Across the sea, the continent of Isha, my little queendom of Yenheim, in the catacombs beneath the palace. I had it. Now I had to hope that Sirileth was right.

I drew on the Source that was killing me and ripped open a portal. On the other side was a gloomy hall lit only by a dim ethereal blue. Sirileth was right. I had done it. I had just opened a portal that led to the other side of the world.

"I knew it!" Sirileth shouted happily. "I mean, I theorised it. I was all but certain." I would have glared at my daughter, but I was weeping blood and trying to blink it away.

"*Hurry.*"

Kento was busy twisting her way out of her jacket. It was solidified with hellion spit, but she contorted her way free and let it fall to the ground with a ripped section of the pahht girl's tunic. Kento staggered towards the portal without a word, passed through.

Sirileth turned to the pahht family still cowering in the middle of the street. "I promised I would protect you," she shouted over the howling of the storm. "I will. You have a place in Yenheim, if you want it. I'll…"

The pahht woman took a single step forward and spat at Sirileth. Then she turned, gathered her children to her, and fled down the street. She was soon swallowed by the swirling, stinging sand.

As Sirileth slumped to the portal, I saw the confusion and hurt in her eyes. Could she not understand that she had just murdered their husband and father? Did she think the family would welcome her? Fool of a girl.

I was the last one through the portal and I snapped it shut behind me, staggering into the cool, dark of the great cavern. All was silent again, the howling of the storm nothing but a memory. Ssserakis fled, diving deep into my soul and curling there like a wounded dog. All my aches, pains, cramps, and everything else flooded back in. I was so close to catastrophic rejection. I could see everywhere I had been for days, a hundred images all layered atop each other. I was coming apart, fraying at all the edges, my essence scattered across our two worlds. It hurt. Fuck me but dying hurt.

CHAPTER

SIX

THE HOST FOUGHT AGAINST THE GOD
fragment. She couldn't win on her own. Ssserakis leant the host
strength. It had much to spare. The fear the host had inspired in the
feral beasts below had been a feast. They had thrown themselves at
her, fear and anger mounting, and she had slain them with fire and
lightning. And Ssserakis had grown fat. It could feel it even now,
even within this strange barrier the gods had erected. Fear, like all
emotion, transcended realms. No barrier could keep it out.

The god fragment snapped her fingers and sound battered
the host. She collapsed to her knees, clutching her ears. Ssserakis
heard the noise only as a distant thing. It took control of the host's
shadow, filled in her ears for her, protecting her. It was for the best.
Ssserakis had never found a host quite so comfortable with its
presence. Most were driven mad by sharing their body and soul
with a horror, but this Eskara host was different. She welcomed
Ssserakis. She needed to be kept alive, though that was more

difficult than it sounded.

The host was determined to end its own life. Even happy, or perhaps especially when happy, the host wanted to die. Ssserakis could feel it, even now. She would sacrifice her life for others, for revenge, for love, for anything. The host was looking for a reason to die, an excuse to end itself. So was the god fragment. They fought each other, loved each other. Both wanted to die here, wanted to be killed by the other here. Both wanted the other to survive. Yet both tried to kill each other. Such madness was beyond comprehension. More importantly, it could not be allowed. The host had to survive, so the host had to win.

Ssserakis poured more of its strength into the host, manifested her shadow as wings. It felt good to control the host's shadow, a way to directly interact with the burning world. Together they fought now, shadow and god magic side by side. The god fragment fell back under the onslaught. Ssserakis revelled in it. Such power they had together. It had never imagined finding a host that fit so well. Even the other lords of Sevorai would be forced to bow against such power as they could wield.

The barrier around them shattered. The god fragment stumbled, confused. The host darted in for the kill and… stopped. Placed a loving hand against the god fragment's chest.

"It's over," the host said.

She didn't know. The host had never experienced the treachery of the gods. She thought this god fragment to be like her because it looked like her. She did not understand the depth of her mistake. Ssserakis would not let the host die. It took her shadow, forged it into a blade, and thrust into the heart of the god fragment.

The god fragment died in the host's arms. For a moment that lasted an eternity, all fear vanished. Not just the fear of the host, that delicious lake that never ran dry, but all fear everywhere. Ssserakis couldn't sense it. Not from the host, or from the host's companions, of the feral beasts below. There was nothing. Nothing but useless grief. A drowning tide of it that swallowed everything. Such a mortal construct, more useless than anything else. Even love was an emotion with a use, Ssserakis could twist it into fear so easily. But grief was all-consuming, blotting out thought and feeling, leaving a horrible numbness in its wake. That numbness was true pain to Ssserakis. An absence so deep it felt like it was drowning, being smothered in nothing. Dwindling away until it just stopped.

Ssserakis felt fear then. Not the host's fear. Ssserakis felt its own fear. It couldn't drink this in. Couldn't use it. Ssserakis was ancient. A horror. The embodiment of fear. It was made to inflict, to feed upon, not to feel.

Something shifted inside the host. Not a physical thing, but a change in perspective. Anger exploded into life, filling the void of that grief. Ssserakis soared with it. Anger, it could use. Anger was close to fear.

"You killed her," the host whispered the words but they thundered through her like a deafening gale that threatened to blow Ssserakis away and apart. It struggled to hold onto itself in the face of such overwhelming fury. Ssserakis knew with certainty if the host turned such a tempest on it, focused all that rage upon it, the host could blast Ssserakis into nothing. Ssserakis was not mortal. Was not made to be extinguishable. Could not allow it to happen. It needed to direct the rage elsewhere before the host obliterated it.

"I protected you, just as I said I would. Just as you asked. Lay the blame where it deserves to be, Eskara." The host liked to be called by its name, as if such a thing was worth remembering. "Not on me, and not on yourself. All this is a product of a war none of us ever wanted a part in. You want a culprit, a target for your grief and pain? There is one right there."

It worked. The host set its sight on the god and shifted

the blame so easily from Ssserakis. She lay the body of the god
fragment down with such tenderness. The host had truly loved
the god fragment. Not such a fleeting desire as lust. But love.
Ssserakis felt something strange at that realisation. It understood
the feeling as guilt but had never thought to experience it. Yet, it
had corrupted the love the host felt for the god fragment, used it to
plant seeds of suspicion. And Ssserakis was guilty to have had a
hand in destroying such a thing.

The host stood, summoned her magic. Ssserakis pushed
the guilt aside and manifested in the host's shadow once more.
Together, they leapt into battle against a god.

"Why did you show me that?" I asked as soon as I
came awake.

Sirileth frowned at me, her darklight eyes blazing in
the gloom of the great chamber. She had her back against
one of the pillars. Kento was next to me, snoring softly in
sleep. Sirileth had been watching over us.

"Are you talking to me?" Sirileth asked. "Or..." She
snorted and shook her head. "Of course not."

Show you what?

"That dream. That... memory."

What are you talking about, Eska?

"I saw..." That wasn't the right word. I didn't
see it. I experienced it. I experienced Silva's death from
the perspective of my horror. Tears stung my eyes and I
squeezed them away to roll down my cheeks. Fuck! Twenty
years and reliving that moment still felt like digging rusty
nails in my chest. Of all the moments to relive, why that one?
Why the moment of my greatest regret?

"Are you *you* again, Mother?" Sirileth asked.

She refused to speak even a word to me. Our daughter is as stubborn as you, Eska.

I nodded, unwilling to open my eyes. I could still feel it. Me as Ssserakis, my shadow sliding into Silva's heart, ending her. I felt her flesh part and her life spasm and then fade. Why? Why? Why that fucking moment?

A sob tore free and I struggled for control. Despair crept up on silent feet, thrust a bag over my head, cinched it tight around my neck, cutting off my breath. I was so damned tired. Tired of the fight, of the struggle, of being me, of living. I never believed in any sort of afterlife. I had seen too many ghosts to fool myself into thinking death was anything but an eternal half-life. Yet at that moment, I wanted to believe. Some people were so certain that when they died they would be reunited with all those they loved in their lives, all those who had passed on already. It sounded wonderful. I wanted it. I wanted to die and be reunited with Silva. To see her again. To smell her again. To melt into her arms and let her soothe the pain away like no one else ever had. I knew it was the call of the void, that treacherous little voice that promised relief. I knew it was a lie. But right then, I just wasn't strong enough to fight it anymore. If I'd been standing on a cliff, I would have thrown myself off. For a single damning moment, I gave in entirely and begged silently for death.

I am sorry, Eska. Ssserakis said the words quietly in my head, and it meant them. I knew them for truth. It was sorry for killing Silva. Not for itself and not for her. Ssserakis still believed it had done the right thing, protected me. But it was sorry for the pain it caused me. It wasn't much. It was everything. It was enough.

The wave of despair washed away, dragging one last ragged sob from me. It left me numb, but the call of the void was gone again. For now.

I wiped my eyes on my filthy sleeve and opened them to find Sirileth watching me. She sat cross-legged, a hand fiddling with her braided hair.

"Thank you for saving me," I said, guessing she had been the one to shove spiceweed in my mouth even as I passed out. "And for watching over us."

Sirileth shook her head. "You're my mother. Kento is my sister." She looked away, refusing to hold my gaze. "I mean, what else would I have done?"

Ask our daughter why she will not talk to me.

"You planned this, Sirileth."

She frowned again, rubbed at her braid, then purposefully pulled her hand away and clutched them both together in her lap. "Not everything went to plan. I mean, I know Kento doesn't believe me, but I meant for Irad to be evacuated. I did. I did. I did." She looked at me, tears sending the light from her eyes sharding in every direction, flaring the coronas. "I knew some would die, but I never meant for so many. I don't know how to..." She was breathing heavily as though unable to catch her breath. "I don't. So many. Too many. Too many. Too many."

I crawled over on hands and knees and wrapped my arms around my daughter. She went stiff for a moment, tensing so suddenly I thought she would push me away. Then she softened, collapsed into me, and sobbed. She clutched to me, hands bunching around my shadow cloak, face buried in my chest.

"I'm sorry about Imiko," she slurred between sobs. "It wasn't meant to be her. I didn't want... Not her."

I floundered, unsure what to do. This was a side of my daughter I had never seen before. Always, she was proper, strong, formal. She had never broken down in my arms. When Vi died, Sirileth had been stoic. When she first killed a man, she had been detached. When the Maker took her and then spit her back out, she had been cold. But here was my daughter, vulnerable and hurting, and I didn't know what to do. So I held her. Pulled her tight and didn't let go while she sobbed, wailed, poured out her sins.

I have watched friends die. Brought empires to ruin. Slaughtered an entire city in my madness. My sins pale in comparison to Sirileth's. But everything she did, all the atrocities she committed, were for a good cause. At least, she believed them to be. She was trying to save our world, to defeat the Maker. She was trying to do good, even knowing that the method would be evil.

I held my daughter a long time there in that cavern. Until our tears ran together, mixing in the fractured light of our eyes. Until our tears ran dry and I felt Sirileth finally slouch, her hands losing their grip. Until for the first time in her whole life, my daughter fell asleep in my arms.

CHAPTER SEVEN

I LET SIRILETH SLEEP, HER HEAD PILLOWED IN my lap. Ssserakis made sure my shadow was cool. There's nothing worse than a hot pillow. My bones ached from sitting still for so long but I refused to move. I was there, and my daughters were with me. Peaceful. Despite everything that had happened, it was as close to a perfect moment as I can remember. But my mind never stays still for long and soon I was considering what we might do, how we might rally an army to march against a world-eating monster.

Kento woke first, seeming more herself. By that I mean she frowned down at Sirileth and stalked away. Sirileth woke not long after and composed herself quickly. The pain and vulnerability she had shown me before was gone, pushed down. But that is the way things often are. Emotions are volcanoes. When they erupt, they do so messily, spewing molten pain or grief or anger or joy all over the landscape, changing things forever. But then the eruption calms and the volcano falls back to sleep, and those emotions that been fiery and molten harden into something solid and cold.

We were all thirsty and hungry, still tired despite the rest. Bloodied and buried. At least we knew the way out. Sirileth had come to the cavern recently enough to create the minor rift.

I spent a minute before we left staring at the rift. It was tiny. You could walk through it and not even realise it was there. Occasionally a soft spark of energy built up and released, arcing to the floor and striking the stone harmlessly. That was it. It made my senses tingle though. I felt it like that odd sensation of being watched. When I was close, I knew something was wrong, but none of my senses could agree what. And when I closed my eyes, I swear I could see Sevorai. A grey mountain climbing into the sky, a city clinging to the side of the mountain like goats to a cliff face.

Xirei, city of Myth. Turn around.

In the other direction I saw a vast valley filled with bones, corpses, ghouls scavenging off the carrion. So many bones. Tens of thousands must have died to fill such a valley.

More.

At the other end of the valley rose another mountain, climbing sharply into the sky. A city clung to that mountain too, a mimic of the one Ssserakis named Xirei.

Ierix, city of Fable. Ssserakis chuckled. *Idiotic names. This is the home of Aire and Dialos, the one that is two that is many that is two that is one.*

"The twins," I said. I imagine Sirileth and Kento were already getting used to me talking to my other self.

I would not suggest calling them that to their faces. This is the Valley of Many where they do battle every day, sending out their thousand selves to fight.

"Every day they send out minions to fight?"

No minions. Aire and Dialos are their own minions. They send out their many selves to fight, to see which one of them gets to make the decisions that day. Fools! They bicker amongst themselves while my world falls to ruin under an overgrown tumour.

"Eska," Kento said. I felt her hand on my shoulder. "It's time to go."

I opened my eyes and Sevorai vanished. I was back in the cavern. Though, I suppose I had never really left. I didn't realise it at the time, but I had spent too long with the Portamancy Source inside me. The damage was done. Much like when I had rejected the Geomancy Source and it had turned my arm to stone, the Portamancy had changed me.

We started our trek up to Yenheim palace. It was a sombre journey. I think much of it stemmed from Kento. She was sullen and that quiet seeped out of her like water leaking from a sponge.

"These minor rifts." I couldn't take the silence anymore. It ate at me, clawed away my sanity. I had too many memories of these decrepit halls. I had lost too much in this ruined Djinn city. And I'd never found the time to scratch the bloody faces off the walls. The faces were the work of the Damned who had once infested the place. I never did find out why they carved faces into all the walls, but the eyes had this unnerving feeling of following you. "We can portal between them all instantly?"

"Yes," Sirileth said. "I set up a few around Isha. But there are others on other continents. All over the place. I mean, wherever someone died from rejection with at least three Sources in their stomach."

"Three?"

"Yes." Sirileth trailed a hand across the wall as she spoke. At first I thought she was purposefully touching all the faces. Then I realised there was a line of white chalk just above. I smiled at that. Vi was leading us home. "If someone dies from just one Source, the Source acts upon them. Turns them to stone or metal or burns them up. If they die from two Sources, the magics conflict and cause a violent explosion, but it's not enough to rip the barrier between realms. If they die from three of more Sources, the reaction tears a hole in reality. A rift. The more Sources, the bigger the rift."

"That's why the rift the Iron Legion left was so much larger," I said. "He could carry ten Sources."

Sirileth nodded. We came to a doorway in the corridor, the chalk stopped. Sirileth peered into the yawning room. "This was our headquarters," she said. I saw an old fireplace, filled with ashen remains. Chairs pulled up around a crude drawing on the ground in white chalk. "Tris would gather us here and detail the plan of attack. Vi would sketch out the directions for our exploration. I stood in the corner and watched." So many years ago, now. So much suffering.

Sirileth bit her lip and stepped past the room and continued on, hand trailing below another line of chalk. "I have plans drawn up in my rooms. A gateway we can build at each minor rift. Each gate needs some of the conductive alloy of ore from our moons, and a Portamancy Source. But they will allow people to open the portals between rifts without a Sourcerer. I mean, anyone could use them. Instant travel from one rift to another. For anyone."

Kento stopped then, stared at her sister in wonder.

"How? How would the gates know where to portal to?"

Sirileth smiled at Kento, warm and genuine. "Augmancers can create enchantments that point to each other. I devised a series of runes that could be entered on a dial. Each rune would point to its counterpart on a specific gate. I mean, you'd select the rune and it would direct the gate. Then just enter the Portamancy Source and the portal opens. It's actually quite simple." She started rubbing at her braid. "It will take time and money to set up though. Lots of ore, lots of Sources. I have the plans, but... Not the resources."

Stable portals to the other continents for anyone. My daughter had just revolutionised travel on Ovaeris and she called it quite simple.

We moved on. Much of the sombre atmosphere evaporated and Kento quizzed Sirileth on the rifts as we walked. I strolled behind my daughters, smiling as they chatted. Some say pride is a sin. Fuck them. I basked in it. My daughters were healthy, strong, smart, more capable than I ever was.

Our daughters. Ssserakis corrected me.

The first guard we encountered was lazing at her post. At the entrance to the catacombs, a small watch station had been set up. It had long sight lines down the corridor, plenty of cover, and a small armoury worth of bows and the arrows to use with them. In my time as queen of Yenheim, the post had always been occupied by at least four soldiers. But the catacombs had been quiet for years now, and I supposed the soldiers were needed elsewhere.

The guard had her chair tipped back, feet resting on the table in front of her. Her helmet and armour were off, stacked haphazardly in the corner of the little guard

station, and she was reading a book. A cup of something hot
steamed away next to her on the table and whatever it was it
smelled good enough I felt like snatching it and downing the
contents. I was quite thirsty. She startled when she saw us
pass the door to her little watch room and dropped her book,
almost fell backwards off her chair. Then she snatched up
her spear and ran outside to accost us.

"Halt!"

It took only a glance from Sirileth to silence the guard.
She all but dropped her spear in her haste to kneel. "Queen
Sirileth. You're back."

"I am. You don't have to kneel." Sirileth extended a
hand and the guardswoman took it with a look of awe, let
herself be pulled back to her feet.

"The regent will be pleased."

"Regent?" Sirileth asked, narrowing her eyes.

"Your brother. He's been ruling in your stead."

Sirileth was silent a moment, then sucked in a harsh
breath. "Has he?" She turned and started striding away.
Kento hurried after her.

I paused before the guardswoman a moment. I don't
think she recognised me. She was old enough to have been
in my employ back when I was queen, but then I guess I
looked much older now. Also, Ssserakis had my shadowy
cloak pulled close, the hood up, obscuring much of my face.

"Can you send for Hardt, ask him to find us." He
might not be working for the crown anymore, but everyone
in my queendom had heard of Hardt. I wondered if he still
lived in the palace, or if he had finally made good on his
many threats to build his own house.

The guardswoman peered at me a moment. Leaning
in, she stared into the depths of my shadowy hood. Then

my eyes flashed. Recognition dawned. She was back down
on her knees a moment later. "You're back, My Queen." She
bowed her head.

I coughed awkwardly. Glanced aside and found
Sirileth had stopped, was staring back, a deadly look on
her face. This poor guardswoman had made a dangerous
mistake. I was not queen here. Had not been for a long time.
I did not deserve the reverence I was being shown.

Yes we do, Eskara. We are mighty, regardless of throne.

"Stand up. I'm no one's queen."

The guardswoman did not stand up, but she did stare
up at me, that same look of awe on her face that she showed
Sirileth. "You are the Corpse Queen."

"Well... yes. That's true. But I'm not queen of
Yenheim. Just stand up and find Hardt."

"My Queen." The guardswoman sprang up and ran
off, leaving her post at my command.

Sirileth glared at me a moment longer, then strode
away. I hurried to catch up and had a feeling I was going to
regret giving out orders.

Sirileth set a determined pace. That's another way of
saying she was clearly pissed off and damn near running.
I never thought my daughter cared all that much about the
throne or her queendom. She did leave it, after all, just like
I had. But she was clearly angry that her rule and authority
had been usurped.

The halls were strangely empty. Few servants,
fewer guards. No children. Most families in Yenheim lived
in the town surrounding the palace these days. I missed
the bustle of my early rule when the halls rang with the
footsteps of people old and young alike. There were still
cats everywhere. They slunk around in packs and hissed at

us if we walked too close. Well, they hissed at me. They ran towards Sirileth, tried to wind themselves about her legs even as she walked.

Sirileth stormed into the throne room with me and Kento only a few steps behind. She immediately slowed to a stop, staring around at the occupants. There was a council in session, though I recognised few of those in attendance. Most of them looked like soldiers, dressed in armour, swords at their hips. A dozen or so, some with faces painted in red and white. Tris' warriors. Those who had taken up residence in the Forest of Ten and refused to stop their raids into Tor territory.

Presiding over his council of warriors was Tris himself. My adopted son lounged in the Corpse Throne's morbid embrace as if he had been born to sit it. The carved stone skeletons clawed up and around him, black and horrific. It was not a comfortable seat. It had never been comfortable even when I stacked it with cushions, yet Tris made it look like opulence.

He was stockier than I remembered. Nearly a decade of warmongering had filled him out. He wore leather armour painted black, his arms bare and heavily muscled. His hair was shorn so short he looked bald. He had a new scar on his left cheek right where I had mine. I had a feeling he had probably done it to himself. To make himself look more like the Corpse Queen. He always did like to trade on my name. He grinned down at us, his eyes half lidded as if it was all just too amusing for him.

"Sister, you're back. And here I thought you were gone for good." Tris' voice was merry, but there was a dangerous edge to it. A wolf jovially greeting a rabbit.

Sirileth slowly paced into the room. She didn't even

spare the audience a glance but kept her darklight gaze locked on Tris. Veteran warriors stepped back, moving out of her way, some with minute bows, others with hungry eyes. Predators waiting to see if she'd stumble.

"And who else..." Tris fell silent, leaned forward a little. He was staring at me. The smile slipped from his face. "Mother?"

I reached up, one flesh and blood hand and one claw made of shadow and pulled back my hood. My eyes flashed. One of Tris' gathered warriors gasped. Another, a giant of a man with only one eye, sank down onto a knee, bowing his head. He was quickly joined by a few of the others. It was the older ones, I noticed, that paid such respect. The younger warriors sneered at me and waited to see which way the wind would blow.

For his part, Tris coughed and sat straighter in the Corpse Throne. He was suddenly a boy again, caught in the act of something he knew was wrong, his mother scalding him for it.

I suppose we never quite lose that fear, that discomfort when we disappoint our parents. I wouldn't really know. I last saw my parents when I was six, as they handed me over to the Orran recruiter without so much as an argument. I've never been back to Keshin. I don't even know if they're still alive. I wonder about it sometimes, but I know I'll never go back. I'm scared what they might think of what their little girl has become. Besides, no matter how backward my home village was they must have heard of the Corpse Queen, and Keshin is not so far from Yenheim they couldn't have come to me. I guess they've never wanted to. And who can blame them? I never really knew them anyway. So fuck them! I choose the family I made over the

one that abandoned me. I choose Sirileth and Kento and Tris.
I choose Hardt and Tamura. I choose Imiko and Vi. They are
my family.

Tris squirmed in the grasp of the throne. I think
he had been ready for Sirileth to return, but my presence
unsettled him. I crossed my arms and stared at my son from
across the hall until he looked away.

"What happened?" Tris said bitterly. "Got bored
of your little village? I suppose that's why they call it
Tiresome."

I could have corrected him. But what would be the
point? He knew the village was called Wrysom as well as I.
Some rebukes are better said with silence.

Sirileth reached the foot of the throne and stared at
Tris. She spoke quietly, but her voice was tempered steel.
"You're in my seat." She started up the steps.

Tris shifted. "I wasn't sure you were coming back,
sister. Someone has to rule."

Sirileth reached the top of the steps and stared down
at Tris now. I wonder if he knew how vulnerable she was
in that moment. Sirileth had no Sources to protect her. She
was exhausted, hungry, dehydrated. Her black tunic and
trousers were ragged and stank of sweat and grime. Her hair
had pulled free from the braid in many places, becoming a
fraying tangle. Her face was dirty, caked in dried blood from
suffering Source rejection. Her eyes still blazed with their
furious darklight, but the bags were heavy enough none
could have missed them. A savage riot of streaking burns
on her arms were still healing, the flesh pink and raw and
tender.

Tris could have thrown Sirileth back to the ground
and crushed her, assumed the Corpse Throne for good. But

I had raised my children better than that. I had failed them all in so many ways, but not this one. Family. I had made them a family. And they would not hurt each other. Not for power, or rule, or pride. When the whole world is set against you, you learn to rely on those you can trust. And with the Corpse Queen for a mother, the world was most definitely set against my children.

Tris shifted, scooted a little, then stood and slipped around Sirileth. "I was, uh, keeping it warm for you, sister."

Sirileth took a moment to stare at the throne, then turned and sat easily in the uncomfortable seat. Thrones should always be uncomfortable. It is the nature of power and rule that those who sit at the top should feel the same discomfort as those at the bottom. How else can one appreciate the consequences of actions that affect everyone, even those they have never met? Sirileth swept her burning gaze over the council of warriors.

"Why are they here, brother?" Her voice was different on the throne. As queen, Sirileth spoke with iron certainty, the usual lilting cadence vanished behind her authority. Her ticks similarly gone.

Tris coughed and flicked his gaze to me. I stood with my arms crossed, ignoring my aching back.

There is a subtle fear in this hall. Like prey waiting to see if a predator will pounce.

I smiled. "More like waiting to see which predator will pounce first."

Finally, you begin to understand.

"They are…" Tris paused, then threw up his hands dramatically. "They're here to inform on the war against Tor." Again, he met my eyes.

I snorted. "Don't tell me that stupid war still persists."

Tris opened his mouth and I saw his face tighten in rage, but Sirileth spoke over him. "It doesn't. I ended it years ago."

"Well, yes," Tris said. "But you were gone and with this new resurgence of the Cursed, I thought now was the perfect time to strike a final blow against our most hated enemy and…"

"No," Sirileth said loudly, her voice carrying well throughout the throne room. I knew the technique. There is a way some people can speak that almost convinces me they must be using Vibromancy to enhance their voice. It is projecting and it is a skill I could never quite master. Tamura used it well, though, and I could see his teachings in my daughter. "The war is over. Pull back any soldiers you have extended. Secure the borders."

"But—"

Sirileth swung her darklight stare to Tris. "No! The war is over, Tris. Say it now or you will not leave this hall alive."

I could taste my daughter's fear. A nervous, fruity energy cascading from her in stuttering waves. But she showed none of it. She masked her tick too, that strange need she always had to re-explain herself as if she could never quite make the words fit right.

Tris clasped his hands behind his back, fingers wrenching into a knot. He clenched his jaw, screwed his eyes shut. "The war…" His voice was tight with anger, but the fear was thick on him, cloying. "The war is over, sister."

Sirileth stared at her brother a moment longer, then turned to the council. "You are all dismissed."

It was telling which of the council left immediately, and which waited to see if Tris would react. In the end, my son kept his peace, and one by one all the council left. I stayed in their way so every one of them had to walk past me. I drew on Ssserakis' strength to keep my back straight and my knees steady. Once they were all gone, I sagged. I wasn't the only one. Sirileth wilted upon the throne.

Kento stepped up beside me, her presence as steadying as her hand on my arm. "I need to get back to Ro'shan, Eska. I need to see my daughter. And my mother will want a report."

I had to bite back a retort that *I* was her mother. I knew it wouldn't do any good, but I really wanted to say it.

I heard a door open somewhere behind me, footsteps ringing on the cold stone floor. Then a voice I hadn't heard in so long. A voice I had not realised how much I missed. "Eska? Eska, is that you?" Hardt had come to see me.

CHAPTER EIGHT

SOME BONDS ARE THICKER THAN BLOOD, stronger than steel, more solid than the foundations of the earth. Hardt had been with me through everything. Our time in the Pit, the torture at the hands of the foreman, our struggle to escape, and the death of Isen. He'd been in the room when I gave birth to Kento and was with me down in Picarr when I absorbed the Arcstorm and placed Vainfold's crown atop my head. He came with me to Do'shan, was killed by the Iron Legion, and it was me who brought him back to life. No one else suffered alongside me down in the Red Cells, and no one else saw the madness that Emperor Aras Terrelan had put in me. No one else stood beside me as I murdered the Terrelan bloodline from existence and set loose a curse on Juntorrow that reduced the city to flaming ruins. He even came with me to confront the Iron Legion, brought me back after I took my life. And despite all that, he stayed with me in Yenheim, helped me raise my little queendom and my children. There is a bond between Hardt and I that I can never fully put into words. He is the rock that keeps me anchored.

Hardt's voice put tears in my eyes even before I turned to face him. I had missed my friend so much. There was so much I wanted to tell him. So much we needed to catch up on. So much… Too much.

When I turned to face him, Hardt froze. I had been looking forward to this reunion, but in that moment, with his eyes wide and shocked, I wanted to hide. I was old, grey, wrinkled, stooped, all long before my time. Hardt had aged too. He was still tall, but much of his muscle had softened. His shorn hair had some grey in it, along with his beard, and his dark skin had more lines than I remembered. His stomach was no longer flat but bulged beneath his tunic. None of us escape the rigours of time, but he wore it well.

I clasped my hands in front of me and saw his eyes drift down and lock onto my shadowy claw. I quickly hid it behind my back.

"Eska?" A voice so quiet it was a rumble of distant thunder.

I nodded. My tongue felt leaden in my mouth and there were no words that could bridge the gulf. But then, there was no gulf. There never had been. Not between Hardt and me. In two great strides he was on me, arms wrapping me up, tightening around me into a crushing hug. Then I was crying. Then he was crying. We spent a while like that. Some bonds transcend time, and some reunions need no words.

I'll spare you much of the babbling we did into each other's shoulders as very little of it made sense. What's important is that we were together again and it was like coming home and putting on an old pair of shoes that fit your feet like no other. Hardt had always accepted me for who I was, followed me despite it. I still don't know why. Out of love, I suppose. Not romantic love, nothing so temporal and fragile. But love built from respect and from hard times shared together that no one else could ever understand.

By the time we separated we were both puffy cheeked and red-eyed. And we were both grinning.

My shadow shifted, bubbled, reared up beside me. *"Hardt!"*

Hardt scrambled backwards, fear pouring from him. "What the fuck, Eska?" In all our years together, the only time I'd heard him sound so scared was when we almost fell from the great chain of Ro'shan.

I sighed. I should have known this was coming from the moment I agreed with Ssserakis that it no longer had to hide anymore. My shadow turned slightly towards me. *"Yes. You should have."* It was a little unnerving that Ssserakis could both speak out loud and still hear my thoughts. I'm not sure why, but it seemed wrong.

"It's alright, Hardt. This is Ssserakis. It's a horror from the Other World."

"I am a Lord of Sevorai," Ssserakis announced.

Hardt stared between me and my shadow. The inky darkness wavered and danced like a candle flame. "This is what you've carried all these years?"

I shrugged. "More or less."

"Your fear has been a delight, big terran."

It took a little explaining. As with most things, Hardt accepted it in the end as just another quirk about Eska.

He's always accepted me, even after I've done things he's
disagreed with. I never deserved the support Hardt gave me.
In the end, Ssserakis agreed to retreat, and I think everyone
was happier without the constant reminder that I was
possessed by an ancient fear incarnation.

Sirileth descended from her throne and Hardt treated
her to the same hug he had given me. She startled for a
moment, I saw that in her darklight eyes, and then softened
into the embrace. I think her demons, the figurative kind
rather than literal, still hounded her fiercely. It was an
extraordinary act of will for her to remain strong. Hardt
didn't tell her off for leaving, but rather pulled back and
grumbled over her arms, asking why no one had cleaned or
bandaged the burns. Sirileth smiled and blinked away tears.

Then came the part I was truly dreading. "Where's
Imiko?" Hardt asked. "She left to look for you, Eska. I
thought, with you and Siri coming back together, Imiko must
have found you. She…"

He must have known. By the way Sirileth and I didn't
answer. The look we shared. The way I slumped, suddenly
too weary to hold my head up. He must have known.

Kento stepped forward, back straight and hands
clasped before her. She saved us from that moment. "Imiko
sacrificed herself to save us all. Everyone."

"She…" Hardt peered at Kento for a moment,
frowning. Then to me. "Sacrificed?"

I nodded.

Hardt stumbled then as surely as if I'd hit him. He
caught himself on a candelabra, big hand wrapping around
the haft. Tris collapsed. He'd been standing halfway up
the steps to the throne, but at Kento's words he sat heavily,
buried his head in his hands, wept. Sirileth went to him, all

conflict between the two forgotten. She sat next to her big brother and laid an arm across his broad shoulders, pulled him close. He screamed wordless tears into her shoulder. They grieved together then, for an aunt who had loved them like her own.

I went to Hardt and the big man fell into my arms. He must have weighed two of me, but I held him up as he sagged. Ssserakis gave me the strength to do it and I slowly lowered Hardt until we were both sitting.

Grief and despair. Such useless emotion.

"Not now, Ssserakis."

We spent some time there. Hardt and I in each other's arms. Tris and Sirileth doing the same. Kento stood by awkwardly, waiting. She could have joined us, shared in our grief, but she didn't. She held herself apart. I think, perhaps, she was hoping for a joyous reunion. Not this shared sadness.

I will not say we dealt with our grief over Imiko there and then. We did not. You cannot deal with grief, not really. It is not a monster you can slay and be done with. Grief is an ambush predator, and we are the prey. It stalks us our entire lives, hiding in smells and sounds, in solitude and in crowds. It waits in items and in thoughts. Memories are the hunting grounds of grief, and when it pounces, its bite is venomous. It inflicts sadness or rage or sometimes despair. But grief is not an adventurous predator. Always it stalks old memories, not new. And that is how we move on. New memories where it is not welcome.

Hardt and I have spent many evenings since going over our old memories. We share them, even ones we have reminisced a hundred times before. The time Imiko stole my Source and beat me bloody for good measure. When she tried her hand at cooking only to create a soup so salty the ocean would have throw it back at her. The way she'd vanish every time Kento or Sirileth needed cleaning. The time I forced her into a dress and she looked like a cat trying to swim. Her heartfelt plea, the only thing that dragged me back from the edge when I was set on unleashing an army of monsters upon Isha. So many memories. Those evenings often ended in tears, but better were the ones that ended in laughter.

Eventually Hardt stiffened a little in my arms. It was a subtle change, as though he had been a sack of grain and then all his muscles remembered they formed a man. "I don't know you, do I?" he said to Kento around a sniff.

Kento smiled and nodded. For the first time since I had met my eldest daughter, she actually seemed a little shy. "You knew me once. Briefly."

Hardt shook his head and looked at me.

"Hardt, this is Kento."

Realisation dawned slowly and he shook his head. "No. You said she was dead."

"I did. I thought she was. But she's alive and…"

Hardt surged to his feet and stormed over to Kento. She actually took a step backwards. He reached out with one hand, paused with it held just beside her face, peered at her so closely. "You look just like him."

I think it a wonder that Hardt coped as well as he did with that day. Here your oldest friend has returned after almost a decade away. Oh, and she's possessed by a horror and always has been. Also, one of your closest friends is dead. And to top it off, here's that long lost niece you thought died over twenty years ago. Sometimes our emotions are tugged in so many directions we stop dealing with them and just ride the flow.

I left them there. It was a happy moment. Hardt and
Kento were finally reunited. She was the one thing he had
never accepted from me. My decision to give her up had
always been a thorn sticking in both of us. I didn't belong
in that reunion. I didn't deserve that happiness. Tris joined
them. He'd never known Kento as a babe, nor Isen, but he
was family and he had a new sister to introduce himself to.
I slunk away like a shadow. Sirileth made to follow me but I
shook my head at her. What I needed to do now, I had to do
alone. There was another reunion awaiting me. Perhaps the
most important one of all.

I stopped a passing servant and asked after Josef.
The squat, balding man gawked at me a moment, then
stammered out directions to what he called 'the temple'.
I followed those directions with a sour feeling in my gut.
Temples were usually dedicated to religions or mythological
figures. The Rand and Djinn had temples all over Ovaeris,
not that the fuckers deserved to be worshipped. I had
never allowed temples in my queendom. But it was not my
queendom anymore.

I paused at the door to the temple. I knew the place
well. It was a large chamber; the same one I had once used
to train my children in Sourcery. The same chamber where
Vi had died so many years ago. I wonder if Josef chose it on
purpose.

The door was gone, removed from its hinges. It was
a purposeful choice, I think, to promote openness. I heard
voices within, many softly spoken words. And something
else, too. It sounded like children playing at stones, that
game where the aim is to thrown small stones into concentric
rings scrawled on the floor.

Enough waiting. I've never been one to skulk outside rooms. I straightened my aching back as much as my age would allow and strode through into the temple. I must admit, I was not expecting the sight I found.

When I left Yenheim almost a decade earlier, Josef had been in a pitiful state. Maybe one day out of ten he was lucid enough to talk. The rest he was either unable to remember himself, or he was made of stone, or living fire, or had no wits to even speak his name. He had a few attendants, those servants I had assigned to him, to take care of him through all his various issues. But largely, he was forgotten. Josef was a broken man. I might not have made the first crack, nor even the last, but many of his fractures were mine. And worst of all, after he shattered, I wasn't there to put him back together. I just shoved him aside to forget about. I feared so much what I would find in that temple. Ssserakis gorged itself on my fear.

I needn't have worried. It seemed, like most things, Josef was doing much better since being removed from my presence.

The chamber was almost stiflingly warm. A number of hearths had been carved into the walls, and the smoke drifted up through cracks in the stonework. There were also lanterns hung over the black stone walls and on free-standing posts set up at regular intervals. It was probably the most well-lit room in the palace. At one side was a heap of blankets and bed rolls all overlapping each other. I saw a few bodies sleeping on that padded mass. Not beds or pallets, but one communal sleeping area. Over the other side of the chamber were tables and chairs and children sitting and learning from a wizened old woman. From the sounds of things, it was a history lesson about the continent of Isha and how one kingdom had become one hundred had become one had become one hundred again. That last breaking was my doing.

In the centre of the chamber, I saw what looked a lot like worship. People standing around or kneeling, all eyes turned towards a small wooden stage built in a circular design with steps leading up to it all around. There were dozens of people. And there, in the centre of the stage, was Josef, kneeling and playing with a bunch of rocks, each the size of an adult's head. He appeared to be rolling them about like a toddler playing with toys. I thought little had changed. Almost, I turned around and left. I wanted a reunion with my friend, the other part of me. Not some addled fool who could not even remember he was an adult grown. Almost. I chided myself for my foolishness and strode on towards the stage. Whatever madness he was afflicted with today, he was still my friend. I owed him an explanation for my years of absence.

I had to pick my way through the crowd watching him. Most were dressed in normal clothes, tunics and trousers. Some wore multicoloured robes and ridiculous hats that made their heads seem twice as long as they were. Whispering started up immediately and before long, I found the crowd turning to stare at me. Well, fuck them. I was well used to being the centre of attention. By the time I reached the stage, Josef had quit playing with his rocks and turned to smile at me. There was too much in that smile. I realised then it was not some addled, mind-injured fool I was facing. It was Josef. It really was my Josef.

He hadn't aged a day since we were thrown into the Pit. Still a youth, with a pale tuft of hair on his top lip, and a scattering of stubble about his chin. His skin was smooth and unmarred by scars or the weird discolorations of time. He sat cross-legged, a skirt pooled around his feet, and his pale chest uncovered. I stopped at the foot of the stage and stared at my friend and had no fucking idea what to say. Of course Josef didn't help. He just stared back at me, cocked his head, a slightly beatific look on his face.

I realised then, even though he'd stopped playing with them, the rocks were still moving. They rolled about the stage as if pulled by invisible ropes, occasionally changing directions. Whenever two bumped into each other, they'd stop and little rocky arms would extend out from the main body, flail at each other, then retract. Then the two rocks changed directions and rolled away from each other.

I gestured at the rocks with my shadowy claw. "Golems?" I thought that strange. Josef wasn't attuned to Golemancy, but perhaps he had bought the little constructs from a Polasian.

"Not exactly." He chuckled and the gathered crowd of… what were they? Attendants? Too many of them for that and I'm sure Sirileth wasn't paying over fifty people to fetch Josef food and bathe him. Worshippers, then? They called this place a temple. In my experience temples usually went hand in hand with worship. Whatever they were to Josef, my skin prickled at being laughed at.

They are far too calm. Tranquillity is a useless emotion. We should show them fear. My shadow began to bubble beside me.

"No. That's not why I'm here."

Ssserakis didn't listen to me. My shadow reared up, a horror of sharp edges that drank in the light. The people around us gasped, a few of them even dropped to their knees and bowed their heads, but I felt no fear from them.

What is wrong with them? Ssserakis inflated in an

instant, my shadow swamping the room casting everything and everyone in darkness. I looked around to find them all frozen. I could see them, but I knew each one of them was isolated, locked in their own prison of nightmares. I had been where they were now, trapped inside a terrifying construct of Ssserakis' making.

They do not fear me. What is going on? Ssserakis was right. Even as it inflicted nightmares on these people, none of them feared. They were so fucking peaceful. It was disgusting.

"Stop it, Eska," Josef said in a calm, cheery voice. I hated him in that moment. No one should come face to face with their greatest fear and be happy.

The darkness faded, my shadow retreated, Ssserakis hid inside of me again. I could feel how unsettled my horror was. It was almost like it was scared because others didn't fear it.

"What is this, Josef? Why do these people act like fanatics?"

Josef patted the wooden stage beside him and nodded to me. "Sit, Eska. Please."

I mounted the stage warily and lowered myself to sitting beside him. The moment my saggy arse touched the floor, I heard new gasps and mutterings from the crowd. Fuck, but it was unnerving. They stared at us with such weird reverence.

One of the little rocks rolled into my leg and it stopped, rocky arms pawing at me. As I looked closer, it was more like a collection of smaller stones all stuck together into one. Its surface was uneven, knobbly. It stopped flailing, turned, and rolled away.

"Not golems?" I asked.

Josef shook his head and plucked one of the odd creatures from the ground. It squeaked like a puppy at play, then settled in Josef's lap and went still. "They're children," Josef said. "My children. I made them."

"They're alive? You think you made life? With Sourcery?"

"Yes."

I shook my head at that. "Only the Rand can make life through magic, Josef."

He frowned at me and shook his head. "A lot has happened while you've been away."

I glanced at the crowd still watching us. More had joined them, the children at class had been drawn over. All were silent, as though hanging on our every word.

"Clearly," I said. I tried to wrench my attention away from the onlookers. "You're doing better, Josef."

My friend nodded. "It's a constant struggle. I lose control maybe one day in ten still. It's worse if I've exerted myself. I…" He paused, frowned, looked at me so earnestly. He looked just like the boy I remembered from my youth. I wanted to hug him, to tell him everything that had happened to me, to take comfort in his presence just like I used to. But those days were long behind me. I could not bear to burden him with my troubles.

"I have learned to use Biomancy to fix myself," he said slowly. "That's not the right word. To contain myself. To keep myself me. It's a struggle, Eska. Some days that constant use of magic is too much. Some days, I can't."

The gathered crowd muttered, a pulsing wave of noise I couldn't quite understand without focusing on it.

"Constant use of magic?" I asked. "You use Biomancy to keep your body stable? Even now?"

Josef nodded.

"How?" This wasn't how I wanted our reunion to go. I'd meant to catch up, not to quiz him. But my mind has a habit of latching on to mysteries and doesn't let up until I solve them. "Don't you suffer rejection?"

He looked at me then, smiled as though at a joke I hadn't quite got. "I don't suffer rejection. Not from Biomancy, at least. Neither do you."

"Oh trust me, Josef, I do." I realised I still hadn't had chance to bathe. My face was probably still stained with dried blood.

"Not from Necromancy."

I opened my mouth to argue. Shut it again. I hadn't swallowed a Necromancy Source in… More years than I cared to count. Not since my first days at the Orran Academy of Magic. Not since induction when we were tested for our attunements. The sad fact is, Necromancy is a mostly useless school of Sourcery. Congratulations on your ability to raise a few impotent ghosts. I suppose I also started the whole Cursed plague thing, but I'm really not sure that's a good example of benefits of Necromancy given the constant threat they pose to Isha even twenty years after I created the curse. But the point is, I did all that with my innate Necromancy. I hadn't swallowed a Necromancy Source in a very long time and had no idea if I would reject it.

"You still don't really understand what Loran did to us, do you, Eska?" Josef said. He stroked the little rock in his lap. "He put gods in us. You a Djinn. Me a Rand. He made us… something else. Something new."

"You're talking about the Auguries?" I asked. That damned prophecy again. The Chosen One to end the fucking war eternal. What a load of shit that turned out to be. It was the Iron Legion who figured out the truth, that the Auguries were guidelines to creating vessels to resurrect our dead gods.

Josef frowned at me and shook his head. "You should talk to Tamura, Eska."

"It's on my to-do list." I couldn't quite keep the bitterness from my voice. I wasn't sure what I had wanted from Josef, but this wasn't it.

I found myself fiddling with my hands. It had been a long time since I'd been able to do that. It all just felt so awkward. There was a time we were closer than siblings. Two parts of one soul. Now... I didn't know what to say to him. I didn't know who he had become. Didn't know how to bridge the gap and find the common ground that had always been there between us. When I looked up, I found Josef doing the same thing. Wringing his hands together over the rock in his lap, a deep frown on his face.

I smiled, laughed. "I missed you."

He looked up at me and grinned. "I..." He shook his head, his eyes distant for a moment. "There's something I still need to do. Sorry, Eska. I... I sometimes think I've seen too much. Know too much. What happened to you?" He leaned forward, reached out and cupped my wrinkly cheek. The moment he touched me, I heard the crowd around us gasp, but tried my best to ignore it. It felt good to feel his hand against my skin again. We had once been so close. I had slept next to him every day for over a decade, curled up against him, taking comfort in that closeness.

"Do you remember the Pit?" I asked. He nodded. "I swallowed a Chronomancy Source to... well, to force you to surrender. I suffered rejection and it aged me. Continued to age me."

"Ahh." He smiled at me. "You absorbed it. The Chronomancy became innate within you. But you don't have control of it. Your eyes flash with Arcmancy. The ground beneath you trembles with Geomancy. Your body ages with Chronomancy.

And the dead rise around you with Necromancy." His voice had taken on a strange chanting cadence. "Have you ever noticed how all those Sourceries are the domain of the Djinn?"

To be honest, I hadn't, but now I thought about it, he was right. The physical Sourceries belong to the Djinn. The biological Sourceries belong to the Rand. I had been injected with Necromancy and Josef with Biomancy. We are two sides of the same coin, he and I. He is life, healing, immortality. I am death, destruction, a lifespan made ever shorter by the magic consuming me. We are a duality, linked, just like the Rand and the Djinn are linked.

I suddenly felt wearied by the conversation. By Josef and his strangeness. By the crowd of people watching us. By all I had been through so recently. And of course by the magic eating away at me. I made to stand. "I should go."

"Wait!" This came from the crowd. One of the robed people with the stupid hat. She stood and rushed forward, stopped at the foot of the steps. "The prophecy."

Well, that sealed it. If there was one thing I was most tired about, it was prophecies. First cataclysms, second cataclysms, Auguries. I wanted nothing to do with any of it anymore. I wasn't even sure I wanted to fight the war that was knocking on our world's door. I felt that familiar despair rising within me. It had been coming more and more often ever since Imiko's suicide. Yes, I call it what it was. Some people might name it a sacrifice to make it noble, but that belittles the pain my sister was in. It was suicide. Because she could no longer take the pain of living. Well, I understood that. I felt it all too well. I sagged under the weight of it and...

"Do you trust me, Eska?" Josef asked.

It took such effort to lift my head and look at him. I was so tired and every bit of me suddenly weighed as much as the earth we were buried in. I nodded once and found it was true. Despite everything between us, all the hurt and pain and betrayal. I still trusted Josef with my life. I always would.

He smiled at me so warmly. "Good." He leaned forward again and placed a hand against my chest. "I'm sorry."

The pain cut me in two and blasted both halves away to nothing.

CHAPTER NINE

DOWN IN THE DARK, THE HATEFUL WORLD
burned less. Away from the sky and its searing light. It
burned less, but still burned. There was no place safe. No place
comfortable. No place for Ssserakis to escape the pain of existing.
It needed to find a way home. Back to Sevorai, to its cities and
minions, to the endless task of keeping the Beating Heart small and
manageable.

Ssserakis drifted through the tunnels. It had ridden a
temporary host down into this darkness. Some creature that called
itself terran. From the first moments of Ssserakis' possession it
had felt the host deteriorating. Madness clawing at it. An innate
understanding that something was wrong and needed to be
exorcised. It ended as all hosts did. In death. The host could not
take the nightmares, the fear, the instinct that something was
wrong inside. Its death had set Ssserakis free.

The creatures down in the dark spent their days digging,

digging, digging. Useless lives. Such pitiful things. Alive for a moment and gone. But their fear was delicious. Such variety. Such distinctive flavours. No two of these terran creatures tasted the same. They all had different terrors and the delight Ssserakis took in drawing them out was as pleasurable as the fear itself.

But the world still burned.

Ssserakis came upon three of the terran creatures and snuffed out their light. They panicked. It was wonderful. Ssserakis trapped them in the dark, took its time showing them fears ripped from their own minds. One dreamed of watching others die, smaller versions of itself, their faces melting, eyeballs popping within their skulls. Another feared the chase, being pursued through the dark by a formless predator. The third was terrified of a big terran covered in scars with eyes that gleamed in the dark. Ssserakis pressed their fears upon them, drank in the emotion, and snuffed out their lives as easily as the little light they had been gathering around. Then it rested for a time. It couldn't end all the terran creatures at once, after all. It needed to keep some alive. They had to feed it until it found a way back home.

Ssserakis sensed new creatures gathering at the chamber entrance. More of the terran creatures, come to investigate the dead. Ssserakis was not full. Was never full. Not here in this world where its strength was constantly burned away. It could feed some more. It made itself small, hid in the darkness and waited. The chase could be fun, but it was even more so when the prey walked willingly into the trap.

A young terran creature entered carrying a light. It was dirty and small and smelled vaguely of the gods. A child of a child of a child of a fragment of a god. So far removed from the power it once held. It was nothing but an ember of a once mighty flame. It mattered not. Ssserakis had come to realise these godlings died all the same as the others; in fear and pain and all alone.

Ssserakis rushed in, swamped the terran creature in darkness. It showed the terran fear; slithering things in the dark pulled from its own imagination. It ran icy blades across the terran's skin, drawing gasps of pain. Paralysed by its own terror, the terran creature was the most delicious yet.

"ENOUGH!" the terran creature screamed. Ssserakis pulled back a little, confused. The prey down here had never spoken to it before. "What are you?"

There was something about this creature. It was still scared, but it mastered that fear, used it to draw forth its own strength. Ssserakis respected that. It answered the terran, and almost as though the creature were feeding on those answers, it asked more and more. Soon Ssserakis grew tired of the questions. It surged back in for the kill, ready to bring new heights of terror to the prey before it died.

"What do you want?"

Ssserakis paused. Considered. Answered. It wanted to go home. Back to Sevorai where the light didn't burn.

"I can help," the terran creature said. "I can send you back."

Again Ssserakis pulled back and paused. It could not decide if the creature spoke true. Sure enough, it was a godling that had pulled Ssserakis from Sevorai. Perhaps a godling could send it back. They came to an agreement then. A bargain struck. The terran would carry Ssserakis home, and in return Ssserakis would let the creature live. Ssserakis held back much of the truth though. The creature didn't need to know it would have to die in order to fulfil the bargain. That realisation would come later and the fear Ssserakis would draw from the truth would be wonderful.

Ssserakis closed on the terran, rushed inside of it, coiled around body and soul. Possession was instant but settling into a new body took time.

*The host left the chamber, talked with some other terrans,
then lumbered away. Ssserakis hid inside, watching through the
host's eyes. The host didn't speak to Ssserakis. Didn't acknowledge
it. It was almost as if the host was pretending Ssserakis didn't
exist. It was amusing. But there was something about this host.
Always before, the light of this hateful world still burned, but not
in this host. It was different, as though the darkness inside the host
was a shield from the light. Ssserakis curled deep, nestled inside,
felt safe for the first time since being dragged to Ovaeris. Here
was a home away from home. A creature made of fear, desperately
masking it with anger. Already, Ssserakis knew this host would
serve for a long time. Assuming it survived the nightmares.*

I woke to pain. That in itself is nothing new or
significant. I often woke with an aching back or a throbbing
ankle or a pulsing headache. But this pain was different.
My body felt wracked with tightness, like I had overexerted
myself and was paying for it, my muscles letting me know
they were not used to being worked that way. I shifted,
groaned, tried to find a comfy spot on the bed. Then realised
I wasn't in a bed. I was on a hard wooden floor. I heard
many voices mixing into one, chanting and whispering. I
groaned again as I remembered.

You're back. Something is right, Eska.

I tried to make sense of that statement, decided I
couldn't and had far more pressing matters anyway. The
whispering grew louder as I sat up, some gasps interspersed
with it. Lursa's Tears, but these people were fools.

*They act like minions should, but they do not fear us. I do
not like it.*

"Neither do I, Ssserakis," I said. I had decided that as
long as my horror was no longer bound by the need to hide,

I would no longer purposefully hide it. Let people know
I was talking to a demon in my head. It couldn't hurt my
reputation.

Many of the gathered fools were on the stage now.
They surrounded me, some prostrate as though in prayer.
Idiots. There was also a steaming pile of ice on the stage.
That was a bit strange, but odd seemed to be the order of the
day.

"You are awake, Pariah," said one of the robed fools.
She had a large nose that only seemed larger under the
ridiculous hat.

"What did you call me?" I winced. My head was
pounding. My shoulders were tight like I had been stooped
for days. Or months. Or years. I leaned back a bit, stretched
out my back, felt a few pops and a crack, followed by
blessed relief.

"You must be hungry, thirsty," the woman said.
She waved to someone and another robed idiot rushed
forward with a tray. There was a clay cup full of water, a
hunk of brown bread, and a bowl of meaty stew on that tray.
Suddenly I realised I was both ravenous and parched, so I
set to the tray with a passion. I downed the cup of water and
pointed at it for a refill even as I snatched the bread, dipped
it in the stew and tore into it with my teeth. Perhaps it was
the hunger, but I felt oddly alive. A strange fucking thing to
say, I know. I always felt alive, except for that one time I was
actually dead. But this was… different. I thought maybe it
was just the result of rest after such an extended period of
exhaustion, but I could move easier than before. I didn't feel
quite as fragile.

Look closely, Eska.

"Where's Josef?" I asked around a mouthful of stewy

bread. There was a chunk of meat floating in the stew and I hoped it was abban.

"I will wake the Paragon," the robed woman said. I frowned at her. Paragon, Pariah. I had a feeling I wasn't going to like where all this was going.

Look, Eska.

The robed woman approached the pile of ice, knelt before it, spoke something softly. Immediately the ice began to melt, Josef at the centre of it. So, he wasn't able to keep the wild Sourcery at bay all the time. His Biomantic healing had limits.

Eska!

"What, Ssserakis?"

Look at yourself.

Well that was tough to do. It's not like I had a mirror lying around. As Josef stirred within the melting ice, I remembered the pain. He'd put his hand against my chest and it felt like I had been torn in two. What had he done to me? Why had it knocked me out? Why had it taken so much from him that he needed to turn into ice for a while?

I scooped up the piece of meat with the dwindling bread in my hand and paused, staring at that hand. Smooth skin, barely a wrinkle or a blemish. I stretched my back again. I was sitting straighter than normal, without the usual tightness that brought on my stoop. I dropped the bread on the tray and lifted my hand to my face. My wrinkles were gone. My skin felt softer, fuller, less papery.

Josef sat up amidst the melting ice. He looked out of sorts, frowning like he wasn't sure where he was.

"What did you do to me?" I asked as he blinked groggily.

Josef gave a tired laugh as the robed woman lowered

him to sit opposite me. "Gave you back... what was stolen from you, Eska." He patted the woman on the arm. "A mirror, please, Senna. And some food. For me."

"At once, Paragon." The woman, Senna, rushed away, her stupid hat bobbing as she ran.

Those around us, watching expectantly, bowed low, extended arms along the floor toward us. I heard a few whisper the word *duality* which seemed far too close to some of my own thoughts for comfort.

I noticed there were more people in the chamber now as well. A few soldiers stood around, no weapons drawn, but they were still in mail coats. I do not think they were there to guard, but to watch. Many others, too, milling around in small groups. Not the weird worshippers, but normal folk. I couldn't help but feel I had just been dragged into something I was going to regret.

Senna reappeared with another tray of food and set it before Josef, then reached into her robe and held out a hand mirror for me. I took it and stared into the past.

How old was I? I had been alive for under forty years. Recently I had felt like an ancient. My body had been wracked by aches and pains; my skin sagged. Chronomancy had maybe doubled my age. And now that was gone. I was young again. My skin was smooth, my hair dark with no grey to be seen. I still had my scars, some crow's feet around my eyes and looked a little gaunt as though I needed to eat well for a few weeks, but I no longer felt the frailty I had.

I dropped the mirror and stood quickly, easily. My knees didn't pop, my head didn't spin. I stretched and enjoyed the feeling of flexibility. My clothes hung awkwardly on me now. Too short, too baggy, too tight across the shoulders. I still only had the one arm, the other

a skeletal claw formed of shadow, but I suppose rewinding
time and regrowing limbs were two very different things.

"How?" I asked as I marvelled at my renewed youth.
The Iron Legion had resurrected gods in order to beg them
to give back the years Chronomancy had stolen from him.
But there were no Rand or Djinn here, only Josef and me.

Josef raised the bowl of stew to his lips and
swallowed a mouthful. He chewed on it for a few moments,
thinking. "I learned a lot from Loran," he said, then frowned.
"You need to understand how rejection truly works first,
Eska." He sagged and Senna rushed forward to steady him.
The crowd murmured in response. Josef sat back up again,
breathing heavily, eyes slightly unfocused. He patted Senna
on the arm and took a deep breath before continuing.

"Every moment a Source is in your stomach, bits of
it are dissolving into your body. Tiny bits. So small it would
take hundreds of years for you to notice. The more you
draw on the Source, the faster it dissolves. There comes a
point where there is too much magic in your blood. Your
body cannot handle it and it begins to react violently to the
Sourcery."

I stretched my flesh and shadow arms above my
head, interlocked my fingers, and reached out as tall as I
could. Damn, but it felt good to be able to move freely again.

"That's how the ore Sirileth was using could stave
off rejection," I said, knowing it was true. "That ore absorbs
Sourcery. With it piercing her skin, it was drawing the magic
from her blood."

Josef nodded and took a bite of the bread, chewing on
it. He spoke around the mouthful. "But *we* react differently
to rejection, Eska. Loran changed us. He put gods in us.
A Rand in me. A Djinn in you. When too much Sourcery

is in our blood, our bodies start to absorb it. Arcmancy, Geomancy, Chronomancy, your innate Sourceries. They are all schools of Sourcery in the sphere of the Djinn. As is Necromancy."

"Huh," I sat down opposite Josef. "So I can absorb Sourceries from the Djinn sphere. And you can absorb Sourceries from the Rand sphere. How does that explain how you turned back time?"

"Because I realised the gods weren't needed. We needed three things, Eska. Chronomancy. That's in you already. It's a part of you just as surely as your Necromancy. We needed Biomancy, and that's a part of me. And we needed a lot of energy. I supplied that. It was quite draining." He did look drained.

"I gave you back the years Chronomancy stole from you, but the Sourcery is still in you, Eska. Unless you learn to control it, it will begin to act on your body again. But if you do learn to control it." He grinned at me. "Immortality comes in two forms. My Biomancy renews my body constantly. You can learn to use your Chronomancy to freeze your ageing. You can be immortal, Eska. Like me."

I stared at Josef aghast. He meant it. He thought he was offering a boon. Immortal, like him. Could it really be he understood me so little? I did not want immortality. The very idea of living forever was abhorrent. Lursa's Tears, some days I didn't want to live at all. But he didn't need to know that. Except he already did. Josef was there, in the library, the day Lesray Alderson put the call of the void in me. He had been the one to save me. Somehow he had realised what I was about to do and caught me as I leapt to my death. Josef had pulled me back from the edge and he wrapped me in a blanket of love. Used his own Empamancy to wash away my pain.

The people around us hushed and I felt as though they were leaning in closer. Josef, too, was quiet, expectant.

"Thank you?" I said, not sure if I meant it as a question or not.

Josef grinned at me and the crowd set to talking again. I heard someone say Pariah and another utter Paragon. I didn't see it. Too blinded by what had just happened. Too bewildered by my new youth. There was a new mythology forming around us, Josef and I the kernel at its centre. It made a sick kind of sense. He was immortal, one day a man, then stone, the next blazing sun. Of course people would come to see him as special, as greater. I had never thought to see that turn to worship. I had never thought to see my friend revel in it so.

Suddenly I needed to be elsewhere. To be away from Josef and the fools worshipping him. I felt the need to run. To lose myself in that exertion like I hadn't in so many years. I stood suddenly, almost overturning the tray. Josef looked up at me, a frown creasing his brow.

"I have to go," I said.

"It will take power," Josef said quickly. I didn't understand. Didn't care. Started backing away through the crowd. They shuffled away from me, still lying prostrate on the ground.

"To use the Chronomancy inside you will take power, Eska. More than you have."

I nodded, stumbled over someone too slow to get out of my way, kicked them aside probably more savagely than they deserved. A few people gasped and I heard that title muttered again. Pariah. That was what I was to them. Not Eskara. Not even the Corpse Queen. The Pariah. Outcast.

Whatever this fucking horrible emerging mythology was, I wanted no part of it.

I reached the door leading away from the temple, glanced back to find Josef on his feet, supported by his attendant in the silly hat. He was staring after me. "Your Necromancy is the key, Eska. You can use it just like Loran used…"

I turned and ran, legs pumping, breath heaving. It was fucking wonderful.

CHAPTER TEN

MY FEET CARRIED ME THROUGH THE PALACE
of Yenheim. Guards and servants alike watched me pass.
What must they have thought? They had no doubt heard
the Corpse Queen was back but was an old lady now. Then
I go streaking through the halls in the prime of my life once
again, whooping as I ran for the sheer joy of it. All thoughts
of frailty or guarding how I moved to stop the inevitable
twinges, were gone. I ran with abandon. And I didn't stop
until I passed through the great palace doors and out into
the cool Autumn air of Isha.

The air burned in my lungs and I doubled over. My
legs ached and I knew I'd feel them tomorrow. My body
wasn't used to moving like that. I had been too long at rest,
blaming old age and infirmity. I'd be paying for that for
months while I got some fitness back in my bones. But fuck
did it feel good to be young again. I wiped sweat from my

forehead and stood straight, struggling to breathe and loving
it.

The sky was an ugly brooding orange behind gloomy
grey clouds that stretched from horizon to horizon without
break. It cast the ground in dark shadows that almost
seemed like night. There was a smell on the air, too, a hint of
smoke but not a clean kind like wood smoke. A filthier, more
acidic burn that stung the nostrils.

It almost feels like home.

Yes, that was it. Between the oppressive clouds and
the creeping gloom, the cool air and erupting smell, it did
feel a lot like Sevorai.

Yenheim was built upon a hill, or a collection of hills
really. It had grown since I had last seen the city I founded. A
sprawling mass of wood and stone buildings and dirt streets
running haphazardly up and down four different hillsides.
Yenheim palace sat at the highest point of the tallest hill. A
commanding view. From it, I could see down across much of
the town and out towards the distant Forest of Ten. Which
is how I saw then that the forest burned. A great rent had
been cleaved into the earth, running through the expansive
forest. I could see it clearly, and I could see the orange flames
spewing forth from underground. Much of the forest had
already burned away, leaving blackened husks all around
the rent earth.

"I did this," Sirileth said. I spun around to find my
daughter sitting on a step next to the palace doors. She had
one knee drawn up to her chest and was hugging it fiercely,
her other leg stretched out before her. "The earthquakes and
tsunamis. Fires. Storms. Clouds blotting out the sun. The
Damned and Cursed have crawled up from their homes to
wreak new havoc on Isha too. I didn't mean to but... I did it

all." She looked up me with her darklight stare and her eyes narrowed. I could see her trying to figure it out.

"You went to see Josef." She cocked her head at me. "I mean, he's turned back your age just like the Rand and Djinn did for the Iron Legion. Chronomancy and Biomancy together." She smiled. "You look… like I remember you. I mean, when I was young, I guess."

I will ever be amazed by what Sirileth was capable of. It took her all of twenty seconds to figure out what I was still trying to comprehend.

I sauntered over and sat next to her. I contemplated hugging her but wasn't sure she'd let me. I don't know how long I was unconscious for, but she had bathed and dressed in fresh clothing. I was still stinking like a scab and wearing sweat-and-grime coated rags.

"I'm sorry for abandoning you," I said suddenly, before my stubbornness could kick in and squeeze the apology down until I swallowed it. "I really did think I was doing the right thing."

"Oh," Sirileth nodded. She glanced at me and away quickly. "And now? I mean, do you still think it was right?"

"Probably not." I bumped my shoulder against hers and she didn't move away. "I couldn't see any other way at the time."

That is an excuse.

"It is," I said. "An excuse. I'm sorry, Sirileth. I should never have left you to shoulder everything on your own."

She leaned against me then, rested her head on my shoulder. I had to blink away tears that threatened to ruin the moment. "I didn't care about the responsibility. Or ruling Yenheim or any of that, Mother. I just wanted you to come home. I just wanted you to be here with me. And you weren't."

"I know." I wouldn't say sorry again. It wouldn't mean anything if I did. "I'm here now."

She was silent for a few moments and when she did speak, it was liltingly, as though she were afraid of the answer her question might drag from me. "You'll stay then? Help me fix things?"

"Fix what?"

She tilted her head to stare at me with shining eyes, the coronas around her pupils flaring so bright. "I broke the world, Mother. And I don't know how to fix it. I'm trying to find a way. I mean, to think of a way. But I can't. Kento was right. I didn't stop the second cataclysm. I caused it." She drew in a hitched breath. "I have to fix things. I have to put it back together. But I don't know how. Help me. Please."

That might have been the most soul crushing moment of my life. More than Josef's betrayal. More than Silva's death. More than the madness that the terrelan emperor turned me into. My daughter begging me for help with an impossible task. Fix the world she had broken. I wanted to say yes. We all want to say yes when our children ask us for help, but she asked too much. It couldn't be done. Not by one person. Not by two. Not by a thousand. The events she had set in motion were a global catastrophe. But that wasn't what she needed to hear. And breaking her spirit now would do no good.

"Of course I'll help, Sirileth." The words tasted sweet on my lips. Like for once in my crooked life I had swallowed pride and said the right thing. "I don't know how to fix it either, but we'll figure it out. Together."

Sirileth sniffed, trembled against my shoulder. "Thank you."

A child should never have to thank their parent for the help they are offered. It should be a given. But then a parent should never abandon their child to rule a queendom and fight a war all at the age of thirteen. It was time to make amends.

"You're welcome, Sirileth."

She sniffed again. "Mother…"

"What?"

"You smell."

We laughed then, both of us together. Even with the world ending around us, and the threat of the Other World, that was the happiest I had been in years.

CHAPTER ELEVEN

THE OTHERS DID NOT ACCEPT MY CHANGES so easily. Kento glared at me, then at Sirileth, then back to me. She was angry for some reason, as though my getting younger was a personal affront to her. While some women might have screamed and raged with that anger, that, I was realising, was not Kento's way. She went icy and distant.

The truth is, I don't think Kento blamed Sirileth for my new age. I think she saw the way I was growing closer to my youngest daughter, and it hurt her. I had chosen Sirileth over Kento. I had taken a side and Kento, I believe, still considered it the wrong choice. That Sirileth and I continued to grow closer must have plucked at the threads keeping her anger woven in. I should also remind you, my eldest had been given the rage of a god. I think she was far stronger than I gave her credit for at the time, to keep such anger in check.

"I need you to send me home," Kento said. She looked away, staring at the ground instead of meeting my eyes or Sirileth's. "I've done the calculations and Ro'shan should be passing over Rolshh in a few days. Is there… You can open portals to any minor rift now? Is there a rift in Rolshh?"

I had no idea. I had only been to that forested continent once back when Do'shan was moored to it. It was a strange place where the forest grew back as fast as it could be cut down, and giant monsters roamed between the trees. I had never actually set foot on the ground itself.

"There is one minor rift that I know of," Sirileth said quickly. "I can send you there."

"Now!"

Sirileth shook her head. "No. Tomorrow maybe."

Kento took a menacing step towards her sister. Sirileth didn't move. "I need to go home. Now, sister."

"I understand…"

"I need to see my daughter." Kento threw up her hands and turned away. "I need to report to my mother, too." She sagged. "But mostly I need to know Esem is alright. Tell me you, at least, understand, Eska."

Of course I did. But that didn't change the facts. I couldn't send Kento to Rolshh, I had no idea where the rift was. Only Sirileth could help her.

Sirileth simply shook her head. "Tomorrow, sister. Trust me." There is perhaps no faster way I know of to lose someone's trust than to tell them to trust you. I think Sirileth was struggling to form some kind of plan. And she wouldn't release any of her pieces until she knew what to do.

Tris goggled when he saw me, but a wild grin quickly spread across his face. Regardless of Sirileth's threats, my

son was still holding secret councils with his warriors,
and I had a feeling he would tread a fine line. The queen
of Yenheim may have declared the war with Tor was over
and done with, but I doubted Tris would let it go so easily.
Something needed to be done about that and I hadn't yet
decided whether it was my responsibility or Sirileth's.

While I ruled, I often trusted Imiko to act in my stead,
sometimes knowing nothing about what actions she took,
but knowing they were for the betterment of the queendom.
Perhaps that was what Sirileth needed then, people she
could trust to take matters off her hands.

Tris dismissed his warriors with a wave and leaned
back on the chair, putting his feet up on the table. He had
commandeered a tavern down in the city for his council
and there was no one else around save for the owner. Tris
summoned the man with a shout and before long I was
sitting around a table with all my surviving children, sharing
wine and ale and crusty bread.

I do not understand why you call this one your son.

"I rescued him from the Iron Legion's cells," I said.
"Adopted him. Raised him."

Tris sipped at his ale and shook his head. "A
wonderful way to start this little meeting, Mother. Remind
everyone I'm the only one here not your natural child."

I shook my head at him. "Don't be so dramatic, Tris."

"Why not? It clearly runs in the family." He grinned
and sipped at his ale again.

I grabbed one of the crusty bread rolls from the table,
cracked it open, and smeared it with butter. "What's the
situation with Tor?"

Tris' face darkened. "Bastards don't know when to
quit, Mother. Oh, I've pulled back our forces just as queen

sister demanded." Sirileth glared at him, but Tris just shot
her a fleeting smile. The two had always had a strange
relationship, part mocking and part rivalry. I think Vi
might have helped smooth things over between them but…
well, Vi was dead and Sirileth's refusal to destroy Tor for
her murder was part of the conflict raging between them.
"They're still gathering new troops on the border. I think
they may have heard about your return. It has them more
spooked than anything I've done to them."

"News travels fast," I said. I'd only been back in
Yenheim for two days. I bit a chunk off the crusty roll and
quickly followed it with another. I had my youth back, sure,
but I was stick thin and weak. Too many years of idleness
and growing old, and the reversal of my age had drained
my body's resources. I was ravenous all the time, and
desperately needed to start training again. There were battles
coming and I was in no shape to fight them.

"Oh, you have no idea," Tris said. "Did you know
Yun is gone?"

"What?" Sirileth looked up sharply.

"Yes. The entire city is gone. They evacuated a lot of
it before the tsunami hit, but you can't evacuate buildings.
The wave crushed the city and drowned anyone who
didn't get out in time. The waters are receding now, but
from what I hear, there's nothing left. It's not the only one
either. Most ports on the northern edge of Isha have been
destroyed by the waves and surging seas. Oh, and half of
Tefts was swallowed by a sink hole that opened up when the
earthquake hit us four days ago. The same time the big hole
in the Forest of Ten happened, swallowing half the town I
built there. Thanks for that, sister."

Sirileth was silent, staring at the table intensely.

"And it's not just Isha," Kento said. "You saw the Polasian desert. That storm is massive. And I have a feeling it's being held in place by the great rift."

"Great rift?" Tris asked.

I explained. About the rift, and how Sirileth had reset it, closing off the Maker, and redirecting the rift to Sevorai. I left out Imiko. She meant as much to Tris as she did Sirileth and I'd spare him the pain of knowing the truth if I could.

"Shit," Tris said once I was done. "You really have fucked us all, sister. Well done."

I was on my third bread roll and was eyeing up the fourth. Nobody else seemed hungry, but my stomach still rumbled.

As does mine.

"You don't have a stomach," I said quietly. All my children looked at me and I just shook my head at them. If I had to explain myself every time I spoke to my horror, we'd never get anywhere. Just like Hardt and Tamura and Imiko had so long ago, they'd soon get used to strange outbursts.

Sirileth was staring at me, eyes burning. "What do we do, Mother?"

Fuck if I knew. I was always much better at breaking things than fixing them. But Sirileth needed to hear I had a plan. They all did.

"We take it one step at a time," I said. "Tris and I will head to the border, meet with whoever is in charge of Tor's armies these days."

"I should go," Sirileth said. "I'm queen."

"You are," I agreed as I reached for the last bread roll. I'd already used all the butter so I just bit into it. "But sometimes you have to let others treat in your place. Tris and I will deal with this situation." I looked at my son and found him staring back, a quizzical look on his face, one eyebrow raised. I think he knew my mind. He knew I would try for peace, but if that failed... well, I really hoped it wouldn't fail.

"While we're gone," I said, spitting a few crumbs onto the table. "You need to send Kento home."

"Finally," Kento growled. She grabbed her glass of wine and drained it.

Tris chuckled. "Oh yes, she's definitely a Helsene."

Kento levelled a hostile stare at Tris. "I am not."

Tris shrugged and rocked back on his chair again. He really could be an insufferable little prick at times. We love our children and can overlook many of their faults, but sometimes you just want to punch them.

"Send word to Lanfall, too," I continued. "Address it to Jamis per Suano. We need to meet. Not just us and him, but everyone. A true council of those in power. The Merchant Union, anyone on Isha who calls themself king or queen. The Polasian Empress, if she's still alive."

Tris whistled. "She is. Lost half her demonships in the tsunami, but she's docked the rest up the river from Lanfall. Probably waiting to see how much of Polasia is left after the moon fell on it."

"Kento, I need you to convince Mezula to attend as well."

Kento just stared at me, neither agreeing nor disagreeing. I decided that was probably about as much as I deserved.

"We need to see whoever is ruling Itexia, too. And the garn. Mur, too, if possible."

Tris laughed. "A gathering like that has never been done before, Mother."

He was right. But we were living in unprecedented

times. The world was ending, broken by my daughter. We either stood together and worked to bring our raging world back under control. Or we died apart.

You are forgetting Norvet Meruun.

Ssserakis was wrong. I wasn't forgetting the Beating Heart of Sevorai at all. But I thought… I hoped that if I could convince the people of Ovaeris to work together once, to save Ovaeris. Well, if they could come together once, then maybe they could do it twice.

As I have said before, there is a reason I hate hope.

I was standing, staring at the Corpse Throne, my back to the chamber when Hardt found me. Ssserakis let me know he was coming and he wasn't alone. My horror watched from my shadow, protecting me, gorging itself on the background fear of a city full of terrified people.

"Siri," Hardt said as he approached, footsteps ringing on the stone floor. "Have you seen Eska? I…"

I grinned and glanced over my shoulder at him, my eyes flashing. Hardt froze mid step, goggled at me, shook his head. "Lursa's Tears, Eska. How?"

There was a younger woman behind him. Younger than Hardt anyway. She was almost of a height with him and not far off his brawn either. By the muscle of her arms and the way she stood, I guessed she was a soldier, but she wasn't wearing armour. Loose trousers, a half-buttoned blouse, and the type of boots one wears when you expect to get your use of them. She was beautiful. She carried a babe in the crook of one arm, and a toddler clung to her trousers, sucking on his thumb. She glanced at Hardt, frozen to the spot, then to me, then back to Hardt. She shook her head, curly hair bouncing, and strode past him.

"You said she was old, fool-of-a-man. Lady Eska," the woman said as she reached me and thrust out her right hand to shake. Not queen, I noticed. Not even Eskara. She claimed a formality with me she hadn't earned and I felt my ire rising.

I do not like this one. There is fear in her, but it is not of us. Make her fear us.

I swept back my shadowy cloak and held out my claw to her. She glanced at it, shifted the child in her arm to the other one, then took my skeletal hand and shook it. "Beff," she said with the barest flash of a smile. "This little one is Tam," she thrust the child in her arms at me so suddenly I had no choice but to grab it or let it fall. He was a heavy babe, probably not surprising given the size of his parents, and smelled like shit. Well, they all smell like shit at that age. "And this one is Sen." She nudged the other boy forwards and he stumbled a step then went down on one knee.

"Kop Ken," the child mumbled around his thumb. I stared at him and wondered if he was stupid.

"That's right, Sen," Beff said. "She is the Corpse Queen."

Sen nodded, still kneeling. "Kop Ken."

The child in my arms squirmed, flailed, smacked me in the face with a pudgy little arm, then continued to stink. I should point out now that while I love my children and never found any fault in them for their early years, I cannot stand other people's children. I discovered this while in Wrysom. Helping to deliver babes is messy, but then you hand the child over and it's done with. When they're old enough to run around and speak, they can be quite fun to tease and chase, and they sometimes come out with the oddest and wisest things you can imagine. But there are

those years in between where they do nothing but cry and
shit themselves. Mess and noise and nothing else. I want
nothing to do with those years or any child in the midst of
them.

"I wanted to say thank you, Lady Eska," Beff said.
"For getting my husband through all those scrapes."

The child slapped me again. I glared at it, my eyes
flashing. It was too young to understand and slapped my
cheek again, laughing. My storm crackled around me, little
bolts of lightning striking the ground, searing the rock.

"Eska," Hardt rumbled, the warning clear. I quieted
the storm before any of the lightning could strike his
children and he grabbed Tam out of my arms. The babe
immediately clutched at Hardt.

Free of the burden, I turned my attention back to Beff.
"You don't need to thank me. I'm pretty sure most of our
scrapes were my fault. Besides, Hardt pulled me out of as
many as I did him." Neither of us had ever kept a tally, but it
would be heavily weighted on both sides if we did.

Beff nodded and pulled Sen up and back to her side.
I tasted the slightest tingle of fear from her now. Not for
herself, though. For her children. She needn't have worried; I
wouldn't have hurt them. But a little fear is healthy.

"Even so," Beff continued. "He's told me all about
you and he wouldn't have got himself out of the Pit if not for
you. Thank you."

She introduced herself properly after that. She had
indeed once been a soldier, a Terrelan guard stationed at the
top of the Pit of all things. But that changed when she met
Hardt and popped out the first of her brats. She was now
a council member for Yenheim town. The council was an
ingenious idea of Sirileth's taking many of the more tedious

issues of rule off her hands. They sorted most of the people's problems and delivered weekly reports to the throne. I wish I had thought of it during my time as queen. I might not have hated it so much. Eventually the children got bored, as they do, and the younger one started wailing while the older one chased one of the palace cats until it got angry enough to swipe at him. Then he was screaming too.

One thing I can say of Sirileth with eternal gratitude is that although she was noisy for her first year of life, she was a quiet child after that.

Beff bundled the children away and left Hardt and me sitting on the steps of the Corpse Throne. I had considered sitting in the seat, but it wasn't mine anymore and I thought it might set a bad precedent to anyone who saw it. I told Hardt about Josef and the Chronomancy. I think he understood about half of it, but Sourcery was never really in his understanding. We talked about Tor and the war that was brewing between the two nations once again. He warned me to be careful of Tris, that my son was not the same young man I had known.

Then we came down to it. Hardt pulled a small flask out of his coat pocket and popped the cork. I took a swig and winced. Whiskey, a fruity, smoky flavour and strong enough my eye twitched and my throat burned. Hardt always did have more of a taste for the cheap, nasty stuff. But then, it wasn't about the drink.

"Tamura should be here," he said, his voice a gravelly rumble. "But the old fool is away and this needs doing." He sniffed, took a swig, handed me the flask. "To Imiko."

We toasted my sister. The whiskey tasted like ash and regret. I leaned against him and he against me and we drank to Imiko in silence. Up until the point Hardt could hold that silence no longer.

"Tell me the truth, Eska. Did Sirileth do it?" He choked on the words, took a moment to steady himself. "Did Sirileth kill Imiko?"

How to answer that question? To say no would be a lie. To say yes would also be lying. In the end, I settled for *a* truth. "It was me. I killed her."

I didn't explain myself. Didn't feel like I could. It would only come out wrong anyway. Hardt went rigid, sat beside me for a while. Then he downed the last of the flask and stood without a word, striding from the throne room, hands balled into fists. I didn't blame him. First Isen, then Silva, and now Imiko. All dead because of me. Hardt probably wondered which of our family I'd kill next.

He'd left the flask on the steps beside me. Empty. Cracked from where he'd gripped it so tightly in his hands. I picked it up carefully so none of the cracks spread too far. I wanted to keep it. I couldn't say why, exactly, but it felt important, meaningful.

Sentimental crap. It was just a cracked, useless old flask. I crushed it in my shadowy claw and scattered the pieces across the throne room.

CHAPTER TWELVE

THE NEXT DAY, I SAID GOODBYE TO KENTO before I left. She claimed once she was closer to Ro'shan, she could send word to her mother and Mezula would dispatch a flyer to pick her up. I tried to hug my oldest daughter, but she pulled away from me. The wariness in her eyes hurt, but I suppose I couldn't blame her. I had just shed thirty years of age, had a skeletal claw that was also an ancient horror, and was draped in a cloak formed of shadows. It still hurt though.

I asked her to consult with Mezula, to beg the Rand to send an envoy to Lanfall for the council of rulers we needed to assemble. We couldn't do what needed to be done without the Rand, and if anyone could convince Mezula it would be Kento. She agreed to ask but made no promises. I also asked Kento to tell Esem about me. To that request she replied only with stony silence.

I left Yenheim with Tris by my side and one hundred
soldiers at my back. It was a small escort, though larger
than I would have liked. I would have gone alone, tried
to convince Tor that war was the last thing we wanted or
needed. Sirileth wouldn't allow it. My daughter pointed
out, quite rightly damn her, that I was still weak and if the
soldiers of Tor did decide to attack, I needed help. All it
took was for her to gesture at my stick thin arms and legs to
prove her point. I was eating heartily, my flesh beginning to
return, but I also tired quickly.

The soldiers marched on foot. Tris sat a trei bird as if
he had been born in the saddle. There was one for me, too,
but I chose not to ride. The march would do me good.

A vast gathering turned out to watch us leave
Yenheim city. They crowded the streets, hung out of
windows, sat on the gutters of rooftops high above us. Word
had spread of my return and the people of Yenheim jostled
to catch sight of their once queen. The people had always
taken a fierce pride in my reputation, even as dark as it was.
They had no doubt heard I was old, and then that I had my
youth again. I put on quite the spectacle.

I wore my old leather armour. It was creaky and
tough from disuse and needed a good oiling. It was also
scored in a number of places from the battles I had seen, and
it no longer fit me very well. It was the same armour I wore
the day I fought Silva up on Do'shan. A couple of the scars in
the leather reminded me of that fight still. Ssserakis draped
my shadow around me as a cloak and I stared out with
flashing eyes that seemed to delight the crowd. It had the air
of festival about it.

Fucking fools! None of them even realised this
was why I had left in the first place. Creating idols out of

monsters is lunacy. I wanted to scream at them all that I wasn't a hero.

"Smile, Mother," Tris said, leaning down a little from his saddle. His trei bird plodded on, taloned claws tearing up the dusty road, feathers ruffling in fright from all the noise. "Maybe give them a wave with that shadow hand of yours. Let them see you."

I scowled in reply.

"You know, Mother, I never quite understood how you did it. These people love you. They'd follow you into hell itself. But you're such a sullen grump at times. I've been jovial, approachable. Downright charming. I've stolen from Tor and given as much as I could back to the people, and yet they never loved me quite like they did you." He smiled radiantly and blew a kiss to a doughty woman in the crowd.

I stepped around a pile of droppings in the street, kept the scowl plastered to my face. "It's not me they love, Tris. It never was. It's the reputation. The symbol I represent. Power, strength, the will to act against those who rule. They see me as the Corpse Queen, the woman who rose up alone and tore down an oppressive empire."

"Well, you did." Tris waved to the crowd.

"You're missing the point." I snapped at my son. "I destroyed an empire that was no more or less oppressive than any other. I did it by unleashing a plague of monsters that turns people's loved ones into monsters. I did it by burning a city down to its foundations. By slaughtering an entire bloodline. I did it in pain and in madness and in grief. It might have been right, but how I did it was wrong. I shouldn't be idolised for it."

"So you wouldn't kill the Terrelan Emperor again if you had the chance?"

I snorted. "Oh no. What I did to Aras Terrelan I'd do again a hundred times over. That fucker deserved it." And more. Killing him three times simply wasn't enough. I just regret killing half of Juntorrow with him.

We marched out of Yenheim and spent the first day on the road, one weary foot falling in front of the other. Marching is a soldier's lot in life, really. More than fighting or standing guard or glorious battle, marching is what defines a soldier's life. That's why they're always so fixated on boots. Tris dozed in his saddle, shadowed flesh under his eyes, the evidence of a late night catching up with him. The soldiers behind us joked, or grumbled, or played stupid little games. I plodded on, lost in my thoughts.

Occasionally I closed my eyes, saw visions of the Other World as if I were moving through it. I almost startled out of it the first time it happened. There was a battle raging around me, only I wasn't really there.

"Do you see this?" I asked.

"Huh?" Tris said lazily, cracking open one eye. I wasn't talking to him anyway.

See what?

"In Sevorai. I'm in the midst of a battle."

Do they all look the same?

I tripped on a rock, stumbled, got my feet beneath me. It was strange marching through one world but seeing another. No sound of the battle reached my ears, nor the smells I knew must be stinking up the butchery, but everywhere I looked creatures were flinging themselves at others. Some of the combatants were small, no larger than a terran, others were huge, towering giants. Some had horns, others had wings, others still were beasts charging about on all fours, or slimes oozing forth. One lumbering hulk scuttled past me on a thousand little legs that looked like they belonged to children. But all the creatures fighting and dying on that field had the same face. A kindly, chubby little face with puffed-out cheeks, watery eyes, fat lips, and a hawkish nose.

"Yes. They all have the same face."

Aire and Dialos. They are fighting for dominance again. The fools squabble while their home is devoured.

I opened my eyes, tried to forget the gruesome images I had seen. I also tried not to blink for a while, scared my new portal sight would put me right back in the middle of it.

When we made camp that first night, Tris slipped from his saddle, handed the reins to a soldier and yawned dramatically. "Time to do the rounds." He set about wandering through the camp as it was erected around us, sharing words with every soldier, a sneaky drink with some, a joke with others. He was amiable, loved as one of them. He did not help raise the camp but bolstered the spirits of everyone around him. A leader, but a terrible general.

What is the difference?

"Distance," I said as I moved away from the camp a little and found a suitably open space. I had an hour before full dark and that was enough for now. "I guess a leader needs to be seen with their troops. Loved by them. These soldiers, they'll follow Tris' orders, but they're not inspired by him. He's one of them. A general however, can hold themselves apart, but they need to inspire those they lead. A general's ideals become the ideals of the led."

Ssserakis chuckled. *Yes. Minions are nothing but mindless cattle.*

"No. Not mindless or cattle. Just lacking cohesion. Direction." I sighed, struggled for a way to explain it to the horror. "People are water…"

What?

"Just… shut up a moment. People are water. Without direction they will blanket the land and either dissipate or drown it. But give them direction, purpose, make them a river, and they have such power and potential. They can carve through the earth, sweep away anything in their path, catch up and crush anything caught in their momentum."

My horror was silent, considering. *It is easier when they are minions. No thought of their own. I command, they do. Simple.*

"Maybe. But with so much less potential." I lunged into a stretch, knowing I would need to limber up for what I had planned. "You tell a minion to attack, it will do so. Throw itself at the enemy until it is dead. But they won't care either way. If a soldier has something to live for, a family to protect, a life to return to, they will fight so fucking hard. If they have friends they will protect each other."

Stronger together than apart. Ssserakis said thoughtfully, finally latching on to something it understood. It retreated inside me to think.

I ached. A day of marching had taken it out of me, but I didn't have time to rest. While our little army of one hundred raised our camp and set cook fires to burning, I trained. I formed a Sourceblade in my hand and launched myself into the old forms Ishtar had once beaten into me. It was awkward at first. My arms and legs trembled from the exertion and weariness. I was weak. Sourceblades might weigh next to nothing, but it's the effort of movement that made me sweat. My muscles, what was left of them, remembered the old forms, but I couldn't reach them. It had easily been a decade since I had last fought with a blade. It showed.

I trained for an hour. I'm a little ashamed to say it was all I could manage. By the end, I was trembling so much I had to cross my arms to keep still. Every part of me burned from exertion. And worst of all, I had an audience. Three soldiers, two women and a man, were standing close by, watching me intently. I hadn't even noticed them while I was going at it. I saw other eyes turned my way from the circle of tents. Well, fuck them. They could plainly see what their mythical Corpse Queen had become. A weakling too frail to hold a blade, and definitely not ready to be swinging it at anything other than air.

I nodded to my watchers, hoping to put them at some unease, then made my way to the river to wash some of the sweat from my skin. After that, I found the nearest cook fire and devoured two bowls of porridge and as many strips of dried meat as I could stomach. Then I crawled into my tent and collapsed.

As exhausting as that first day was, the next was worse. I woke early, mostly by choice, and forced myself out of bed. I was stiff and every step was aching agony. I think I'd have struggled to move if not for Ssserakis lending me strength, drawn from the fears of a hundred nightmares.

Dragging myself up and out of my tent, I found the morning light dull and as weary as I felt. It seemed such a muted thing behind the thick cloud cover. The sentries greeted me even as the rest of the camp slowly came awake. I immediately went back to my little clearing, just away from the camp, and set to moving through the old forms again. An hour in the morning and an hour at night, just as Ishtar had long ago demanded. It was a good practice to adopt, but I recommend never falling out of the habit. Getting started again after time off is gruelling.

By the time I finished, I had watchers again. There were more of them this time, eight soldiers staring at me in something like puzzlement. Some nodded to me in greeting and I returned it as I set off to find food.

The second day was harder than the first, but I expected that. My legs were wooden, caught in that hell between painful as fire and numb as ice. Often I found myself dragging my feet. The day passed in a monotonous blur of dull light and gentle hills. We saw a few people, farmers or villagers come to see what was happening. We also passed a cacophony of abbans and I stared longingly after it, wishing for freshly cooked steak. The clouds never thinned and the sun never poked through. Ssserakis appreciated it, but my horror was from another world where there was no sun. Things worked differently there. Here, on Ovaeris, life needed sunlight to grow.

My legs barely worked by the end of that second day. Sharp pain shot like hot knives from my soles all the way up to my hips, and my thighs burned. I was sweaty and so tired it was a struggle not to curl into a ball and weep. Still, I took myself apart from where the camp was springing up from the dirt, and formed a sourceblade in my hand, lurching into motion as I staggered through the forms again.

I was only halfway through the set of forms when I realised I was not alone. Five soldiers, two men and three women, had joined me. They'd dropped their armour, and they certainly weren't going through the same movements I was, but they were there beside me, training.

Guilt can be a powerful motivator but only as far as the initial prodding we need to act. Pride, on the other hand, is a much longer lasting stick we use to beat ourselves with. It was guilt that convinced those first soldiers to stand beside me, practicing their forms. Guilt that even after a day's long march, their old queen put herself through another hour of torture to make certain she was ready for what was to come. But yes, it was pride, of standing beside me and earning the sweat and ache and exhaustion, that convinced them to continue.

The next morning I had well over twenty people training with me. Not only that, but one of them was a bloody drill instructor. He marched up and down and berated those who were slacking or out of step. He even stopped in front of me, his fat lips pursed and beady eyes frowning. I knew that look; he had something to say but was afraid to voice it.

I paused mid-swing, panting and sweating, both hand and claw on the hilt of my sourceblade. "Go ahead," I said between breaths.

"Thank you. You're dropping your elbow on the follow through," the man said in a gravelly voice.

I sighed, saw him blanch. "You're not wrong."

I stepped back, flowed into the strike again. Well, flowed isn't quite right. Sputtered into it maybe. Anyway, I lifted my elbow a little more. "Better?" I asked.

The man's fat lips puckered like he was sucking on a lemon. "Not really."

"I'll keep working on it. Thank you..." I let it hang.

"Taxon. My name is Taxon, Corpse Queen."

"Well, Taxon. Thank you." It took some effort to say, but he was right. Besides, he was positively polite about it compared to the teachers I'd had in the past. Hardt often beat me bloody in our sparring. Tamura was a ruthless taskmaster in his own cryptic way. And Ishtar could never utter two words to me without an insult flying from her jowls.

By the fifth day of marching, I was utterly sick of walking, outwardly seething at the permanent shroud of gloom the brooding clouds cast us in, and covered in a motley of bruises. We started sparring on the fourth day, an hour of matches just after form practice. I got the painful end of every fight I threw myself into. I knew it would be very different if I could use my Sourcery, or my claw, or just fucking move the way I once had.

It is so blisteringly frustrating to see a strike coming, to know the perfect way to block it, but not be able to get your blade up in time. Or to finally force your body to move fast enough to parry, only for the slash to break through your defences because your arms are so weak you can't stand before a single blow. I took my beatings with as much dignity and humble humour as I could manage. Which is to say I stalked away and didn't shatter their existence like an avalanche through a glass window.

I found Tris watching me on the sixth day. By then I had more of the soldiers joining me for sparring than not. We paired off, a dozen different bouts taking place at once, and the winners had the reward of sitting out the next fight. I obviously had very little time to stare after my son, but when I saw him he was standing around with five others I recognised from the little war council he had been holding in Yenheim palace. I realised then at least some of the soldiers in our little band were loyal to Tris, not to Yenheim. Not to Sirileth and not to me.

On the eighth day out from Yenheim I knew we were getting close to the Tor border. Even in the permanent sullen overcast light I could see a proud watchtower far in the distance. There were no villages so close to the border, on either side of the line, and the road was less well-travelled. The war had been going on for so long, and although hostilities had all but ceased recently, tensions were still high between the two nations, and travel between them was scarce.

We struck camp at the bottom of a valley. It had once been green and lush and full of life, but now was near barren. Nothing but rocks and scree and dark rents in the earth that when peered into gazed back like the emptiness of the void. I did not like camping there, but there was a stream and good space for the tents. Still, something gnawed at me. An itch I couldn't scratch. The ghostly tingle of my missing arm, even so long gone.

We fell into the form training and then to sparring. I lost my first and second matches handily and had just taken a padded sword to the ribs, signalling the end of my third match, too. I leaned heavily on my sourceblade, gasping for air. The soldier who had just beaten me looked caught between apologising, checking I was alright, and running away. I gave the young woman a brief smile, then told her to fuck off. She met my flashing gaze and jogged from the field. I watched her go admiringly.

"Mind if I have the next bout?" Tris asked. He dropped his coat in the arms of one of his waiting sycophants and sauntered into the training arena to face me. He stopped opposite, standing tall where I was slouching and barely able to keep upright. The air shimmered around him and a kinetic arm formed in his hand. His weapon of choice was a scythe. Bloody horrible weapons to wield and even more horrific to fight against. Which, of course, he knew all too well.

I shook my head at him wearily. "You don't want to

do this, Tris."

"I think I do, Mother." He grinned smugly like a wolf had cornered a mouse and knew there was no escape.

I stood my ground. That should come as no surprise. I am stubborn and defiant and refuse to back down. I always stand my ground. But there was more to it than my own wilfulness. Some people, like me, have no give in them. The harder you push, the more they push back until one or both of you break. There are no other options. Others will back down the moment someone stands up to them and says *no more*. And then there are people like Tris. I knew my son well. I had raised him, failed him, fought him. Tris was the type of person who pushed everyone around him, tested everyone. Friend, foe, family, lover. It didn't matter. Ever since Vi died, it seemed like he was on a mission to test the limits of everyone close to him. And because he never stopped pushing everyone away, he found them all wanting. Even me. When I expelled him from Yenheim so long ago, I failed him. I stopped pushing back. I wouldn't do it again. I wouldn't fail him again. I couldn't lose him again.

I stepped forward to meet him. It was more of a limp given my hip was aching, but I tried to make it look dramatic. I stood to my full, inconsiderable height and stared up at Tris, my eyes flashing. Then I lowered my voice so no one else would hear. We were surrounded by soldiers, and most eyes were turned towards us. Even the other sparring bouts had stopped to watch. I realised we had been here before, Tris and me. When he had tried to force me to abdicate and let him take the throne. We had fought. He had lost. We both knew the outcome would be different this time around.

"This doesn't end how you think it will, Tris," I said.

"You'll win here. We both know it. But it won't earn you the respect you're after. Nor will it knock me down in their estimation." I grinned at him even as his smile slipped away into a scowl. "Most of the soldiers here have already beaten me in a match. They all know I'm not at my best. You, a young man in his prime. Me, out of shape and weak from the matches I've already fought. You'll look like a bully, and a petty one at that."

"What makes you think that isn't the point, Mother?" His mask had slipped, his joviality gone. This was the dark, brooding boy I remembered. The real Tris always simmering below the surface. So full of pain and anger.

"Because this is a play for power." I shook my head at him. "And it's the wrong move. Fight me here and you'll win the match but lose the respect."

He glared down at me, cold fury in his eyes. "You're wrong, Mother. It's not about power, or respect. When you're at your best again, you will fight me."

The wind changed. A slight thing, the breeze shifting from one direction to another. It brought the scent of death. A foul, rotting, sickly sweetness I knew all too well. Suddenly I realised why this place had felt so strange to me. I had just been using the wrong senses to determine why. It took only a moment to reach out with my innate Necromancy. I felt them beneath us, down in the holes, hiding in the dark. Hundreds of rotting bodies. Thousands of them.

"Strike the camp," I said.

Tris met my gaze, sniffed, nodded.

"Strike the camp," I shouted. "Now!"

Soldiers milled about for a few seconds, then Taxon took up the shout and suddenly people were running for the tents, pulling them down double time.

"What is that stench?" Tris asked.

I glanced up at the darkening sky. We had maybe thirty minutes of dingy light left. It would be dangerous marching in the dark, especially through an area pockmarked with holes. More dangerous to camp near a hive. Especially at night.

"Use your Necromancy, Tris," I said. There were soldiers running all about us, but we two stood in the eye of that storm of motion.

His eyes went wide. "Oh, fuck. The Cursed."

CHAPTER THIRTEEN

THE CURSED ARE MY LEGACY, MY ROTTING gift to the world. They are people caught somewhere between life and death. Their bodies rot. They are mindless. That's not quite true. The people they once were are still there, trapped inside the shell, forever locked away and unable to do anything but watch. It is a horrific thing I did, creating such a plague. The Cursed have no will of their own. They follow a command I gave when I created the first of them. I was not in my right mind. Driven mad by Aras Terrelan's months of torture. I was fuelled entirely by anger and hate and...

Excuses. It's all just excuses.

I killed one of my torturers, took hold of his soul as it left his body and forced it back into his corpse. And I gave him one terrible command. Kill them all. Spread my curse and kill them all. And that is what he did.

I still do not fully understand how I created the curse. A strange fusion of Sourceries, I think. At first, I could control them, command them this way or that, or simply make them stop, give them the peace of a final death. At first. As my curse spread, each generation of it slipped further and further from my control. The monsters that plagued Isha these days were so far removed from my original curse that even Necromancy could not affect them. And worse still, they had somehow spread outside of our continent. My curse. My legacy. No longer even confined to Isha. Now it was the whole world's problem to deal with.

We marched through the night, which, in case you're wondering, is a fucking stupid thing to do. Even with lanterns lit, it was so dark we could barely see a few feet ahead of us. An insipid mist rose from the ground and made it even more treacherous. We lost three people, though none could say how. When the sun finally rose and gave us the barest hint of light to work with, we checked our numbers and found three missing. I sent scouts back to search for them, but there was simply no trace. Maybe they had blundered into one of the many holes that dotted the valley, or maybe the Cursed had come above ground and taken them. Maybe they just deserted and who could blame them?

We finally made camp at the base of the watch tower that sat on the Yenheim-Tor border. It was strategically placed to have a commanding view of a good swathe of land. It was also where I had agreed to meet with a Tor ambassador so many years ago. Where Tris had been waiting instead, the ambassador slain.

My people were weary. A forced march through the night, nerves on edge. The chatter was sullen, forced, a blade hidden behind every jest. Tents were erected in silence and fires started to heat the cookpots and fill empty bellies. I dragged my feet to the watch tower to meet with whoever was stationed there. Even before I climbed the steps, from the vantage point atop a hill, I could see a camp of Tor soldiers splayed out before a forest edge. Their camp was bigger than ours. A lot bigger.

I was met at the base of the watch tower by a burly old soldier with more hair on his chin than on his head. He looked a little flustered when he saw me and quickly dropped to one knee.

"I heard but didn't think… didn't think it were real. You're back." He spoke with a familiarity. I wracked my brain to remember him but couldn't.

"I am," I said cagily.

He looked up at me, smiled. "Corst. That, uh, that's my name. I was with you down in the Pit. Spent years digging. Even saw you stab that fat twat Prig in the neck. You, uh, gave me bread once, for knocking some fool senseless. I was, uh, younger then, bigger too."

I nodded and waved at him to stand. "Corst," I said as if committing the name to memory rather than forgetting it a few moments later. "What are we dealing with here?"

Corst stood and pushed open the watch tower door, starting up the rickety wooden stairs. "Well, those Tor bastards have an army. Bloody big one. They, uh, turned up a few days back. Bad sign, I reckon. First the sky goes all dark, and then the ground shakes, those, uh, holes open up. Now we got an army to deal with. They've not done much yet though. Just seem to be, uh, sitting there. Watching me watch them."

"You're alone here?" I noticed a section of the tower wall had fallen away, stone tumbled out to litter the grassy ground below. It was not an insignificant hole.

"Have been for near ten days now," Corst said. "Bolder was here with me, but, uh, went out for a piss one night and never came back. I had a look around but couldn't find sight of him."

This one is riddled with fear. Watch.

My shadow rippled, streaked ahead of me, ahead of Corst. It rose up against the stone wall of the staircase and Ssserakis formed the face of a screaming terran there. Corst staggered, cried out, fell backwards so I had to shove my shoulder against the wall or risk us both tumbling all the way down to the bottom of the tower.

"Di-di-d-did you s-s-see that?" Fear flowed off him in great waves. Ssserakis gave me some of that strength, enough to allow me to push against Corst and get him upright again.

"See what?" I asked innocently. His fear only grew stronger. "Get up, man. Go."

Imagine how strong we could be if I fed off an entire city this way. The true purpose of minions, not thrusting useless steel into their hands.

We continued up the tower, Corst trembling and looking around frantically. There was a storage room full of sacks and barrels, likely containing food to keep whoever was stationed here going, and a small bunk room with two beds, a couple of chests, and a table. Then we were at the top. A covered rooftop with regular slitted windows for peering out. Corst pointed to one of the windows and I stared through it.

With a better vantage point I could see the Tor camp quite well now. Well enough to know that if it came to a fight, we were fucked. They outnumbered us by a good

ten to one, and I saw flags fluttering in the breeze that I
recognised from long ago. Tor treated its Sourcerers like
royalty. As I watched, I saw a small procession of people
riding those damned horse creatures, leave the main
encampment and start up the hill, a white flag held high.
That was a good sign, at least. It seemed they wanted to
parley. Always good to have a bit of a chat before bloodshed.

I rode out to meet the Tor delegation. I would
probably have walked if I had my way but Tris demanded he
accompany me and that it would look better if we rode. I can
ride trei birds, but the long-legged things are so awkward.
They plod when walking and bounce when running, and
they didn't seem to like my shadow, always shying away
from it.

Six people of Tor were there to meet us. They had
picketed their horses nearby and stood waiting. I guessed
at least two were Sourcerers by the way their hands kept
near the pouches at their hips. All wore enchanted armour,
the runes etched into metal and leather and glowing faintly
pink. They took no chances. I think they expected to find
Tris. But they certainly didn't expect me. That was good.
Nothing like a surprise Corpse Queen to ruin someone's day.

Eyes went wide at my approach, the impact marred
only slightly at my ungainly dismount from the trei bird as
it tried to step away from my shadowy cloak. It was scared
of me, but the blunt fear of the mindless. I let my cloak settle
back into position and approached with Tris at my side. We
stopped a few paces away, in easy striking distance. My
storm flashed at them through my eyes.

*All six of them are terrified. Shall we give them a true
reason?*

My shadow started twisting beside me, bubbling and

growing, sharp angles and snaps as it lurched into the hazy shape of a terran. I glanced at Ssserakis and a leering patch of darker black stared back at me from my shadow.

"No," I said. "We agreed. I'll deal with the people from Ovaeris, and you'll deal with the lords of Sevorai."

Ssserakis laughed loudly enough all six of the fools from Tor fell silent. *As you wish.* My shadow deflated and slivered back under me.

"I like it, mother," Tris said quietly. "Put them at ill ease from the start. You haven't lost a step."

I ignored him and waited for the Tor delegation to work up the courage to face me. It took a few minutes. Eventually a man stepped forward. He was short, perhaps even shorter than me, but had wide shoulders and a look about him that spoke of muscle and hard work. His face held a patchwork of scars that made him look like he had been assembled from at least six different people and none of them had started pretty. He wore a silver breast plate, glowing pink with enchanted runes, and had a sword buckled at his hip. He was also a Sourcerer. I felt a tingle as he came close and would have put money on him being an Augmancer at the very least.

"Corpse Queen," he said by way of greeting. Then he glanced at Tris and his lip curled. "Reaper."

I nudged Tris in the ribs hard enough he flinched. "Reaper?"

My son shrugged. "It's a nickname *they* gave me. I think it's because of the scythe. I quite like it." He grinned, turned the rictus smile on the Tor man. "And who are you?"

"Richter," the short Sourcerer said. "Richter si Poe."

"Wonderful," I said, unable to hide my impatience. I've never liked formal proceedings. "We're all introduced.

Now how about we get down to business. Take your army, fuck off back to Tor, and we'll do the same. Queen Sirileth wants peace."

"We've heard that from you before, Corpse Queen. Do you really think I'd be so stupid as to believe you again."

Tris chuckled. "I told you, Mother. They won't listen." His dark eyes were fixed on Richter and there was no humour in them, despite the smile on his face. "Entirely intractable."

Richter returned the dark look and I sensed there was maybe some history between him and my son. Well, Tris had been waging his war for over a decade now so it probably shouldn't have surprised me. I was starting to wish he hadn't come along after all, but it was my choice. I needed him to make amends if peace was a possibility.

"This doesn't come from me," I said. "I am not the queen of Yenheim. I'm not queen of anything."

"Except corpses," that came from one of the fools behind Richter. Fucking idiot probably thought he was being unbearably witty.

"Queen Sirileth wants peace," I stated very firmly. "We're only here to deliver the message. Because believe it or not," I raised a hand and a claw and pointed to the sky, "there are more important things for us to be dealing with."

These fools have no idea what is coming for them from my world. Would you like me to show them?

"You can do that?" I asked.

Yes.

"What?" Richter asked.

"I said can you do that? Can you fuck off back to Tor and us to Yenheim, and we can have the peace we need to deal with more pressing matters."

My shadow started twisting again.

"Stop," I said quietly. "I'll deal with this."

Ssserakis chuckled and my shadow settled back down. *You sound very certain.* I wondered when my horror had picked up sarcasm.

"I didn't do anything, Mother," Tris said.

Things really would have been easier if I had just spoken to Ssserakis with my thoughts. I knew the horror could listen in on them, but I'd never liked communicating that way. It is strange but admitting my horror could hear my every thought broke down a barrier I wasn't willing to lose. Even if it was only an imaginary barrier.

Richter was staring at me, but he had turned, was consulting with the rest of the Tor delegation. I saw them whispering, nodding, shaking heads. One of them pointed at me, then her finger waved sideways to Tris.

"We could just attack," Tris suggested a little too loudly. "There's only six of them, Mother."

Richter frowned and one of his hands went to his breastplate, absently stroking the rune glowing there.

"That's not helpful, Tris," I snapped. "Perhaps if you apologised for all the atrocities you've committed."

"Sure. Sure. Anything for mighty Yenheim." Tris stepped forward and sketched a bow that was somehow both dramatic and mocking all at once.

"Grand warriors and people of noble Tor," Tris said in a simpering voice. "I, Tris Helsene," he straightened from his bow, "some of you call me Reaper. Do apologise for any wrong doings I have visited upon you." The smile slipped from his face. "For any sisters murdered unfairly. I apologise. May you all choke on our peace and rot in hell."

He stepped back in line with me and gave a sullen

shrug. "There. I tried my best."

"Really spoke from the heart with that one," I said. I couldn't blame him though.

I wanted peace. I did. But I also couldn't forget how the war had started. I might blame myself for stealing a few abban from the bastards, but the truth was it was an inconsequential theft compared to the retaliation. Tor had sent assassins to kill me and had instead killed Vi. My adopted daughter and Tris' sister. Little Vi who loved to chatter about anything and everything. She filled my life with joyful noise. I think she also kept much of Tris' darker nature at bay. Just as Josef had with my own for so long.

I saw so much of myself in Tris. He was who I might have become had I not Josef's steadying presence throughout my years at the academy. If I had not had Hardt's solid moral conscience to lean upon after the Pit. If Imiko had not pulled me back from the edge after Silva's death. I had almost become who Tris was now so many times, but every time one of my friends had saved me. I realise now no one had been there for Tris. Vi was gone. Sirileth was not a steadying presence by any approximation. I was… No. I never tried to pull him back from the edge. Just the opposite. After Vi's death, I dragged Tris over the edge with me. Only he didn't have the experience to pull himself out again. And when I did, when I finally woke up and clawed my way from the darkness and despair… Damn me, but I didn't take him with me. I left him there. I abandoned him.

Tris glowered at the Tor delegation, his hands flexing, curling into fists. There was no fear in him, not a drop of it. There was nothing but rage and hate in his heart. I reached up, put a hand on his shoulder and he flinched away from me, eyes wide and dangerous.

Richter cleared his throat. I almost skewered him with a shadowy spike for that. The little, scarred man from Tor stepped forward and drew himself up to his full, inconsiderable height as though he was about to deliver the most important speech of his life.

Or maybe just his last one.

"We accept," Richter said.

I sighed in relief.

Richter cleared his throat again. "With one condition."

Oh, fucking save us all from puffed-up cocks with an inflated sense of self-importance.

Richter raised a hand and pointed at Tris. "We demand the Reaper surrender himself to the people of Tor for justice."

Tris snorted out a laugh. "Justice? What the fuck would you know about justice?"

"You have murdered countless people of Tor…"

Tris stepped forward. "That *was* justice!" he shouted.

"Murder is never justice," Richter snapped.

"A fitting thing for a murderer to say." Tris held his hand out to the side and formed a sourceblade, a giant scythe.

Richter stumbled back a step, eyes goggling in his patchwork face. "You threaten me at a parley?"

"*I* threaten *you?*" Tris advanced, claiming the space Richter ceded. "What would you call demanding my head if not a threat?"

Could I really do it? Could I sacrifice my son to save Yenheim from a war it couldn't afford to fight? To save Ovaeris from falling beneath the encroaching tide of Norvet Meruun? Do not misunderstand me, I did not for a

moment believe that Yenheim as a queendom was all that
stood between Ovaeris and annihilation, but I also knew
that Sirileth and I stood in the centre of it all. We were the
lynchpins that our world would stand or fall on. We couldn't
afford to fight a war against Tor. Couldn't afford to get
distracted from the real conflicts stacking up around us. I
had done it before, sacrificed someone I loved for the greater
good. I could do it again. For peace. For resolution. For
Ovaeris.

*You have a strange way of convincing yourself to do what
is necessary.*

Fuck it! I paced forwards, putting myself between
Richter and my son. Their snarling quickly stopped and both
sets of eyes turned to me, Richter's with suspicion, Tris' with
hesitation. A man bracing for betrayal.

I let my eyes flash and pierced Richter with the
stormy glare. "You will not take my son from me."

"Hah!" Richter snorted, raising his arms as if I had
just proven him victorious. "I was right. You come here
claiming to seek peace and negotiate with bad faith."

Tris bristled behind me, but I forged on, not letting
him speak. "Bad faith? Bad fucking faith? You started this
war by murdering my daughter, and now to end it you
demand the life of my son as well. Which one of us, Richter
si Poe, is negotiating in bad fucking faith?" My storm burst
forth, crackled along my skin, arced from my shadowy cloak
and traced searing lines in the dirt.

Richter stood his ground, but I could taste the fear
on him. The rest of the delegation was no different. Some
shoved Sources in their mouths, others drew swords. All
were terrified. My reputation and anger unmanning them.

Send them back to their city in fear. Have them spread it

like a plague. We are weak now, but with a city afraid, a continent feeding us, imagine what we could accomplish, Eska. Even Norvet Meruun would shrivel before us.

"Is this it then, Corpse Queen?" Richter said, the smile on his patchwork face claiming a victory he had not earned. "Your false peace shattered for the lie it is?"

My shadow rippled beneath me, crept along the ground towards the Tor delegation. It seemed negotiations had broken down. It had happened so quickly. Really, you'd think I'd have learned to make peace and negotiate by now. Apparently not.

"So be it," Richter said, backing up. One of the other members of the delegation handed him the horse's reins and he swung up into the saddle. The horse stamped back and forth, hooves crushing the wilting grass. "We'll drag you both back to Tor in chains and see justice done."

Threats. There are two types of people who make threats. Those who are assured of their victory, and those who are certain of their loss.

"Perhaps you don't remember the last time someone dragged me in chains back to their city," I said.

He did, of course. Tor was raised out of the bones of Juntorrow, the very city I had been dragged to, imprisoned under, and had destroyed on my escape.

Richter's horse danced for a few more seconds as the man stared down at me, fear running off him like rain down a mountain. Then he tugged on the beast's reins, kicked its flanks, and was racing back down the hill to his camp, the others right on his heels. I watched them flee for a few moments, making certain they were out of earshot even if one of them was a Vibromancer.

"We're fucked," I said, turning to Tris.

My son was staring at me, a slight smile on his lips. I think it was pride. "We'll destroy them together, Mother."

"Idiot," I shoved him with my elbow and pushed him towards his trei bird even as I struggled up onto mine. "They outnumber us ten to one." I snapped the reins and got the bird moving.

Tris fell in beside me. "Their soldiers are worth a tenth of ours. And between the two of us we…"

"*I* am not exactly at my best, Tris," I said a little too sharply. I was struggling to control the damned bird and think at the same time. "I can't beat a soggy pillow in a fight at the moment and…" I fell silent. I had not tested my limits with Sourcery since having my age reversed. I had no idea how much power I could currently draw on. "Ssserakis?"

Still weak. If we could turn their forces to terror I could feed on them, but even now their fear dwindles in the face of blood lust. Anger is a weak mask over fear, filled with holes, but the anger of many forges strong bonds.

Whip an army into a frothing red haze, and they would fight to the last against overwhelming odds.

"We can take them, Mother," Tris insisted. It was easy to forget he still had the foolishness of youth about him. At his age, I would have marched against a thousand strong army by myself, secure in the feverish belief I would win. I had done just that. And I had lost.

"No. We can't."

We reached the top of the hill and whirled the birds around to stare back down. The Tor forces were already moving, streaming out of their camp and forming up to march up the hill towards us. It was a slight rise, but it would give us an advantage if we chose to defend it. Not enough of an advantage, and the watch tower was not a sound structure to defend. But we were a hundred, while they were a thousand. That gave us one advantage.

"Order the troops to form up behind the camp, ready to retreat. Leave everything. Tents, packs, supplies." I reached for my Source pouch and rolled the crystals around my fingers.

"We're running?" Tris asked, incredulous. "They'll chase us."

I nodded. "I know. But we can't win a fight against them here."

"Our troops are too exhausted to march," he argued.

"Then they're too exhausted to fight, too."

"Do you have a plan at least?"

I plucked the Portamancy Source from my pouch and pinched it between my fingers. I had a plan. It was a fucking awful plan.

CHAPTER FOURTEEN

I GAVE US A HEAD START WITH A PORTAL. I DID not take us far. Holding open a portal for a hundred people to cross through is draining. Our forces were still in sight as the Tor army crested the hill at a league-eating march. They had cavalry, fifty men and women on horses, but they did not charge us. I think they were scared. They wouldn't engage until they could bring their whole strength to bear.

We marched on, retreating, slower than I would have liked. Our troops were exhausted. A full day of marching, a forced march through the night, set up camp, but no time to rest, back to marching with dogs snapping at our heels. We were all tired.

Tris kept turning in his saddle, staring back at the advancing Tor wave, hands clenched on the reins like he wanted to charge into their midst and die a glorious battle death. There's no such thing as a glorious death, in battle or

otherwise. Death is messy and painful, and as devastating
to those you leave behind as emboldening to those who
tear you down. Trust me, I have unwoven enough ghosts to
know that most of those who believed they died glorious
deaths would much rather have lived long, unfruitful lives.

By early evening, we were all flagging. The Tor force
had chased us for a full day and did not look like they were
ready to give up. They were fresher than us and closing fast.
My soldiers could no longer keep up the pace.

The land turned rocky again, the pockmarked valley
we passed through the previous night lay before us. The
stench of death and decay surrounded us and set nerves on
edge. It was not just a smell to me, though. I could feel it, my
innate Necromancy tingling like a nerve coming back to life.

I rode my bird to the head of our column and
dismounted, then tore open a new portal to the end of the
valley. Let our enemies cross this cursed, pockmarked land.
We'd skip it. My soldiers trudged through, many of them
sent me weary looks. Many of them sent me angry ones.

They do not want to retreat. No creature wants to be prey.

"Better fleeing prey, than dead predator."

No. It is not. I felt it from Ssserakis too, then. My
horror didn't want to run. It had already fled its world like a
tiny prey animal before a lion. Ssserakis was sick of running.
It wanted to fight. It wanted to win, and it wanted to reap
the rewards of feasting on our enemy's fear.

Tris was the last one through the portal and he turned
weary, sullen eyes on me. "You cannot portal us all the way
home, Mother. They are going to catch us." He smacked his
bird and sent it through the portal.

I stared back as the Tor army surged into view once
more. In the failing light, and the dark blanket of clouds

smothering the sky, I could barely make them out until they lit torches all along the line like an advancing forest fire.

Just holding the portal open was taxing me. I'd suffer from rejection long before we made it back to Yenheim. We could take refuge in one of the little towns, make a call for reinforcements, but that would only bring misfortune to the townsfolk, and reinforcements would arrive too late to matter. Even if I did somehow manage to get us all the way back to Yenheim, that would leave an army a thousand strong in our lands, wreaking who knew what damage. The bastards from Tor were set on war and would not stop until both my and my son's heads were decorating a spike. I couldn't allow it. So I made a decision. No more running. It was time to make a stand.

Yes! It is about time. We are together again, Eska. Remind them all why they fear us.

"You sure about this?" I asked coyly.

Of course.

"No matter what it takes?"

I sensed a moment of hesitation from my horror. *Yes.*

"Right then. This is going to hurt, but I need them to see us." While I still channelled Portamancy through my hand, holding the portal open, I raised my shadowy claw and lit it on fire with a gout of Pyromancy. Ssserakis hissed in pain inside of me. The horror had never liked fire. I let the flames burn bright, illuminating me in the dark. I gave those Tor bastards a good look, then I stepped through the portal and let it close.

"What's going on, Mother?" Tris asked as soon as I was through.

I let the fires around my claw die out even as I set my hand ablaze instead, holding it up like a beacon. I swept my hand around me and released a searing plume of flames that set the ground ablaze.

"Come on," I said loudly over my shoulder. "Step forward, show them your arses. Let them know we're done running."

My soldiers rushed forward then, much of their spirits restored, if only for a short time. They shouted at the advancing Tor force, waved at them, mocked them. A few even took my advice, dropped their trousers, and put their arses on display. I stood at the head of it all and let my storm spark around me so our enemy would have no trouble picking me out against the darkness.

"Come on, you fuckers," I whispered. "Come and get me."

The wave of torches swept up the pockmarked valley towards us, moving faster now we had stopped. They were eager to reach us. Eager to kill us. As they reached the midpoint of the valley, my troops fell silent. They were seeing for the first time exactly what we were up against, and how outnumbered we were. In the dark, with each Tor soldier carrying a torch, they didn't look like a thousand soldiers. They looked like ten thousand warriors with heads aflame. They looked like demons coming to claim our souls.

A foolish thought. You are the only creature I know of who feeds on souls.

"Me?"

What else would you call it when you devour ghosts to syphon off what little strength remains to them?

"I call it giving them peace. Unravelling them to save them from an eternal half existence."

And the power you take from them?

I had no answer to that. It put much of my past into a

new damning perspective. I knew Biomancy could be used
to feed off the living. The Iron Legion had used it to funnel
power through Josef and me into Sources to bring the Rand
and Djinn back to life. Could Necromancy be used in a
similar way, to feed off the dead? Is that what had kept me
going down in the Red Cells? When I had lost hope after the
emperor had broken me, was it the strength I took from my
ghosts as I unravelled them that gave me the will to go on?

*You do not have time for your usual self-flagellation, Eska.
Your enemy comes.*

Tris echoed my horror. "I'm usually all for a good
brood, Mother, but I don't think now is the time. Do we fight
or flee?"

"Neither. But I do need your help, Tris."

Innate Necromancy. The magic I was injected with
so long ago. The Iron Legion had done the same thing to
Tris. In his insane attempt to reproduce what he had done
to Josef and me; he injected Vi with Biomancy and Tris with
Necromancy. Tris had an innate Necromancy, just as I did,
and I needed his strength to join with my own.

The Tor force was surging forwards, driven into
greater speed now we were so close there could be no more
fleeing. I heard my troops muttering about a last stand,
taking down as many of the enemy as we could before they
overwhelmed us. Fuck that! It was time to turn the tide.

I looked at Tris, pulled his gaze away from the force
charging towards us. "You can feel them below us, can't
you?" I asked.

My son frowned, nodded.

"Call them. Help me call them. I can't control them
anymore, they're too far removed from the curse I created,
but they will come. They are mine, after all." My legacy. My

curse.

Tris' eyes widened as he realised exactly what I was asking. Then we set to it. No time to waste. I reached out with my innate Necromancy, felt Tris doing the same beside me, and called to the dead. Begged them to rise. Demanded it. The Corpse Queen and her Reaper called, and as our enemies surged towards us, screaming for our heads, my children answered.

It was almost quiet at first, subdued. A few hoarse, guttural screams, entirely unlike those baying for blood. Some of the torches vanished, snuffed out. I don't think the Tor soldiers realised the trap they had run into until the noose snapped shut around their necks, and the Cursed tore up from the earth.

Panic crashed in waves. At first, the rear of the column was in disarray. The Cursed poured out of the holes in the earth. Bloody, oozing fingers broke on the rocky ground as they crawled out of the holes, but the dead don't care about injuries or pain. They don't care about anything but that command I put in them decades ago. *Kill them all. Spread the curse.* Some wore rags, decaying strips of cloth reminiscent of those ghouls swathed themselves in. Others had fresher clothing, indicating they had not long since been cursed.

They threw themselves at the Tor soldiers, clawing, biting, punching, dragging. The soldiers panicked, tried to draw steel, bring spears to bear. They stabbed, slashed, kicked, tried to get away. Soldiers crashed into each other. Torches dropped, snuffed underfoot. Men and women went down, dragged by the cursed or tripped in the press. Many didn't get back up.

More and more of the Cursed came out from the

earth, drawn by my and Tris' call. They didn't understand
it but knew only that they were summoned. And here was
prey. Fresh lives to take.

The Tor soldiers fought back, forming panicky
groups, holding the dead at bay with shields as spearmen
stabbed out at them. The Cursed took wounds that would
have felled the living, but kept on regardless, throwing
themselves onto shields, dragging them down, breaking
teeth on armour, gouging thumbs into eyes. Shouts turned to
screams. Pain and fury mingled into a sickening miasma of
noise. Sour fear gushed forth and both sickened me and set
my mouth watering all at once. Ssserakis fed well.

As more of the dead surged forth, the front lines of
the Tor soldiers finally realised what was happening. They
tried to turn back, were set upon from behind. Flames lit
the valley as Pyromancers drew on their Sources to turn
Cursed into shambling pyres. Fire is a poor weapon against
the dead. It makes them more dangerous until the flames
consume too much of their bodies. Many a Tor soldier died
to burns as the flaming Cursed grabbed at them.

I saw Richter si Poe at the front of the army,
desperately trying to get his horse under control as it
stamped this way and that. I think he tried to form up his
cavalry for a charge, but there wasn't the room. Two of the
horses sidled too close to one of the holes and disappeared
in a dual scream of man and beast. Lost. The dead swamped
forth, crashing into the cavalry. Richter swung left and right,
sword crackling with enchanted energy. He must have killed
a dozen of my Cursed before a ragged woman in the remains
of a blue dress sunk her teeth into his ankle. He screamed,
stabbed her through the head, but it was too late. That brief
lapse in concentration and a burly Cursed man in a heavy

smith's apron and nothing else dragged Richter from his horse. That was the last anyone saw of Richter si Poe. Alive at least.

I watched it all with Tris beside me and my meagre Yenheim forced crowded behind, staring in horrified silence. Fear of the massacre robbed them of the thrill of victory. The Tor force put up a valiant struggle. Many won free to retreat. Others fought to their last. For everyone who fell, the Cursed numbers grew. Though I will admit I think the soldiers killed easily as many as they lost.

"This is it, Mother," Tris said, striding forwards, energised by the slaughter. I think he viewed it as victory, but nobody won anything that night. The fires reflected in his eyes and made him seem manic. "We can push the Cursed ahead of us all the way into Tor. We can finally end the war once and for all."

The dead do not fear. An enemy is far more useful alive and cowed.

"End the war," I said quietly, musing. "You mean slaughter an entire kingdom. Then what?" I had not the heart to get angry with him. It is hard to get angry when you feel so numb and witnessing slaughter on that sort of scale has always left me insensate.

"Then we'll have won. Vi will finally be avenged."

"Vi? You think this is about Vi?" I shook my head at him and took a few paces down the valley towards the site of the battle. There were still a few small groups of soldiers holding out, but they were horribly outnumbered. Many had fled, some chased by the dead. Large hordes of the Cursed were milling about now, lacking direction. Tris was right. We couldn't control them, not anymore, but I could feel them and we could certainly push them in the direction of Tor. His plan was horrific, but it could work.

"What are you talking about? Of course it's about Vi."
Tris rounded on me, face contorted with rage.

"This," I shouted, waving at a hand at the slaughter
in the valley below us. "Has nothing to do with Vi. Everyone
who had anything to do with her death is already dead."

"How can you know—"

"Because I killed them," I screamed at him. "I tried to
make peace with Tor, yes, but do not think for one fucking
moment I forgave the people who murdered your sister. I
made sure everyone who had a hand in her death was killed.
I just did it quietly." I had used Imiko's contacts. And she
had known, of course. Something I made her complicit in.

Tris stared at me, open mouthed. I couldn't tell if
it was horror or anger or disappointment. "Then this was
about—"

"This was about putting an end to this stupid fucking
war so we can concentrate on what really matters, Tris.
Look around you. Look up, look down. Think about Polasia,
destroyed. Think about Yun, drowned. Think about all those
people right now flocking into Yenheim because there's
not enough light for the crops to grow. Because the earth is
opening up beneath their homes. Because the sea surged
over land and swept their lives away. Because the Damned
and the Cursed are crawling out of the deep places and
doing this." I finished by waving my hand at the slaughter
in the valley below.

Tris frowned. It was a face of concentration I knew so
well. His brow crinkled, the right side of his mouth tugging
up just a little. He was still my son, no matter how much
blood swirled around his boots.

"Your sister did this," I said. "Sirileth did this. And

she needs our help to fix it. Your war means nothing, Tris. Vi is avenged. Your sister. Your living sister needs your help. And I do, too." That got through to him. No matter how I might have failed him, failed all my children, I did one thing right at least. I instilled in them all the importance of family. Of protecting those you love from danger, avenging them when they fall. And most importantly, being there for them when they need you most.

Tris nodded slowly. "This threat from the Underworld, Mother. It's real, isn't it?"

I was getting tired of correcting people. It seemed everyone was calling Sevorai the Underworld these days.

Other World, Underworld. What you call it matters not. You name it anything other than what it is to distance yourselves from it. Shall I show him the truth?

I nodded. "Do it."

"Do what?"

My shadow boiled beside me, expanding so quickly neither Tris nor I had time to react. One moment we were standing at the head of a valley, the earth burning around us, troops at our backs and slaughter below. Then the meagre light was gone and we were swallowed by Ssserakis' darkness.

"What the fuck, Mother?" Tris staggered about in shock, his head swivelling one way then the other, but there was nothing to see.

I reached out, gripped hold of his arm with my claw. "Try not to move around too much, Tris. You're still at the top of the valley. This is just a…" I tried to remember the word Ssserakis had used so long ago.

"It is a construct of thought."

Tris startled. "What was that? Was that you, Mother?"

"It's Ssserakis."

"Your demon?"

Ssserakis chuckled, the sound echoing all around us. I could feel Tris' fear. Taste it like the scent of cooking bacon on the wind. Ssserakis drank it all in and I grew stronger by the moment.

"Demon. Horror. Words. I am ancient." I heard a noise like the fat, wet slithering of a thousand snakes. A soggy squelch of something huge lumbering close. A noise like a butcher's saw shredding flesh and grinding bone. A terran scream cut short. It was all an illusion, one Ssserakis had trapped me in when we first met. Tris was not so fortified. He twisted in my grip, tried to pull away, slapped at me.

"Something has me. Mother. Mother where are you?"

I sighed. "Ssserakis, stop it. Just show him."

My horror laughed. As far as Ssserakis was concerned, it was simply having a bit of fun with my son. No damage was done, no blood or cuts like the horror had once inflicted on me. Nothing but nightmares and fear as food.

The darkness between Tris and I fell away so we could see each other. His eyes were wide, panicked. Sweat stood on his forehead, his hands held before him as if to defend from who knew what. He blinked when he saw me, started breathing too heavily.

"It's just an illusion, Tris. It's not real."

"I could make it real."

Tris jerked his head, searching for the source of Ssserakis' voice. "I would very much like to be free of this now, Mother." I heard the edge in his voice. Fear quickly masked by anger. Ssserakis was amused by that. My horror considered my son's anger and thought it a fragile mask.

A sound like a rusty blade scraping across a plate

shrieked at us, and Tris' mask shattered. He clutched at me. What a strange feeling that was. One part of me held my son close and wanted to protect him from all the pain and evils of the world, and another part of me exulted in his fear and knew we could feed off him for so long.

"Enough, Ssserakis," I growled. "Stop playing with him and show him."

My horror considered defying me, then relented with a chuckle. The darkness fell away from us, but we were not in the valley surrounded by flames and our troops. We were flying through Sevorai. Or, more accurately, we were standing on nothing and Sevorai was moving below us. It felt like we should be falling, but we did not. The ground was solid beneath us, but what we saw was something else. My stomach kept lurching, expecting the drop, and from the way Tris clutched me I knew he felt it too. I think Ssserakis did it that way on purpose, to keep Tris scared, to keep feeding on his fear.

The grey landscape of Sevorai swept along beneath us, and then we were flying over the exposed fleshy mass of Norvet Meruun. She extended as far as we could see. Her flesh pulsed with a low crimson, and she grew again, extending outwards in all directions. Hairy tentacles flailed, slapping at the rock. There was no life around her, nothing that didn't belong to her. Her minions, most of them with those little fleshy worms sticking out of their skin, buzzed about, bringing her more to feed on. More to absorb. It was a desolate wasteland, and it was all her.

I told Tris what she was as we stared down at her, flying over her endless bulk. The Beating Heart of Sevorai. The death of that world, and of ours now the two were linked by an open portal. My son finally understood the depth of the shit we were drowning in.

When Ssserakis dropped the construct and retreated inside my shadow, I could see how shaken my son was. Our troops were pretty shaken, too, though none of them had seen the enemy. They had simply seen us vanish in a ball of darkness for a time.

Tris staggered when I let go of him, then fell, sitting down heavily on his arse, drawing his knees up and hugging them, crumpling in on himself like a paper crane crushed in a steel gauntlet. He stared across the valley blindly. He was silent for a long time, contemplating. When finally he looked up at me, there were tears in his eyes. He nodded.

"What do we do, Mother?"

"First, we clean up my mistake."

CHAPTER FIFTHTEEN

WE PUT A LOT OF CURSED TO REST BEFORE WE
left that valley. I say it that way because it is more palatable
than the truth. Though the Cursed were no longer mine to
command, Tris and I could call them. Like dogs herding
sheep. We gathered all those we could, all the dead who
would listen, and corralled them in the centre of the valley,
then set it ablaze. They did not die quickly, but it was the
safest way to do the deed. Still, many of the Cursed escaped,
too far from our call, or too set on chasing down their prey.
I did not think the people of Tor would thank me for that
new wave of plague I set upon them, but with the army they
had assembled destroyed at least we would have peace for a
time.

The next morning, as soon as the sun crested the
horizon, we set off toward home. Tris and I rode that first
day, both of us exhausted. The rest of our troops marched,

though they were not in much better condition. We were
poorly rested, under-supplied, and had no tents nor pots to
cook. We ate what little we carried and descended upon the
villages between us and Yenheim like locusts. The people of
those villagers might be under Sirileth's rule, and many of
them said they were glad to see me alive. But I think mostly
they were glad to see us leave and wished we had not taken
so much as we had. Times were tough.

The sun never once made an appearance. Not truly.
The blanket of clouds was a roiling, churning mass of
darkness that blotted out almost all light. The grass beneath
our feet wilted, turned yellow, died. Ill winds blew, snapping
into different directions every few seconds. We had to skirt
one small valley as there appeared to be molten fire running
through it rather than water. The smell was foul, like eggs
left to rot and then cracked open. We pressed on.

The march to Tor had been full of pleasant evenings,
even if I had been beaten bloody during many of them,
and a jovial atmosphere. Despite winning the battle, after
a fashion, that journey back to Yenheim was oppressive.
Tris brooded for much of it, I think considering his place
and where he now fit in within Sirileth's queendom. I
spent much of my time considering our plights. I had some
ideas about breaking the cloud cover, but it was nothing I
could execute myself. I didn't have the right attunements.
The raging oceans and fires breaking through the earth
were another matter entirely. The world was coming apart,
broken as Sirileth had named it. I saw no way we could fix it
without Sourcery.

When we finally reached the streets of Yenheim, dirty
and dishevelled and footsore, we were not greeted with
the same fanfare as when we left. The mood had soured in

the city and not even their returning ex-queen could raise morale. Our soldiers wandered off to see their families or drink their woes away. Tris and I rode our birds through streets that seethed with sullen resentment and people sharing dark looks. Still, evil looks and angry whispers are always better than thrown rocks and mobs with murder on their mind.

There is a wonderful fear in this city, Eska. It surrounds it like a cloud of flies. They are all terrified.

"Yes," I agreed. "They're afraid with everything that is happening, they're going to die."

They are mortal. They all die.

"Which is why they fear death. Do you?"

Of course not. I am a lord of Sevorai.

"You're immortal. Life and death have never been an issue for you. You just are. All this fear you're drinking in, Ssserakis. It's because these people's lives balance on a razor's edge. And they can feel themselves teetering."

I sighed and turned the trei bird up towards the palace. "And they expect their queen to do something about it."

What can our daughter hope to do about a world ending?

"Maybe nothing. But they expect her to do something."

Ssserakis mulled over that for a few seconds. I looked around the street and saw a young boy covered in grime digging through a pile of refuse in an alleyway. He stopped to stare at me as I passed and our gazes locked. He lifted his chin in something like defiance, then turned and fled.

You should control your minions better. That they fear is good, but they should not expect you to help them. They exist to serve you.

I laughed. Tris glanced back at me, a frown creasing his brow again, but I shook my head at him. "They're not my minions, Ssserakis. I'm not their queen anymore. And I don't think Sirileth would give back the throne if I asked for it."

Then do not ask. Take it.

"I don't want it. I don't think I ever did. And she sits it far better than I."

My horror fell silent again, but I do not think it was pleased with me. Ssserakis was a lord of Sevorai, created to rule. I wonder how much of my original desire to forge my queendom had been based on Ssserakis' desire to be in power? Well, not anymore. Sirileth could come crawling, begging me to take the throne back, and I'd still say no. I'd hand it over to Tris before I allowed my head into that noose ever again.

When we reached the palace doors, I slid from the trei bird, happy to be free of it. The bird immediately sidled away, staring at me with one huge eye. Tris did not dismount. He kicked his bird forward, collected the reins of my mount and stared at the palace doors.

"Not coming in?" I asked.

My son shook his head wistfully. "I'll leave you to report to queen sister. If you need me, Mother, I'll be at the Dripping Bucket, trying to drink away the taste of…" He waved his free hand in the air. "Everything." He tugged on the reins and pulled both birds away.

Tris had always been one for melancholy brooding, but there was something darker about it now. I think I robbed him of purpose when I told him Vi had already been avenged. He had been a raging fire, burning everything in its path, and I had divorced him of his fuel. Without it, he guttered out into drifting embers, flickers of light and the ghost of warmth.

"I do need you," I said quickly before I could think better of it. Tris stopped, turned in his saddle to look at me. "Not just for what is to come. You're my son, Tris. I'll always need you."

The bird fidgeted beneath Tris and for a few seconds he stared at me in silence. "Pretty words, Mother." He turned and kicked the bird back to walking. I couldn't miss the implication. Words were easy. He needed actions, though I had not the wit to figure out what. "I still want that match. Whenever you feel you're at your *best*."

I watched him go. My son was a grown man now, tall and broad and strong. He was a leader, and a good one. A warrior, a powerful Sourcerer. A killer. And yet, there was still much of the sulky boy in him.

My shadow twisted beneath me until Ssserakis hovered there, a vague blur of inky darkness. "*His fear is… strange. Sickly sweet. He doubts himself and fears his worth.*"

I nodded, still staring after my son as he rode away. "I don't know how to help him."

Ssserakis fuzzed and shivered beside me, its shadowy outline trembling. "*Keep him close. That fear will make us strong. You have such a wonderful way of putting deep, lasting fears in people, Eska. So much more complex than fear of death or monsters. You make people fear themselves. An inexhaustible feast.*"

I ground my teeth and glared at my shadow. "I don't want to make him fear himself. I want to help him."

Ssserakis turned and stared back at me, its coal-dark eyes burned. I could feel my horror trying to figure me out. "*Maybe… ask the big terran? He always had a way of quenching your fear. For a time.*" There was a hesitance to Ssserakis I wasn't used to. I was asking the horror to think outside of its usual patterns. Not as a lord of Sevorai or an ancient horror. I was asking it to think as a parent, as a friend. And though it went against Ssserakis' nature, it did so. For me.

I made my way into the palace, nodding at the guards who stared wide-eyed at me. Probably not surprising given they had just witnessed me talking to my shadow. There were lanterns lit all along the walls of the corridors. The palace was a dark and dreary place on the best of days, and those were far behind us. There was a chill in the air, too.

I found myself not heading for the throne room, but to Sirileth's chambers. I needed to speak to my daughter, but I also wanted to catch her alone. There was much we needed to discuss and I... Well, the truth was I was a little ashamed. I had gone to Tor to treat and make peace. Instead, I had fallen back on my old ways and forced the dead to rise to crush my enemies. We are creatures of patterns, preferring well-trodden paths to hiking through undergrowth.

Perhaps it was thoughts of who I had once been that made me remember how my palace had also been. Once, early on in my rule, the halls of the palace rang with footsteps. Servants, guards, people just trying to make a living, children, animals. At one time, all of Yenheim had lived within these halls. There was laughter and tears, shouts of anger and moans of intimacy, dogs barking and children teasing each other. All gone now. Gone. Just bare, empty stone devoid of life and love and heart.

Sirileth's rooms were located in the east wing, along with mine, so long disused. I stopped outside Imiko's door, my hand hovering over the handle. She had only ever used the room infrequently, so often outside the capital on official business. Or unofficial, I suppose. But the room was hers, filled with her things. So many nights we had spent there, talking about my children or her exploits, half of which I'm certain she made up on the spot. We shared stories, reminisced, sometimes drank ourselves into a stupor.

I missed her so much. I would have torn the world in two to hear her voice. Mocking me, teasing me, accusing me. Anything just to see her again. A wild part of me thought it was all some elaborate act. That it was Imiko and disappearing was her thing. I thought… I hoped… I half convinced myself that I'd open the door and find her sitting on her desk, legs dangling and a wide grin on her face. She'd mock me, tell me she couldn't believe I actually thought she was dead. I wanted it. I wanted it so much I put my hand on the door and pushed.

The door swung open easily and that was the most damning proof I needed. Imiko always locked her door when she left, but not this time. Because this time, she had known she wasn't coming back.

Her desk was covered in papers held down by candlesticks draped with old wax. Her chest and wardrobe, doors open and half empty. The climbing post Hardt had made for Imiko's old ringlet that she had never gotten rid of even after the little beast had died. And her bed, the sheets rumpled and piled from the last time she slept in them.

I staggered, caught myself on the doorframe. My legs wobbled and gave way. I sank to my knees, leaning against the stonework. My breath felt ragged in my chest, tears streamed down my face. I was so utterly, unbearably tired. Even leaning was too much. I wanted to lie down, to sink into the earth and be crushed. I wanted it to end. The pain in my chest, a gnawing ache of emptiness. The bone weariness that made my limbs feel like they were made of stone. The words running through my head over and over. You did this. You did this. You. Did. This. It was all too much. Too fucking much. Imiko was gone, dead. My fault. The world was ending and Sirileth expected me to fix it and I didn't know how. The Other World was rising up against Ovaeris and no one even knew how fucked we all were. It was too much! I couldn't deal with it all. I couldn't keep being the strong one people looked to.

Eska? Eskara, what is wrong?

I was on the floor, my scarred cheek against the cold stone, dust puffing away from my breath. Imiko had been gone for weeks. There were footsteps in the dust. Two prints leading into the room, then turned and left again. I noticed it, didn't understand. My mind wasn't working right. Took in the details, didn't care.

"*Eska?*" Something shook me lightly, pressing my shoulder, pushing me back and forth. "*I cannot reach you. Eskara, what is happening?*" My shadow. My shadow knelt before me, rocking me. I stared up at it. At my shadow. Shadows weren't supposed to do that. They weren't supposed to be tangible.

Fear. Not mine. Trickling past the numbness. Making me feel. Making me hurt. Gnawing, clawing, scraping emptiness inside. A hollow deeper than hunger. A maddening void that could never be filled. Not mine. Not me. Something else. Something alien.

The bubble burst, my numbness shattered and everything came crushing back in all at once. The stone floor beneath my cheek was cold. The dust tickled my throat, made my lips feel fuzzy. My mouth was dry as the Polasian desert. I ached. Oh, Lursa's fucking Tears, I ached. Not just the gnawing emptiness inside, nor the beatings I had taken

from the soldiers I trained with, nor the rigid burn of my
core from sitting in a saddle for so many days. I ached…
inside, in a way I can't quite explain. Like that horrible tingle
of a limb waking up, but all of me.

My shadow shook me again. *"Eskara, I do not
understand."*

I tried to speak, opened my mouth, couldn't
remember how to form words. They seemed such ungainly
things. Noises made with mouths, meanings lost in
translation from the space between lips and ear. We all speak
different languages. My mind was racing now, thoughts like
lightning there and gone in an instant.

"MMM…" I licked a leathery tongue across my
lips and tried again, closing my eyes to think about what I
wanted to say. "I'm… all… alright. I'm… alright." The words
came out slurred, the meaning barely reaching me.

I sat up with help. My shadow picking me up and
leaning me against the doorframe of Imiko's room. Ssserakis
knelt before me, flickering and fuzzy. I could feel its concern,
its fear. I smiled, laughed weakly. I was making fear *fear*.

"Eska?"

I felt drunk. Out of control. Just a few moments
before, I had welcomed it, wanted it. Now I hated it. I hated
feeling out of control. My mind was coming back to me,
slowly. Too slowly. What had just happened to me?

"What happened?" Ssserakis lingered before me, a
shadowy limb outstretched, keeping me upright. I realised I
was leaning against it and straightened up.

"It was nothing, Ssserakis. It was just…" Not quite
the call of the void, but something linked to it. A wave of
depression that crashed over me.

I thought I had long since passed through these

drowning waves of depression that rose up so suddenly.
It had been years since they assailed me with a regularity,
or any potency. But this was not the first time I had felt
it recently. They were back and I struggled at first to
comprehend why. I wondered if it was my rediscovered
youth. Somehow the years falling away reawakening old
demons.

But no. I knew the truth, even if I was afraid to admit
it. It was about Imiko. My best friend, my sister had gone
ahead of me. She had taken her life to escape the pain. And
damn me, but I was jealous of her.

There it is, the truth I found so hard to admit, even
to myself. I was jealous of a woman for being dead, while
I had no choice but to go on. And I wanted so much to join
her. Not in any sort of afterlife, I am not so stupid as to think
there is anything but a ghostly half-life after we die. I wanted
to join her in oblivion. In nothing. In freedom.

I swallowed past the awful taste in my mouth, wiped
tears from my cheeks and eyes, and stood shakily. My
shadow hovered nearby, Ssserakis waiting in case I needed
help again. I would not. It had passed. For now.

I took one last look at the floor of Imiko's room.
At the footprints in the thin layer of dust. I already knew
who they belonged to: Sirileth. My daughter had come to
Imiko's room, perhaps for the same reason I had. She was
grieving, even if she refused to show it. I thought, perhaps
that was something we could do together. Maybe it was
time I stopped running from my grief and confronted it, and
helped my daughter do the same.

CHAPTER SIXTEEN

SIRILETH'S DOOR WAS LOCKED. I KNOCKED, thinking she might be sleeping, but there was no answer. The throne room would be the next obvious place to look, but I did not want to go there and be seen by people. I was still feeling shaky and did not want to face the attention.

"No matter how many times its sets, the sun always rises again."

I knew that voice. The lilting sing song way of speaking, the words that seemed to make no sense. I spun about, a grin already stretching my face. Tamura stood before me. He was unchanged, but of course he was. Tamura was immortal. He was old when I met him, many years ago down in the Pit, and he would be old when I finally called it quits for the last time. His dark hair was shot with steel and braided into a hundred cords each carrying a single bell on the end, making it all the more amazing he had snuck up on me. His dark skin was as wrinkled and leathery as ever. He wore a bright yellow tunic that did not suit him at all, and a dusty satchel hung at his side. And he had a pair of very sturdy boots. Tamura was quite specific about his boots.

"Old Aspect," Ssserakis shouted by way of greeting. My shadow leapt to life and surged ahead of me, stopping just in front of Tamura. Of course, just like with Hardt, Ssserakis knew Tamura almost as well as I did, but they had never really met. I had kept my horror hidden from those I loved.

Tamura cocked his head, squinted at my fizzing shadow, and reached out a single finger, tapping Ssserakis. "Djinn bane. Dark pearl of the spirit." He grinned. "Hello, Ssserakis." His gaze flicked past my horror and locked on me.

I had never told Tamura about my horror. I had a feeling the old Aspect knew, but quite how he knew its name, I could not fathom. Not that it mattered anymore. Ssserakis was done hiding and I was done hiding it, and none of that mattered anyway because Tamura was here.

I all but ran, brushing my shadow aside and leapt at Tamura, wrapping my arms around his skinny body, I lifted him from the floor and spun him about before dropping him again. He giggled like a child. I was quite amazed by my strength, just a few weeks ago I'd have paled at the thought of lifting someone from the floor, now I felt like I could crush the old man in my arms.

As soon as I put him down, Tamura gave another giggle and spun about on the spot. Then he stopped, reached out quick as a lightning strike, cupped my left cheek, rubbing a thumb over the old scar there. "I once knew a girl who ran these halls and looked just like you. Full of fear and anger and terrible purpose."

"Terrible purpose," I echoed, feeling my joy drain
away. Of course I couldn't deny it. He wasn't wrong. It's
just hard to have your most damning aspects laid out by
someone you love.

"No!" He slapped me. Not hard, but enough to make
my cheek sting. "No. No. No. Terrible purpose. Not terrible
purpose." He snorted and turned, waving over his shoulder.
"Come, woman who looks like girl I once knew."

He is as crazy as the Rand that spawned him. You
wouldn't think the living embodiment of fear was capable
of affection but I suppose I corrupted Ssserakis as much as it
corrupted me.

"Stories sink into the heart as history does into stone,"
Tamura said as he walked, his hair jingling like a choir with
each step. I hurried to catch up and he took my shadowy
claw in hand, not caring that it must have felt cold and bony
to the touch. We walked, hand in hand, and I let him guide
me.

"I missed you, Tamura," I said, giving his hand a
squeeze.

"Yes, I suppose you would." It was something of a
gut shot that he didn't admit to missing me. But I think time
moved differently for Tamura, years passing in what must
have seemed such brief spans. Did he know how long I had
been gone?

"One queen, two queens, a lord and more," he
sang as we walked. "Lokar weeps for his fallen love while
sisters battle for life." He stopped and pulled me to a halt,
spinning me to face him. "The Maker searchers for her still."
He smiled a sly, knowing smile. "But cannot find her." He
gasped and pulled so close to me I could smell stale ale on

his breath. He poked at my face again. "Renewal. There is still hope."

"Slow down, Tamura."

He barked out a laugh and started walking again, faster than before, dragging me with him by my claw. "When fishes flounder on dry land they suffocate. When abbans dive too deep they drown. We all must stick to our substrate. But what then of one who can move between? Teach a fish to fly and watch it explore a new world."

I tried tugging him to a halt, but the old Aspect was always so much stronger than he looked. He pulled me on. We turned a corner and there were steps ahead. I realised he was leading me into the catacombs beneath the palace, though I wasn't sure why.

"Tamura, you said renewal."

"Yes!" He waved his free hand in the air as if swatting at a fly. "Renewal." He stopped, poked me hard in the chest. "Time doesn't flow backwards." He pulled a confused face, brows wrinkled. "Occasionally it stops." He held up a single finger and was silent for a few seconds. "There! It did it again. Very strange."

The crazy old man had always been tough to understand and I was oddly comforted that nothing had changed. He pulled me down the steps behind him. "Not healing. Not reversal. Renewal." He laughed. "Prophecy is a bug. Always growing. Always leaving old skins behind."

"You're talking about the Auguries again, Tamura."

Raither, the Rand who had created Tamura had been an oracle. She had seen the future and it had driven her to madness. Not much of a leap, I know, given the Rand are all fucking crazy, but Raither was apparently worse than the rest of them. In a bid to free herself of the burden of

knowledge, she made Tamura, her Aspect. She gave her
child two gifts. The first was immortality, her immortality.
She did it to remove from herself the thing keeping her alive,
and she died mere moments after Tamura was… born, I
suppose. She also gave him knowledge. All her knowledge.
All her experience. Everything she had seen in the past and
the myriad possible futures. It was too much for a terran
mind to take and it broke Tamura. Silva once described
the old Aspect as a man surrounded by cracked mirrors,
each one showing him a different bit of himself. He seemed
happy enough with his madness, though I have to wonder if
it was because he didn't know any better.

"The Iron Legion proved the Auguries false, Tamura,"
I said.

He snorted at me. "Ask a blind man to describe green
and you're as like to hear about purple."

I tugged Tamura to a halt. I had to put quite some
force into it. "Are you saying the Iron Legion was wrong
about the Auguries?"

Tamura rolled his eyes at me. "Yes," he said very
slowly. "Now come. You have to meet the Corpse Queen."

He poked his head through a doorway into the
corridor beyond and sniffed, made an appreciative noise,
and dragged me on. I suddenly realised it was beyond dark
in the corridors. There were no lanterns or torches, or any
light at all. I could see, though everything was in shades
of grey. That was Ssserakis' doing. The horror could lend
me its night sight, though it was odd seeing everything in
monochrome. And it didn't explain how Tamura could see
clearly enough he was striding along not stubbing his toes
on any of the rocks.

"Tamura, I don't understand. I am the Corpse

Queen."

"Really?" he asked, sounding sarcastic. "Have you met yourself recently?"

We kept on and Tamura never took his hand from my claw, always leading me unerringly, though I couldn't say where. Finally he slowed to a stop outside a dark doorway. I could hear wind howling far off. He waved at the doorway. "A mirror. A girl. A woman. A start. An end. A life. A death. Gods from seeds, from nothing but dust. All here. Once here."

I stared into the room, my night sight picking out all the details in sharp shades of grey. There was stone rubble on the floor, the remains of a bench maybe. A discarded lantern, long since empty and now covered in dust, lay on its side on the floor. Next to it, an ancient brown stain that was almost flaked away. There were bones in the far corner, bundled together on a pile of old rags.

I know this place, Eska. We know this place.

"I don't understand."

Tamura gestured to the room again. "Time to meet yourself. Hah. Time. No time. He can't hurt you, only show you to yourself."

I stared at the crazy old man for a few more seconds. He made a shooing motion. I didn't know what I would find in the room, but whatever it was it seemed important to Tamura, and I trusted him. I stepped over the threshold and braced for… something. But nothing happened. It was just a dark, old room. Thousands of years buried and forgotten, like the rest of the ruined Djinn city. Maybe someone had been here for a time. The bones, bloodstains, and discarded lantern certainly seemed to suggest it but… Ssserakis was right. We did know the place. I had been there before.

Like a flicker of realisation I saw myself. A younger me, smooth-skinned and bold, brash even. I still had both my arms. I was wearing prison rags, my hair stuck up in odd angles. The scar on my cheek was barely healed, the flesh still proud. Then it was gone. Nothing but a memory. Oh yes, I recognised the place now. This was our last stop before we escaped the Pit. This was where Josef had killed Isen. Where I had faced my best friend, screamed at him, and suffered his cold rage in return. This was where I swallowed a Chronomancy Source and set my will against his. This was where Josef had died. Where I realised Ssserakis was joined with me in a way I couldn't understand at the time.

I looked at the bones in the corner. Isen's bones. Right where we left him. I'd never really thought about what must have become of his body, but then his ghost had followed me about for years, damning me and judging me for all the poor choices I made.

"Why bring me here, Tamura?" I asked. He was leaning against the doorframe, smiling benignly. "What do you hope I'll see?"

"Sources are important," the old man said. "It is important to understand the source. This is where it all began."

"Surely it began back in the Pit, where we met? That's where you made me realise we could escape. Remember, *this one is not as promising as the last* and *starfish spider cross section* or whatever it was."

He smiled as if remembering, but I wasn't sure he could. Tamura's mind was so broken there were times he couldn't remember yesterday. "Will is important. Will set on escape was not will set on becoming. Here, you were renewed."

I shook my head, pinched my nose. "Are we back to the Auguries again? Please, Tamura, speak plainly."

"Hah! Ask the mountain to flow." He fell silent for a moment, frowning. "Prophecy only exists in hindsight." He shook his head, groaning. "Here was where you set your will, but you have not yet become what you burned into the world."

I decided to take control of the conversation before Tamura gave himself a nosebleed trying to be cogent. "You have Raither's memories," I said. "All of them, past and future." He snorted. "How much of the future do you see, Tamura?"

He giggled and danced into the room with me, pointed up at the rocky ceiling above. "None. All. What is there to see but patterns in the wind?"

"I don't—"

"You cannot see what is not set. The future is now. No. That's past. Now. No. Still past. Hmm."

"Are you saying Raither couldn't see the future?"

He pointed at me. "Ahh. She's in there still."

That would mean their vaunted Auguries were nothing but lies. I could feel Ssserakis' disdain. *Typical of the Rand and Djinn.*

"But what of her predictions? The Auguries were only part of Raither's many predictions."

"Defend yourself." Tamura sprang at me, lazily swinging an arm my way. I blocked with my claw. He swung his other arm at me and I blocked with my hand. Then back to the other arm again. For a few seconds he attacked me, one slow strike after another, and I blocked.

"Raither was smart," he said as he kept up his offence. "And desperately wanted her sisters to know it, too, but could not reveal the truth for fear they would see the ruse. The world is formed of patterns and when you see those patterns... Close your eyes."

I did as he asked. I had long since learned it was best to do what Tamura wanted or risk being assaulted with a spoon. I don't know why he loved spoons so much. I kept my defence of his attacks even with my eyes closed.

"How are you blocking me?" Tamura asked dramatically. "Can you see the future?"

"I understand. If you can see the patterns of the past, you can make predictions about the future."

"Yes! Except..."

I raised my claw to block and the expected strike did not come. I opened my eyes as Tamura pushed me hard in the chest. My feet tangled, caught, and I tripped and fell backwards. Ssserakis made my shadowy cloak solid, spikes striking out into the ground and arresting my fall. Then it pushed me back onto my feet and my cloak fell loose around me once more.

Tamura grinned. "Impressive." He stared hard into one of my eyes and waved. "Hello in there."

Should I skewer him?

"No," I said. "He'd only make a riddle out of it."

Tamura cocked his head.

"So Raither couldn't see the future but made predictions based on the past."

"All to convince her sisters she knew more than she did. The Auguries..." Tamura shook his head and laughed. "Her greatest work and nothing but a joke. Renewal. Unity. Life and death. A prophesied one to break eternity. She vomited the joke into the world, made her sisters believe, then created me to run away and hide so none could doubt."

"The Auguries weren't real?"

"Never real. Never anything but the ravings of a mad god who needed to feel important before she took her own life." He spread his hands. "And there ends the tale of Raither, the Calm in Chaos. Mad gods make for poor mothers."

I struggled to comprehend. So much of my life had revolved around those damned Auguries. Mezula had thought me capable of ending the eternal war between the Rand and Djinn, but that had been a lie. The only way to end that war was to kill them all and I never had the power to take on a god. The Iron Legion had thought the Auguries were an instruction on how to create vessels to give rebirth to dead gods and… well, he had been right.

"But the Auguries were real, Tamura. They had to be. You know what the Iron Legion did. What he did to me and Josef. It worked. He brought one of the Rand and one of the Djinn back to life through us."

Tamura shook his head. "Will is important. The Auguries meant nothing until Mezula and Loran decided that they did. The Iron Legion set his will on resurrecting gods and that is what he did. He manifested his will and called it destiny. It was not. No more than you might say *I will have a child* and then *Here she is. Destiny in action.*"

He is right. Ssserakis sounded strange in my mind, almost reverent. *Think, Eska. Our battle against Vainfold. I saw an image of us working together in that shield and made it happen. Did it predict the future, or did it offer a future that I made manifest?*

That made an awful kind of sense. I had looked into the shield, Madness, more than once. Each time it had shown me glimpses of possible futures. At least one of those I had avoided.

"So I'm not a chosen one?" I felt oddly relieved at that. Even decades after the apparent prophecy had come to pass, being free of it was liberating.

"Are you not?" Tamura asked, smiling. "You were the Iron Legion's chosen one. He made it so."

Like the sun breaking through clouds, I finally understood. The prophecies were a lie, but we could manifest them by choosing to make them real. The sun's heat turned to burning as the realisation of that dawned on me. "The second cataclysm…"

"Yes."

I shook my head at Tamura. "You cannot tell Sirileth any of this."

"She is stronger than you think."

"Oh no. I think she's stronger than anyone I've ever known, Tamura. But she's more fragile than *you* think. As long as she believes, as long as everyone thinks the second cataclysm was destined to happen, there's a chance we can pull her back from the edge." I had to protect her from this.

Tamura gave me a sad smile. "Destiny cannot be used as an excuse, Eska."

"What do you know?" I snarled at him. The truth can kill us as surely as the cold. Excuses are the lies we clothe ourselves in so we don't die of exposure to icy truth. "You could have told me at any time that all this Augury stuff was nothing but shit, but you let me live up to now thinking I was some fucking chosen one destined to be great and terrible."

I advanced on Tamura, saw him shrink before me, stepping back. I could taste his fear and it tasted of dust and disuse. "Keep this to yourself. Do not destroy my daughter,

Tamura. Please."

His eyes were wide, head jerking about as if he was searching my face for something. He nodded once. I took it as a promise and stepped past him, suddenly eager to be away from the place.

"Was that all?" I asked at the doorway. "You brought me here to tell me my life was nothing but being forced into other people's lies?"

I heard Tamura shuffle behind me. "There was… Will. Will is important. New gods rising in defiance of the old. You are not finished…"

"Enough, Tamura." I was suddenly weary of it all. First he tells me prophecies are nothing but shit, then goes right on spouting a few new ones. It was all too much to fucking take. Still, I look back now and I wish I had let him finish. I wish I had listened.

CHAPTER SEVENTEEN

I EVENTUALLY FOUND SIRILETH IN THE GREAT cavern with the minor rift we had used to travel to Yenheim. She was alone, exhausted, suffering from Source rejection. A metal arch stood over the exact point of the rift, or at least most of a metal arch. Sirileth was in the process of constructing it using both Ingomancy and Augmancy, two Sourceries she was not attuned to. And with none of the ore to stave off rejection, she was building the damned thing in five-minute bursts of activity before the rejection got too bad and killed her. My daughter was nothing if not determined.

I asked her why she was doing it. Why was she so determined to see the thing constructed even at the cost of her health. She told me about the reports she'd been receiving. The earth splitting open, raging fires erupting, monsters crawling out of the depths as if the Underworld had opened inside Ovaeris. She was not far wrong with that. Creatures of Sevorai, once no longer bound to the Sourcerer who summoned them, sought the dark places of our world where the light could not hurt them. With the sky blanketed in cloud, creating an unnatural, permanent night, they could roam the surface without suffering the pain of the sun's light. All in all, it made traveling along the roads a dangerous prospect.

The seas were not much better. Storms ravaged the deep oceans, churning them to maddening froth and sending forth tsunamis to wreck the coasts. In places, the water boiled as though something unfathomably hot was cracking open and spewing heat into the oceans. Travel by ship was impossible in such conditions and ports the world over had been destroyed.

That left travel by air, but flyers were not commonplace. The methods of building them belonged to the Rand and the Djinn, and they were powered by Kinemancy Sources. I had no doubt many of the more wealthy or influential people of our world had purchased a few, but their use would be heavily policed. And even the skies were not safe. The storms that battered the seas would easily dash a flyer from the air as well, and the wind was far from predictable, gusting in every direction, currents slamming together to form twisting funnels that sucked up dust and dirt and anything they touched and flung them out to join the hateful clouds above.

The world was ending. And bereft of any way to stop it, Sirileth was doing what she could. If she could convince the leaders of kingdoms and nations to construct similar archways above minor rifts in their own lands, she was certain she could create a stable network of portals that would allow instantaneous travel between them. It would not fix the world, but she hoped it would convince the separate nations to work together. I think much of the reason she pushed herself was to assuage her guilt. She was both punishing herself and desperately trying to create something useful and lasting to give back to a world she had broken. She was also running away, burying herself in a project to keep her mind from her grief.

Sirileth let no others see the doubt and fear and guilt she was suffering. To the Yenheim council, to her advisors, to her people, and to her friends, she played the part of a confidant ruler in control of things. But not to me. When we were alone, she let her mask slip, her resolve crack.

Kento was gone, sent to the minor rift on the continent of Rolshh. Sirileth said the jungle was alive with the stomping monsters that roamed it, but Kento went through the portal regardless. I hoped she was alright. That she had made it back to Ro'shan and was even now holding Esem in her arms. There was probably no safer place on Ovaeris for them to be. The Rand would keep Ro'shan flying and safe. I still hated Mezula, but she would keep my daughter and granddaughter alive.

Sirileth had sent word to Jamis per Suano and had received a response. There was to be a summit in eight day's time. Representatives from all over Isha would be there, and the Polasian empress, too. Invites were also sent to the terrans on Rolshh, the pahht of Itexia, the garn, the mur, and even the tahren. I held out little hope of the tahren attending and wasn't sure I wanted them too, either. They had tried to destroy the world once by bringing the Maker across after all. I doubted the little, furry fuckers would help us try to save the world instead.

Sirileth paused after telling me about the summit,

her darklight stare burning in the cavern lit only by the blue mineral veins.

"Jamis per Suano also sent me a note declaring he had weeded out all the supporters of my cult." She frowned and wiped a trickle of blood from her nose. "I assume he's talking about the merchants who helped me in Lanfall?"

I smiled at her. Between her burning eyes and mine flashing, the gloom between us danced with colour and light. "Yes. We thought you were leading a death cult set on bringing the Maker into Ovaeris."

She laughed. "I suppose it was a cult really. I never intended to… I mean, they were just useful. For a time."

"How did you convince them?"

"Hmm? Oh, it was easy. I mean, lies mostly. I approached some of the lesser merchants, those clearly hungry for more wealth and power. You know the type. I told them what they wanted to hear. They'd be spared, a new world order, them in charge once the dust settled." She grew suddenly sombre. "I guess the dust won't settle."

A false cult to scam a bunch of greedy merchants into doing what she wanted. I was more than a little proud of Sirileth right then. "And the tahren?"

Sirileth shook her head and smiled again. "They were even easier to fool. I mean, they already believed in the cataclysm. I just had to convince them I was…" She paused, rolled her eyes. "I mean… I guess I convinced them I was their messiah. It was simple. I had already fooled the Maker. That wasn't simple, though. I mean, fooling the Maker. Every time I was near a portal it kept trying to force me… I mean, get inside my head. Read my thoughts. I had to fortify my mind with lies, partition off what I wanted it to read. I mean…" She stopped, squeezed her eyes shut.

Sirileth could grasp things I never could. Her mind seemed to work so much faster than mine, than everyone else's. Yet, she struggled to choose the right words to make others understand her. I kept silent, gave her the time she needed.

"I had… I had to show the Maker the me I wanted it to see. I mean, I kept the real me hidden from it and let it see the lies. What? Why are you staring at me like that, Mother?"

I shook my head. "I'm awed, Sirileth. By you. You tricked a god. The God of gods, and you fooled it. Hid your true self from it inside your own head."

She laughed, looked down, embarrassed. "It was nothing really. Nothing special. I mean, you once pulled a city from the earth."

"You pulled a moon from the sky."

Sirileth let out a wild laugh, clamped a hand over her mouth and smiled around her fingers. "I did, didn't I."

I couldn't take it anymore. I was so unbearably proud of how strong my daughter had become. I scuffled forward and pulled Sirileth into a hug. She wrapped her arms around me. I rested my chin on her head and breathed in deeply. My daughter smelled of dust and sweat and raspberries. I thought that strange. I'd never known Sirileth to wear perfume before, but then I had to admit I did not truly know her at all.

"We need to talk, Sirileth," I said before I could think better of it.

"About what?" she murmured.

"Imiko."

"Oh." Sirileth pulled away from me, sat up straight. "Do we?"

"I saw your footsteps in her room. She's gone, you

know."

"I see. You think I don't realise that?"

"I think you lost someone close to you, and a part of you is…"

"Stop it, Mother." Sirileth stood, patted herself down. "I am well aware that Imiko is gone. And how. And when I need to talk about it, believe me, it will not be to you."

She strode away, leaving me floundering and more than a little devastated. Well, what did I expect really? I had never been there for her when she needed me, so of course she had found others to fill the roles that I vacated.

Preparations for the summit went quickly. Mostly because we had little to prepare but an argument that seemed to me like blatant common sense. Convince the leaders of separate nations to work together to save the fucking world we all lived on. I honestly didn't think they'd need that much convincing. What an idiot I am.

Sirileth assured me there was a minor rift just outside of Lanfall that no one knew about. That meant we could be in the city within an hour of leaving Yenheim. Useful things these rifts my daughter had set her will to creating, even if each one did come at the cost of a life. And multiple Sources, I suppose, but honestly I couldn't give a fuck about the coffins of our gods.

Hardt found me the day before we left for the summit. I was at the training grounds in the city barracks. The regime I'd set myself as we marched to Tor, I decided to keep. Once a day I made my way to the barracks and spent a few hours practicing my sword forms, getting my body back into some sort of shape. It was tough, exhausting, painful, and made me wish I'd never let myself grow so weak even

when age had all but crippled me. I then spent another hour
at sparring matches with anyone who was willing to take a
swing at me. I still lost more than I won, but I was starting
to find my footing again. That bolstered me. Pride has ever
been one of my failings and it felt damned good to land the
occasional hit.

The soldiers cheered for me. My improvement
was something of a point of pride for them, I think. After
sparring, I often joined some of the soldiers for a drink or
two. They found me more approachable now I wasn't queen
of Yenheim. Oh, I was still the Corpse Queen to them, but I
think they thought of me more as one of them now I wasn't
in charge of anything. It rankled Ssserakis that they didn't
fear me but liked me instead.

I noticed Hardt waiting near one of the torches
around the sparring ring. It was the middle of the day, but
we had to have torches burning all around just to be able to
see anything, it was so dark. I took my eye off my opponent
for one second and she darted in and gave me a solid thwack
on the arm that let me know I was dead.

My sparring partner laughed, clapped me on the
same arm she had just assaulted, and made her way out of
the ring. By my own rules, my loss meant I had to stay in
the circle for the next challenger, but I bowed out to talk to
Hardt, rubbing at my throbbing arm as I went. My shadow
shifted, Ssserakis forming it back into a cloak that draped
from my shoulders and I absently pulled the hood up over
my head. I saw Hardt frown at that but tried my best to
ignore it.

"Hi," I said as I reached him. I was unsure of where
we stood. Last time I had seen him I had admitted to killing
Imiko. It had left things strained between us.

Hardt crossed his arms, uncrossed them, tugged on his nose, sniffed, rubbed a hand up his forehead, scratched at his head. I don't think I'd ever seen him look so awkward. "I, uh, talked to Sirileth. She told me the truth, Eska. About Imiko."

"Oh." I really wasn't sure what to say. Truth is such an awfully subjective thing. I may not have killed Imiko, but I felt responsible.

"You should have told me, Eska." He locked eyes with me and his jaw clenched. Hardt was slow to anger, but when he worked himself up to it, he could do smouldering fury like no other. Ssserakis basked in my fear. "Why claim you did it?"

One of the nearby torches popped, flared brighter for a moment. Burning so many torches made the air feel close and oily and warm, but I still felt cold. I shivered and almost reached for my Pyromancy Source.

"Because I didn't stop her." I let out a bitter, humourless laugh. "I didn't help her and…" I shrugged. I had nothing else to say. Could not find the energy to continue. Suddenly I felt so weary. I almost lay there in the middle of the sandy court. Ssserakis flooded me with strength, not understanding that I wasn't truly weak. Just tired.

"You know that's a lot of shit, Eska. You're an idiot, girl, but you're smarter than that."

I managed a weak smile at him. "History might suggest otherwise."

He shook his head. "You did a terrible job of raising those kids."

I prickled. "Thanks. I don't think they turned out too bad."

"You gave them love, taught them to be strong, sure. But you protected them from consequences, Eska. Never told them off even when they were being little shits. Never gave them boundaries. You're doing it again, now. You're trying to take away blame that rightfully belongs to Sirileth. Stop. Let her reap what she's sewn."

I winced at the hard truth. "Why would I step back when I can protect her? It doesn't matter how old she is or how old I am. She's my daughter and I'll do whatever the fuck I can."

"She's an adult, Eska. She's not a girl anymore. Let her deal with the consequences for her actions."

I ground my teeth, clenched my claw so hard I felt the shadowy bones creak. My eyes flashed like a brooding storm threatening to break. "No," I said. It felt somewhat empowering. Hardt was probably right. He was always right. But not this time. "You're wrong," I ground the words to dust between my teeth. When I looked up at him I saw his own jaw writhing. What a pair we were.

Shaking my head, I tried a smile instead. "You're right, Hardt. But you're wrong too. I did do a terrible job of raising them. But I will never stop protecting Sirileth. Or Tris. Or you. I'd pull our other fucking moon from the sky before I stop protecting the people I love."

The big man sighed and rubbed a hand across his eyes. "Stubborn to a fault. I didn't mean to come here and start a lecture, Eska. I just... urgh..."

Things used to be so easy between us. I might have shed the years like a snake its skin, but they had still happened. We had still grown apart. I desperately wanted us to be friends again, like we used to be. I wanted that comfort Hardt had always provided me with.

"How about a match instead then?" I suggested, thumbing over my shoulder towards the empty sparring ring. "I assume you still know how to throw a punch."

Hardt laughed and slapped a hand against his belly. "I haven't fought anything nastier than a touch of gas for years, Eska."

"Perfect," I said, grinning. This was something we both knew. It was the way we could get back to where we had once been. "I might actually win a bout against you for once."

I didn't.

CHAPTER EIGHTEEN

SSSERAKIS WAITED AT THE TOP OF ITS CITY, *staring down at the gathering masses as they thronged through the crowded streets. The Djinn had created the city, and the tower, and the pulsing Evergloom light that even now drew Ssserakis' minions from the furthest reaches of its territory. Most of the mindless beasts did not even know why or how they had been drawn here. Scuttling geolids and crawling creakers, ghouls slinking from shadows and hellions swooping in from above, khark hounds loping along the streets in vast packs and lumbering yurthammers shaking the ground with each step. They flocked to the calling light. They came to be fed upon.*

Ssserakis drank in their fear, swelling with the energy. Most of these minions were dull minded beasts with little thought past feeding and breeding, but even they provided a bland meal, lacking flavour but providing some scant sustenance. Some were higher of mind, the ghouls and sighthorders and imps. Their fears

were sharper, full of strength and flavour. They could be made to
fear in such wonderful ways, and Ssserakis could feed upon them
for days if it needed to. Far different from a khark hound that
would die of fright if stimulated for too long.

As the streets grew more crowded, Ssserakis sent tendrils
of darkness creeping down the outer wall of the tower. Each
time a tendril touched a minion, Ssserakis leapt inside its mind
and formed a construct, treating the creature to its worst fears,
inflicting stilling dread and blind panic. A yurthammer reared
up, flared blinding bright for a moment, then collapsed, curled in
on itself and trembled, caught in a sticky web of terror. The fear
rose like heat and Ssserakis gathered it all, swelling, becoming fat,
becoming powerful. Soon it would be strong enough to venture out
and do battle once again.

It needed to come back here regularly these days, to call its
minions, to drink their fear. The enemy was growing larger, and
it was taking more power to prune it back. It only feared when
Ssserakis was strong enough to truly do it damage. That was when
Ssserakis could harm it, when the enemy feared. There was no taste
quite like it, no source of power could match it. But even that was
fleeting. When the enemy became too scared, it would detach that
part of itself and retreat to another section of its flesh. The detached
part was truly a mindless thing, unable to feel anything, even
fear. It would slither around and feed and grow larger, eventually
returning to the whole. This was how the enemy had learned to
combat Ssserakis. It was why the battle was slowly being lost.

But soon. Soon Ssserakis would be strong enough to do
battle once more. It had no choice but to carve the enemy apart,
make it fear while it could. Ssserakis knew of no other way.

"Interesting," a voice Ssserakis didn't recognise. A
creature stood before it, on the top of the tower. Ssserakis had
seen the kind before. It called itself terran and came from before.

Another world, another time? Ssserakis had been born from the mind of a creature like this only smaller and so long ago.

The terran stepped forward to join Ssserakis at the edge of the tower and stared down at the city and the gathered minions, bowed in fear and supplication. The terran creature glowed softly around the edges, shimmered, the light penetrating its form as if it wasn't truly there at all.

"You're parasitic," *the terran creature said, smiling. He was old and grey, stoop backed and wrinkled. But he radiated power like nothing Ssserakis had ever felt.*

"What are you?"

The terran glanced at Ssserakis. "Loran tow Orran. I've come here searching for... not important, I suppose. This green light." *He pointed a finger at the pulsing Evergloom, tapped at his chin.* "It's a summoning cantrip, isn't it. Plants a compulsion in the mind of all those who see it, drawing them to this place for you to feed on them. Ingenious. Not your design, obviously. Left over from the Djinn?"

Ssserakis did not understand this creature. It had no fear. It talked like a lord of Sevorai, all confidence and strength. It trespassed on Ssserakis' territory and did not even know well enough to make an offering.

"ENOUGH!" Ssserakis surged towards the terran creature and wrapped it in darkness, searching for its mind. It would trap it in a construct of terror and feed off it, drain it dry and...

The terran creature laughed. It did not fear. "You're a horror." *He squinted into Ssserakis' darkness, stroked his chin as he considered.* "More advanced than most of your kind. Your emotion is fear, I believe. You might just serve."

"I do not serve."

The terran creature smiled. "Oh, but you will serve me." *He reached out a fuzzy hand.*

Ssserakis pulled back, drawing its tendrils in, puffing up to an intimidating size. It would envelop this terran creature entirely, show it darkness, show it fear, peel its skin from its bones...

The terran creature stepped forward, and lightly brushed Ssserakis' shadow with a hand. The world burst into blinding light so painful Ssserakis screamed. It tried to flee, struggling one way and then the other, but couldn't. It was as though something were tethering it in place. Ssserakis couldn't see, had never known light could be so hateful and painful. It burned. It burned. It burned.

"Smaller," the terran creature's voice was a booming command Ssserakis couldn't ignore. It fought it, rebelled against it even as it obeyed without question. "Smaller."

Ssserakis raged, screamed, thrashed, shrank. Smaller and smaller still, compressing itself into a tiny ball of darkness. So much power contained in such a small form was agony, but at least the light hurt less.

"Did you know, energy can be compressed almost infinitely. Here I hold the power of a god, perhaps even the same one that created you, pinched between two fingers. Smaller."

Unable to resist, hating that inability, Ssserakis forced itself so small it felt like it would burst. Its power fizzed at the edges, demanding to escape, to rip free. Ssserakis wanted to let it, to spread out, to flee, to find somewhere to hide from the light. It could not. It could not disobey the terran creature's command.

"That's better," *the terran creature said. Something moved around Ssserakis and encased it. It quested out with darkness, the light searing it to a wisp, and found something hard and unyielding. Glass. Strangely, the glass tingled to the touch, pushed back when Ssserakis thrust against it. It was all around, a ball of glass surrounding Ssserakis. It tried to escape, pushed against one wall, was repelled. Ssserakis raced towards the top, the opening, desperate to escape.*

"Stop!"

Ssserakis stopped, unable to defy the command. Compelled to do nothing but watch past the burning, hateful light as the terran creature reached down with a hand covered in flame and twisted the neck of the glass, sealing it tight.

"There we go." *The terran creature knelt down in front of the glass, smiling in at Ssserakis.*

Ssserakis screamed and rushed at the glass, desperate to shatter it, break free, escape. The glass tingled, pushed back, compressing Ssserakis further into its tiny, painful ball of darkness. It whined, pleaded to be let go. The light burned. The glass constricted it. It held too much fear, too much power to be pressed so tightly.

"Soon," *the terran creature said, breath misting the outside of the glass.* "Soon you'll be tested. I need to know exactly how much power you contain. I need to know what your life is worth."

He plucked Ssserakis' glass container from the table. More of the world was visible now. They were in a room, large enough to contain many shelves, many cages. Ssserakis could feel the fear of so many from inside those cages. Khark hounds and ghouls, a terran child. The fear was sickly, warped and wrong.

The terran creature slotted Ssserakis' glass bubble on a shelf between two others. Ssserakis heard a scream, a fellow horror, Vessir who fed on joy, grown so small it was a dust mote inside its prison. To the other side was a lesser horror, one so primitive it did not have a name. The shelf was thick with them, dozens of glass bubbles, each containing one of Ssserakis' kind.

"There you are," *the terran creature said. He tapped the glass bubble with a single finger.* "Don't worry, horror. It will be your turn soon." *He turned and walked away.*

*Ssserakis screamed. The noise was lost amidst the
cacophony of its fellow inmates.*

The day of the summit came and Sirileth and I
made our way down to the minor rift. She had finished
construction of her archway. It was wide enough to walk
an abban through, and just as tall. There were two dials on
one arm of the arch, each one with a dozen strange symbols
on it, and below them a small depression where a Source
could be placed to power the portal. Sirileth assured me
it would work once other similar arches were constructed
with corresponding symbols. The dials were for determining
destination.

We dressed for the occasion. Sirileth wore a black suit
with golden trim, a deep blue sash around her waist, and
thigh high leather boots. She had her long hair in a single
braid and wore no jewellery save for metal hoops through
her ears. She turned up her sleeves, exposing her scarred
arms and I had a feeling it was for the shocking effect of
seeing such a motley of pitted, melted flesh.

I wore a dress. I've always liked to whenever I get the
chance, though it has not been often. It was a rich red colour,
with a deeper red in cloudy patterns, split at the side for ease
of movement, and artfully tattered at the hems. It clung to
me loosely and proved that though I had put on a fair bit
of muscle since my age reversed, I had not yet regained my
fullness. I wore a black shawl draped over my left shoulder,
hanging low enough to conceal my shadowy claw.

We made such a pair, my daughter and I. Both of us
dressed as queens. Sirileth's eyes burned with her darklight
and mine flashed with my storm. We were ready to meet
with those who called themselves rulers. We were ready to

beat them into line and demand their cooperation.

I did not know the location of the minor rift in Lanfall so Sirileth swallowed her Portamancy Source and tore open the portal. It crackled around the edges, a hole in the world from one place to another. I smelled stale dust and mildew wafting in from the other side. I stepped through first and drew on my Pyromancy Source, flaring orange fire in my hand to light the basement we had entered.

"I will never get used to that feeling," Ssserakis said from my shadow. *"Portals feel like they are tearing at me. Trying to separate us."*

Sirileth glanced at my shadow, and then away, saying nothing. She still had not said a word to Ssserakis and my horror brooded over it. Ssserakis did not understand the passive aggression Sirileth was directing its way.

Sirileth snapped the portal shut and placed a pinch of spiceweed in her mouth, sucking on it for a few moments before lurching aside to heave up her Source. I would have gone to her, held back her hair, but I knew she wouldn't allow it.

We were in a large basement with crates stacked on one side. I did not know what they contained, but there were also some barrels that smelled of oil. I pulled my flames away from them. The floor was stone, but the walls and roof were wooden. Apart from a layer of dust and some mouse droppings, there was nothing else to see but a set of stairs leading up.

The stairs led to a small barn piled high with hay. A single abban, female with six legs, dozed on its side in an unlocked stall. Its snores were enough to rattle the flimsy wooden walls. A young man was sitting on a stool. He wore farmer's overalls and had a cloth cap tipped jauntily on his head, covering his eyes.

Sirileth reached into a pouch beneath her sash and popped something in her mouth, sucking on it. "Mint," she said. "I mean, it's a sweet flavoured with mint. I don't like my breath smelling like vomit. It's unpleasant."

I'd never really considered it before, but it was probably something most Sourcerers should carry.

"Mistress," the young farmhand said as he pulled his hat from his head and leapt to his feet. "Right on time, you are."

Sirileth shot the man a very brief smile. "Of course I am. Is the carriage ready?"

"And waiting. Just outside. Pulled by horses, hope you don't mind it."

Sirileth started towards the barn door. "You're going to want to clear out before nightfall. This farm will be swarming with Lanfall soldiers soon and they will not be leaving."

We left the barn to find the carriage waiting. It wouldn't do to simply walk into Lanfall. We were not there as travellers, but as queens. Ruling a people, any people, is just like acting on a stage; mostly it's about making shit up as you go and pretending you know what the fuck you're doing. People follow confidence and direction, even when the confidence is feigned and the direction is over a cliff.

It was the midmorning and yet the sky was dull and dark. The clouds occasionally lit with lightning rippling above them, the thunder that followed was forceful enough to make stones on the road jump about. The crops in the nearby farms were dead, the grass well on its way to joining in, wilting and yellow. The few farmers I saw from the carriage window were busy harvesting the grass to dry

into hay to feed the abban. It wouldn't last. Isha was dying.
Ovaeris was dying.

Entering the city was a subdued affair. Last time I
had come to Lanfall, I had been old, weary, footsore and
all but unrecognised barring the flashing of my eyes. But
the city had been vibrant and alive. Lanfall was a chaotic
mismatch of architectural styles, but the people were terrans,
living their lives as best they could. Merchants had been
trying to sell their wares. Farmers brought goods to the
city. Craftsmen were busy making bread or horseshoes or
whatever the fuck they did with their days. All that was
muted now. I saw a lot of beggars on the streets, wrapped in
thick cloaks and shivering from the cold, throwing pitying
eyes at everyone who passed, trying desperately to make a
single connection so the passers-by would feel guilty enough
to spare a coin. There were far fewer merchants, and the
stalls they had set up were scarcely provisioned. One man
with a rickety cart was selling fruit that was quite clearly
rotting. And yet it had people lining up to buy from it. The
prices the merchant was charging were ridiculous, even if
the fruit had been fresh and picked by the gods themselves.

"Fuck," I said as I peered out the window, the curtain
pulled back. "Things are bad." I immediately realised that
was a bloody stupid thing to say, turned to find Sirileth
staring out the other window, her scarred hands clenching
the curtain in a fist.

"We'll fix it," I said, still with no idea how.

*The fear in this city is marvellous. A festering cloud oozing
from the minions kept here. We should stay, Eska. I could feed
off this place for weeks, make us strong again.* I already knew
Ssserakis' words for a lie. Well, not entirely a lie. The horror
could feed for weeks, but it struggled to hold that energy

it harvested inside itself. Here, on Ovaeris, even with the clouds covering the sky, the light burned away so much of Ssserakis' power.

The carriage trundled on and I found I no longer had the heart to stare out at Lanfall. I pulled back inside, let the curtain drop, went over arguments in my head, ways to convince the people we were meeting to help us. Sirileth kept her vigil at the window. I saw her trembling, reached over and put a hand on her shoulder. She shrugged it away.

The carriage finally stopped at the gates to Fort Vernan, the driver banging on the roof to let us know we had arrived. I flung the door open and found armed guards in enchanted armour waiting for us. The runes on the breastplates glowing a faint pink to let me know they were prepared to face a Sourcerer.

I stepped from the carriage and approached the first of the guards. He was taller than me, but that was nothing new. His right hand trembled by his side and I knew he was itching to reach for his sword. My shadow writhed across the floor towards him.

He is terrified. It would be so easy to break his mind. There is nothing like the fear of a sentient creature.

My eyes flashed and the man swallowed hard, taking a tiny step back. I pointedly looked down at my shadow and the man followed my gaze. "Leave him be, Ssserakis."

Ssserakis laughed, not inside my head, but out loud. My shadow retreated. The guard sweated.

"They've provided us an escort, Queen Sirileth," I said loudly.

"Right, yes, of course." Sirileth stepped down from the carriage, her back straight, her face composed, her ticks under control. Whatever guilt she had been feeling she pushed it down. "How kind of the union. Lead the way."

The guard nodded, took a shaky step, followed quickly by another. Sirileth and I followed, and the other six soldiers marched behind us in silence.

Fort Vernan had not changed much since I had last been there, save for the fact that it was a lot busier. Guards were in mass attendance, but there were also servants scurrying about everywhere, carrying food or wine or messages. I spotted a group of pahht lounging in a room with a steaming pool but had no chance to investigate. I smelled a swampy scent on the air like unwashed socks I knew came from garn. There was a host of Polasians, too, their sun-darkened skin almost as much of a giveaway as the veils all their men wore.

I shouldn't have been surprised. If anyone could call a summit of Ovaeris' most powerful people in just a few weeks, of course it would be Jamis per Suano. I felt an odd mix of desire and anger at the thought of seeing the man again. I wondered how much of it was mine, and how much of it was left over from the Empamancer's detestable meddling.

We were led to a waiting chamber. There was wine and food, but I touched neither, and Sirileth was far too distracted to contemplate it. The guards waited outside our door. I paced along a very fine ochre rug, hoping to wear my footsteps into it. A painting of an old man with wispy white hair on his head and chin watched me all the while. Sirileth went to the window and stared out, ignoring the metal bars that made this place nothing more than a comfortable cell.

We waited for hours. Or at least it felt like hours. I gave up pacing and sauntered over to the table of food and wine. The wine smelled sweet and fruity. The food was mostly cakes with frosted spices, and a selection of grapes and apples. A younger me might have dashed the table to the floor in frustration, but I couldn't help but remember the beggars in the streets below. The people of Lanfall, of Isha, of Ovaeris going hungry, starving. The Merchant Union did not appear to be suffering the same fate. But that is the way of the rich. Fuck the destitute and who cares about the end of the world, just so long as there's a way to profit from other's misery.

A woman in the doorway cleared her throat. I'm sure she was aiming for polite, but I truly hate that little cough people perform. It never puts me in a good mood. I had seen the woman before. She was tall, dark skinned, with a mass of hair coiled into dozens of thick braids. She wore a red suit that hugged her figure and did very little to hide her cleavage. That was how I recognised her. I had seen her painting last time I was in Fort Vernan and had assumed the artist had accentuated her features. They had not.

The woman's dark eyes roved from me to Sirileth and back again. She frowned, her brows crinkling. She was quite stunning. "I was told to expect Queen Sirileth and an old woman."

I grinned at her and took a step forwards, forced my eyes to flash. "I'm sure you were told a lot of things. Who are you?"

The woman bowed just a little and was smiling when she rose. "Othelia per Suano, of the Merchant Union."

"Is Jamis your brother?" I asked.

Othelia per Suano smiled at me and I felt a hunger like I hadn't in a long time. "Jamis is my husband."

"Ah, how unfortunate for you."

Othelia frowned at me and a damning silence erupted

into the room. I felt my cheeks grow horribly red.

What is happening, Eska? Is this woman a threat?

Sirileth stepped up beside me, shooting me a quizzical look. "Merchant Suano," she said respectfully.

"Queen Sirileth," Othelia bowed again. "The summit is gathering. I thought I would lead you there personally."

I cursed myself for acting like a fool, but I suppose it was no worse than the last time I was at the fort. I decided to keep a tight control on my emotions in case any other Empamancers tried to manipulate me.

I will know if they do. But I have never been able to stop you from drooling after your affections.

"Shut up," I whispered to my horror.

Sirileth glanced back at me, reproach in her stare.

Fort Vernan is constructed of five separate towers. It was originally designed with defending Sourcerers in mind during a time when Orran was a rich nation. Each block of stone used on the outside walls is enchanted against Sourcery. It's by no means an ultimate defence, but it's enough to stop an energetic Sourcerer from trying to blow the towers to rubble with a well-placed blast of magic. The top of the towers provided a commanding view of the city and the surrounding land for Sourcerers to rain down hell upon attackers. I know because I did exactly that once. The towers are connected by sky bridges at various levels, running between them like strands of silk in a spider nest.

Othelia led us out onto one of the sky bridges. Rock stretching from one tower to another, the cold air rushing in on all sides. The bridge was wide enough for ten people to walk abreast. There was only a waist-high railing of metal on either side of the bridge to protect anyone from falling over the edge. I wondered how many drunken fools had plummeted to their deaths from these bridges. Othelia walked with confidence. Servants rushed past us the other way, some stopping to bow, others hurrying on. The wind whipped at us with determined gusts.

It would be a perfect place for an ambush. No way to escape, death waiting on either side. A single Aeromancer could whip up a gale to dash us from the bridge with ease.

If only we could fly. Ssserakis flared my shadowy cloak into wide wings of purest darkness. A servant carrying a pitcher of water screamed, fell back. Othelia and Sirileth turned to the commotion.

Sirileth's eyes went hard. "Mother, stop showing off."

"I—" There really was no point in arguing. Ssserakis pulled my wings back.

We continued our trek across the bridge and entered another of the towers. Othelia led us to a large, open room with raised seating all around in a circular design. It was lit by a series of frosted glowing globes set into the walls, casting everything in a soft, fuzzy luminescence.

There were servants everywhere, hurrying to and fro. I recognised a few merchants in fanciful attire. There was the fat bastard with six chins who had tried to mock me last time I was here. He stared at me, clearly confused for a few seconds until my eyes flashed. Then he gasped and hurried away to talk to a tall, painfully thin woman with a shaven head and piercing grey eyes.

The door opened again and a garn slithered in. Three terran servants trailed behind it, frantically mopping the floor and failing to clean the mess it left behind. It was a greenish yellow colour and its huge mouth drooped at the corners. It seemed to be breathing heavily. Garn typically live in hot, humid swamps. They are quite capable of leaving those climates, but cold weather makes them slow and sluggish. They breathe quickly to speed their metabolism and keep warm.

The garn turned its body slightly as it slithered on and glanced at me with two huge eyes. I will admit, I've always found garn to be quite intimidating. Partly because each one is the size of a large carriage and could happily crush a terran beneath its bulk, and partly because they remind me of the Abominations, Norvet Meruun's children.

Not children. The things you call Abominations are a part of Norvet Meruun. Separated for a time, but still under her control. Imagine that you could detach your finger and order it to crawl around the room and then come back and reattach it. It is part of what makes her so dangerous.

Two more terran merchants arrived. I recognised them both from the ball Jamis had thrown. They gawked at me and quickly moved away. Next came the representatives from Tor. A tall man wearing a robe of dizzying yellows, and a shorter fellow with the same robe in reds. I knew they were from Tor because they spotted me and spat on the floor, then whisked away to find their seats and glare daggers. I noticed there was quite a bit of glaring going on and most of it was directed at either Sirileth or myself. Well, fuck them. They could sneer all they wanted as long as they helped us save Ovaeris.

"Terrible student, is that really you?"

I turned, grinning. A pahht woman with more grey in her fur than I remembered half swaggered half limped into the hall. She was wearing tight leather armour, a vast cloak of crimson, and a brace of swords at her hip. Ishtar, my old sword tutor. My old friend. She held out her arms as she approached and I stepped to meet her. We embraced and she bashed me on the back in fond greeting. I smelled wine on her breath and was oddly glad to know that hadn't changed about her.

We pulled apart and she gripped the side of my face in one clawed hand. "I heard you were old now," Ishtar said, her accent as strong and clipped as ever.

"I was," I said. "Age is fluid."

"Hah! For you, maybe. For some of us not so much. You see the grey?" she gestured at her face. "I wear it well, no?"

"You do." I stepped back and waved at Sirileth. "Ishtar, this is Sirileth."

"Ahh," Ishtar looked my daughter up and down. "I still cannot believe you had a child, Eska."

"I had a child before we ever met, Ishtar."

"Really? I did not think you liked men. Do not glare, I heard the noises you and the Aspect made at night. Made me consider trying to find my own Aspect, eh?"

Sirileth gave a slight, respectful bow. She was always so much better at playing queen than I. "It's good to meet you, Ishtar. My mother told me a lot about you."

Ishtar laughed hard. "That cannot be good." She returned the bow. "A pleasure to meet you too, Queen Helsene. I should, ah, introduce you to..." She turned and gestured to a young pahht man standing quietly behind her. He had flame orange fur and darting eyes. He wore hide armour with metal plates sewn into it, and an axe hung from his belt. He stepped forward, past Ishtar as if she wasn't even there. He held out a clawed hand to Sirileth, ignoring me.

"Envoy Ystelo," the pahht said in an accent far more practiced and gentler than Ishtar's.

"Sirileth Helsene." My daughter and the envoy proceeded to exchange some brief, inconsequential words, both doing their parts as polite diplomacy required.

Such posturing and pandering. Lies and half-truths. Pointless. Force them into submission.

"You're an envoy now?" I asked Ishtar.

"Hah! Me? No. You think I would do well in politics? Terrible student. I am guard. Eat well. Drink well. Limp about after child." The envoy sent a brief glare at Ishtar and she bared her teeth at him. "The ankle will not let me mercenary like I used to."

"Sorry." I could not forget it was my fault she had been injured in our first struggle against the Iron Legion.

"Do not apologise, Eska. It was my choice I was there."

"Because I was paying you."

Ishtar shrugged. "It was my choice to take your money."

The envoy cleared his throat. Clearly he was finished talking to Sirileth. "Ishtar, come." He strode away.

"Ahh," Ishtar said, baring her teeth again, this time at me. "Like a dog, I am summoned. I come, master. Woof, woof." She laughed and limped away a couple of paces, then stopped, turned back to me, lowered her voice. "Be careful, terrible student. You have no friends in this room, only enemies." With that rather ominous statement, she left.

Neither Sirileth nor I had any idea where we were supposed to sit, so we remained standing in the centre of the vast hall. We watched others enter. Mostly terran, Merchant Union members or kings or queens of minor nations. Three more pahht envoys appeared, making their way to join Ishtar's envoy. No more garn slithered in. Then came the people of real importance. I guessed most had been waiting to make a late appearance to flatter their egos. Idiots thinking status is more important than surviving the end of the world.

The room was closing in on full when Kento strode through the doors. I almost ran to her, desperate to hear how Esem was fairing, but there was something in my eldest daughter's posture that warned against it. She was rigid and cold, wearing a rich blue and gold dress. She was here as the Aspect, the representative of the Rand. And it would probably serve us all best if it remained that way. Not many knew that she was my daughter, after all.

Kento was almost to her chair at the head of the hall when I heard the doors open again and a commotion flowed through. The queen of Polasia, Qadira al Rahal, was preceded by ten slave men whose muscles gleamed with oil. They were half naked and wore red veils over their mouths. That meant they were royal guard, the most elite of the elite Polasian male troops. They were also nothing but a distraction. The real danger was the six women who followed them, looking demure in their soft, wispy yellow robes. I knew those women might appear soft, but each one was a veteran warrior trained from birth to fight, and they were all Sourcerers, too. Oh, the Polasian queen tried to hide it all from the world, but every ruler worth an inch of land knew those six women were the true royal guard. They swept into the room, casting wary glances, trying to look intimidating. I think they managed it for the most part. I know I didn't want to test myself against them, but then I was still losing fights to the logs we used as targets.

After the extensive royal guard, came the Polasian princes and princesses. There were twelve of them. Qadira al

Rahal had been quite prolific in popping out children in her younger years. Credit where it's due, it never stopped her from ruling Polasia despite its vast size.

Lastly, Qadira al Rahal herself made an appearance. She was sitting on a ridiculously plump chair mounded with cushions and carried by four Polasian slaves. She was a hard woman when I met her years back and age had only sharpened her lines. Her hair was black as oil, though I wagered she dyed it so. Her eyes were dark, but a little clouded as though her sight were failing her. She wore her many wrinkles poorly, like a discarded dishcloth, and age had burned what flesh she once had from her bones, leaving her skinny to the point of emaciation. She ignored everything as her slaves carried her in, then stood from her chair to sit in another next to Kento. Her children crowded behind her, silently jostling for the best spots. Her many guard spread out, lining the walls.

Such a show of power, that entrance. She was a guest and yet she acted like she owned the whole continent.

Then came a woman I didn't recognise. She was alone, dressed in a simple, white gown with golden hemming that fit her well and seemed to almost shine. Her hair was short and blonde, just starting to lose its colour, and she wore a porcelain mask that covered the right side of her face from her brow down to her bottom lip. She flowed into the room confidently and glanced at me, a single blue eye piercing and steady. Then she swept past me and took her place next to the queen of Polasia.

I leaned a little closer to Sirileth. "Who is that?"

Sirileth also leaned in. "That's the Queen of Ice and Fire, Mother. I believe you know her as Lesray Alderson."

"The bitch whore?" I asked incredulously. My voice

carried surprisingly well in the room. I swear it echoed about for a few minutes just to make sure everyone fucking heard me. Lesray's eye found me again but I could read nothing in her cool regard.

I will admit, I struggled with my emotions. It had been many years since I had last seen Lesray Alderson, and so much had happened. Besides, we were both products of our upbringings. We were both conditioned and tortured by the Orran Academy of Magic. We were both experimented on by the Iron Legion. We should have had that in common. Perhaps even been allies because of it. And yet. She had tried to kill me. She had used Empamancy to implant the call of the void inside of me and no matter how many years since, that echoing desire for oblivion still shook me. Still brought me close to throwing myself down and ending my own life. I hated her. I couldn't escape that hate despite the years and distance between us. I fucking hated her still.

My storm crackled around me, sparking from my skin, arcing down to score the stone floor in lines of searing fire.

Kill her, Ssserakis hissed in my mind. *Pull her head from her neck and shower them all in blood, Eska. Think of the fear. They will cower before us. We do not need them to agree, only to obey. What better way than with fear?*

My shadow rippled, spread beneath me, extending out in every direction as it crawled across the floor. My eyes flashed, my storm raged, my claw clenched tight, taloned fingers digging into my leg. I stared at Lesray with every bit of the hate I felt for her and it only flared hotter when she gazed back with nothing but cold dismissal.

"Mother, stop it," Sirileth said, quiet and demanding. I glanced at her, her darklight eyes shining bright. "Not here.

Not now. We need them."

Damn her and damn them all, but she was right. I wanted to kill Lesray for the Empamantic command she had placed in my head so long ago, but right now we needed her. We needed them. The world was more important than my vengeance. For now.

The door opened a final time and Jamis per Suano sauntered in. "Ahh, excellent. We're all here. I suppose we can finally start." He strode past me, sending but a glance at Sirileth.

My emotions lurched sideways again, desire roaring to life inside me in a way I hated almost as much as I did Lesray.

What is going on, Eska? You want this man?

I clamped down on my feelings, closed my eyes, tried to get my traitorous heart to stop pounding. It was not my desire, I felt. It had never been mine. Just a fragment of another's feelings implanted in me as surely as Lesray's command to take my own life had been. I breathed deeply, slowly, forced everything I was feeling down into a little ball.

I was already starting to wish I had never called for this summit.

CHAPTER NINETEEN

I HAVE ALWAYS STRUGGLED IN SITUATIONS with powerful people. I have begged at the feet of kings, bandied words with the most powerful Sourcerer who has ever lived, told gods to go fuck themselves knowing it was very likely possible. But in situations where I am faced with the attention of those in positions of power, I often find my tongue becomes stuck. I simply cannot think of anything to say. This time was no different.

As Jamis swept a bow at all the gathered peacocks, then pointed to myself and Sirileth, I stood in silence, desperately trying to remember why we were there. Sirileth stepped seamlessly into the breach.

"Lords and ladies, kings, queens, and envoys." An auspicious start, she gave. It's always good to pamper to those who think themselves above the rest of us. "I'm sure you know why we are here."

"To see your head struck from your shoulders." That was shouted by one of the Polasian princesses standing behind her queen. I didn't catch which as she was hiding amongst her siblings. Her mother did not reproach her for the outburst. Did not react at all. But a wave of muted laughter passed through the gathered merchants and aristocrats.

Sirileth waited for the murmuring to die down, then stepped forward into the centre of the hall. She glanced back at me once, and I nodded. It was her floor, her summit, her plea.

She swept her gaze across them, turning in a circle, then stopped facing the far end where Jamis and Qadira and Lesray and Kento sat. "The world is breaking," Sirileth said loudly. "The seas thrash and boil. The land bucks and splits. The air is rent by storms. We are living in an unnatural winter. People are dying. Starving, set upon by monsters crawling up from the earth, drowned in floods or buried in quakes. None of us can fix it alone." She paused, swept her gaze again, found only stony faces and hard silence.

"I… um…" Sirileth frowned, glanced down, her confidence broken. "I have a plan. I mean, I have some ideas. That might… Might… I mean, there's a possibility that if we all work together." She was fiddling with her hair, rubbing the end between her fingers.

What is wrong with our daughter?

"She's nervous," I whispered.

Why?

"I need Sourcerers," Sirileth blurted suddenly. "Your Sourcerers. All of them. I mean, in order to…"

Qadira al Rahal stood, her silken robe hanging awkwardly on her bony frame. "The world *is* broken," she said. "Because *you* broke it."

Sirileth looked like she'd been punched. She pulled her hand from her braid, clenched it hard by her side and looked up, meeting Qadira's eyes. "I did." There was iron in her voice. I was both proud and terrified, because this was the Sirileth I had seen just after the cataclysm she wrought. This was the Sirileth who had defended her actions even knowing the cost. "I did what was necessary."

"Necessary?" Qadira hissed. "You dropped a moon on my city."

"It was the only way…"

"You murdered hundreds of thousands of Polasians." The Polasian queen turned her spiteful attention to the rest of the summit. "Why are we entertaining this murderer? She has admitted blame. There is nothing left but judgement."

"You don't understand," Sirileth shouted over the rising tumult as people added their voices to Qadira's demands. "I had to stop the Maker."

The painfully severe merchant stood, waving a hand for attention. "Speak clearly, girl. Maker of what?" I winced at the words. Already these people were reducing Sirileth to *girl*. She was a queen and should demand that right.

"The Maker," Sirileth said. She turned, trying to find the merchant who had spoken to her, but the woman had already sat again. "The… I mean, the eye in the Polasian desert."

Another of Qadira's mouthy spawn, a fat princess who I was certain was wearing a robe too small for her, stepped forward past her mother's chair. "The eye has always been above the desert. It drives a few fools mad each year, but nothing more."

The murmur of voices was quickly harmonising into a

damning choir.

"You don't understand," Sirileth shouted, struggling to be heard. "The eye... I mean, the Maker was trying to come through the rift. It made the Rand and the Djinn and it wanted its power back. It was..."

"Where is your proof?" the voice that boomed into the hall was the sole garn representative. The words almost sounded like he spoke from underwater.

"I... I am the proof," Sirileth said. "I mean, it showed me was it wanted to do when it took me as a child. I..."

Qadira poked her fat daughter in the leg and the princess bellowed, "First, she claims the eye wished to kill us. Then, she admits she was in league with it."

"I was not..."

The fat princess had a better set of lungs on her than my daughter and shouted her down, "She has admitted guilt. A hundred thousand Polasians dead. How many others? These storms she claims to want to fix are her doing. The seas and the quakes, all her."

"I had to pull the moon through the rift. It was the only way to reset it." Sirileth shouted, but I don't think anyone heard her over the rest of the voices.

Jamis was staring at me. He cocked a single eyebrow, gave the minutest of shrugs. Fuck him and his blatant arrogance. My daughter was struggling to convince these fools to do the right thing, and all Jamis could do was smirk at the chaos. No doubt the greasy arsehole was planning a way to make it all work to his advantage.

These fools squark like startled bonehawks. My shadow started bubbling beside me. *And you have yet to even inform them of the greater threat. Take control, Eska. Silence them.*

I tried to focus on the summit. Though still calling it

a summit was being generous. I've seen more composure in Damned fighting over a corpse.

"We demand reparations," the Polasian princess shouted.

Ishtar's pahht envoy barked a laugh. "Of course you do," he bellowed and I had to admit he had good volume for a smaller man. "People are dying and you wish to be paid."

"It is Polasia that has suffered most from this tragedy," the fat princess roared.

Someone else joined in then, I'm not sure who. And then another and another. Suddenly everyone was shouting and I couldn't make out what a single one of the stupid fucks was saying. It was chaos.

I caught Ishtar's eye. She cocked her head to the side dramatically and yawned at me. She had been telling the truth when she said we had no friends here.

Even Jamis was shouting now. A screamed conversation with his fellow merchants from the union. Only Lesray remained silent amidst that storm of noise. Well, only Lesray and myself. I caught her staring at me with her one uncovered eye. I found myself curious about the point of her mask. Was she scarred underneath that porcelain facade? Or what it just an ornament to make her stand out. Damn her, but it worked. In the madness the summit had so quickly devolved into, Lesray Alderson sat still and serene, dressed all in white, her face as expressionless as her mask. The fingers on her left hand drummed leisurely on the arm of the wooden chair.

"The bickering of parasites," Ssserakis said. *"It is fear, Eska. Tell me you can feel it."*

I could, all too well. Everyone in the room was scared but determined to cover it up with angry bravado.

"Idiots, all of them," I said. "I don't know why I thought coming to them would work."

"Then kill them all and take their power, Eska. Rule is nothing but the application of superior strength. You wish to unite Ovaeris against the threat from my world, then do it under us. We do not need these simple creatures, only the minions they command."

I was starting to consider the possibility, I won't lie. Jamis and Qadira, the Merchant Union, the pahht and the garn. All just scheming to their own ends even in the face of annihilation.

I smiled at my horror. "Maybe you're right," I said. "They're already afraid. I can taste it. All we need…"

"Mother," Sirileth's voice stopped me and I suddenly realised the room had gone silent.

All eyes were turned to me. Well, me and Ssserakis. My horror floated beside me, a fizzing patch of darkness, twin to my shape and size. Jamis was staring with eyes wide. Qadira was suddenly shrouded by her bodyguards. Lesray's expressionless mask had finally slipped to reveal a slight smile on her lips. I looked around, searching for friendly faces, found none. Ishtar had her head in clawed hands. Kento was staring at the floor so intently I was surprised it didn't crack under the scrutiny.

Well, fuck! When you're dealt nothing but losing hands, you might as well try to bluff.

I stepped forward slowly to join Sirileth in the centre of the floor. "Idiot children playing at importance," I snarled. "The world is falling apart around you, breaking into pieces, burning. And you wish to assign blame." I paused, let their fear fill me, buoy me.

"Will it help? Will killing my daughter fix the

world? Stop your people starving? Drive the monsters back underground? Calm the fucking seas?"

"She is possessed!" shouted one of the pahht.

"QUIET!" I roared the word and Ssserakis flared my shadow so large it darkened the room for a moment. I threw back my shawl to reveal my claw. No point in hiding it anymore, let them all see exactly what they were facing.

"My daughter wishes to save you." I smiled grimly. "I cannot think why. And yet all you do is squabble. The world is ending, and you fight over who gets the largest piece of rubble.

"Will it help? Will deciding which of you gets paid the most stop your people from dying?"

The fear was intoxicating. They all tasted different. The many-chinned merchant was sweet and sticky like overripe tangerine. Qadira was dusty and bitter like cocoa. Jamis was rich and moist like a good ale. Only Lesray showed no fear. That isn't quite right. It wasn't that she wasn't showing any fear. She held no fear at all. She was a bastion of calmness that gave me nothing. That annoyed me. I could grow fat and happy on the terror from the rest of them, but I wanted hers. I wanted Lesray to fear me.

"And the worst of it is," I continued. "You still don't even know about the greatest threat you face. There is a monster coming. The great rift in the Polasian desert now leads to Sevorai."

A murmur of voices rippled through the summit. The garn representative slithered forwards. Even towering over me and fully capable of pulling my limbs off without trying, the garn feared me. It tasted of spices, hot and tingly. "There is a portal to the Underworld?" I found it somewhat interesting that the garn was the one to ask despite their people having no Sourcerers.

"Yes," I hissed at it. "And the monster that devoured that world is coming for ours."

Qadira stood again. She was afraid. Of me, of my horror beside me. But she had that fear in check. It is rare to find a person who's will is stronger than their terror. "Threats," she said in a voice as dry as her desert. "One after another. The eye wanted to kill us all. The world is ending. There is a monster coming. It is all nothing but threats. A distraction. You came here…"

"*Do you want to see?*" Ssserakis said in a distorted version of my voice. "*Shall I show you the Beating Heart of my world?*"

Qadira ignored Ssserakis and stared straight at me. "Another threat." She turned, spreading her arms to address the summit. "Do you see what they are now? This is all they can do. Threaten us with portents and shadows. The Corpse Queen's time has passed. We see her for the frail creature of reputation long since eroded. Now her daughter wishes to take her place as the new queen of fear. It is nothing but empty threats." She focused her gaze back on me. "We will not listen to more of your lies."

I stared at her for a few seconds and let my anger simmer to a boil, then turned to Ssserakis. "Show them."

Ssserakis laughed out loud. "*With pleasure.*"

My shadow expanded, swallowing the entire assembly hall in an instant.

The many-chinned merchant screamed. To be fair, he wasn't the only one, but his voice was the shrillest. I might have killed him for the offensive noise, but honestly I was enjoying the taste of his fear. So strong. We could feed off him for days, sucking him dry until all that was left was an insensible husk unable to feel anything. Enough terror does that to a person, castrates them of all emotion. They become numb. Responsive, but... no longer really there.

It was a construct, one larger than I had ever seen before, and in it was nothing but darkness. A black so complete none of those locked inside it could even see their own noses. Except for me, of course. I could see it all. Some of the fools stumbled around as if trying to find a way out, others shouted to be released, some just curled into balls and wept. One of Qadira's daughters staggered, bumped into a brother, swung at him. The brother went down, clutching at his face.

I will give it to Qadira's guards though, they held firm. They stayed in position, ready in case a clear threat presented itself. Qadira herself was almost as stoic. Her hands clutched at the arms of her chair and her lips drew back into a snarl, but she didn't panic.

Lesray remained entirely still save for the drumming of her fingers on the arm of a chair she couldn't even see. Bitch! I swear, I think it's her life's purpose to piss me off.

"Mother, tell Ssserakis to get on with it," Sirileth said. She was also trapped in our construct, but her fear was not of the dark. It was something deeper and sicklier. I did not like the taste of it.

"*Ahh, so our daughter does remember me. Stop ignoring me, daughter.*"

Sirileth did not respond.

"Show them, Ssserakis."

The darkness faded, leaving us standing on a rocky cliffside in Sevorai. Below, stretching out as far as the eye could see was Norvet Meruun. Her infested hellions and wind thrashers buzzed about her. A pack of three giant, fire-spewing yurthammers plodded along before the pulsing mass of the enemy, dragging a cart that could have housed half of Lanfall. Wrapped in so many chains I could barely make out the flesh beneath, a giant insectoid figure with a thousand segmented legs twitched in the centre of the cart.

Now the merchants and queens and guards could see again, they started shouting, pointing, arguing. Three of Qadira's elite guard stalked towards me. Jamis was on his feet, obviously trying to calm everyone. Kento glared at me with frustration.

"Is this real or just a creation of your construct?" I asked Ssserakis.

"It is real." My horror sounded oddly sad. "She has captured Lodoss. The last lord of Sevorai that truly opposed her. There is nothing to stand in her way now. Nothing to delay Norvet Meruun's march upon your world."

The chained mass of legs twitched again, dark gore oozing out and running to the side of the cart, dripping down to stain the grey earth. I realised the chains were anchored in Lodoss' flesh, giant metal stakes driven through his legs and body at a hundred different places.

"He cannot die. Like Norvet Meruun, Lodoss cannot die. But he can suffer. It is his purpose to suffer."

"Where are we, Corpse Queen?" Qadira's fat daughter shouted after being prodded by her mother.

I strode towards them, away from the cliff's edge. "Technically, you're still in Lanfall. This is a construct. Ssserakis is using it to show you what we face."

"This is your demon's doing?" Ishtar's envoy asked.

"I am no demon. I am a lord of Sevorai." Ssserakis roared the words from everywhere and nowhere at once. "I am ancient. I am eternal. I am fear itself." Too much bluster, but it seemed to have the desired effect and the envoy shut his mouth.

"Nothing but illusions and trickery," Qadira said coldly. "Is this all you are, Corpse Queen?"

"This is real, Qadira," I said, taking a few steps forward. Her lead guards drew their blades, pointing them my way. I stopped within striking distance, hoping none of them got it in their head to take the initiative and stab me. "Everything you see here is real. Happening right now in Sevorai. That," I pointed over the cliff edge towards the pulsing tumour of Norvet Meruun. "Is coming. It will not stop. It will devour everything in its way. If it reaches the great rift, if even a piece of it crosses over into Ovaeris, it will consume our world just as it has this one."

"What would you have us do?" This from Kento.

Qadira spoke before I could. "Finally the Aspect speaks but only to take her side?"

Kento stared down the Polasian queen. "The Rand take no sides. I only ask a question to take the answer back to my mother."

Qadira waved a bony hand in the air and snarled. "Bah!"

"What should we do?" Kento asked again. I think she was trying to help, in her way.

"Stop fighting us," I said. "Stop fighting each other. We need to unite, raise an army, march through the rift and into Sevorai. Stop this monster before it reaches our world."

The garn shook its massive head. "First you tell us Ovaeris is tearing itself apart, and you need Sourcerers to fix it. Now you demand we wage war against Hell itself?"

I shrugged at the garn. "That's an overly dramatic way of putting it. But yes."

"How would you have us fight that thing?" One of the pahht envoys asked.

To be honest, Ssserakis and I were still working on that part of the plan. "We need to beat it back, carve enough of it apart that it shows its true self and…"

Qadira shouted over me. "Giant eyes in the sky, earthquakes and floods, monsters from hell. It is all nothing but a distraction." She wasn't talking to me now, but to all the others. And damn them all, but they were listening. "We need to focus on the real issue here." A bony finger snaked out and pointed at Sirileth. "She is a murderer and must be brought to justice for her crimes. Not just against Polasia, but against us all."

Again they all burst into shouting and noise. It was as if they didn't even see the hellscape around them, the monster slowly crawling its way closer to our world.

"Shall I kill them all now, Eska?" A few eyes turned my way, proving that at least some of the merchants had heard Ssserakis. I had a feeling it wasn't going to help our cause.

Sirileth stared at me, caught my gaze, shook her head slowly. She looked tired.

Lesray stopped drumming her fingers. She stood smoothly, elegantly, every bit of her the Queen of Ice and Fire. Like a drop of water hitting a pond, ripples of silence spread from her as she walked. By the time she reached me, everyone, even Qadira had quieted.

"Put your demon away, Eskara." Lesray's voice was silken with a slight dry rasp of crinkled paper. "You will convince none of us with threats or coercion."

I stared at the hateful bitch, my claw flexing, talons eager to tear out her throat for all she had done to me. Lesray just stared back, impassive and unyielding.

"Release the construct, Ssserakis."

"But they still bicker like ghouls over a corpse."

"Do it."

Sevorai vanished and we were all in the summit hall once again. A few of the Polasians staggered as if dizzy. One of the merchants ducked away to heave up their breakfast.

Lesray's uncovered eye never left my face. Up close, I could see the left side of her mouth drooped a little underneath her porcelain mask. I was suddenly certain the mask was not just ornamentation but hid an injury.

"You can leave now," Lesray said. "Wait outside. We will discuss your matters outside of your…" Her eye flicked to Ssserakis standing beside me in my shadow. "Influence. You'll be notified when we have reached a decision."

No one argued with her. Not Jamis nor Qadira nor the pahht or garn. Just like that, with only a few words and an aura of cold calm, Lesray had assumed control of the entire summit. I'll admit, I was a little in awe of her. That awe was not enough to quench my hatred for the bitch.

I lingered, fighting my desire to get in the last word. I didn't like being dismissed like a servant. But then, what could I do? *Kill them all.* They were kings and queens, powerful merchants, and envoys to foreign nations. I was nothing but a name and a dark reputation. The bogeywoman of Isha. Not even a queen anymore. So I treated Lesray to a few more seconds of glare, my eyes flashing with raging lightning, then I turned and started towards the big doors.

Sirileth remained. "I have one more matter I need to discuss," she said. "I mean, it's an offer, really."

One of the merchants started shouting her down, but Lesray held up a hand to the man, commanding silence with only a gesture. "Queen Helsene has as much right to speak here as any." There was some grumbling but none argued with the bitch whore.

"There are rifts," Sirileth said. "I mean, other rifts, not the great rift in the Polasian desert. I call them minor rifts. They're everywhere. Dozens at least, I mean that I know of. All over Ovaeris. I have plans. Detailed instructions to build gates around each one. They will allow portals to be opened between them. I mean, long distance portals without need of a Sourcerer. Instantaneous travel between any of the rifts."

The severe merchant stood. "You want us to build one of these gateways so you can move your forces against us with ease."

"What? No."

"This is nothing more than another ploy."

Sirileth shook her head. "It's not. I'm trying to..."

"If we build these gateways, the savages of Yenheim will have easy access to us all."

Sirileth clutched her hands before her. "If I wanted to use the gateways to attack, I would not have told you about them. Yenheim already has access to them. We can already use them to travel between rifts. There is one here in Lanfall. If I wanted to, I could have marched my forces through and attacked you here."

"Another threat," the severe merchant shouted.

"It's not a threat," Sirileth shouted as the tumult rose. "I'm telling you this so you can build your own gateways. Instantaneous travel between all your nations. I mean, think of the possibilities this offers."

A slow smile spread across Jamis' face. He stood and cleared his throat loudly, waving his hands in the air for attention. The voices faded to a dull throb rather than a roar. "We will need to know where this rift is, of course, Queen

Helsene. You say there are many of them. We will need to know where they all are."

"Yes," Sirileth said. "That's part of the point. I mean, the gateways I've designed can be used to access any other gateway. But I can't build them all myself. They take a lot of the ore that comes from the moons."

Qadira poked her daughter again and the fat princess took a deep breath. "That ore is rare and extremely expensive. You would have us drain our coffers to build your network of gates."

Sirileth sighed, her hands wringing. She stared down at the floor a moment, then looked up straight at the Polasian queen. "It just so happens a massive amount of that ore has recently landed in the Polasian territory. In fact, I imagine if you moved swiftly enough, before the tahren lay claim to it, Polasia will soon be the richest nation on Ovaeris."

A tense silence fell over the summit as everyone considered Sirileth's words. Even Qadira sat back in her chair, a thoughtful expression on her face.

We left the summit then, Sirileth and I. The arguing had already started before the door closed behind us. I had a bad feeling worming its sour way through my gut. These fools wouldn't help us. I don't think they cared enough past lining their pockets and making sure they still had a throne to sit on. They would soon find a throne of corpses an uncomfortable seat.

CHAPTER TWENTY

THEY SHOWED US BACK TO OUR CELL. IF THEY thought a couple of iron bars and a locked door would hold me, they were sorely mistaken. I picked at the food, found a withered apple to devour.

They might have poisoned it. Choking to death, face purple and bloated, all your dreams unfulfilled.

"Stop trying to scare me, Ssserakis. Let them kill me, I'd welcome the peace."

Sirileth shot me a darklight glare. She was pissed off at me for some reason. There is a silence some people can give that is more accusing than a scream. Hardt was a master of those silences and he had apparently taught my daughter well.

"What?" I snapped.

"You took over, Mother. You made the entire thing about this war with Sevorai, and you turned it into a chaotic shouting match."

I snorted. "It was already a shouting match before I said a word."

"What point is there of fighting Norvet Meruun if our world dies while we are doing it?" Sirileth shook her head and stood, flounced dramatically towards the window, and stared through the bars. "You said you would help me. What you did in there was make it all about you and your war."

"My war?" I laughed bitterly. "You're not the only one trying to save the world, daughter. Just the only one who broke it first."

Sirileth's silence grew legs, eyes, wings, mouths, and it swallowed us all.

"Fuck," I said. "I'm sorry, Sirileth. I didn't mean it like that."

I tried to go to her, but my daughter turned and there was danger in her eyes, a warning to stay back written in darklight shards. One more proof, if ever it was needed, that I ruin everything I touch.

We stared at each other, tension mounting. My shadow twisted and rose. *"You both speak as if only your world is in peril. Norvet Meruun has already all but consumed my home. I will need both of you to beat her back and save it."* It comes to something when the living incarnation of fear is playing peacemaker.

Sirileth didn't so much as glance at Ssserakis. "I am talking to *you*, Mother. I need *your* help." She shook her head. "If you cannot give it, then at the very least stop getting in my way."

My shadow shifted, Ssserakis turning to regard me with pitch black eyes. *"I wish to speak to our daughter alone."*

Sirileth startled, glanced at Ssserakis, then back to me.

She looked uncertain. I couldn't blame her.

"How?" I asked Ssserakis. "It's not like I can leave the room without you." I poked at my shadow, found it soft but resistant like unfired clay.

"*Do not panic, Eska.*" Ssserakis chuckled. "*Or do. Your fear has always tasted sweetest.*"

Before I could answer, my shadow engulfed me. Ssserakis locked me in a construct of darkness. I could see nothing, hear nothing, smell nothing. I was alone in a void.

Panic? No, I didn't panic. I quite liked it. It was peaceful, serene even. I wondered, was this what death was like? Eternal nothing. A vast and empty space with no one to make demands of me?

Suddenly I felt tired. Weary beyond belief. I dropped to my knees, had to fight the slick, seductive urge to lay and melt into the floor. I knew it wouldn't help. This wasn't death. This wasn't peace. I was alone here, yes. But *I* was still here. My mind, my thoughts, my guilt and anger and pain. Here, in this space, there was nothing to stop my memories picking at me like wolves darting in to take bites, to draw blood.

Memories of my childhood came back to haunt me. So many times, I dragged Josef into trouble. I was an awful friend to him. When I used to lie to my parents to get my brother in trouble. A horrible child. The call of void echoed around me so strongly if I had been facing a wolf I would have shoved my head in its jaws.

Then it was over. The darkness vanished and I was in our cell again, on my side on the floor, cold and insensate. Sirileth rushed to me, spewing words at me I couldn't make out. She tried to help me up, gripped my arm and leant me that support.

*What happened, Eska? There was nothing in the construct
to attack you.*

"Nothing but me." My words came out slurred,
tripping over each other. I think Ssserakis took it as
confirmation. My horror didn't understand. No monster it
could conjure could hurt me more than I myself. None could
be as vicious or as deadly.

"Mother, are you alright? Ssserakis, what did you
do?"

Sirileth got me into a chair and fetched me a glass
of wine. I'd have preferred whiskey, but the wine was
watered enough to quench my thirst at least. I came back to
myself slowly. I didn't admit it to her, or to my horror, but
my attacks were getting worse. Lasting longer, tearing me
down quicker, taking longer to recover from. The feeling of
depression faded, but I was left with one inescapable truth
that clung to me no matter how I tried to deny it. I would
have answered the call of the void if I could. Trapped in that
construct, I would have taken my life and been happy for it.
I wondered, was it Lesray's doing? Had she reaffirmed that
Empamantic command she put in me so long ago? That seed
of self-destruction she planted, now was she watering it,
forcing to grow? I didn't know. Couldn't tell.

I fucking hate Empamancy.

The sun was setting by the time the door to our cell
opened again and Jamis sauntered in. He brought no guards
to protect him, nor his pet Sourcerer. That was probably
wise. My emotions tugged the moment I saw him and I felt
myself growing warm from the unnatural desire I felt. I was
already feeling fairly fragile and I've always been one to
hide any fragility behind anger. If the Sourcerer had made an
appearance, I would have made certain it was his last.

"Well," Jamis said as the door closed behind him. He made his way straight to the wine. "That was an utter mess, wasn't it." He poured himself a cup, downed it, then poured another. I noticed a slight stoop to his shoulders, a crack in his composure, and there were bags beginning to show beneath his eyes. He took his cup, retreated to a plush chair, and sank into it with a grateful sigh.

"What did they decide?" Sirileth asked. "I've been thinking. I mean, I have plans. A way I think we can…"

Jamis waved a hand in the air. "Where to start?" He sipped at his wine. "Coordinated efforts to put an end to this cataclysm. That's what we're officially calling it now. It took about half an hour to decide on that. Coordinated efforts are unlikely."

Sirileth wrung her hands together. "But we can't hope to…"

"Lursa's Tears, let me finish." Jamis closed his eyes and rubbed at his temples. "I've had enough of interruptions and outbursts for the day. The pahht have the most powerful Aeromancers and Meteomancers, and they've already been experimenting with pushing back the cloud cover to allow the sun to shine again. It doesn't last. It takes an enormous amount of energy and Sourcerers are rejecting within hours. And as soon as they stop, the clouds rush back in to shroud everything all over again. They say without a way to remove all the ash and dust from the sky, there simply is no point in trying.

"That brings us to the next problem, bizarre weather patterns are creating violent funnels across the world, sucking dust and earth into the sky. New volcanoes are springing up on Rolshh, in Itexia, in the oceans. Each new volcano throws up more debris. Until we can stop them, there is no chance of clearing the cloud cover." He sighed. "At this point I don't think any of us will see the sun again in our lifetimes."

I sat opposite Jamis and could see just how tired he was. It was not just the summit. He'd been moving to put himself as head of the Merchant Union, and I had no doubt his eyes were set on Isha next. What was the point of a crown if all you could rule over was corpses?

Jamis sipped at his wine again and shook his head. "Hydromancers have no idea what to do about the seas. Apparently the magical energy involved in calming even a turbulent pond is significant."

"And Geomancers agree about the land," I said. My innate Geomancy was weak, but even I could feel the constant tremors beneath us.

Jamis nodded. "No one believes stopping any of this is possible. They're all focused on riding it out. Being the ones to survive. I know you wanted to unite everyone against a common threat, but the threat is too great."

"So that's it?" Sirileth asked, her voice cracking. "I've ended the world because everyone has decided it's too hard to fix so why even try."

Jamis was relentless. "Essentially yes. What did you think would happen when you crashed a moon on top of us?" He didn't even try to hide the bitterness. Sirileth retreated to the window again, stared out at the dark sky.

Jamis drained his wine and looked mournfully at the jug on the table. Then he turned his gaze to me. "As for you and your monster from the Underworld."

"The Other World," I corrected him. "Sevorai."

He sent me a scathing look. "Bringing out that demon was a terrible idea."

My shadow writhed, rising beside the chair. "*I am a lord of Sevorai.*"

Jamis startled. His fear oozed lazily from him and tasted oily. He was too tired to be properly afraid. "Again," he said between gritted teeth. "It doesn't help. They won't follow you."

"I'm getting that."

"Honestly, Eskara, they're scared of you. Believe it or not, fear doesn't breed loyalty."

"*Clearly you have never known true terror. I will show it to you.*" My shadow surged toward Jamis.

"Stop it, Ssserakis."

My horror paused, then pulled back, retreating inside of me, letting my shadow fall naturally again. Jamis released his claw-like grip on the chair arms. I sensed a puzzle piece floating around me but couldn't grasp it. There was something, a part of the solution had just been handed to me, but I've never been one to solve puzzles by concentrating on them.

"So that's it?" I asked. "Both worlds can fall just because a bunch of bureaucrats and politicians don't like me? All of you are such a bag of self-serving, cowardly pricks!"

Jamis stared at me, his lip twitching as he held back a snarl. "Well, that aside. They won't follow *you*, Eskara. But I do believe they might line up behind someone else."

"So do it," I snapped. "Take control. That's what you've always wanted anyway."

"If only it were that easy." Jamis stood and poured himself another cup of wine. "It can't be me." He looked at the chair again, sighed, then turned away from it, standing straighter. "My position as head of the Merchant Union is too new and fragile to drag us into an alliance without support from others first. Additionally, I have too recently had dealings with you, specifically."

Yes, I remembered the function he had thrown atop the tallest tower of Fort Vernan. I also remembered how his Empamancer had twisted my emotions all to use me so Jamis could claim he had mastered the Corpse Queen. All for this, his new position at the head of the union. All fucking pointless unless he was willing to help.

"If I were the first to back you and start rallying support, my people would claim I'm in league with you. I'd find my position quickly revoked before I could secure it, and they'd make me a pariah. You wouldn't gain an ally, but a pauper without a connection to his name. It can't be me."

He poured another glass of wine and held it out to me. "You're going to want this."

"Why?" Suspicion made me snappy but I took the glass.

"They need someone to back you. Someone to line up behind. Someone well thought of by the Polasians, the pahht, the garn, the mur, all of them. They need someone they like, someone they're not afraid of."

I shook my head. "Don't fucking say it."

"Someone who is entirely beyond suspicion of already being in league with you. Someone who, they believe, can control you."

"Fuck off!" He was right about the wine. I drained half the glass in one gulp.

"Who?" Sirileth asked.

"Lesray fucking Alderson," I said.

Jamis nodded, sipping at his wine. "The Queen of Ice and Fire fits every single requirement."

I scoffed at that. "You think Lesray can *control* me?"

Jamis rolled his eyes. "I don't think the gods could control you, Eskara." He probably thought he was being charming. "But she is your only chance of making this work. You need to get Queen Alderson on your side."

I'd let the moons fall, the world crack open and burn, the giant tumour of a slug from Sevorai suck out everything left before I bowed to Lesray Alderson. She who had implanted the call of the void in my mind, tried to kill me over and over again as children. As fucking children! She might have convinced the rest of these idiotic fools that she was a just ruler, a calm and steadying hand, a good person, but not me. I knew better and I would not let her win.

"What about the gateways?" Sirileth asked. "Will they all build them?"

Jamis stared at me a few moments longer, then turned to Sirileth with a weary smile. "We didn't get to those. We'll discuss them another time, but you can be sure I'll push for them. They are… an intriguing opportunity."

"I'll leave the plans and locations of all the rifts with you," Sirileth said. "I have to return to Yenheim."

"You truly offer this technology freely?" Jamis asked, sceptical himself. "You want nothing in return?"

Sirileth shook her head. "They can be the future of travel between nations. They need to be built."

I sought out Kento before we left but was already too late. She had taken the flyer she had arrived on and was already flying back to Ro'shan. I thought that bad sign. My daughter did not even spare the time to talk to me. I desperately wanted to know about Esem, but it would have to wait.

Jamis had already sent a contingent of guards to

the location of the minor rift outside of Lanfall. They were
instructed to let us pass and did so without complaint, but
they were already setting up barricades and stationary
weapons to defend against incursion through the rift. Sirileth
might be willing to gift this new form of travel to the world,
but I had no doubt the people in charge would corrupt her
dream. I imagined the taxes on using the gateways would be
high.

We returned to Yenheim defeated. There would
be no unified attempt to save Ovaeris, nor armies raised
to fight Norvet Meruun. We had tried, and in the end we
had defeated ourselves. Sirileth slunk back to her rooms,
ignoring the servants requesting her attention. She locked
the door behind her without a word. My poor daughter. I
knew I had to find a way to help her. No matter the cost.

CHAPTER TWENTY ONE

THE NEXT DAY WE FOUND TRIS LOUNGING ON the corpse throne again. We'd only been gone a day and yet he draped himself over it like he'd been born in the damned thing. Despite that, he looked harried. He also happily leapt out of the chair. Apparently he had been receiving reports of troubling activity all day and was at his wit's end as everyone was looking at him to help.

The cloud cover was killing the crops. Half the Forest of Ten was either burning or just plain gone, sunk into the earth. There were monsters prowling the countryside and at least one patrol of soldiers sent to deal with them had been found dead. Dead, he informed us, was putting it mildly considering how they had been found. I was just happy they stayed dead. Clouds of deadly vapours had started forming and sweeping across Isha. He had no idea what that was about at all, but he'd received reports of hazy mists blanketing the land, enveloping entire villages, and leaving nothing but corpses behind. And the ghosts of Picarr were missing. That last one was delivered as something of an afterthought, but it piqued my attention.

I set out the next day, but before I went I visited the Source vault. The guards there let me in without question. All our Sources, though I suppose I should say all Sirileth's Sources, were clearly divided into type and labelled as such. We had many of some, and few of others. It was a fortune worth, either way. I noticed there were not many Biomancy Sources left. It had been a decade since the vault and its contents had been mine, but I remembered we had over a dozen Biomancy Sources. Now there were only two. Had they been lost, stolen, traded? I didn't know.

I took one of our three Necromancy Sources, a small thing no larger than a pebble with two sharp ridges.

On the way out, I asked the guards who had access to the vault. The answers were predictable for the most part: me, Sirileth, Tris, a couple of Sourcerers Sirileth had in her employ, and three of Tris' most trusted comrades. And Josef. I had a feeling I knew where the Biomancy Sources had gone and would need to talk to Josef again and soon.

I made my way down to the gateway Sirileth had created. A useless, if somewhat atheistically pleasing construction. It was functional only when at least one other gateway existed. In the meantime, I could access any rift I knew of with a Portamancy Source. And luckily, I knew of one in Old Picarr, though I will admit I was not looking forward to going back there.

What is it you fear you will find? He's dead.

Ssserakis did not understand. I don't think it could. It was a horror, built differently to us terrans. The Iron Legion was dead, yes. My memories of him weren't. Trauma is a disease you can never be rid of. No matter how many times you treat the symptoms, it will always come back. Like fucking herpes.

You hesitate.

My horror was right. Didn't have to sound so smug about it though. I opened the portal to old Picarr. To the Iron Legion's laboratory underneath the ruins of the Orran Academy of Magic.

It was not as dark as I was expecting. There were torches burning in sconces on the walls. It gave the grand chamber a cosy glow. The iron cages still stood to my right all along the walls. Most were filled with bones from the last lot of sacrifices the Iron Legion made. My memories of that threatened to claw their way up and drag me down into another attack of depression. Not just my memories either. The Iron Legion had funnelled over two hundred lives through me into the Source. I had absorbed memories from each person he killed that day. Glimpses of their lives. A terran family at dinner, laughing. A young girl terrified and fleeing through dark alleyways, shadows chasing her. A man on a boat, floating on a lake, a fishing rod in hand and an air of peace all around him. Memories laden with emotion that wasn't mine. I had long ago sorted through them all, made peace with them, and all the others I contained too. But to have them suddenly clamouring for attention at once was distracting.

Behind me was the hole the Iron Legion had created when he detonated. It was a place of wild magic, a bottomless void. A bolt of lightning shot out of it, arced towards me, struck me in the back. I stumbled from the shock and force of it. It would have killed anyone else, but

not me. I absorbed the Arcmancy, felt it pass through me
and into the Arcmancy Source sitting in my stomach. My
storm flashed stronger, my eyes casting jumping shadows
all before me. That was new. Of course I had absorbed
Arcmancy before, but never like that. Never had I somehow
injected energy back into a Source. I didn't even know it was
possible... except that was exactly what the Iron Legion had
forced me to do to rebirth one of the Djinn.

I had no time to consider it further as a man sauntered
into the cavernous hall from one of the side corridors. He
had a lantern on a stick strapped to his back, dangling over
his head, and carried a stack of books in one hand, and a
metal cylinder in the other. He was humming to himself as
he walked into the hall.

The rift behind me sparked again, the Arcmancy bolt
seeking me out, striking me in the back. I gasped somewhere
between searing pain and debilitating pleasure as the energy
coursed through me into the Source in my stomach.

The man looked up at the flash and his eyes goggled
at me. He dropped the books, they hit the floor, the top one
bouncing open spine up and pages bending. I winced at the
poor treatment of the tomes.

"What are you doing here?" the man shouted, rushing
towards me. "Get away from there, it's dangerous."

I didn't want to move. I wanted the lightning to strike
me again. I wanted to feel that strange sensation again. To
know what it was doing to the Source inside of me.

The little man reached my side, tugged on my arm.
I let him pull me away but turned back to the hole and
watched another arc of lightning streak across it. It felt like
wasted energy when it could have been mine.

"Don't know where you came from, lass, but you

can't go standin' near that hole," the man was saying as he
led me away. "Dangerous things come out of that hole. They
don't bother me much if I don't bother them. Means I hide a
lot of the time, but worth a little risk, eh?"

*What happened, Eska? You took the power but no
memories.*

"I don't know," I said.

"Don't know?" the little man asked. "Don't know
where you came from?" He glanced around, then looked
back towards the hole. "Strange things come out of that
hole." He let go of my hand, took a step back, staring at me.
"Dangerous things."

*I felt like I was pushed out of the way by that energy. I
shouted to you, but you didn't hear me.*

I tried to focus on my situation. "Who are you?"

The little man narrowed his eyes. I realised he had led
me off to the side of the hall. There was a patchy tent set up
here, a small fire before it and a pot dangling above the fire,
the contents bubbling away merrily.

"Who are you?" he asked.

I shrugged, saw no reason to lie. "Eskara Helsene."

He barked out a laugh, looked at my face, let the
laugh die. "Oh, shit."

I grinned at him. "Dangerous things come out of that
hole."

He backed away towards his tent. "Listen, miss, uh,
queen, hmm. I don't want trouble. I'm just here makin'
a livin'. You know, scavengin' the place. You can take
whatever you want, yeah? Just, uh, don't take me."

"Take you?"

He shook his head quickly. "Like you do the
children."

"Oh, that."

I looked away from the man and around the hall. It was a lot more barren than when last I had been there. The shelves on the far wall were empty, all the books and scrolls long gone. Most of the cages stood open, the bones insides scattered as though they had been thoroughly searched. The place still bore the scars of my final battle with the Iron Legion, though. Rent walls, scorched stone, rubble strewn about. My gaze found its way back to the hole in the ground and the occasional spark of lightning.

My shadow rose beside me, earning a squeak of alarm from the little man. *"I do not know what that was, but you should stay away from it, Eska."*

"Scared, Ssserakis?"

"Yes. For you. Do not forget, Eska, the things you carry inside are dead Djinn. Do not forget the last time you fed one of them enough energy."

I could not forget. But this did not feel the same. When the Iron Legion had forced energy through me into the Source, it had not been inside of me. And the energy had been different. It was life energy, taken from the living. This was… I stared at the hole and another spark of lightning. I longed to go closer, to feel it strike me again. It was different. It was not feeding the Source life. It was not fuelling the rebirth of a Djinn. Instead, the Source inside of me felt charged, nearly thrumming with energy it couldn't contain. I remembered the Iron Legion's words to Ssserakis: *Energy can be compressed almost infinitely.* Another puzzle piece floated before me, but it was like trying to pluck a fly from the air, it kept zipping away when I concentrated on it.

I tore my attention away from it and back to the cowering man as he put the bubbling pot and fire between us. "You've been scavenging this place?" I asked him.

"Aye. All fair. All legal. I risk my neck here, sell what I find to folk in New Picarr."

I shrugged. What did I care? This place was nothing but the past.

I spent a few hours strolling through the ruins of old Picarr. It was a desolate corpse of a city, long ago destroyed by battle. Sourceries had clashed here and had ripped buildings apart, slaughtered thousands. I had been here a few times since then. Dodging around magical traps was easy for me, I could feel them tingling my skin, but it was clear many scavengers were still caught by them. I saw a fresh corpse gripped in a stone fist that had risen from the cobbled streets and crushed the poor woman. In a charred wreck of a house, a dark basement smelled of carrion. I heard growls rumbling from within. Ssserakis informed me there were ghouls hiding down in the dark, a pack of them.

I had spent a decade here, learning Sourcery, being moulded into the weapon the Orrans needed. Then I had come back, after its ruination, to absorb my Arcstorm, to wear Vainfold's crown and set half the ruins ablaze once again. And I had come back a second time to face the Iron Legion and free Josef. Old Picarr was a place of dark memories, and drifting ghosts. Except that it wasn't anymore. Tris was right. All the ghosts were gone.

I even swallowed my Necromancy Source, extended the senses it granted me. There were corpses here, some fresh, many nothing but picked clean bones. But there were no ghosts. For over two decades the city had been known as a haunted ruin, ghosts so thick they gathered, swamped people, drifted out into New Picarr. Not anymore. I extended my Necromantic senses as far as I could and still felt no ghosts.

It was confusing, and though most people would probably think it a good thing, I found it alarming. Ghosts did not tend to roam too far away from their corpses, not unless someone like me dragged them away. And though their forms faded over time, they did not vanish entirely unless someone like me unravelled them. I did not think either thing had happened here. They were simply gone.

I had no answers, only questions. I returned to the Iron Legion's lair. The little scavenger greeted me warily, offered me soup. I declined and approached the hole once again.

It sparked as I drew close, but I stayed far enough back that the lightning didn't strike me. It was more than just Arcmancy dancing about the hole. The Sourceries here were wild and unpredictable. Ssserakis tried to drag me back, sensing my desire, but I won that battle of wills and reached out a hand to the rift.

A bolt of Arcmancy shot out, circled my arm, struck me in the chest. Again that rush of pleasure and pain so mingled I couldn't separate them, so intense I wanted to lose myself in the thrill. The gentle touch of a lover finding just the right spot to make my knees buckle and my thoughts melt away. The searing jolt of a paper-thin knife slipped underneath a fingernail and twisted to pull the nail free. All at once. I held onto my senses this time, felt the energy sucked into the Arcmancy Source in my stomach. It fuzzed and vibrated, charged with an energy it couldn't hold. My storm reacted to it, growing stronger, the two sources of Arcmancy feeding off each other in a loop of ever-increasing volatility until I couldn't take it. Couldn't hold it in anymore.

I staggered back away from the hole, flung out my

arm and unleashed a storm of electricity that surged across
the hall and struck the metal cages. Iron smoked and twisted
from the heat and energy as the storm ripped from me.
And then it was gone. The iron bars steamed and sparked,
deformed by the attack.

I searched inside, found my storm still strong, not
empty like it often was after a violent release like that. The
Arcmancy Source hummed inside my stomach, like that
moment of anticipation before a first kiss, but it was no
longer a violent charge that needed dissipating. I had not
given rebirth to a Djinn. But whatever had happened had
been new.

That was dangerous. I felt pushed out of the way again.

Something clicked in my mind, that moment of
inspiration. "I gave birth to a Djinn here," I said.

Yes. And now there are two of them in the world.

"Exactly," I said. "The Rand and Djinn grew weaker
every time two of them were killed. So they probably grew
stronger when two were reborn. Maybe they grew strong
enough."

Strong enough for what?

I laughed, mostly because I knew how bad an idea it
was. "To save the world."

*Last time you met Aerolis… He knows about me. He hates
you for harbouring me.*

It didn't matter. It was the only plan I had. The
only chance we had left to save the world that Sirileth had
broken. It was time to return to Do'shan.

I went to bed that night with a new sense of purpose.
Direction. It would be difficult, but at least all was not yet
lost. I threw up my Sources before settling into bed. The
Necromancy Source hurt on the way up, its edges drawing

blood along with the bile. The Portamancy Source was small and smooth and easy to come up. But then there was the Arcmancy Source. It caught in my throat and I coughed up blood and bile and eventually spat it onto the floor. It glinted a cool blue glow, quickly fading, but that was not what caught my eye. There was a crack in the Source. It had not been there before. I knew this because I also knew that Sources were damned near indestructible.

CHAPTER TWENTY TWO

TRACKING DO'SHAN WAS EASY ENOUGH. AS
soon as I told Sirileth the plan, she made the calculations
and determined Do'shan was flying over southern Isha and
should be nearing the eastern coast. Unlike its sister city,
Do'shan had no chain to drop to anchor it in place. It never
stopped moving, though the Djinn could slow it down or
speed it up by some process I have never understood.

Sirileth was enthusiastic. She saw it as the final chance
to make right what she had done wrong. I was less so. My
trepidations were one thing, but I could feel my horror's
anxiety over the upcoming encounter with the Djinn. They
had made its world, after all, and they were not impressed
with the creatures the Rand had filled that world with.
Ssserakis was old enough to remember the start of the War
Eternal.

There was a rift on southern Isha, located in a tiny

fishing village on the coast. It was also in Tor lands, so I fully expected us to receive a welcome warm enough to melt skin. Hopefully we wouldn't be staying long before we spotted Do'shan. Then it would be up to me to portal us onto the flying city. And then we had to hope the feral pahht that lived there were not as combative as last time I dropped by unexpected. Hope. What a seductive drug it is. Trust to it once and it's so easy to take another hit and another and another.

Tris joined us on our trip down to the Yenheim gateway and he wasn't alone. He had six of his best and most loyal warriors with him. When I asked him why, he pointed out we were going to Tor and would need an escort. I was about to argue, but he also reminded me I might need the backup on Do'shan too. I would still have sent him home, but Sirileth nodded her assent and that was that. It's tough not being queen.

I will admit, I have a problem with not being in charge. Yes, you've probably already noticed. It is a failing of mine, I do not like it when things are out of my control. But I was learning. Never too old to pick up a new skill or drop a bad habit. Sirileth was queen of Yenheim. She was in charge. I was but an advisor. For now.

As Sirileth took a few deep breaths and prepared herself to open a portal halfway across the continent, I noticed Tris and his warriors painting each other's faces. Death seemed to be the theme. It was all blackened skin and white, leering skulls. Some wore paint like snarling pahht, or decaying terran faces with insects crawling out of deadened sockets. The artistry on display was quite magnificent and I was impressed at the same time as being a little repulsed.

Tris wore the face of a simple terran skull, with a

mouth stretched up into an impossibly wide grin. Like a skeleton had clawed its way to life and told a terrible joke it couldn't stop laughing at.

"What are you doing?" I asked him.

Tris grinned at me, the painted skull stretching even further. "Do you like it, Mother? Certainly strikes fear into the hearts of enemies."

Perhaps we should paint your face, Eska.

I rolled my eyes. "I never needed a painted face to make people fear enough to feed you."

Tris frowned at me. It turned the painted skeletal face into a comical thing. "Well, no I suppose you didn't, Mother. But then I am not you and I will take any advantage I can get."

I sighed. "I was talking to Ssserakis."

"Of course you were," Tris said flatly. "We started painting our faces after the people of Tor started calling me Reaper. Figured we might as well play into it."

"Take away an enemy's courage and you also take their will to fight," I said, quoting Belmorose. "Unless they're backed into a corner and then they might fight twice as hard to get free."

Tris shrugged and turned to start painting one of his warrior's faces. "In my experience, most people are more likely to beg for their lives when scared, rather than swing a sword."

I might have pointed out that his experience was far less than mine, but I knew an argument starter when I encountered one. It is the incurable ailment of youth to believe they know more than their elders. While age often wears tracks we can't help but follow, even when there might be a better road.

Sirileth tore open the portal. We stepped across Isha and reappeared in a half-drowned hovel. The brackish water lapped lazily against our knees. The little house had a distinct slant to it, and there was more hole than roof above us. Thin, reedy grasses clogged the ground underfoot, breaking free of the water in an attempt to find sunlight that was hidden from them. They wilted then, forming a swaying mat on top of the slosh. And the insects... bitey little fuckers everywhere, nipping at skin and dining on blood. I had but one consolation and that was that every single insect that bit me, died. It is a peculiarity of Sourcerers, something to do with our blood and the magic that runs through it. I think that was when the last puzzle piece appeared to me, and they just slotted into place so easily.

We emerged from that hovel into a dying village. It was small: a few dozen homes at best, one rickety tavern, a smithy with the forge gone cold. The village had flooded recently, more than once by the looks of it, and the ground was muddy and squishy underfoot. The ocean, no more than a hundred paces away, was a turbulent, roiling monster. It thrashed and raged, rushed in towards the land, took bites of the earth, retreated to gather before attacking again. I saw the remains of a dock, now nothing more than a few wooden posts valiantly thrusting out of the thrashing waves. There were boats on the water, fisherman braving the anger to cast nets into the madness. If they caught anything, I did not see it, but they tried. How else were they supposed to feed their families?

We squelched our way to the centre of the village unmolested. I saw a few pairs of eyes peering out of windows, but shutters were quickly closed, children pulled away. They probably thought we were here to cause trouble.

Fear flooded the village as surely as the ocean had.

"Ssserakis," I said, moving away from the others. "We need to talk."

Tris and his warriors skulked the village, peering in through shutters, poking through the dead smithy. The fear rising from the place grew thick as porridge.

What is it, Eska?

I tried to decide how to explain. "I have a plan. A way to fight Norvet Meruun."

Finally.

"The Iron Legion told you power could be compressed almost infinitely."

I remember. My horror's words were laced with bitterness. *Being forced so small was painful. Energy can be compressed, but it demands to be free. It hurts. And I cannot hold much of it in your world. It is constantly burned from me by this hateful light.*

Given how dark Ovaeris was all the time, I almost found it funny. "Can you store it? The energy you take from fear. Can you push it into a Source?"

Ssserakis was silent as it considered. *I do not know.* Not surprising, it had never been tried before. But I knew energy could be directed into a Source. *When you absorbed that magic before, it could not be contained, Eska. It burst out of you.*

I nodded. "I know, but I think that was different. I was absorbing Arcmancy into an Arcmancy Source, and it was reacting with my storm, creating a feedback loop of power sparking off itself. Your energy is different, Ssserakis. If you can store it in a Source and pull it out at will. You can store up the power we need to fight Norvet Meruun."

But Josef said when power is drawn from a Source, bits of the magic enter your blood, Eska. That is why you reject the

Sources. If this works, it will kill you.

I reached into my pouch and pulled out a Necromancy Source. Such a small thing, holding so much power. "Josef also said that he no longer rejects Biomancy, and that I will not reject Necromancy." I popped the Source in my mouth and swallowed hard. "Try it."

Ssserakis never stopped drinking in fear. As long as there were people or animals nearby capable of being scared, my horror sensed it and fed upon it. This little village was rife; a stagnant, watery fear. My horror sucked it in and funnelled it into the Necromancy Source. I half expected to feel the same pleasure and pain as before, when the wild magic had struck me, but there was nothing. No pleasure, no pain, no fear. Nothing.

It works! Ssserakis shouted. *I can fill the Source, but it is so vast and the energy I can squeeze into it so small.* Strength surged into me then, making me stand straighter. I felt the restlessness of it, the need to move, to run, to do... something.

I can draw it out again, too. A moment of elation from my horror. Then the strength left me and I felt a little dizzy, stumbled on the spot and almost fell. It took a few moments for that dizziness to clear.

It is too little, Eska. There is not enough here. A hundred times as much would be too little. If I had my minions, I could feed well, fill this coffin and more besides. But they are gone. The enemy has taken them, consumed them or controlled them. It works, Eska, but it is not enough.

"Then we need to feed you more," I said. Already, I knew how. And I knew what it would cost me.

You will stop denying me then?

"Yes," I said. I had spent so long trying to hide from

it, my reputation. Trying to soften it. Trying to be something else. No more. It was time to be the Corpse Queen. Time to make the world fear me.

The boats had reached the shore, the men and women fishing them clearly having realised there were armed soldiers in their village. They rushed up the muddy banks to face us, oars in hand as if such paltry weapons could chase us away.

A door to my right banged open and an old woman brandishing a solid, iron cooking pot, barrelled her way out, taking a wild swing at one of Tris' warriors. "Get out of here. We don't want trouble, but we'll give it ya." I saw a small child behind her, clinging to her apron, eyes wide, fear oddly tasteless.

The young creatures are often so. It takes time for taste to develop.

Scaring old women, people struggling to survive, children. Was this how I was going to start?

Yes! They are minions, Eska. They exist to feed us.

I swallowed my disgust and stalked towards the old woman. She stepped forward very bravely. I'll give her that. She swung her pan at me and I blocked with my shadowy claw, wrenched it from her hands, flung it away. My eyes flashed and she quailed. Ssserakis fed.

"Get away from them," one of the returning fisherman shouted. He ran forwards, oar raised. Tris intercepted him, knocked the oar away, pushed the man into the mud. Others moved to defend him, but Tris' warriors were there, disarming them all. Some were hurt, but none seriously.

Good. Pain is good, Eska. Not too much, just enough to let them know that more is to come.

"I know," I hissed through clenched teeth. I
remembered all too well the lessons of pain taught to me by
the Terrelan emperor.

I grabbed the old woman by her apron, dragged her
out into the muddy street, threw her to the ground. Then
I stalked into the building and dragged the child out too,
threw him down next to the woman. "Round them all up," I
shouted to Tris' warriors. "Everyone in the village."

The fear was an intoxicating aroma. Watery, salty,
thin. We drank it in, but it was not enough. It didn't fill the
Source in my stomach. It was barely a meal for Ssserakis. My
horror was still perched on the edge of starvation.

Sirileth watched me, frowning, her darklight stare
accusing. I ignored it.

In short order, Tris' warriors had been through all
the rickety buildings, disarmed all the villagers, corralled
them in the centre of the village. I prowled around them, my
shadowy hood up, my eyes flashing. Ssserakis fed on them
and their terror and needed more.

I drew on my Pyromancy Source, lit my hand with
green flames that sputtered and sizzled with the light rain.
"Is this all of you?" I asked, forced a savage smile onto my
face. "If there is anyone else, I suggest you tell them to get
out here." I pointed my flaming hand at the nearest building.

One of the men shouted, screamed, spat insults at me.
He was terrified. Eventually he called out a name. A young
boy came running from the building, streaking past me,
before launching himself into the man's arms. I shot flames
from my hand and set the building alight.

"Burn it all down." I gave the order, but it didn't feel
like me. I pushed down my disgust and anger and did what
I needed to. Sirileth took a step toward me. I gave her a brief

shake of my head. She relented, but I knew she hated what I was doing. She'd understand. Once I explained it to her, she'd understand. She had to.

The people in the village cried, insulted, begged. Some tried to resist, were quickly knocked down. I stood over them, feeding on their fear as their homes burned. Ssserakis funnelled power into the Source, informed me it was not enough. Not nearly enough. We needed more. So much more.

"Run back to Tor," I shouted once all the houses were burning. They'd be safer in Tor anyway, more likely to find food and better shelter.

Such weak justifications for evil.

"Tell them the Corpse Queen has not forgotten them." Ssserakis flared my shadow, wings bursting from my back. "Tell them I'll be coming for them soon."

We let them go then, kicked them into fleeing. Some stopped, looked back, but eventually they all ran from the village. I took to the skies, wings flapping lazily, hovering above the fires, lit well enough that every time the villagers looked back, they saw me there.

Once the villagers were out of sight, I floated back down and staggered the moment I hit the ground. I felt wretched. Sirileth came to me then, but I waved her away. I needed time. Only the strength Ssserakis fed me kept me upright.

You cannot do this every time, Eska. If this is to work, I need to store the power, not feed it back to you.

I nodded, unable to form the words to agree. The villagers would carry word of this back to Tor, spreading the rumours everywhere they went. I consoled myself with the knowledge that their terror would save them all. I stared into the flames of the building I had lit on fire and considered throwing myself to them.

"It's time, Mother," Sirileth said, laying a hand on my shoulder.

I startled to realise how much time had passed. The sun had set, casting us in sheer darkness. Do'shan had arrived. The shadow of the great flying mountain was an ominous presence above, an odd shift in the atmosphere. The scale of Ro'shan and Do'shan is nothing short of mind boggling. They dominate the sky when they pass, bizarrely soundless as they soar above.

I ripped open a portal. So great was the distance, almost straight up, it was a struggle just to hold it open, so I hurried through. Sirileth and Tris were a step behind me, his painted soldiers following quickly. We were all smudged with mud and ash, and there was a grimness about us.

We emerged on the edge of Do'shan just where the outskirts of the city gave way to dead, open land. A killing zone where Source weaponry could be turned on any invaders. Last time I had assaulted the flying city that's exactly what had happened. Feral pahht attacked us. This time there was nothing. No sizzling bolts of lightning came our way, nor discs of metal propelled to frightening speed. No ferals came charging at us with claws and teeth. A freezing wind howled through the streets of Do'shan's ruins and it was the only noise save for Tris' warriors' chattering teeth and curses about the cold.

"Your old stories didn't do this place justice, Mother," Sirileth said as we started in towards the city. The Djinn would be at the centre of it, I was sure. Where once there had been a sphere of utter darkness, now there stood a great tower. We could see the top of the tower even from so far out, and the pinnacle shone with a blinding light like some flying lighthouse. I could not divine its purpose, but then our gods are quite mad so purpose and reason might not enter into it.

I snorted. "Last time I came here, we were under attack

before we set foot on land." I was still wary of ambush, keeping my hands free to create a kinetic shield at a moment's notice.

Tris caught up with us, walking on my other side. "I remember those stories. You were always so morose when talking about this place."

I glanced at my son. "Well, Silva's grave sits at the base of that big stone phallus, so this place brings back some ill memories. Where have all the ferals gone?"

"Underground, maybe?" Sirileth asked. "I mean, you always said there was an extensive network of tunnels and caverns."

There is no one here, Eska. No fear rises through the rock. This place is as barren as it looks.

We walked through empty streets seeing signs of recent habitation. An overturned wheelbarrow here, a broken cup there, little bones not yet bleached by the sun. But there was no sign of life. We went farther, making our way to the centre, always towards that great fucking tower, the light seeming to pull us in.

We reached the base of that tower without incident. I took but a moment to look towards Silva's grave. There was nothing there but a slight scorching of the stonework that had never been scoured away. The last remnants of the woman I loved. Strange that even after two decades, I still felt tears stinging my eyes. Still wished I would see her ghost hovering over her body so I could get one last look at her. I'd have given anything to see her again. But she was gone, and I had nothing but old memories of her so worn by age they were as much fiction as history. Like an old book I had read so many times, the ink was smudged, and some pages missing.

"Now what?" Sirileth asked. She approached the tower, placed a hand against the rock. "It's solid stone," she said. "Warm though, despite the chill."

Tris' soldiers had spread out, keeping themselves in pairs. They were searching the area. It had been a coliseum before Aerolis raised his tower in its centre.

"Now…" I said, waving both my children over towards me. "Now we get the attention of a couple of arrogant gods." I stepped forward, stared towards the tower so high up I couldn't even see the top. I took a deep breath and forced down my anxiety. Three times I had made a deal with Aerolis, and three times the Djinn got the better of me. Some lessons I never learn.

"Aerolis," I shouted. "The Changing. Lord of Do'shan. Oh mighty god." It was always best to lead with a flattering of egos. "Show yourself, Djinn. Or I will tear down your stupid fucking tower."

The wind howled around us. The earth rumbled beneath our feet. Lightning sparked and dust rose to float in the air. Yes, we had their attention now.

CHAPTER TWENTY THREE

STONE SHATTERED BENEATH ME AND I
stumbled back out of the way just as a dense collection of
boulders shot up to hang in the air. They twisted and turned,
spinning, connected by a translucent haze. Aerolis had come.

"You dare return here, terran?" the god roared at me.

Ssserakis retreated inside, making itself small. *It will
kill us, Eska.* My horror had always been scared of the gods. It
was instinctive and a good survival trait. Honestly, I shared
its fear, but I've always been far too stubborn for my own
good.

"Your bluster never scared me off before, Aerolis.
What makes you think now would be different?"

The stones floated closer, spinning faster. "I can sense
the Rand's creature inside of you." Wind gusted, whipping
at my shadowy cloak. The Djinn extended a rocky protrusion
towards me. Damn me, but I started trembling. We'll call it

adrenaline rather than fear. I let my eyes flash and my storm crackle. I flexed my claw, ready for a fight.

I wanted it. I had tested myself against Aerolis once before and the Djinn had barely felt it. So much had happened since then. I was both stronger and weaker. I wanted to test myself. I wanted to throw everything I had at this creature and see how much I could tear from it before it killed me.

Stop it, Eska. This self-destructive streak of yours will get us all killed. Our daughter will die with us.

It took a lot of effort to draw back from that fight. I let my storm dissipate, lowered my eyes, staggered back a step. A wave of weary depression threatened me. I could feel it rising, another attack incoming, but I forced it away. I couldn't allow that right now. I had to…

Suddenly I couldn't find the effort to fight it. It was all just too much. Too much work. Too much to struggle against. It was a shit time for an attack, but then aren't they all.

I collapsed. Except I didn't. I tried. I let go, let myself fall, but my body stayed upright. Ssserakis, despite its fear of the Djinn, rushed in to assume control of my body. It was a surprise, but I couldn't bring myself to care. It didn't matter. Not in the end. Nothing mattered. I just didn't have the energy or will to care.

Get over this quickly, Eska. I can keep you standing, move your body about like a puppet, but I cannot pretend to be you. The words sounded so far away, screamed across an endless abyss.

Aerolis was shouting something, the rumble filling the air, the grating of rock, the screaming of wind. And yet the god still had not struck me down. What more did I have to do? What other blasphemy could I level at it to make it kill me?

Sirileth stepped forward, striding past me to face Aerolis. "Mighty Djinn," she shouted over the raging of his winds. "My name is Sirileth Helsene."

Aerolis' attention shifted. It is not wise to come to the attention of the gods, but Sirileth took it upon herself without hesitation. I should have saved her from that. I should be the one to put myself in harm's way.

Yes, you should. Now stop wallowing in this false exhaustion and be you again.

How little my horror understood. This was me. This wearied shell that wished things to end. It is so hard to explain. It felt like drowning. Like a current pulling me under, sucking me down to the depths, but when the waters closed over me, it was not panic or pain I felt, but rightness. I was too tired to struggle, too numb to feel anything but exhaustion and the slightest hint of relief that I didn't have to fight anymore.

"You smell of her, terran," Aerolis rumbled, the stones forming its body twisting.

Sirileth bowed her head respectfully. "She is my mother."

"Then you will suffer her punishment as well."

All such self-important bluster. Aerolis didn't want to punish me or Sirileth. He just wanted us to show him respect.

Sirileth glanced back at me. It was like seeing her through a dirty window, like my eyes were not my own. She turned back to the Djinn.

"Aerolis, the Changing," Sirileth said. She knelt on one knee before the Djinn. "I've come here seeking your aid. We cannot save the world without you."

The winds calmed a little, the rumbling beneath us grew fainter, the spinning of Aerolis' rocks slowed. "At least this one shows some respect."

A vortex of twisting purple smoke drifted down from above, lightning flashing within its depths. All around the creature time was distorted, fractured. This was Terthis, the Never. I remembered the Djinn because I had given birth to it. Through me, the Iron Legion had funnelled enough terran life force to bring it back from its crystal coffin.

"Foolish terran," Terthis said, its voice like cracking ice. "There is no threat. What you call end is nothing but change."

Aerolis shifted, the rocks falling away, and became a blur of golden light. "I have told you, brother, these creatures are liminal beings. They do not understand the passage of time and see only what is important to the weak flesh they inhabit."

Terthis swirled for a few moments, energy flashing in its core. "A failing of the Rand. Our sisters should have enlightened their chosen pets."

A part of me bristled at that. I did not like being called a pet. I tried to ignore that part of me, but I could not. It snagged me, wrapped around me, anchored me to my flesh.

Yes, Eska. Come back.

And I did. Not by choice. Not really. I was dragged back, thrust back into my flesh and given control once more. Ssserakis retreated a little but flooded me with its strength to keep me standing. I gasped, struggling to catch my breath.

Sirileth stood, looked between the two Djinn. "But Ovaeris is tearing itself apart," she said. "I mean, you can see it. You must see it. Look at the sky. The sun, I mean, it's gone."

"The sun is not gone," Terthis crackled. "See." The Djinn sparked, a thread of light streaking towards the sky. Like a cup of water with oil dropped into it, the clouds peeled away to reveal the darkness of night, stars glittering, Lokar's cracked flesh shining blue upon us. "Oh, it's night. Still, the sun is not gone. If it were, you would not be able to see our prison." The Djinn settled a little, the swirling vortex of smoke slowing. Above, the clouds rushed in once again to cover the sky and blot out the stars. Such power they showed and made it seem like nothing.

"But it is ending," I said, finding my voice croaky and strange. "For us."

Aerolis turned to me again, his golden light searing around the edges. "Such drama from one so brief it cannot begin to understand. Change is not end. It is beginning."

"We can't survive this change," I said, still struggling to catch my breath. "We'll die."

"Many of you, yes," Aerolis said. "Perhaps most. Not all."

Terthis drifted closer. "And those who survive will be better equipped to the new world."

"But it doesn't it have to be like that," Sirileth said quickly. "You can change it back. Make the world how it was. You just proved it."

"Why would we?" Aerolis asked.

"Because you are a god." I licked my lips, coughed, continued. "You're our gods. Do not try to deny you like being worshipped as such." I thought I saw a way through the argument now. "The Rand took that from you once." I focused on Aerolis. "Mezula trapped you here, turned the world against you. And now everyone worships her, worships the Rand. And they all fear you."

"Never make a deal with a Djinn," Sirileth said, picking up the argument. "That's what they say. They have cast you as villains. Mezula collects your trapped brothers, torments them."

Aerolis flared blinding bright for a moment. "What do you hope to accomplish here, terrans?"

"Don't you understand?" Sirileth asked. "I mean, I thought it was obvious. The Rand have spent hundreds of years squashing out worship of you, while drawing it to themselves. But here, now, you have the opportunity to undo it all in one great act. The Rand can't save us. Only you can. Aerolis, Terthis." She lowered to one knee and bent her head. "You are gods and should be worshipped as such. Save us all. Please. I beg you."

Again Aerolis' light flared and I had the feeling it was shining at me. He was watching me. I warred with myself for a moment. Lost. Stiffly, I went down on a knee next to my daughter. I even bowed my head. "Please." I had to force that word out and I still hate myself for it.

Aerolis flashed, Terthis twisted.

"It would be gratifying to see our sisters brought low," Terthis crackled.

Aerolis blinked out and a huge drop of water pooled then rose into the space he inhabited. "By the very creatures they created, no less."

"Their own pets hating them and worshipping us."

The two Djinn orbited each other and I had a feeling they were communicating beyond my perception.

I do not like this, Eska. They cannot be trusted.

I looked at Sirileth, she kept her head bowed, eyes screwed shut.

"No," Aerolis announced, his voice like air bubbles

popping on water's surface.

Terthis spun a little faster, the light fracturing around it. "It will be just as satisfying to watch all their pets die."

Aerolis bubbled again, more drops of water flowing upwards to inflate his size. "A fitting punishment for their corruption of our dream."

Fuckers! It was still about their stupid bloody war. Thousands of years, countless deaths, and still they held a grudge for Sevorai.

"But..." Sirileth shot to her feet. "You... I mean..." I saw her grit her teeth. "I sent the Maker back to its realm. Closed it off. I saved you. Help me."

Both Djinn were silent for a moment. Then Aerolis bubbled again. "No."

Sirileth clenched her hands into fists, squeezed her eyes shut. The dirt trembled around her. "Please," she ground the word out, begging.

Tris stepped forward beside me, clapped his hands loudly to gain attention. "How about a game?" he said in that jovial tone of his. "I've heard the stories and in them you Djinn always love a game. A riddle. A challenge. That's how it always goes, no? *Face these challenges and we'll grant you a boon.*" I glanced at him and he grinned back at me. "How about it? Let's wager for the fate of the world. What could be more fun?"

Aerolis bubbled again, floated towards Terthis. The two orbited each other more energetically than before. Sirileth joined Tris and me, looking pained. I reached out, gave her hand a squeeze.

Aerolis splashed apart, his water showering the ground. A moment later his rocks rose into the air again, spinning excitedly. "We accept. Our terms are this, terrans."

Terthis crackled. "Three challenges, one for each of you, each designed to test the limits of your strengths."

Aerolis rumbled. "And the depths of your weaknesses."

"At any time you can forfeit."

"But should you fail, all you have lost is forfeit, too."

Aerolis floated towards me. One of the rocks twisted my way, floated there like a face, mocking. "Do you accept?"

I glanced first at Sirileth and then at Tris, both nodded to me. "We accept." And with those two words, I damned us all.

CHAPTER TWENTY FOUR

AEROLIS WAS THE FIRST TO RESPOND. THE Djinn burst apart, rocks falling to the floor and then reassembled itself into a new configuration of floating madness. "We shall start right away. For you, a puzzle." It extended a rocky limb to Sirileth and chips of stone, pebbles, rocks flew up from the floor, colliding with each other, splintering, cracking, reshaping themselves until the Djinn held a box formed of stone. It dropped the box into Sirileth's hands and she stumbled from the weight of it.

"A puzzle?" she asked.

"Open it," Aerolis rumbled energetically. "That is all you need to do. Just open the box."

Sirileth glanced at me, then smiled. She loved puzzles and I could already see her eager to get to it. She gave me a nod, then retreated a few steps and sank down cross-legged, the box in her lap. She immediately started turning it over in her hands, inspecting every side, every edge, every dimple and groove. I trusted she would figure it out and soon. No puzzle had ever eluded her for long. She was grinning, I noticed. Absorbed in her challenge.

Do not trust them, Eska. They are Djinn. Whatever game they are playing, we are all in danger. The fear sent a bolt through me. It rang too true and already I wondered what was behind the little puzzle they had given to my daughter.

"Next we come to you," Terthis crackled as he floated up to Tris. The Djinn spun before my son for a few moments, then away again. Time distorted around it and I saw flashes of a hundred different scenes, all splashed with blood. "A warrior," the Djinn said. "A leader. Such pride in command."

Tris turned to me, shrugged.

"A fight then," Terthis said. "To test your skills and resolve."

"Sounds fun," Tris said. He rolled his shoulders, held out a hand, and formed a Sourceblade scythe in it, gave it a spin for effect.

"Be careful, Tris," I said quickly. "You don't know these creatures."

"I'll be fine, Mother," Tris said. "Watch. You'll see how strong I've gotten."

Terthis crackled. "But we will need something for you to fight. How fortunate." A bolt of fractured light shot from the Djinn, zigzagging across the old coliseum until it struck one of Tris' warriors in the head. The man was knocked off his feet, slumped against the stone wall at his back. Then he jerked upright like a puppet with its strings pulled. He shook his head as if to clear cobwebs from his eyes.

"Boss?" the man said. He jerked forward, arms snapping out to the side as he moved, legs jittering. "What...

what... what's going on?"

"These creatures are strange," Terthis said, turning to
Aerolis. "They are so uncoordinated."

"Yes, brother," Aerolis rumbled. "Primitive things, all
pumps and pulleys."

"Ahh, you're right," Terthis crackled. "I'm getting the
hang of it now."

The puppeted soldier stopped jerking as he walked.
His eyes were wide and fear drenched him. It tasted like
sour ale. "Boss? Boss, I can't stop myself." He reached down,
drew his sword from its sheathe.

"Primitive constructs," Terthis said. "Primitive
weapons."

"They will do," Aerolis rumbled. "They take so little
to end."

"Is one enough, do you think?" Terthis asked.

Aerolis was silent for a moment. "Why not take them
all?"

"An excellent idea, brother." Five more bolts of
fractured light shot from Terthis, each one seeking out one
of Tris' warriors, striking them, controlling them. They all
staggered forward, each of them shouting that they couldn't
control themselves, begging to be set free.

"Stop this!" Tris roared. He let go of his scythe and it
popped, the energy dissipating. "Let them go, Djinn. I'll fight
you. Or some constructs. Or anything, but not them. Let my
people go."

"Too late," Terthis said. "You have already agreed to
the terms."

Tris shouted, threw a kinetic blast at the Djinn. It
breezed through Terthis to no effect.

I made to join Tris, but Aerolis rumbled towards me,

blocking me. "Their challenges are their own, terran. If you try to help, the terms are forfeit."

I glared daggers at the Djinn, then leaned to the side to watch my son in his struggles.

The first of Tris' warriors, a brawny man with a thrice broke nose, reached Tris. "I can't stop it, Boss." He swung his sword wildly. It was clear, though the Djinn was controlling him, it could not mimic any skill with a blade the man had. Tris ducked the sword's arc, rose into an uppercut that thundered into the man's gut. Broken Nose sputtered, vomited down his chin. He was clearly in pain, but it didn't affect the control the Djinn had on him. He lurched forward, wrapping meaty arms around Tris and bearing them both down to the ground.

Another of Tris' warriors, a woman with a half-shaved head, staggered forward on jerky limbs, a spear in her hand. She raised the weapon and stabbed down. Tris threw Broken Nose aside and rolled away, the spear breaking on the dirt where his head had been. He leapt to his feet, not seeing the man behind him with his sword raised.

"Dodge!" the man behind him shouted.

Tris flung himself to the side as the blade sliced the air. He had to fight back. All six of his soldiers were closing in on him, jerky movements making them seem nightmarish. Some begged, others shouted, clearly trying to wrench control back to themselves. Pointless. They were in the grasp of a callous god.

I tore my gaze away, glanced back to Sirileth. She was absorbed by the puzzle box, turning it over in her hands, twisting bits, pulling others, moving stones about into new configurations. She didn't even look up at her brother's struggle.

"Sirileth," I said.

She raised her head as if to look at me but kept her darklight stare fixed to the puzzle box, still moving bits of it about. She mumbled something I couldn't make out, then bent her head to her task once more.

We have to stop this, Eska. You know these creatures. They will destroy us.

"How?"

Aerolis rumbled dangerously in front of me. "You dare speak to your abomination before us?"

I didn't bother answering the arsehole.

Tris had a kinetic bubble up around him, weathering a storm of attacks as his warriors beat upon it with sword, spear, rock, or fist. He shouted, threw his arms out, released a wave of kinetic force that knocked them all away. Normally it would have at least dazed them, but they all lurched upright as one, and launched into a jerking run towards him.

Tris ran at Broken Nose, slid underneath his sword swing, pulled the warrior's legs out from under him. Broken Nose let out an *oof*, and then congratulated Tris on the move. Tris slapped the ground with an open palm and the dirt went liquid for a moment. Broken Nose sank into it up to his waist, then the ground hardened again.

Shaved Head came at Tris from the side, broken spear stabbing at his chest. Tris spun around the haft, placed both hands against her chest, released a burst of kinetic energy that sent her tumbling fifty feet away across the old coliseum. Two more of his warriors reached him, both with swords, one from each side. Tris stepped in to meet the attack on his left, knocked the blade aside with a flat hand, flung an elbow into the woman's face, kicked her legs out from under her. Then he launched himself at the man on his other side, spun away from the sword stroke, grabbed his wrists, and twisted. The man shouted, let go his sword. Tris flung the sword away, pivoted around, still holding the man's arms, and launched him in the other direction.

Two more of his warriors reached him, apologising even as they tried to carve him up. Tris created a kinetic shield in one hand and warded off blows as he gave ground before them. Over the other side of the coliseum, Shaved Head stood from where she had landed. One arm was twisted, clearly broken, and her head lolled on her shoulders. She was unconscious and yet still under the Djinn's control.

"Tris," I shouted. "They won't stop coming. Even unconscious and broken, they won't stop."

My son spared me a glance, shook his head, screamed. He released his kinetic shield in a wave of force that knocked his attackers down. Broken Nose had already clawed his way out of the dirt, hands bloody from the effort. He joined another two of Tris' warriors and stalked forward, movements jerky.

"It's alright, boss," Broken Nose said. "We knew what we were signing up for. If it saves the world, it's worth it. Do it."

I had a sudden moment of clarity. I felt like I had been here before. Because I had. I had been here and I had been in Tris' exact situation.

I tore my attention from my son's struggle and levelled a flashing stare at Aerolis. "Does this amuse you, Djinn? Putting my son in my place."

Aerolis twisted before me, rocks spinning. "Yes."

I had been here. I had fought Silva here, killed her

because I could find no other way out. And now the Djinn
was putting my son in the same position because of it.
Because of me.

"Stop this, Aerolis," I hissed. "Just tell me what you
want from me."

Terthis spun closer, still effortlessly controlling Tris'
warriors even as it crowded me. "It believes this situation is
about her?"

Aerolis rumbled. "This terran is arrogant, brother, I
have dealt with it before."

"Please, Aerolis," I begged. I fucking hate begging,
especially to our useless cuntish gods, but I did it anyway.
"Stop this."

Aerolis regarded me for a few moments, rocks
spinning like leaves caught in a current. "Your turn will
come soon enough, terran."

Tris screamed again; raw anguish torn from deep
within. He held out a hand, formed a scythe, and cut Broken
Nose in half with a single slice. The battle, if you could call
it that, ended so quickly. Even had his warriors been in
control, I don't think they could have stood against my son,
but puppeted by Terthis, they were but wheat before him.
But then, that was the whole point. It was never meant to
be a challenge of strength or skill, never meant to be a fight
Tris couldn't win. It wasn't about the fight. It was about the
sacrifice. About his resolve.

What else will these creatures take, Eska?

My son, surrounded by the dismembered corpses of
his warriors, his friends, let his blade puff away. He sank
to his knees amidst the slaughter. He wept, buried his head
in his hands, screamed, sobbed. I should have gone to him,
given what scant comfort I could, but Ssserakis' words

echoed inside of me, igniting a new fear. What else would the Djinn take from me?

I spun about to see Sirileth still playing with the puzzle box. Her mouth hung open, eyes glazed over. She gave a final twist to one of the sections, and the box folded open like a flower opening to the sun. It fell from her limp hands, clattering against the ground. My daughter didn't move. She just stared, jaw slack, arms limp by her side. I ran to her, waved a hand before her face, shook her shoulders. She didn't move, didn't respond, didn't even blink. I shouted her name. No response. Slapped her cheek. Nothing. It was as if she were simply gone.

I rounded on the Djinn. They both hovered nearby. "What have you done to her?"

Aerolis rumbled closer to me. "An interesting puzzle isn't it, terran. Simple to solve for one as methodical as she, but the only way to open it, is to give yourself to it." The Djinn extended a rocky limb and the opened box lifted from the ground, floated towards it. I made a snatch for the box but an invisible force shunted me aside. "Her mind is ours now."

"Give it back," I snarled. "Give her back."

Aerolis floated for a few moments in silence. "No."

Tris staggered to his feet, stumbled a few steps away from the carnage he had wrought, looked down at the blood on his hands. He threw up. Sirileth sat, drooling and mindless behind me. And our arsehole gods, a floating rockslide, and a tempest of time, somehow managed to look smug about it. Oh, how I fucking hate them!

Terthis sparked as it drifted closer to me. "Would you like to know your challenge now, terran? We designed it just for you."

Careful, Eska. There is more planning to this than we realised. There was distress in my horror's voice. I could feel Ssserakis' fear as an echo of my own. Not fear for itself anymore, but for Sirileth. For what had been done to her.

"What do you want from me?" I bit off each word, barely able to control myself. I wanted to attack them, to tear them apart, to expend every bit of myself and Ssserakis and see exactly how much it took to kill a god. But I also knew it would be pointless. I tried it once before and failed. Even if I managed it, it wouldn't save Ovaeris. Wouldn't bring back Tris' fallen comrades. Wouldn't give my daughter her mind back. I had no choice, but to do whatever the Djinn wanted.

Aerolis twisted. "Your challenge, terran, is negotiation."

"What do we want?" Terthis crackled. "What can you offer us to secure our cooperation?"

Fuck! Negotiation and diplomacy, never exactly my strongest skills. No. They were Silva's, and she had never managed to teach me. I was too hasty, too direct, too honest, never able to hide what I wanted, nor divine what others desired from their games. What did the Djinn want from me? What did I have to offer? They were gods, could have anything they wanted. I was a mortal, with nothing to offer but myself. And suddenly it seemed obvious.

"My life," I said. "You hate me, want to kill me. Do it. Take my life and…"

Aerolis rumbled. "If we wanted to kill you, terran, you would be dead."

It is not you they want, Eska.

"You want Ssserakis?" I asked. Could I give up my horror to save the world? Ignoring the fact that separating us would still kill me, I was not sure I could sacrifice Ssserakis to these creatures any more than I could agree to give them Tris or Hardt or Kento. Ssserakis was my family, a part of me. And I would protect it with everything I had.

Terthis floated closer, sparking, time fracturing all around it. "If we wanted your abomination, we would rip it from you."

"Then what?" I asked. "If my life is already yours to take, what more can I offer? What do you want?"

They could take anything they wanted from me without consent. They could create anything they wanted with a gesture. They were Djinn. The only thing they couldn't make was life, but they had already proved that they could control it. They puppeted Tris' warriors about like marionettes, all while they begged and pleaded to be released, to be spared.

They can control bodies, but not minds.

I glanced back at Sirileth, sitting legs splayed, arms limp, mouth open and drooling, eyes vacant. They took my daughter's mind, trapped it in a box. Held it. But could not control it. That was it, I was sure. What did they want from me? What could they not take from me? Not my body or my life or my mind. Something they couldn't touch. Knowledge, memories. Something.

Ssserakis realised it at the same time I did. *You cannot give it to them.*

It was a secret I had sworn to take to my grave. And I would. I would. If only my life had been at stake, I would. But it wouldn't just be my grave. It would be Sirileth's and Tris', Kento's and Esem's. It would be everyone's grave.

The funny thing about choosing the lesser of two evils; it's still evil, and still enough to damn you.

"You want to know how the Iron Legion did it," I

said. "You want to know how he brought Terthis back to life." There were only three of us left who knew the truth; Josef, Ssserakis, and me. A truth that might break the world all over again, even as it saved it.

You cannot, Eska. You would be giving the Rand and Djinn back their power. With each death, they grew weaker. With each rebirth, they grow stronger again. This war of theirs will continue as long as one of them lives. If you give them this secret, they can bring themselves back as many times as they like.

Ssserakis was right. And my horror did not even consider the cost. Over four hundred terran lives every time two of them were resurrected. We would be nothing but fuel to them, fuel to the fires of the War Eternal.

"I can't."

Terthis crackled. "Then you fail your challenge, and all your children have sacrificed is forfeit."

I looked to Tris. My son stood amidst the bodies of his friends, splashed with their blood, eyes red with grief. I feared for his sanity. I looked to Sirileth. My daughter was gone. Her mind, everything that was her, sacrificed to this fucking game the gods played. I couldn't let their sacrifices be in vain.

They planned this from the start.

I laughed, but there was nothing but bitter edges to it. "You said I was arrogant to think this was all about me. But it was, wasn't it? From the beginning. All of this was to force me to tell you how to bring yourselves back from the dead. Fuck you, Aerolis. Fuck you!

"I'll do it. I will tell you. But what you offer is not enough."

Aerolis rumbled. "Not enough? We offer to fix your world, make it liveable again. How is that not enough?"

"Give my daughter back her mind," I hissed.

Terthis crackled. "But it was part of the payment. Her challenge. Her sacrifice."

Aerolis' stones fell away, and a gust of wind surged into the coliseum, swirling about in a sand timer shaped vortex. "We did say this was a negotiation, brother. A compromise, then."

Compromise is nothing but a pleasant word for when someone has you so fucked you have no choice but to give them whatever they want.

"Acceptable," Terthis said. "Your daughter's mind. We will restore your world to liveable conditions again. Now tell us, terran. How can we bring our brothers back to life?"

"Still not enough," I growled at the gods. "I need to borrow your flying city, too."

CHAPTER
TWENTY FIVE

THE AUGURIES. THE PROPHECY. IF TAMURA
hadn't already told me they were shit, I think I might have
guessed it then. I was supposedly meant to end the War
Eternal. Instead, I had just assured that it would trundle
on long past the death of both worlds. I am nothing if not
contrary to expectation.

Sirileth came round slowly, blinking groggy eyes,
unsteady on her feet. She couldn't remember anything after
sitting down with that damnable box. I told her what the
Djinn had done to her, what they had forced Tris to do, and
what I had given them in return for their help. I think she
grasped what it had cost right away.

Aerolis and Terthis fled Do'shan immediately, but
they would be back. They had assured me the city would be
where I needed it and when. As they streaked across the sky,
rain fell heavily on the coast of Isha, and I could see it was

black with dust and detritus. Bastards, they might be, but the Djinn were true to their word. Already they were working to undo as much of the devastation as they could. It would not be a quick or easy transition, and I feared there was much that would never go back to the way it was, but like a shift in the wind, I could feel it. Ovaeris would not fall apart under their care. They are, after all, our gods. Shitty gods, they might be, but to be fair to them, they had a shitty role model.

As soon as Sirileth was back to herself, I went to Tris. I tried to console him, but he pulled away from me, shook his head. He would recover. I knew the anger and disgust he was feeling, all too well. It ate at him, sucked the joy from the world, and replaced it with bitter rage. It would pass. And there was nothing I could do for him but be there when he broke from the strain of holding it in.

I portaled us back down to Isha. The villagers had thankfully not returned to their burning homes. That was good. I'm not sure Tris could have coped with seeing the hate in their eyes. I think he was finally starting to realise what it truly was to be my son.

We returned to Yenheim a successful but beaten trio. I had given away the one thing, the one secret I had sworn I never would. And the worst thing about it, I knew I would never pay the price of it. That was for the people of Isha to pay. The gods wouldn't hesitate to reap their lives to be reborn.

There was a strange air in Yenheim palace. It felt almost like celebration. I didn't think the Djinn's changes could have taken hold so quickly. As Tris slunk away to find a tavern to drown himself in, and Sirileth slogged her way to the throne room to see what needed her attention, I let them go and asked a passing servant what was happening.

The woman bowed low to me, far too low for my liking. "Pariah," she said in a voice like reverence. "The Paragon is making his pilgrimage."

I all but ran to Josef's temple only to find the place abandoned. The pile of blankets gone, the tables and chair cleared away, the wooden platform stood empty. Josef, his followers, his strange rock creatures; all gone. I ran for the palace gates and emerged into the dull gloom of morning light. I could not see Josef, or any of his followers, even with the advantage point atop the hill.

I strode out onto the path, staring all around me, down into Yenheim town, but there was no sign of my friend. An insect buzzed at my face and I swatted it away. It zipped angrily down and I watched it as it ducked inside a flower blooming in the middle of the path. It was not alone. All around me, new shoots of grass were erupting through the earth, flowers had sprung up, were blooming despite the lack of sun. The path of grass and flowers led off down the hill, following the main street leading from the palace.

"Ssserakis, wings."

Now the Djinn are fixing your world, it is time we deal with Norvet Meruun, Eska. We need to secure the alliance of the other lords of Sevorai. Especially now the enemy has captured Lodoss.

"We will," I promised. "Give me my wings, Ssserakis." They burst from my back, great shadowy things, and Ssserakis gave me control of them. I leapt into the air and beat them hard, carrying us up into the sky. It gave me a commanding view of Yenheim town and from that vantage I could follow the path of blooming life all the way to the western outskirts. There I saw a large procession of hundreds of people, dozens of packs animals. They were

leaving Yenheim, and judging by the belongings they
carried, they did not expect to return. Even from high above,
I spotted Josef at their head.

I swooped in on wings of shadow and dropped at the
city outskirts just as Josef passed the final wooden building.
He spotted me, grinned. Despite the cold, he was wearing
little, only a loose pair of britches, a light shirt and flowing
half robe over the top. His feet were bare and grass and
flowers bloomed around him. Every step more life sprung
up from where his feet touched the ground. Biomancy,
raging out of control, bringing new life to the world at his
mere touch. Was there any wonder that people had started
treating him like a newborn god? The little rock creatures
he had created, called his children, tumbled along behind
him, threading through the growing grass. And behind
them, his followers. Some of them gasped when they saw
me, others bowed. Murmurs rippled through them all. It all
stank of mysticism. I would not be sad to see the back Josef's
followers, only of him.

Josef strode forward to meet me even as Ssserakis
settled my wings about my shoulders. He seemed to glow,
as if lit from within by a fierce light that shone through
his skin. Life thrust up from the earth around him and he
radiated power like nothing I had ever seen before. Not the
Rand, nor the Djinn, nor the Iron Legion. Whatever Josef was
becoming, it was something different. Something the world
had never seen before. Wild Sourcery contained within a
man.

"Have you come to keep me from leaving?" Josef
asked, smiling.

I thought about that for a moment, wondered if I even
could, then shook my head. "I won't stop you," I said. "But

I am asking you to stay." I suddenly felt like a girl again.
Pulling Josef through the halls of the academy, pleading with
him to join me on my adventures.

Josef frowned, looked away. "I don't think I can, Eska.
This place is too... you. Yours. I need to find a place that's
mine."

It wasn't enough of a reason. I wanted him to stay,
needed him to stay. I knew I hadn't spent much time with
him since my return. I'd been too busy with my children,
with trying to save Ovaeris. More excuses. I'd been too
scared to go near him. He had reversed my age, spoken of
immortality, and reeked of portent. I was scared, and I had
been avoiding him because of it.

I didn't want him to go. I didn't want him to leave
me. Not again. I know it's selfish, but I'd hoped to be
reunited with Josef. Properly reunited with the young man
I had once known. But he wasn't there anymore. Josef was
no more that young man, than I was the young woman I
had once been. We had grown too far apart, too different. We
would always be linked, not by the Auguries or any mystical
prophecy. Not by Sourcery or what had been done to us.
We were linked by the memories we shared, the people we
once were. The pahht call it *soul-bonded*, and I truly believe
that we are, Josef and me. No matter how far the distance
between us, and no matter what the people of Ovaeris might
say.

"Where will you go?" I asked.

"I don't know," Josef said. "That's part of the point,
I think. I will see where my feet take me. I need space, to
become. You do, too, Eska. I don't think either of us can
become what we need to be around the other."

I sniffed, desperately searched for a way to make him

stay, no matter how selfish it was. "It's dangerous out there. There's…"

"We'll be fine." He took a step forward, the ground blooming to life around him. "I have to go, Eska."

Josef stepped to the side, then walked past me. He was going and there was nothing I could do. It was unbearable, and yet, bear it I would. I looked down, saw life springing up with every step Josef took, yet none of that life reached my feet. I stood on barren ground. I had done this, somehow, pushed him away, and now he was going.

"It's not your fault, Eska," Josef said as if reading my mind. I didn't turn to look at him. His little rock children rolled past me, joyfully tumbling through the grass, leaping on and around each other like puppies at play. Then Josef's followers were moving past me, too. Some whispered the word *Pariah*; others bowed their heads.

"Please, Eskara," Josef said. "Know that I love you, and always will. No matter what you remember I…"

I leapt into the air, using a kinetic push against the ground to give me height. My wings burst out of my back and I let Ssserakis carry us away. I could barely see past the tears and my storm reflected back at me.

CHAPTER TWENTY SIX

SEVORAI IS SUCH A BIZARRE PLACE. THERE IS no sun, no moons, no stars. The sky is empty and grey. There are clouds, and it sometimes rains, but for the most part the sky is devoid of anything. And yet, there is light. I have never been able to determine where it comes from and so can only say that it exists. It is not the harsh, burning light of Ovaeris, but a softer, fuzzier light that glows everywhere but never shines. The Djinn created the Other World at the height of their power, and it is a testament to that power as it breaks so many of the laws that govern Ovaeris. And so do the creatures that call it home.

I tore open a portal at the minor rift below Yenheim and stepped through into Sevorai. I immediately felt stronger, stood straighter. It was as though gravity had less of a hold on me.

"I no longer have to have to hide to preserve my strength,"

Ssserakis said as my shadow formed into a vague terran shape beside me. *"You feel it through me. This place is home."*

It did feel a lot like home. I'd always felt a strange connection to the Other World. It was stronger now. Maybe I was changing. Maybe not for the better.

"Change is never bad, only the new direction it sometimes leads."

"Very philosophical, Ssserakis. Have you been reading Belmorose?"

Ssserakis chuckled. My shadow pulled back. *I have no need to read when I can feel the truth of life with my very existence. Now, we must find the other lords of Sevorai before Norvet Meruun does. They are strong.*

"As strong as you?"

Ssserakis was sullenly silent for a few moments. *For now, stronger. I need to feed. Storing my energy in that dead Djinn you carry is draining.*

"The wings are yours, Ssserakis," I said. "Lead the way."

I will treat with the other lords.

"As we agreed." I ground my teeth but forced the next words out all the same. "I am but a vessel for you, for now."

You are the host. I had a feeling if Ssserakis had a face, it would be grinning at me.

We took to the grey skies and soared above a rocky landscape teeming with life. All creatures were fleeing before the advancing tide of flesh. I saw a large spidery creature with a dozen segmented legs, erupt out of a crevice and skewer a passing khark hound as it loped along. As the creature dragged the hound back to its crevice, I saw a grotesquely large tahren face hidden amongst the legs. Its

teeth were gnashing as if eager to consume the hound. Then
both were gone, disappeared into the dark earth.

A thrickren, Ssserakis said, noticing my attention.
*They usually stay underground and prey on geolids and other
subterranean creatures. The enemy's advance has driven them
closer to the surface to seek prey.*

We flew on. Some creatures looked up at our passing,
sensing Ssserakis and cowering in terror. My horror drank
it in with glee and swooped closer to stoke the fears even
greater. With so much life, so many of the Other World's
creatures gathering together, it was easy to make a feast of
them.

Aire and Dialos were closest and easiest to find. We
came across them mid battle and it was a slaughter the likes
of which I hadn't seen since the days of the Orran-Terrelan
war. The valley between the two mountain cities was a riot
of chaos and battle and blood. Monsters of all shapes and
sizes battered against each other. Some were great, shaggy
beastmen with horns and hooves, others were winding
serpents with glittering scales, or long-legged walkers
wading through the carnage with serrated bones skewering
foes. But no matter what shape the creatures took, all wore
the same chubby, childlike face. Aire and Dialos, the twins,
the one that was two that was many that was two that was
one.

"They don't fear," I said as we hovered above them
with steady wing beats.

*They have nothing to fear. These deaths mean nothing to
them. Aire and Dialos will fight and one will win, proving his
dominance. Then they will spawn more of themselves and fight
again. It has been this way since the dawn of my world. The
ground beneath their feet is so much crushed bone and flesh.*

"How do they spawn more of themselves?"

A winged lizard swept past us, ignoring us entirely. The chubby baby face screaming as it dove into the chaos below, snatched up a beastman in its claws and pulled it apart in a gout of blood raining down on the battle. Before it could escape, a huge ape-like monster reached up with a ridiculously muscled arm, snatched the lizard by its tail, then leapt upon it, slamming fist after fist against the scaly body.

They are Aire and Dialos. It wasn't exactly a satisfying answer to my question, but I sensed it was the only one I'd get.

"So how do we stop them fighting?"

Ssserakis chuckled. *Stop them? Would you like to drop into the middle of that battle? Are you still so eager to die?* I felt like I had asked a ridiculous question and did not like it. *We wait until the slaughter is finished and one has achieved dominance. Then we will approach and convince that one of our need to fight the enemy together.*

It surprised me that Ssserakis could not see the fault in its own plan. The decision to aid our war against Norvet Meruun could not be made by just one of the twins. It would be overthrown the next time they fought and the other one won. They both had to be convinced together. They both had to submit to our will.

"You said it yourself, Ssserakis. The lords of Sevorai respond to strength. So let's show them strength, just like with Brakunus."

We dropped faster than a stone, Ssserakis beating our wings to speed our descent. As we closed on the ground, and the fighting below, I released a massive kinetic blast, infused with Geomancy to crack the earth. We landed amidst broken rock and shattered bones, and I flung both arms out, releasing another wave of kinetic force, this time infused with my storm. Bodies, living and dead, were thrown away. Lightning arced from me to sear lines in stone and set corpses to burning.

A wave of stillness spread out from us like ripples in a pond. It was not our entrance that stilled the battle. That was but the catalyst. Aire and Dialos had been warring like this since the birth of Sevorai, and never once had they been interrupted. That uniqueness gave them reason to pause their slaughter of each other. And now it was up to Ssserakis to use the moment.

My shadow roared to life, not beside me, but above me. Ssserakis flared into an enormous patch of ragged darkness. The edges danced and flickered; the eyes burned with a darkness deeper than black.

A beastman with curved horns, stepped forward, hooves stamping at the earth. The chubby baby face made it an unnerving sight, especially as its voice was a rough bestial thing.

"This is not how things are done, Ssserakis." The words were not just spoken by the beastman, but by half the warring army all speaking in unison, in a thousand different voices all rising to a cacophony.

That one is Aire.

"We should tear the host asunder. Our contest cannot be interrupted." The other half of the army said in thunderous unison.

And that is Dialos.

"*You underestimate us, Twins.*" A ripple of anger passed through the assembled monsters. Ssserakis had said they did not like being called twins. I hoped my horror wasn't about to get me killed. *"I am stronger with this host than I have ever been. If you wish to break yourselves upon me instead of each other, then come. I will beat your subservience into you if that is what it takes."*

By sheer force of will I kept my mouth shut. I had agreed to let Ssserakis handle the lords of Sevorai. Still, I did not think goading a couple of armies in the middle of a battle was a good idea.

"What do you want, Ssserakis?" The roar came from a thousand voices, Dialos' side of the conflict.

"It is time to end your ceaseless struggle for dominance and submit to my will, Twins. The Beating Heart is unleashed, has consumed too much of Sevorai."

Aire's thousand monsters laughed as one. "If Norvet Meruun has grown too large for you to scare, that is your fault, little shade. Our conflict transcends your disagreement with the pustule."

Typical. Even here, a world made of nightmares, those who called themselves lords were too busy assigning blame to fight back against the true threat.

"Do you think you are safe, Aire? Do you think yourselves mighty enough the Beating Heart will not come for you, Dialos?"

"Do not try to seduce us with your fear, Ssserakis," Aire's forces thundered.

"Hyrenaak is dead," Ssserakis screamed, flaring my shadow into a great black flame that roared over the battlefield.

Two separate rumblings spread through the twins, the Aire side saying one thing, the Dialos side another, the noise mixing together into a churning mass of nonsense. "It is not possible," Dialos said eventually, shouting a thousand voices up at Ssserakis.

"Do not lie to yourself, Dialos. We all heard his death scream. But not everyone chose to ignore it. I watched him fall, witnessed the Beating Heart's pieces devour him from the inside. I have seen his bones. Hyrenaak is dead. The balance is destroyed. Norvet Meruun is coming for us all." The twin armies were arguing with each other now, between each other, all resonance seemingly lost.

Ssserakis hovered above us and shouted down. *"Already she has captured Lodoss. Even the Beating Heart cannot kill him, but she keeps him chained, drives him before her. A herald of the death that will consume us all. Brakunus has fled to the other world."*

"Coward!" Aire roared, his voices finding their chorus once again. It was working. Ssserakis had used the death of Hyrenaak as a rallying cry, and it had stoked the fires of fear in Aire and Dialos. Where before they had been happily slaughtering each other, now an insidious, cold terror was creeping through them. If Hyrenaak could die, Aire and Dialos could, too. And they knew it.

"Cease your pointless bickering and submit to my command. I have raised an army from the other world. Soon, we will meet the Beating Heart and prune it back to the pustule it should be. We will restore balance in Sevorai." I chose not to point out we had raised no such army.

"What should we do?" Dialos asked.

"We cannot attack Norvet Meruun directly," said Aire.

"You will not need to." Ssserakis started shrinking down again. *"Come when I call you. Join the army from the other world in battle against the enemy's forces. I will deal with the Beating Heart."*

We had our first ally. And a mighty ally the Twins were, too. An army all by themselves. It was not enough, and I had a feeling it would not be so simple to recruit the others. Even more difficult to recruit the people of Ovaeris. Aire and Dialos knew about Norvet Meruun, believed she existed and were terrified of what she could do. Fear made them willing to throw their lot in with Ssserakis. Fear of me on Ovaeris would make us strong, but as Jamis had already pointed out, it would not win us allies.

I suggested returning to Yenheim, but Ssserakis had other ideas. We had two more lords of Sevorai to recruit yet, and now we were here, my horror was eager to get on with its mission.

We flew fast, soaring over plains of swaying grasses. Valleys full of rocks that peered up at us with fearful eyes. Lakes so deep I could see gargantuan shapes gliding below the surface. Cities that looked like they were formed out of intestines, all fleshy tubes and hairy growths.

It is strange to say, but despite my lengthy studies of Sevorai, I had never seen the ocean in the Other World. We flew over it then. The waves were turbulent things, grey to Ssserakis' vision, but regularly whipped into frothing, white madness. We swooped down low, skimming the water so close I was slapped in the face by spray that was not salty like my world. Fish with oversized eyes and teeth longer than their bodies leapt out of the water, snapping at us as we passed. I spotted larger things moving in the depths, and Ssserakis had to take us higher up when a claw the size of a house thrust out of the water to pincer us. I did not see what the claw belonged to, so I can only hazard a guess and say, it was really fucking big.

"What else is down there, below the waves?"

What do you think mur dream of? What nightmares do their rubbery minds concoct? Remember, everything in my world was plucked from the nightmares of your world.

We flew on. At one point I saw great fleshy, pulsing tentacles erupting from the turbulent waters, waving in the air, then pulling back below the surface. Norvet Meruun was here, too. Even the force of the ocean could not keep her at bay. We veered away, flying along a different route, over vibrantly coloured coral constructs that spiked out of the waves in hundreds of glistening spires.

A mountain rose before us, thrusting from the waters. Though I suppose I should call it an island. As we came closer, the scale of it awed me. This was no mere hill grown too big for the word, the mountain climbed so high I could not see the top. Ssserakis took us higher and higher still, and the peaks continued to elude us. I think my horror was showing off. We dropped back down, soared around the mountain, and Ssserakis assured me it was quicker than trying to summit it.

We flew most of a day, I think. My horror did not tire, but I certainly did. Terrans need rest, no matter how foolish we are to push ourselves. I drifted away, certain Ssserakis would wake me if there was danger.

Wake up, Eska. We are here.

I blinked groggy eyes, rubbed away the grit. The wind was whipping at me, and I was cold, but that was nothing new. I immediately reached for my pouch and swallowed my Pyromancy Source, letting the little fire it lit inside warm me. We had left the ocean behind and were flying over a forest. The trees were grey to my eyes and swayed with a rhythm all their own. To my left, I saw a sheer wall rising hundreds of feet into the air. Above it, I saw dark shapes buzzing about.

Flowne continues to build walls to hold the enemy back. It is a losing war, she fights.

"Sometimes those feel like the only kind."

We soared down into the forest and the atmosphere grew dense and claustrophobic. The light was dimmer here, even with Ssserakis' night sight, and there was a charge on the air. I sensed danger and it felt like it came from all around.

Shall I remind you again, Eska? Everything in my world is trying to kill you. Even the things you call trees.

I looked closer to the trees as we flew in between the great trunks. The wood shifted and flickered, and I soon realised each 'tree' was actually a colony of insects with mottled backs, constantly moving, trampling over one another like an ant nest driven to a frenzy. The leaves, or what I had mistaken for leaves, were great winged versions of those crawling up the trunks.

We flew into a clearing and I was glad to leave the 'forest' behind. There was grass here, or what I took for grass, reaching all the way up to my knees. It swayed as though in a breeze, but there was no wind at all. The ground felt solid enough below me and my Geomancy confirmed that there were odd tremors running through it every few seconds. I put it down to Norvet Meruun trying to tear down Flowne's wall.

"Now what?" I asked. Ssserakis was silent.

A woman with mottled skin rose from the grassy clearing ahead of me. She was naked and stunningly beautiful. I'd already taken a step towards her before I realised what I was seeing had to be a lie. There were no terrans living in the Other World, especially not women who walked around naked and smiled at me like I was the love of their life. My feet dragged another step, and I swear it was not by my doing.

I couldn't take my eyes from her, this picture of perfect beauty. Her legs, hips, breasts, pouting lips, and soulless dead eyes. It was those eyes that stopped me, knocked my senses back into place. How to describe it? There was no sight in those eyes. It was like they had been painted. Then I noticed the seams in her flesh. What I had taken for mottled colouring was not that at all. There were seams running all along the woman's flesh, as though she had been assembled from a hundred different body parts. Because of course she had.

My shadow bubbled beside me and Ssserakis chuckled. *"Flowne."*

The naked woman hissed. Not from her mouth, but from a hundred mouths. She split apart into separate pieces down all her seems as if she had been suddenly diced. A mouth with serrated teeth opened up in each part of her. There was a vine connected to each part, each chunk of flesh. As the bits of her split apart, floated, waving around on their vines, the ground shook violently. More vines thrust up from the earth, thousands of them each one waving a body part about. Not all were terran. I saw a khark hound's jaw, a hand that looked like it belonged to a pahht, a terran man's groin, half of a ghoul's face. Every part of her had a mouth in it, and all hissed. Then Flowne's true body shook itself free from the earth. A great, shaggy plant of overlapping leaves and tufted growths rose from the ground. It was easily five times the size of an abban, and with it came a musty scent that was somehow both itchy and arousing all at once.

I will admit, I gawked. I have since learned that Flowne is an ambush predator. She lures prey in by showing them a vision of desire formed from the many body parts she has collected. There is a strange intrusion of mind there, that she can reach into a person's thoughts and pluck from them a vision that will inspire lust. I cannot deny that it worked on me. When her prey gets close enough, the many mouths open up and devour it, hundreds of sets of teeth tearing the unfortunate creature to bloody shreds. You may wonder where she collects her body parts. She had many belonging to terrans and not many of my kind had ever set foot in Sevorai. Well, her shaggy leaves play home to a vast colony of phase spiders. The little arachnids can travel between the two worlds at will, and their venom is known to phase a person's bitten limb away, leaving a raw wound in its place. Flowne then collects the limbs as they appear in Sevorai, adds them to her collection. In case it has not yet become apparent to you, Sevorai is a fucked-up place.

As Ssserakis consulted with Flowne, I examined her as best I could. There was constant movement within her thistle of leaves as phase spiders scuttled about. Silk webbing draped from her to trail along the ground like a dangling veil. Her musty scent continued to stick in my nose making me quite uncomfortable for a couple of different reasons.

One of Flowne's vines whipped towards us, a pale terran ear dangling on the end. A mouth opened up in the middle of the ear, serrated teeth behind the lips. "I cannot help," Flowne said through the mouth. It's more than a little unnerving when an ear speaks to you. Her voice was the jingling of soft bells. "Norvet Meruun has grown too strong. I can do nothing but flee before her. Even my walls do little to stop her now."

"So that's it?" I asked. "You can't be sure you'll win, so you just refuse to fight?" I was suddenly sick of it. Sick of

people, or monsters, calling themselves lords or queens, and
refusing to help us in favour of saving their skins.

All battle, no matter how prepared you are, is a game
of chance. A stray arrow, an unfortunate patch of ice, a
blinding flash of sunlight. There is always the risk of losing.
Of death. But that doesn't mean you don't roll the dice,
because sometimes you have to risk everything on a bluff or
lose it all by being bullied out of the game.

"The host talks," Flowne said, a dangling hand with
only one finger joining the ear.

I waited just a moment for Ssserakis to tell me to shut
up. I had agreed to let my horror take the lead, but Ssserakis
was silent. I took it as assent.

"The host has a name," I growled up at the
overgrown shrubbery. "Eskara Helsene."

More vines whipped forward, more dangling body
parts. In mere moments, the naked woman from before had
been reassembled, slotted together so perfectly I could barely
see the seams. Then a hundreds mouths opened up along
her legs, thighs, belly, breasts, arms, cheeks, within her eyes.
All the mouths spoke at once. "You have never allowed your
hosts to retain their sense of self before, Ssserakis."

"This one is different. And she speaks truth here, Flowne."

"Your world is almost gone," I said. I tried to stare
past the terran simulacrum to the plant behind her. Partly
because she was distracting, and partly because when she
spoke it was horrifying. "Norvet Meruun has consumed so
much of it. You hide behind your walls and cower, but I have
no doubt you can feel it. This wall will soon fall."

"And I will build another," the soft jingling of bells
was a sharp contrast to a hundred fangy mouths flapping all
along the woman's skin.

"And that will fall, too. It's nothing but delaying the inevitable. Unless we stop her, Norvet Meruun will keep coming."

"Unless you stop her."

"Exactly," I said. "Which is more likely if you help."

"The host does not understand," Flowne said.

My shadow seethed beside me. *"No, she does not. Flowne will hide here behind her walls until either the Beating Heart catches her, or we manage to contain her."*

"Coward," I spat. "My world is in danger, too."

The simulacrum shivered, all her parts splitting for a moment, then reassembling quickly. "How so?"

"The Beating Heart is closing in on the portal."

"Portal?"

"To Ovaeris."

"Eska, stop!"

The simulacrum split apart onto dangling vines, each one snaking back to the main body as the mouths spoke. "There is a way through." The jingling of bells became a harsh, discordant racket.

Flowne shivered and began to disintegrate, her vines, leaves, body parts, all becoming fluffy tufts like dandelions blowing away on a gust of wind. They swept past me in a flurry and floated away. Flowne was gone. I watched her breeze away for a minute, unsure of what had just happened.

Your world will not thank you for this, Eska.

Talk about a fucking understatement. I had not secured us an ally in our war against the enemy. All I had done here was unleash one of the lords of Sevorai on my own world.

CHAPTER TWENTY SEVEN

I SUGGESTED CHASING AFTER FLOWNE, BUT Ssserakis shot me down. Apparently my horror could not fly as fast as the shambling flower in that form and was far from certain we would be able to stop her anyway. She would be a problem to deal with later, and for now nothing but a distraction. We rested in that clearing for a time. It might have been pleasant but for the weird insects posing as trees, and the constant pounding I felt through my Geomancy as Norvet Meruun crumbled the giant wall. But both Ssserakis and I needed the rest. I fed my horror well with nightmares.

When I woke, we took to the skies again. I wanted to return home. I was hungry, the meagre supplies I had brought with me had run out, and we had already been gone for over a day. Much can happen in a day, and I feared what I might come back to. Strange, isn't it? I had left my queendom and children for seven years, but now I couldn't bear to be away for a single day. But we were not returning just yet. We had one more lord of Sevorai to track down. Kekran.

I had met Kekran once before. He appeared terran, for the most part. He stood as tall as Hardt, though rangy rather than brawny. His skin had a swirling look to it, like water circling a drain. I remembered he had a new arm when I had seen him, his last one lost in a battle so he had replaced it with another, torn from the slain creature. He was also surrounded by imps. A large colony of them that followed him about like servants to a king. He was quite genial at the time, and he and Ssserakis were clearly well-acquainted, if not friendly. I hoped for an easy ally.

We soared over territory that was thick with Norvet Meruun's minions. They ignored us; too busy carting off easier prey to feed to their mistress.

I do not like this. Kekran should be protecting his lands, not allowing these cretins to run rampant.

We found Kekran halfway up a broken mountain trail, where the path had evened out for a short distance. He crouched, surrounded by bodies. Most were imps, but I saw khark hounds and ghouls and hellion corpses, too. All were torn limb from limb. We had come across the lord of Sevorai in the aftermath of a battle, one that appeared to have cost him all his servants.

We touched down a short distance from Kekran in one of the few parts of the path not thick with blood. Still, I kicked a dismembered arm away as soon as we landed and had to tear my gaze away from what appeared to be the lower half of a khark hound jaw.

"What happened here, Kekran?" Ssserakis asked from my shadow.

Kekran twitched, glanced over his shoulder. His skin was a dark swirl, his eye lit from within with a glowing red light. Something wriggled below his eye.

"Ssserakis..." I said.

"It cannot be."

Kekran stood slowly, turned to us. All along his face and neck, worms wriggled, the tail ends flailing about in the air. He was infested. Norvet Meruun had taken him, made the lord of Sevorai her puppet.

Ssserakis screamed, a sound of pure rage that split the air like thunder. My shadow lurched, spearing forwards into a stabbing spike. Kekran's hand snapped up, grabbed the shadow spear in one hand, held it for a moment. His grip tightened, Ssserakis howled, my shadow shattered in Kekran's hand. Ssserakis pulled back inside me, hurt and shocked all at once.

Run. The word was a pleading mewl in my mind, but my first instinct has never been to run. That was not what the Orran Academy had beaten into me, and it was not something I was willing to lower myself to.

Kekran burst into a sprint, splashing blood with every step. He snatched a dismembered arm from the ground, shoved the torn fleshy end into his elbow. The skin fused together in moments as he grafted the second arm onto himself. I raised a kinetic shield as Kekran reached me, crouched, and steadied myself to block. Kekran slammed his arms against my shield and the world lurched around me as I was thrown away by the force. I hit the ground hard, rolled through pooled blood, scattered limbs, hit a khark hound carcass and thudded to a stop. I rose to my feet immediately, wincing at pain in my arms and back.

Did you think he was weak because of his size, Eska? How

many have made the same mistake of you? Run.

"No," I growled the word as I formed a Sourceblade in my hand. We could not run. Kekran belonged to the enemy now. We would have to fight him sooner or later and if I could take something away from Norvet Meruun now, I would.

Kekran reached down, picked up another arm, fused it to his flesh, then grabbed another and another. As I watched, he grafted so many limbs to himself he stood like a giant ape, his arms formed of arms many times the size of his smaller body.

He lumbered towards me then, walking on his knuckles as much as his legs. I ran to meet him, formed a kinetic shield around my claw, pushed Pyromancy into my Sourceblade so it burst into flames. Kekran swung for me, I ducked under his giant flailing arm, leapt, and brought my sword down on the limb. My sword cut through flesh and three imp arms fell away from the mass, flesh burning. Kekran spun, smashed an elbow against my shield. I managed to roll with the blow, blood coating my old leather armour, soaking my hair. He grabbed for me. I raised my shield again. His fist smashed against it, knocked me back. His fist opened up into eight grasping hands, each one clawing at my shield, searching, finding the edges. I had to let the shield dissipate before he used it against me.

I slashed twice more, flames charring skin, blade carving flesh. More arms fell away from the mass, but Kekran had the limbs to spare. I backed up, feet sliding through the slick, bloody ground. Kekran lurched after me and I raised my shadowy claw, drew on my Arcstorm, and unleashed a flurry of lightning at him. He raised a meaty arm and the lightning hit him, scoring flesh. He waded through my storm, slammed his free arm into me, knocked me away. My flight arrested suddenly and my leg lit with pain like fire. One of the grasping hands that formed his arm was wrapped around my thigh. Before I could react, he swung me up through the air, slammed me back down on the ground. I gasped, spilled blood rushing into my mouth, choked on it. My vision had gone bright and I felt like something inside had broken.

I felt myself lifted again. I twisted in Kekran's grip, stabbed out blindly. I must have hit him as he let go, staggered back a step. I hit the ground, still coughing up blood as I pushed onto hands and knees and crawled away.

We have to run, Eska.

I was starting to agree with Ssserakis. I had both underestimated Kekran and overestimated myself. I was not ready for this fight. Not strong enough.

Kekran lumbered after me. I stamped on the ground, sending a pulse of Geomancy through the earth. Stone cracked underneath his feet. Kekran pushed off his knuckles, leapt into the air above me. I formed a kinetic bubble just moments before he landed and his fists smashed into my hazy, purple shield. He slammed his giant arms against it once, twice, again, again and again. I cowered before the strength of his blows, feeling cracks appearing in my shield. The earth depressed beneath me from the force.

The pounding stopped just before my shield shattered. Kekran's multitude of arms spread out around me on either side, surrounding the kinetic bubble. He pressed in, grabbed hold of my bubble, with me still inside, and lifted it from the ground. He hugged the bubble to himself, squeezing it. Visible cracks spread all along the surface.

Caught in his crushing embrace, I could clearly see

Kekran's face. There was no anger there, no hate, no pride at his impending victory. I saw no emotion at all. He was about to crush my shield and me along with it, and it would mean nothing to him. So completely was he under Norvet Meruun's thrall.

When a wolf has you by the throat, you might as well stick your thumb in its eye and take the fucker down with you.

I launched myself at Kekran at the same time I dropped my bubble. The explosion of kinetic force staggered him for just a moment and I drove my blade into the monster's neck. I leapt back, ducking under his swinging reach, let go my sword. The Sourceblade exploded in a puff of force, laying open Kekran's neck in a gout of blood that sluiced down his chest.

I rolled away, staggering to my feet, pushed hair slick with gore from my face. Kekran staggered, clutching at his neck, bleeding out. I panted, grinned, shouted at the monster to go fuck himself. So secure in my victory.

Run, Eska. Now!

Kekran reached down with one of his giant arms, grabbed a ghoul carcass, tore out its throat and slapped it against his own. The skin grafted to him in moments and the fatal wound I had dealt him turned out to be nothing but a brief annoyance. It was time to run.

I turned, sprinted towards the edge of the rocky path, leapt out into the drop. My wings burst from my back and Ssserakis beat them hard, taking us up and away from the fight even as Kekran rushed on, arms flailing in a failed attempt to grab us.

I shifted, staring back over my wings. Kekran stood on the rocky path, watching us for a few moments. His mass of arms fell away so he looked almost terran again.

I told you he is stronger than he looks.

"Not strong enough apparently. The enemy still took him." It hurt to speak. I couldn't decide if I had cracked a rib or was just bruised as a mistreated peach.

I felt a pang of loss from Ssserakis. The horror had considered Kekran more than just an ally or fellow lord of Sevorai. Kekran had been as close to a friend as Ssserakis had ever known in its world. Gone now. Nothing but a puppet left behind. My horror was scared, too. Hyrenaak dead, Lodoss captured, Kekran infested. Ssserakis was scared it would be next. The ancient horror had always considered itself immortal. But now it wondered. If everything became Norvet Meruun, and she did not fear the horror, if her minions did not retain enough of themselves to fear, would Ssserakis starve to death? Dwindle away to nothing.

Below us, back on the rocky path, Kekran reached down and picked up the body of a hellion.

"Oh fuck!"

Kekran tore the wings from the hellion, fused them to his own back. He gave an experimental flap, another, then leapt into the air. In mere moments he was soaring after us.

"What is he?" I had never even heard of a monster like him before, one who could take body parts from the dead and make them his own.

He is… was Kekran. I could not mistake the sadness in my horror's words.

We flew like a howling gale and Kekran kept pace. He did not seem to tire, nor struggle with his grafted wings. It was a chase we would eventually lose for Ssserakis was growing weaker. I could feel my horror flagging. It hadn't fed enough to sate it in a long time, and what little fear I was feeding it was going into the Necromancy Source in my stomach. Neither of us was strong enough to beat Kekran in our current state. So we ran. I detest running from a fight, but there is truth in the old saying: When your opponent holds all the cards, it's better to fold than to play a shit hand.

By the time we reached the site of the minor rift, Kekran was almost on top of us. We had seconds before he caught me, and I had a horrible image of being torn apart and then the monster stealing my remaining arm just to be an almighty dick about his victory.

I hit the ground running, feet stumbling over uneven rock, drew on my Portamancy Source and ripped the portal open back to Yenheim. I had a brief glimpses of torches, faces turning to look at me, then I leapt through the portal and let it snap shut.

I hit the ground, rolled, sprang to my feet, turned. There was a severed hand lying on the floor below the minor rift, the end oozing blood. I had no doubt Kekran would replace the lost limb soon enough, but it wouldn't be with my own.

I heard a shuffle of feet, a sword sliding from its scabbard, whispered words. When I turned around, there were six soldiers facing me. All wearing the black and gold of Tor.

CHAPTER
TWENTY EIGHT

"KILL HER. SECURE THE PORTAL," SHOUTED A
bearded man wielding a torch.

A young woman with a spear was first to act. She
charged me, spear levelled, a snarl on her lips. A foolish
attack, but it almost caught me off guard such was my
surprise. My horror, however, was not so slow. My shadow
sliced upwards, shearing the spear in half. The woman's
snarl turned to shock, but it didn't last long. I stepped
forward, grabbed the spear haft in my hand, reached across
with my claw, gripped her neck, tore her throat out. She
dropped, blood spraying from the wound.

I had a moment to look around the great cavern. It
was well lit with the blue mineral veins running through the
remaining pillars, but there was more. Torches everywhere,
soldiers in small groups, going through the rooms at the
cavern edges. A large tent set up on one side, barricades in

mid-construction around it.

It is an invasion.

I had no more time to think. Two more of the soldiers came at me, one with a sword and round shield, the other with a spear, hanging back. A tough combination to beat. Unless, of course, you're a Sourcerer.

I stamped on the ground, sent a Geomantic pulse through the rock. The shield-bearer stumbled as the earth shifted beneath him. I rushed in, forming a dagger in my hand. I grabbed the rim of his shield in my claw, turned it like a wheel, heard his shoulder pop from its socket. I lifted it just enough to block the spear thrust, then spun around the shield-bearer, inside the spearman's reach. I buried my dagger in his gut, ripped it sideways. He fell, screaming.

"Reinforcements!" the bearded man with the torch shouted. "The Corpse Queen is…"

I didn't let him finish. I channelled my storm through my claw and hit him with a blast of lightning that charred his skin and threw him back against the nearby pillar. The last two soldiers did not look like they were in a hurry to come at me. But then, they didn't need to. Already I could see hundreds more streaming from the rooms at the cavern edges, pouring from the big tent. An army to face me.

Not just you, Eska. They have twisted our daughter's vision and used her portals to attack your home.

Ssserakis was right. It was the only explanation. Tor had rushed the completion of their portal and used it just as they had accused Sirileth of doing, to launch an invasion. This wasn't just about me. It was about Sirileth and Tris and all of Yenheim, too. I had to warn them.

The shield-bearer with the dislocated shoulder roared as he launched back to his feet behind me, sword raised

high. Such a clumsy strike. I swayed to the side, just out of
the way of the blade's path, grabbed his wrist in my claw
and twisted hard, heard the bone crack. He dropped back to
his knees, screaming.

They fear us, Eska. I wanted to kill them all. *They are
more useful alive.*

"Not all of them."

I still held the man's arm in my claw. I twisted again,
spun him around, dragged more screams from him so all the
cavern would hear his pain. I forced him back to his knees
before me, his arm twisted and broken behind him.

"Please please please please..." he pleaded with wet
lips, tears streaming down his cheeks.

Do you think he would have hesitated had you begged?

"No."

His comrades were rushing forwards, gathering in
groups, Sourcerers spread among them. Such a sizeable
force. If they caught us unawares...

*What if they already have? You assume this is the
vanguard.*

I twisted the man's arm a little more, dragged another
scream from him. The closest soldiers faltered, unsure of
what to do now I had a hostage. They were waiting for
someone to take command. Well, I wouldn't give them the
time.

*Their terror will make us strong. Give them a reason to fear,
Eska.*

Yes. Not just for Yenheim. Not just for Sirileth and
Tris. For all of Ovaeris and for Sevorai, too. To fight Norvet
Meruun, we needed to be strong. We needed the power
Ssserakis gained from fear. Besides, these bastards had come
to kill us all.

Excuses. I am good at those.

I dropped the man's twisted arm, let it flop to his side. Then I grabbed his hair in my claw, wrenched his head back, formed a Sourceblade in my hand and stabbed it into his neck. He had a thick neck. It took some sawing. He screamed and flailed. Until he didn't. The closest soldiers stared in horror. Some rushed forwards, but too late. I was covered in fresh blood by the time it was done. The man's body fell limp to the stony floor and I held his severed head in my claw.

I heard a sound like tearing paper behind me as the portal opened. I turned to see another army, easily a thousand strong, waiting in ordered ranks. The dim light of morning shone through the portal. A woman in enchanted armour was at the head of the army on the other side. I didn't recognise her, but I recognised the colours she wore. Blue and orange. This second army was from Tefts, another of our neighbours. Too much to hope they were here to reinforce Yenheim. No. Tor and Tefts had finally formed an alliance. To kill Yenheim.

Footsteps on stone, many boots pounding the ground as the Tor forces rushed for me. I tossed the severed head through the portal. It rolled to a stop at the Teft woman's feet. She stared down at it and I felt a wave of fear ripple through her and her soldiers. The cavern was thick with terror. And why not? They had come to destroy Yenheim, and the Corpse Queen had met them, drenched in blood, throwing severed heads around like balls for a dog.

Time to go, Eska.

I could not fight them all. Even if I could, it would serve little purpose. I needed them alive. Afraid but alive. And besides, Sirileth needed to be warned. We needed to evacuate.

I crouched and Ssserakis flared my wings, two great shadows darkening the hall. I leapt into the air and flew, carrying us up and up until we reached the top of one of the broken staircases at the cavern edge. I stepped calmly through the doorway, made sure I was out of sight, then launched into a sprint. I needed to be far enough away from the rift that it wouldn't interfere with my portal.

As I ran, I felt a wave of exhaustion hit me, stagger me. I hit the corridor wall with my shoulder and stopped, leaning against it. I was breathing heavily, and not because of the running. I remembered the sound of the man's screams, the feel of sawing my blade through his neck, the horrified terror of those watching. I felt sick. I felt tired. I wanted to lie down and melt into the floor and stop. Stop. Stop.

"No time," I breathed, tasted blood, not mine. I spat. I did not have time for an attack right now. My queendom was falling, enemies inside the palace. My children were in danger. I had already lost one child to Tor assassins sneaking into my palace, I would not lose any more.

I pushed away from the wall, forced the depression down into a little ball and swallowed it. I did not have time for it right now.

... Eska. There is too much at stake.

"I'm back, Ssserakis," I said. I slowed my rapid breathing.

I do not know where you keep going when this happens. My horror was as scared by what was happening to me as I was.

"We should be far enough away." I drew on the Source in my stomach and tore open a portal to my rooms up in the palace, stepped through.

There were soldiers in my room and they were wearing black and gold. Ssserakis was right, the army in the cavern below was not the vanguard. This was a coordinated attack with vastly superior numbers. And if they were already in my quarters then the palace was all but lost.

A soldier with tawny hair spilling beneath his ill-fitting helm, raised an axe at me. I flung out my hand and hit him with a kinetic blast that threw him away so hard he smashed my bed to splinters and left a smear of blood on the far wall. A woman swung a sword at me, I blocked with my claw, the metal clanged to a halt as if against bone. It did not hurt. I punched her in the throat, reached out with my claw, grabbed the side of her head and slammed it against the nearby wall once, twice, a third time. Half of her face was caved in by the time I stopped. The last soldier, a towering oaf of a man, ran, hit the doorframe on his way out, spun about just in time to see the ball of flame I launched his way. He collapsed into an inferno.

They are more useful alive than dead, Eska.

"Not true."

I grabbed the woman's ghost as it fled her broken body, forced it back into its shell and tore away her will. She rose on unsteady feet, unable to resist my command. Her face was a ruin of pulped flesh, broken bone, and one eye popped from its socket. She was in pain and she was scared.

"See."

I cannot feed on her, Eska. Her fear is… muted, as if too far away to reach me.

I shrugged at my horror. "She can still serve a purpose."

I grabbed the burning man's ghost as it fled his

charred body, forced it back into the smouldering ruin of his flesh. He, too, rose to serve me.

I had six corpses following me by the time I reached the throne room. The palace was thick with Tor soldiers. I found a slaughter waiting for me at the foot of the corpse throne. I recognised many of the bodies. Sirileth's soldiers had died defending her. Others wore the black and gold. It seemed a battle had taken place, and both sides had paid a heavy price. I did not see my daughter.

Tris leapt from behind a pillar as I approached, his scythe cutting through the air. He pulled the strike short as he saw me. A grim smile spread across his blood-spattered face. "Mother," he said. "Behind you. Argh, what the fuck?"

I glanced back at my grisly retinue. They shambled into the throne room behind me. The burned man was struggling to walk, too much of his muscle scorched away, but he could not help but follow my command, regardless of his pain. "They're with me," I said.

Tris eyed the walking corpses with distaste. "One day, Mother, you will have to teach me to use my Necromancy like you do."

I stalked past my son towards the throne. "Nobody should use it like I do."

The fear of you is spreading, Eska. I feel it rising through the stone. So many minds turned to terror. I could taste the fear of the soldiers attacking my queendom. It was sharper than the background fear from the city, more filling. Like a good steak rather than watery broth. Ssserakis was pouring most of the power it syphoned into the Necromancy Source, but it was keeping enough back for us to use.

"Sirileth?" I asked.

"Rallying the troops in the city for a counterattack,"

Tris said. "We'll push the bastards back. I know you wanted peace with these fuckers from Tor, Mother, but that's not an option anymore. We have to break them and their shitty little nation…"

"No. This isn't just Tor. They've allied with Tefts." I shook my head even as I saw the truth dawn on Tris. He was arrogant and angry, but even he could see the shit we were in.

Three of his warriors entered the throne room from the far archway, jogging, weapons dripping blood. They came to a stop before Tris. Two of them, a man with no hair on his head and a woman with a cleft chin, stooped, trying to catch their breath. The third, a wiry man with his lip curled into a permanent sneer, saluted my son.

"The catacombs are lost," the sneering man said. "The last of the palace guard are holding them as best they can, but they've overwhelmed."

Tris looked to me. I nodded. It was time to go.

I took one last look at the Corpse Throne, the symbol of my rule. I had never asked for it to be carved as such, a host of corpses clawing their way from the ground, and I had never found it comfortable to sit in. I hoped they would tear it down.

We fled the palace even as the sound of fighting echoed down the stone corridors. Steel clashing against steel, screams of pain. Calls of surrender cut short.

Sirileth was gathering soldiers just outside the palace. It was a meagre force she had assembled, barely a hundred worth giving weapons to. Hardt and Beff were with them. Hardt had his old gauntlets hanging from his belt and Beff was busy strapping a sword to her thigh. We'd get them all killed if this wasn't stopped.

"Eska!" Hardt said, reproach in his voice as he eyed the six corpses staggering behind me.

I shook my head at him. "It's not what you think." He'd been there the day I created the Cursed and he'd seen what they had done not just to the Juntorrow garrison, but to the city, to its people.

"I think you raised corpses to fight for you again."

I placed a hand on Hardt's shoulder. "It's not what you think," I repeated.

He grumbled but didn't say more.

"Mother," Sirileth said. "You're back. I mean, I'm glad you're here. I've been consulting with Beff and we need to push the Tor soldiers back, secure the entrance to the catacombs and form a bottleneck." She glanced at Beff and the woman nodded at her words.

They didn't understand, so I told them exactly what we were up against.

Sirileth stared at the ground, darklight eyes burning. "But the bottleneck," she said. "Their numbers won't matter."

Beff should her head. "It's too much, my queen. We can't stand against it, even if we could push them back."

"We can't," Tris added. "The palace is already theirs."

"Collapse it?" Hardt asked. "Trap them underground."

"There are more ways to the surface," I said. "Even Sirileth couldn't close them all." Her Geomancy was always stronger than mine, but the city beneath us was a warren with ways up all over the place.

Sirileth let out a bitter laugh. "So that's it. I mean, we convince the Djinn to help, to fix the world. And they are." She gestured to the sky and I had to admit, the cloud cover was lighter than it had been in previous days. "And I still lose my queendom." She breathed in deep, screwed her eyes shut, and for a moment I thought she would scream in frustration. But that is not Sirileth. She swallowed it and opened her eyes, straightened her back; Queen for one last time.

"Beff, call the people to the assembly hall in the valley," Sirileth said. "When the soldiers come, surrender. No fighting. It's not you they want, it's me. Me and Tris and mother. If the city surrenders, they won't harm you."

Beff looked like she'd argue for a moment, but then nodded grimly.

"Eska," Hardt said. "Whatever you're going to do, I'm…"

"Staying right here with your family and keeping them safe," I said.

Sirileth ordered them all to go and they went. Hardt was the last to leave and he hugged us both, squeezing us in a crushing embrace, then hurried off after his wife. That left me, my children, and just short of a hundred soldiers. A pitiful force.

It was quickly decided to flee to the Forest of Ten. Half of it was gone, sunk into the ground or burned to ashen husks, but it would provide the cover we needed to rest up and form a new plan. I let my children go on ahead and assured them I would catch up. I had one more thing I needed to do before I could leave.

I lined up my six corpses. Three barely looked wounded, felled with a single Sourceblade thrust, but the other three were mangled and bloody. They would all serve a purpose. I dropped a knife in front of each of them and gave them their orders. Then Ssserakis flared my wings and we flew up onto the rooftop of a nearby tavern, *The Blind Pig*. There I waited, clearly visible, my armour, hair, and face stained with blood.

The soldiers of Tor and Tefts were not quick to emerge from my palace. They took their time securing it. When they did come, it was in a rush, securing the entrance and the steps. A woman in blue and orange, the same woman I had seen through the portal, stepped out from the great doors, her gaze sweeping over my retinue, and then up to me, clinging to the tavern roof. Beside her stood an extremely tall man in gold and black. I took them for the generals. They didn't matter. It was the rest of the soldiers that mattered, hundreds of men and women from Tefts and Tor swarming forwards.

Make them fear. Ssserakis' words echoed in my head. Yes, fear was the plan.

As the soldiers rushed down the steps, drew close to my corpses, eager to see to their comrades, my orders took hold. The corpses could not fight my will. They reached down, picked up the knives I had left them, and slit their own throats.

I watched their second deaths, watched their ghosts rise from their bodies again. I let them. They had served their purpose. Ssserakis drank in the terror and horror of all those who witnessed the macabre suicide executions. The rumours would spread. Fear is a disease carried on the breath of words. I ignored the shouts and cries of the soldiers as they roared hatred up at me. Bravado to mask the fear. It worked only for a time and would soon fade away. The generals ordered for archers and I knew it was time to leave. I leapt into the sky and flew up and over Yenheim palace. I flew not north towards the Forest of Ten and my children, but south. South towards Tor.

CHAPTER TWENTY NINE

I KNOW WHAT YOU'RE THINKING. ESKA FLEW to Tor and wreaked bloody, foolish vengeance. Well, you would be half right. Ssserakis and I were in Tor by nightfall. I knew we would be beaten there by soldiers through the portal, and that was half the point. I made certain we were seen. I stalked about rooftops and menaced a few watchmen. I killed no one. I can say that much, at least. But rumours of my presence spread fast and wide and soon every ill thing that happened in Tor was attributed to the Corpse Queen.

Old Dorrian took sick with a pox; must be the Corpse Queen magicked him. Tarcy's foal dropped from its mother blind; more of Eskara Helsene's wickedness. Fire consumed half the warehouse down by the river's ford; it was the bogeywoman calling down her lightning. To be fair, I did start that fire. It backlit me very well and I swear half of Tor got a good look at me standing before the blaze.

I will state again: I did not kill anyone that night. But deaths were attributed to me regardless. Whether illness or mishap, they placed the dead at my feet and called me monster. It's fine. It. Is. Fine. They fed my horror well. By the time I left in the morning, the whole of Tor was afraid of me. That sharp, present fear. It filled us well, though the Necromancy Source was still so far from sated.

I winged my way back to Yenheim, keeping low so as not to be seen by watchful eyes. I alighted on the palace roof and spent some time sneaking around, listening for news. Then I launched myself up into the cloud cover and flew towards the Forest of Ten to find my children.

The village Tris had established in the forest was gone. It had fallen into the chasm that opened up the day Sirileth dropped the moon on Ovaeris. I darted through smouldering trees and coughed on smoke and fumes. My anxiety bubbled up in my gut every moment I couldn't find them.

Our daughter will be fine. I have seen her heart, Eska. She is far more capable than you believe. Her fears are such wide things, encompassing everything and everyone. There was a wistful silence from my horror, then *She reminds me of you in that way. Taking the hurts of the world and making them her own.*

I ground my teeth and flew on, zipping between trees, searching.

This thing we do, Eska, is necessary. Your world must fear you. But do not lose yourself in the blame.

"Shut up, Ssserakis." I didn't want to hear it. Strange, isn't it? It was easier for me to accept the blame and hatred of an entire world than to admit the truth that maybe I wasn't to blame. That I wasn't the monster everyone thought I was. My name had been synonymous with evil for so long, even I started to believe it. I fell into that trap, and it was easier to languish there than claw my way out.

We found my children near the northern edge of the forest where the trees grew thin and needly. They had made a camp of sorts, a small fire where they were roasting some gamey creature. I tucked my wings away, hit the ground running, ignored the startled sentries. Sirileth stood to meet me and I didn't care about propriety or her usual distant nature, I flung myself at her, wrapped my arm and claw around her and hugged her tight. She gave a startled squeak, then hugged me back as fiercely. She lowered her head against my neck and I think I heard a stifled sob.

"Typical," Tris said, sauntering over from where he had been sat. "I'm always the one ig…"

I grabbed the idiot with my claw, pulled him into the hug and held them both tight. Ssserakis wrapped us all in shadow, and for a few blessed moments none of us were stupid enough to talk. We just stood there, in each other's arms. My family. All that was left of my cursed family. I loved them fiercely, held them tightly, and hated what I knew was to come next. Even covered in ash and blood and sweat, even exhausted and wounded, even reeling from the loss of everything I had built and everything Sirileth had shaped, those moments were perfect.

But moments are fleeting, and not even the arms of loved ones can protect you from the world and all its sharp edges.

Eventually we separated, sat by the fire. Tris turned the beast on its spit, his remaining warriors moved far enough away to give us the idea of privacy.

"It's gone, isn't it?" Sirileth said at last. "I mean, Yenheim is dead."

I nodded. We all knew there was no chance of taking it back. We had lost too many of our soldiers in that sneak attack. Even if Sirileth could rally those remaining, the forces of the alliance against us were too great, too well entrenched.

Tris added a log to the fire. "I disagree, queen sister. I'm well versed in guerrilla tactics. We can hide out here in the forest for years, raise a new army, peck away at the bastards occupying Yenheim until they have no choice…"

"It's over, brother," Sirileth said, defeated. "I mean, even if I could raise an army and weaken them." She shook her head. "I built the portal below the palace. They can reinforce themselves too easily. I should have built defences around the portal. I should have seen this coming." She rubbed at her fraying braid of hair. With her dark suit dishevelled, her hair a mess, and her face smudged with dirt and grime, she looked more beggar than queen.

"Then we find another rift, take our army through and strike them in the rear." Tris smiled savagely. "See how the fuckers like their own tactic turned on them."

Sirileth buried her head in her hands, spoke sharply through her fingers. "To what end, brother? We don't have time. Do we?"

I shook my head slowly. Norvet Meruun was consuming her way across Sevorai, growing ever closer to the great rift. We had a few months at most. Building a force to fight her seemed an impossible task, but I would not lay that burden at my children's feet. It was my task. My failure.

"What about Yenheim town?" Sirileth asked suddenly. "The people, are they safe? Did Tor…"

I held up my claw to silence her. "It's alright. They're being questioned, Tor soldiers making sure they aren't hiding us. But they were never the target. It was us. Sneaky fuckers, they might be, but they recognise the surrender and aren't harming anyone."

"Good." Sirileth's voice trembled on the word and I saw her shaking. New tears rolled down her cheeks. "I'm sorry, Mother. I tried to hold it all together. I tried." She choked on a sob.

I shuffled over to sit next to her, put my arm around her again and held her. "You did well, Sirileth. Better than I ever did. And I should never have put such a burden on your shoulders anyway."

Sirileth sniffed, rubbed her wet face against my shadowy cloak. "It's alright. You were a shit queen, Mother."

Tris laughed, turned the beast on the spit. "You were."

I nodded along. "I was."

"Thank you, though. I mean, you helped." Sirileth leaned more heavily against me, relaxing as tiredness overcame her. "I asked you to help me fix things, and you did." Her voice was growing airy. "Now it's my turn. To help you, I mean. Whatever you need, Mother. Whatever I can do."

"Sleep, Sirileth." I lay my daughter down and Ssserakis spread my shadow over her like a blanket. "Rest. We'll watch over you."

She grabbed the edge of my shadow, pulled it close, curled up into a ball. I watched until her face relaxed into unconsciousness.

I tried to decide how much I would tell her in the morning. Eventually, I realised it had to be everything. All my cards on the table. No more betting or bluffing, just the plan, as much of it as I had.

I looked into the fire and found Tris watching me over the flames. He nodded when he caught my flashing gaze.

No words were needed there. As wilful and rebellious as Tris was, he would follow me into hell itself. He was a good boy. A good man. Perhaps I hadn't done such a poor job raising him after all.

The next morning the sky seemed a little brighter. The rain fell heavily though. It was thick and left grey smears on everything it touched. It might have dampened some spirits, but I saw it for what it was. The Djinn were about their work. It was no easy task we had committed them too, but they were busy drawing the dust from the sky. How they would calm the seas and still the land, I had no idea, but they had done it once before during the first cataclysm so I trusted they knew what they were about.

When Sirileth woke, she ate heartily. As was my daughter's way, all trace of the vulnerability she had shown the night before was gone. Here sat a queen even without a throne. Back straight, bearing proud, control oozing from her. I smiled to see it. Then I launched into my plan.

I told both Sirileth and Tris all I knew of Norvet Meruun. She was vast, yes, all parts of her working independently of direct control like muscle memory. She could split her own body into smaller sections, the Abominations, and they, too, operated both independently and also responded to her orders. But most importantly, there was a core to Norvet Meruun. A part of her that controlled the rest. It could move freely throughout her mass, and when it was close, her pulsating flesh responded more quickly, more decisively. That was key. The first step to defeating her. We needed to do enough damage to her, slay enough of her minions, that Norvet Meruun would move her core close to the battle, to assume direct control. To do it, we needed an army. More than one. We needed warriors,

Sourcerers, weapons. We needed to unite Ovaeris.

"But can we win?" Tris asked. "If this overgrown spot is as big as you say, Mother. If it has already consumed half a world? Even with the greatest army Ovaeris has ever seen, can we win?"

I chewed on a cold strip of meat left over from the night before and shook my head. "We can't win. But sometimes you don't fight to win. You fight to show your enemy they can lose."

"What good will that do us if we're all dead?"

"Fear," Sirileth said. "I mean, that's the point, isn't it? To show Norvet Meruun she can lose. To make her fear Ssserakis again."

I cannot wait to share her taste with you. You cannot understand its vastness, Eska. The flavour of it is beyond anything in your memories. We will fill those dead gods in your stomach with such power.

"Once she has shown herself, and once she begins to fear again, the rest is up to me and Ssserakis."

"You'll kill her?" Tris asked.

She cannot die.

"Yes."

CHAPTER THIRTY

JAMIS HAD BEEN TELLING THE TRUTH WHEN he said the people of Ovaeris would not follow me. I recognised that now. And so I believed he was likely telling the truth about how I should go about gathering the support I needed. The people in charge needed to believe it was their cause, not mine. They needed to believe they were all in real danger from a threat that wasn't the Corpse Queen. They needed someone to believe in. And fuck, but of course Jamis was right again. They needed the bitch whore.

Lesray had made her empire on Rolshh. A jungle continent famed for its giant monsters. Sirileth knew of two rifts on Rolshh, one of which was close enough to Lesray's palace. All we needed was a rift of our own to portal me there. Unfortunately, I doubted we were getting back into Yenheim. So, despite the pouring, ashen rain, we fled the boundaries of my old queendom, and set out to what was left of Yun.

When I was fleeing the Pit, so many years ago, the trip had taken us weeks of hiking across lush, springtime terrain. Now, the grass was no longer green and growing, and the weather was cold with a side of dreary. However, we made the trip in two days of portal jumps. What we found when we got there was a shanty town of starving people mourning the drowned ruins that had once been their port city.

Yun was gone. The waves had risen, flooded the coast, dragged what they hadn't crushed back out to sea, and left nothing but frothing spray in their retreat. Luckily, the rift stood on a highland, a cliff overlooking the roiling ocean. We made our way there without hesitation. I doubted there was anything the people of Yun could offer us but accusing stares and there weren't enough of them left to provide Ssserakis with more than a morsel.

"It's going to be cold," Sirileth warned us as we stopped just before the sparking rift. Tris and his two dozen warriors set about putting on their warmest cloaks. Sirileth wrapped herself in the same blanket she'd been sleeping on. I didn't bother. I had nothing but my old leather armour and my shadow cloak, and the Pyromancy Source burning inside.

Sirileth tore open the portal. We all rushed through into frigid winds and ice beneath our feet. Of course Lesray had built herself a palace on top of a glacier. It was as fitting as the rumours she once had a palace at the mouth of an open volcano. The self-proclaimed Queen of Fire and Ice was nothing if not a dramatic bitch.

"This wind has teeth," Tris shouted into the gale. He pulled his cloak tighter and turned to put his back to the wind. The last of his warriors hustled through and Sirileth snapped the portal closed, then immediately fumbled at her pouch with shaking hands and sucked on some spiceweed. By the time she was done, she had to chisel the Source out of her frozen vomit. She stood shivering, huddling in her blanket as the wind whipped it about.

We all gathered close. I was the only one who didn't shiver.

"How far to Lesray's palace?" I shouted over the howling wind.

Sirileth lifted a shaking hand, pointed, spoke through chattering teeth. "Half a day's walk or so."

Half a day's walk, across the top of a glacier, directly into the bite of a freezing gale. I was far from certain Sirileth would make it.

"Go back," I shouted. "I'll go on alone." There was a good chance Lesray would just have me killed on the spot anyway. If I could send my children away to let me do it alone, all the better.

In response, Sirileth shivered and shot me a scathing darklight stare that seemed to melt the frost flinging itself in her face. She had gone so pale already.

"And the rest of you?" I asked.

Tris shivered. "Oh, shut up and start walking, Mother. And stop looking so fucking warm."

Why does he complain? It is wonderful here. If the hateful light of your sun would set, I would almost think I was home.

We started trudging on into the whipping wind and frost. "Does that mean others from your world might find their way here?" I asked, the wind blasting away my words so no one else heard.

Yes. Horrors especially will hide here. None of us like the heat or light. Be wary of any dark crevices you find.

The footing was solid enough beneath our feet. I had never been somewhere so icy before, but long ago, during one particularly harsh winter, the Olton lake in Picarr had frozen over. The tutors had forbidden us from going to it, but of course Josef and I snuck out to play on the ice. It had been slippery and strange to walk on. I'd marvelled at the people gliding across it so gracefully. When I'd attempted to mimic them, my feet slipped from under me and I'd landed on my arse. It had taken me hours and many bruises to get the hang of it. But here the ice was hard and there was packed snow crunching beneath our feet. The footing was easy, but Ssserakis plagued me with fears of dark cracks that our entire company could vanish into without warning.

We found strange tracks; lines driven into the snow like carriage wheels. Sirileth immediately set her feet between the two lines and followed them. I walked next to my shivering daughter and Ssserakis draped my shadow cloak over her shoulders as well as mine so I could share my Pyromantic heat with her. She gave me a brief, grateful smile, but it didn't lesson her shivering.

We trudged on and it felt like days rather than hours. I heard howls in the far distance, riding the wind, and could not tell if they were wolves or something from Sevorai that had taken to hunting us.

On we went, each footstep harder than the last. Sirileth staggered and I caught her, held her up. Her eyes were closed, her lashes frosted. I slapped her awake until she pierced me with a darklight stare. I dragged her on.

The city, if it could be called that, appeared suddenly. One moment we were slogging through an endlessly desolate expanse of ice and wind, the next, there were squat domes all around like the glacier had grown pimples. We all gawked and stopped to wonder what we had walked into. I saw a furry figure dart from one dome to another and left Sirileth behind to chase them, but a blast of icy frost slapped me in the face and I lost track of them.

We moved on. The wind rushed this way and that, flinging frost at us, skipping off the domed buildings. It's honestly amazing what people can adapt to if given enough time and the will power to bend themselves to nature. The people who lived here had learned to construct their homes to survive in the harshest conditions I had ever seen. At least, I assumed there were people living there. I had only seen the one, and given how furry they were, it could have been a small bear.

My question was answered a moment later when we found ourselves surrounded. I couldn't say where they had come from. We were walking, then weighted nets closed over us, pulling us to the ground, tangling up our limbs. I was about to burn the net and rise, roaring to take revenge, when I saw the spears. I might escape, but all it would take would be a couple of easy thrusts to kill Sirileth and any of the others.

There were close to fifty of them, all dressed in expansive furs, their eyes the only thing uncovered. They spoke a language I'd never heard before and moved with a brisk efficiency removing each of us from the nets and binding our wrists with rope. When they bound mine, I let my claw fade away, freeing my hand, then Ssserakis reformed my claw. They tried again to the same effect. One of our captures shouted something at me. I flashed my eyes at him.

"Mother," there was reproach in Tris' voice and

I glanced over my shoulder to see him standing beside
Sirileth. My daughter was sagging, her hands bound, her
eyes closed. She wasn't shivering anymore.

The third time I let them bind my wrists, I didn't
remove it. They led us into one of the larger domes and I saw
what I hadn't grasped earlier. There were a couple of chairs,
a small cot, some cupboards, but most importantly was the
winding staircase carved into the ice leading down into the
glacier's heart. Our captors led us down. Tris walked ahead
of Sirileth so the first time she stumbled, he grunted, caught
her on his back, carried her the rest of the way down.

The staircase deposited us into an expansive cavern
that glowed with an azure light. We were surrounded on all
sides by ice, but the air down there was not biting or frigid.
It was cold, surely, but not so much that the inhabitants
were forced to wear their furs. Indeed, the cavern was filled
with people. This was the city I didn't have a name for.
The homes and buildings were wooden things, hammered
directly into the ice at the cavern floor. There were no orderly
streets, but a large thoroughfare did lead directly through
the centre of the cavern. At each of the four walls, was a
large arch carved directly in the ice, leading to another
cavern. A city, as vast and populated as any on Isha, built
under the ice. I had never imagined such a thing.

Our captors stopped, forcing us to stop with them. I
immediately slipped my bonds again and went to Sirileth,
wrapping my arms around her. I drew on my Pyromancy
Source and stoked my fire within until my skin burned like
I had a fever. Ssserakis withdrew into a tiny ball, hiding
from the flames inside, but the horror did not complain. I
could feel its worry over Sirileth as a mirror to my own. My
daughter stirred a little in my arms and started shivering

again. I thought that a good sign.

One of our captors pulled down her hood to reveal light brown, wind-blasted skin. Her hair was as black as my own, and for just a moment I thought she looked like my own mother. I had always known my mother was not originally from Isha, but now I had to consider just where she had come from. Did I have Rolshh blood in my veins as surely as Orran? The woman barked something in a harsh language.

"We're here to see your queen," I said, still hugging Sirileth tightly against my burning body. "Lesray. Alderson. Queen." Why is it when confronted by a communication breakdown we resort to speaking more loudly and slowly? Judging by the cadence of our captor's barking, she was doing the same thing.

Eventually a brute of a man whose furs struggled to contain him, shoved forward, pushing aside Tris' warriors to get to me. Tris moved into his way, but quickly found a knife held to his throat. He backed away slowly and the brute grabbed me by the arm, wrenched me away from Sirileth. My daughter collapsed immediately. I thought about fighting, but we were in a shitty situation and getting us all killed was only going to make it shittier. The brute pulled me away and the rest of my group was prodded into motion, moved to stand on a wooden platform with dangling ropes leading all the way up to the roof of the cavern.

The brute shook me by the arm and I turned my flashing stare on him. "Do that again," I dared him.

"Queen," the woman who reminded me of my mother said. "Alderson. You, Queen Corpse."

Your reputation even spreads below the ice, Eska. Should we fight?

I looked around the cavern. Most of the citizens were about whatever daily chores people did living encased in a glacier. Sewing of furs, gutting of fish, tending to a pack of yapping hounds.

"No," I said. "We're here for an alliance. Slaughter is rarely a good opening move."

The woman stared at me oddly for a moment, then turned and strode away, waving over her shoulder. The brute started after her, his grip on my arm pulling me into motion again.

As I was led away, I glanced over my shoulder to see a Sourcerer waving their hands in the air near my children and Tris' warriors. A cage of ice formed around them, penning them in on all sides. A moment later, the platform started lifting into the air, dragged on ropes and pulleys. A section of the cavern roof opened up and the platform rose into it, exposing my people to the merciless cold and wind once more.

How long can our daughter last up there?

I ground my teeth but didn't answer. I didn't need to. We both knew it wasn't long.

CHAPTER
THIRTY ONE

DESPITE WHAT PEOPLE THINK, I AM NOT
an evil woman. I do not enjoy pain, on either end of the
equation. I am not indifferent to suffering. But when given
a choice between my friends and family, and some random
fuckers I've never met, I will choose those I love every single
time. Well, every time but one, I suppose.

My captors led me at a sauntering pace, taking time to
greet some of those we passed. I could not understand what
was said, but it sounded jovial. I caught the brute staring at
me a couple of times, a small smile on his face, and guessed
the little delays were on purpose. My people, my children,
were in danger on the surface, trapped in the harshness of
the elements. This was a fucking tactic, leveraging the lives
of those I loved to make me more pliable. Good to see Lesray
fucking Alderson hadn't changed at all.

They led me into another cavern. This one stank of

livestock, the smell of manure heavy in the air. I saw blood running down a groove cut into the ice, streaming out to flow away through one of the cavern walls. The stink told me butchery was going on somewhere. I heard the persistent clang of metal striking metal, too. A forge was operating nearby. It seemed odd to me that they could keep a forge fire going while encased in ice, but everything about this city was odd.

I half expected them to lead me to some grand palace built into the ice. I'd find Lesray sitting on a frozen throne, staring down imperiously, gloating like she always had as a child every time she beat me. Every time she almost killed me. Instead, my captors led to me a wooden building set against the far cavern wall. I heard the yipping of dogs and saw a huge wolf lounging on the ice outside. This was some sort of kennels, I supposed.

They are going to feed you to dogs?

"That would be a first," I admitted to Ssserakis.

The woman gave me an odd look, then ducked inside the kennels. The brute kept his grip on my arm. There were others about, but none looked like warriors. Some were tending to the wolves, others pushing carts. A woman wearing nothing but a heavy apron, her arms stained red to the elbow, sauntered past, threw a leg of meat to the wolf outside, then turned and walked off. The wolf immediately set to gnawing on the leg.

Lesray Alderson walked out of the kennels, chattering away in the same language as her people. She wore a bone-coloured dress that stretched down to her ankles, a light fur coat, and that strange porcelain mask over the right side of her face. She spared me a glance, then kept talking to her attendant, who calmly made notes on a scroll of paper.

My other captor positioned herself between me and Lesray and fixed me with a hard stare. I waited. Patiently. Or as patiently as I could. I'm not really known for patience. I may have growled loudly enough even the wolf raised its head. My daughter was up on the surface, freezing to death, while this stupid fucking charade was carried out.

Eventually Lesray finished narrating to her servant and turned her full attention to me. "Eskara," she said, her voice husky as if she had been breathing smoke. "Why are you here?"

To tear you limb from limb. To make you wish for death like you have done to me so many times over the years. To repay you for a childhood of torment. My anger boiled inside. I had spent a long time nursing my grudges against Lesray Alderson. But I would not act on them. I forced them down, swallowed them. They were petty things and my need was far greater than my childish anger.

"To form an alliance," I forced the words out.

"I see," Lesray said. "Then you've come a long way for nothing."

"Listen to me." I started forward and the brute tugged me back. I sent him a scathing glare. "First, tell your idiot to let me go."

Lesray took a slow breath. "No."

I was expecting it and I was done showing weakness. I have never been one to simper and beg. Bet from a position of strength, even when you're one hand from losing the game.

I reached across with my claw, grabbed the brute's hand on my arm and twisted, spinning with it to add force. He tried to resist with brawn alone, but I had been trained by Tamura and knew well how to use a man's strength against him. He cried out as his wrist bent to almost breaking. I kicked his leg from under him and let go, turning back to Lesray. The cold bite of steel kissed my neck. My other captor was close, snarling. I let my flashing gaze drift to her, smiled. She staggered back, her own eyes going vacant as Ssserakis wrapped her in a construct. I reached up, gently pushed the knife away from my throat. The woman dropped to her knees. Her fear was a magnificent thing that tasted oddly of overripe apples. I walked past her, closing on Lesray.

To her credit, Lesray did not run, nor flinch. She met me head-on, back straight, gaze unwavering.

I stopped just a couple of paces from her. She was within striking distance. I could have formed a Sourceblade in hand and driven it into her heart with such ease. But I reigned in my anger, straightened my own back, and met her as the queen I had once been. She was taller than me, but not by too much. I could just about see the scars of twisted flesh beneath her porcelain mask.

The brute gave a roar, charged me from behind. Lesray held up a single hand to stop him, gave an order in that other language. The man halted, walked over to the other woman.

"Release her, Eskara."

I hesitated a few moments, then shrugged. Ssserakis pulled the construct and my shadow back. The woman gasped, burst into tears. The brute picked her up and they walked away.

"That was very dramatic, Eskara," Lesray said. She started walking, her attendant close on her heels. I had no choice but to follow. Damn her.

"You started it," I said. "You have my people in a cage

on the surface, freezing to death."

"Hmm," Lesray grunted. "And they will stay there until you agree to leave." She glanced at me with her one eye. "There is nothing for you here, Eskara." I noticed she wasn't wearing shoes. She walked barefoot on the ice and left melted footprints behind.

"Stop being so bloody petty and listen to me, Lesray."

"Interesting choice of words, Eskara," Lesray snapped. "When you show up in my city covered in gore and stinking of blood." I had to admit, she was right about that. I'd washed my face and hair as best I could, but the blood had soaked into my leather armour and I feared I'd never get the stains out.

Lesray stopped outside a pen holding creatures that looked like silky, fat dogs with flippers instead of legs. She said something to the man tending the creatures and he replied while Lesray's attendant made notes on her scroll.

"Regardless of the misgivings between us, Lesray, I need your help."

She looked at me and her eye went wide with shock. The left side of her mouth opened, but the right side seemed to droop beneath her mask. She quickly regained her composure and schooled her features once more. "My help? To do what, Eskara? Which world are you trying to save this time? Which threat are you trying to beat me into submission with?"

"The Djinn are already working to calm Ovaeris."

"So I see. And I suppose you wish to take credit for that?"

Lesray's attendant said something and she replied. Then they were moving again, faster than before. I caught up easily and paced alongside them.

"I don't care about credit, Lesray. I care about the threat that still exists. You've seen it."

We passed through the great archway into the next cavern. I looked up to see the wooden platform was still raised. "What I have seen, Eskara, is an illusion formed by the demon that possesses you. And on that, you wish me to kneel and raise an army to sacrifice to your command?"

Pride is such a useless emotion. Though I have brethren who feed on it. Much like fear, they say once it sparks in a person, it grows and feeds on itself.

Ssserakis' words jolted me to a stop and I stood, remembering what Jamis had said. They won't follow me. They're too afraid of me. But they would follow Lesray.

"Fuck!" I hated it. I hated the idea of it. I hated her, and I hated the entire bloody situation that made it necessary.

Swallow it, Eska. There are more important things. Our daughter freezes on the surface. Norvet Meruun devours unchecked across Sevorai. Is your pride worth it?

"Oh, fucking shut up, Ssserakis."

You know I am right.

"You're supposed to be the voice of fear, not reason."

I have grown.

"Now who's fucking wallowing in pride?"

I looked up to find Lesray had stopped. She was staring at me curiously, probably wondering why I was talking to myself. I glared back. Hated her for everything she had done to me. For the call of the void she had put in me. I couldn't do it. I had to do it. What is pride worth? Nothing. Everything. It is a currency to be spent and swallowed when the time is right. Well, the time was right. Still, it was hard to do.

"Is that what it will take to make you believe, Lesray?" I asked.

She looked at me quizzically, said nothing.

I closed my eyes, choked down my pride, and knelt before the Queen of Ice and Fire. "I am no queen," I growled the words, the only way to force them between my clenched teeth. "I gave it up years ago. My daughter is no longer a queen. Yenheim was invaded, taken. I do not care about credit or being the one in command." I opened my eyes and met Lesray's gaze. "The threat is real. I swear it. Right now, a monster is consuming the Other World and unless we stop it, it will use the great rift to cross into Ovaeris.

"Please, Lesray, put aside your hatred of me and help me stop this monster." I sighed. "Then you can go back to trying to kill me."

"My hatred of you?" Lesray said, she sounded surprised.

She turned to her attendant. "Have them lower the cargo platform. Take furs and food to Queen Helsene and her people." She turned her gaze back to me. "But they can wait in the cage until we come to terms."

Lesray turned and strode away. "Come, Eskara. We have much to discuss, you and I."

I stood and watched her go, then turned to stare at the platform. I had not surrendered my pride completely and I would not follow Lesray like a dog to heel. I waited until the platform lowered, until I saw the cage drop out of the howling wind above. I could not see them well from such a distance, but it looked like Tris and his warriors were huddled close together, with Sirileth warmest at the centre. I had not known how poorly my daughter managed in the cold. But then, there was still much I did not know about her.

CHAPTER THIRTY TWO

WE SAT AROUND A WOODEN TABLE IN AN icy room, Lesray and I. A fur-clad servant brought wine. I sipped at it, found it oddly spicy with a bite like whiskey. I approved of her taste, if nothing else.

I waited until we were alone in that cold, bare room. "What's under the mask?"

"You claim a familiarity with me you do not have, Eskara," she said. "You have admitted yourself that you are no longer a queen. Well, I am."

"Fair enough." The bitch was right and I was begging for her help. "What's under the mask, Queen Alderson?"

"My face." She shrugged. "What's left of it. I see you escaped Loran's experiments, mostly intact." Her gaze flicked to my claw.

"Mostly," I said. My lost arm had nothing to do with the Iron Legion, but I saw no reason to correct her.

She holds no fear. Ssserakis sounded confused. *Not of us, or of anything that is happening. It is not like Josef's zealots though. She has not muted her fear with blind serenity. She masks it, I think.*

Empamancy. Lesray had always been attuned to that hateful school of magic. I wondered, had she discovered how to turn it on herself? A way to banish the emotions she did not want to feel.

An atrocity. I cannot read her, Eska.

I never could. One of the many reasons we hadn't gotten on as children. The prime reason being that she kept trying to kill me.

We stared at each other like gamblers trying to read the other's hand in their expressions. I held out longer.

"Let's say I believe you, Eskara." Lesray started drumming her fingers on the table. "Let's say I believe this monster your demon showed us was real. What exactly do you expect?"

"Your help in convincing the others. The Polasians, the pahht, the garn, the Merchant Union. All of them. They won't listen to me, but you… you they trust." I scoffed. "They like you, though I can't figure out why."

She stopped drumming on the table. "I see you still haven't outgrown your childish spite."

"My spite? You tried to kill me, Lesray."

She held up a pale, slender hand. "I admit, I did. Once."

"Once?" I could remember at least five times.

"Must we air our grievances before we can move on?"

"It might help if you apologise." Yes, I was being obnoxious, but in my defence, she brought it out of me. I could not look at her and not feel the call of the void tugging at me. I remembered the wave of helplessness, of despair, of self-loathing. I remembered mounting the stairs to the library rooftop, walking to the edge, staring down at the flagstones below. I wanted to end the pain. And I remembered leaning off into the drop, caught at the last moment by Josef. I remembered it all, and every time since I had felt the call of the void rise up inside and the need to end my own life with it.

"Fine," Lesray said. She took a hasty sip of her wine and some of it dribbled out of her mouth under the mask, running down her chin. She dabbed it away quickly. "I tried to kill you once, Eskara. I'm sorry. How is Josef?"

I frowned. "He's a fish. He's an ice cube. He's a prophet. Depends on the day. Why *do* you ask?"

"Because he's the reason, Eskara. Don't you remember?"

I said nothing, only stared into my wine.

"I liked Josef. We shared many of the same attunements, spent time together in class. We were friends. He was kind to me when the tutors were not. When I was not strong enough for their liking." I'll admit that certainly sounded like the Josef I had once known. "But any time I came close to him, you pushed me away and claimed him for yourself."

I snorted and slammed the wine back onto the table. "I never claimed him for myself."

"No? You slept in his bed, Eskara. You followed him around. Anytime anyone else talked to him, you threw yourself into the conversation and made it all about you."

"That's not..." I paused, thinking back. "Not how I remember it."

Lesray stood and paced on the other side of the

table. "I got tired of it. Yes, I tried to kill you once. We were sparring with Pyromancy and I impaled you with an icicle. I knew what I was doing and I'm sorry for that. Besides, it had the opposite effect. Josef almost killed me with a kinetic blast, then spent the next two weeks at your bedside, healing you while I could barely move for the broken bones."

"And all the other times?" I asked.

"There were no other times, Eskara," Lesray said, stopping behind her chair, putting both hands on the back. "I learned my lesson that day, believe me. Besides, Josef wouldn't talk to me after that." She coughed, adjusted her mask a little.

It all sounded so reasonable. My memories of the events were different, but now I looked back, they were fuzzy. I had to question myself. Was I right? Was I misremembering? Memories are such imperfect things, they fade over time and given enough weathering, green can look blue. It all fades to grey eventually. What I knew for certain was Josef had a merciless streak to him when his life or mine was threatened. Or was this all some Empamantic trick by Lesray?

There is no one manipulating you, Eska. Horrors are creatures of emotion, I would know if anyone but me was toying with yours.

"What about the call of the void?" I asked.

"The what?" She sounded earnest.

"The…" I hated talking about it, always have. I hate to admit the weakness in me that I sometimes want to kill myself and end it all. But it was hers to begin with. It was Lesray's fatalistic desire, not mine. Something she put in me. "In the library. You used Empamancy on me. You made me want to kill myself."

"What?" The shock was real. The way she gripped the chair back, the anger and surprise drawing her face into half a frown. "I have never been strong enough in Empamancy to do that, Eskara. The tutors used to beat me for being so weak in that damned school. I can use it on myself. I can use it to feel what others are feeling. But I've never been able to imprint my emotions on others."

Truth is a dogged predator. You can hide from it, run from it, but it never stops chasing you. And when it finally catches you, it devours all the lies that kept you safe.

Lesray was telling the truth. And with her revelation, my memories reorganised themselves, like a curtain being drawn back to reveal the world outside the window. I finally saw what I had been hiding from for most of my life. I saw the truth, about her, about me. About Josef.

I'd been alone in the library, studying. The wave of self-hatred had come on me so fast I'd had no chance to swim against the current. It swept me out to sea and drowned me. Lesray wasn't there. But Josef was. He'd known what I was doing. He followed me to the roof, caught me right before I jumped. He pulled me back, wrapped his arms around me, told me he loved me. And I had felt it from him. I had felt him use his Empamancy on me to convince me that he loved me. It was him. It was all him. His guilt. His self-hate. His pain and desire to end it. He'd put it all on me, in me. Why? As some prank gone wrong? Because he truly wanted to be rid of me but changed his mind at the last moment? Because he couldn't take the self-loathing and thought I could weather it in his stead? I wished he was there to ask, to scream at, to beat to a pulp. I wanted him to account for the crime of making a young girl hate herself so much she wanted to die.

A little part of me had always wondered if my love for Josef was truly my own, or if it was something he had used Empamancy to put in me. Now I wondered, was my self-hatred truly mine? I had no way to answer, and I did not think I wanted to know. I could see no way the answer would do anything but destroy me.

"Eskara?" Lesray asked.

I was still in that cold, bare room. A simple table and chairs and a couple of glasses the only things between Lesray and I. I felt numb. Raw.

Eska! You went away again. I could not reach you.

"It's alright, Ssserakis," I said. I looked at Lesray. I still hated her. That was mine, then. That anger and hatred. Misplaced, but mine. I would have to work on that.

"I'm sorry, Lesray." I don't think I could have said those words at any other time in my life, but right then they seemed like the right thing to say.

Lesray rounded her chair and sat again, giving me a strange look with her one eye. "So am I, Eskara. For trying to kill you. I'm still not sure if the world would have been better had I succeeded."

"Me either," I agreed with her. "Lursa's Tears, but I wish I had never gone to the Orran Academy. Josef put the call of the void in me, and the Iron Legion put death in me." I was feeling strangely nostalgic and open all at once. A good release can do that to you.

"Necromancy?" Lesray asked.

I nodded. "I've been followed around by ghosts for most of my life. Mostly they annoy me with guilt until I unravel them."

"I see." Lesray gripped her wine glass by the stem, twisted it around and around. "It could be worse, Eskara. As long as we're comparing scars." She let go her glass, reached up and unfastened her mask, pulled it away,

The right side of Lesray's face was a twisted mass of melted flesh. Her ear was gone, her mouth drooped, her lips burned away. And in her right eye socket, instead of an eye, burned a fierce orange flame. "Prince Loran put fire in me," she said out of the left side of her mouth, the right side only twitching with her words.

I stared at her in horror for a few long seconds. The sight of the flame burning in her otherwise empty eye socket will never leave me. Then she fixed her mask back into place and drained her wine glass.

"It burns, Eskara," Lesray said. "Every day and every moment, it burns. I have to draw on Pyromancy at all times just to keep myself cool enough so I don't melt through the ice beneath my feet. I fear to touch people lest I scald them. Since the academy and Prince Loran's experiments, I have let the fire out just once." She waved at her mask with a hand. "And this is what happened."

There didn't seem much to say about that. Our misery was not a competition, but if it were, I think Lesray would be winning.

"Why wear the furs?" I asked. "You clearly don't them."

Lesray drummed her fingers on the table again. "My people already know of my affliction, but I see no need to constantly remind them I am different." She glanced at my claw again. For a stupid moment, I felt like hiding it under the table. The moment passed.

"Are we done reliving our pasts, Eskara?" Lesray asked.

I nodded and drained the last of my wine.

"Good." Lesray stood and rounded her chair. For just a moment I thought I tasted a burning fear like hot chillies wafting off her, but it was gone before I could savour it. "Show me this monster again."

"Her name is Norvet Meruun," Ssserakis said as my shadow slowly expanded, filling the room and blotting out all light. *"The Beating Heart of Sevorai. The enemy. I have hunted her for longer than your people have been able to speak."*

The darkness was complete. I could still see, of course. Lesray stood, written in grey hues, her eye darting as she searched for anything.

"You do not fear the dark?"

I saw Lesray flinch, but she was still composed, rigid, calm. No fear. "My emotions are my own, Eskara."

"My name is Ssserakis," my horror roared at her.

Again Lesray flinched, but her gaze went stony. "Get on with it, demon."

Ssserakis reached for her, determined to inflict nightmares and pain, to test the limits of her control and her mask. To make her fear. And I realised, it was my anger and hate that the horror was reacting to. Despite our aired differences, I still hated Lesray, and through me so did Ssserakis. It would serve no one to make an enemy of the only chance we had for allies.

"Get on with it, Ssserakis."

My horror relented. The darkness of the construct fell and we found ourselves standing on a river's flood bank. The ground should have been soft underfoot, but of course we were not really there. Before us and all around us, Norvet Meruun pulsed. We stood in her path. Her flesh was bulbous and towering, strangely loud as though blood roared in her so thunderously it blocked out all other noise. Wind thrashers buzzed overhead, the worms wriggling in their skin. Hairy tentacles slapped the ground, cracked stone, flung mud to the sides. Norvet Meruun pulsed and grew a little closer.

Behind us, the yurthammers forded the river, dragging Lodoss' platform with them. Lodoss writhed in his chains, insectile legs scrabbling against the metal platform, finding no purchase. His body twitched, segments scraping against each other. His blood ran purple down his armoured plates. And around Lodoss, worms wriggled, crawling over him, burrowing into his wounds. Norvet Meruun was trying to infest him. If she managed it, she would have two lords of Sevorai under her control.

Norvet Meruun pulsed again, her heartbeat thrumming through the ground. She grew.

"How long do we have?" Lesray said quietly. I heard her despite the noise of the Beating Heart.

"*Not long,*" Ssserakis said from my shadow. "*She knows about the rift now, surges toward it. A few months at best.*"

"Take us back, demon."

Ssserakis released us from the construct. Lesray staggered and caught herself on the back of her chair. I was far more used to the transition. She called for more wine and was silent until it arrived, then she sipped it. I noticed her hand was trembling a little.

"How can we beat it?"

I told her as much of the plan as she needed to know.

"It's the only way?" she asked.

I laughed. "Unless you can think of something else."

"I will call another summit. I'll need you there, Eskara, beside me and silent."

I ground my teeth at that. "Of course." Just like Jamis

and his merchant union, Lesray needed to show the rulers of the world she had the Corpse Queen under control. Well, fine. I could swallow my pride and their insults one more time if it meant they stopped bitching at each other and agreed to help.

"Your daughter, too."

I shrugged, too ready to comply if it got me what I wanted. I should have known, should have realised. Lesray had plans of her own.

CHAPTER THIRTY THREE

WITH THE BARGAIN STRUCK, I WENT TO MY people and freed them from the cage. I hugged Sirileth tight, let my fire chase away her chill, and told her we had done it. She was not nearly so certain, but then my daughter was always smarter than I.

Lesray sent out the word to the other rulers and a new summit was arranged. I doubted they would be easy to convince, especially Qadira, but then I had little to do but stand there and let them spit insults at me.

We had days to waste and I spent them training. My brief scuffle with Kekran had convinced me I wasn't ready yet. I wasn't strong enough, fast enough. My body remembered the old forms but wasn't yet used to them. I pushed myself hard in those days, taking on anyone willing to fight me. Tris' warriors were eager enough and proved a good challenge, and some of Lesray's soldiers took me

up, too. I lost a lot. I lost again. And again. And then I won.
Again. And again. It was a start, but I was not satisfied.
I needed stronger opponents, those skilled enough to
challenge me. I needed to test the limits of my body and of
my Sourcery.

The day of the summit came upon us all too quickly.
Lesray led us to a cavern deep in the glacier where a
hundred guards were stationed, all with Source weaponry at
the ready and pointed at one of Sirileth's archways.

"You built it," Sirileth said, smiling for the first time in
days. "I hoped you would, but I didn't think here. I mean, I
didn't know there was a rift here."

"Of course you didn't," Lesray said, sending a brief
glance at my daughter. "Useful things, these gateways of
yours, but I am not foolish enough to let others know I have
one in my city. I am having another built over the rift out on
the glacier's surface. That one, I will allow others to use."

We passed through the portal and found ourselves
on Isha once more. The outskirts of Lanfall. The clouds had
thinned to the point where sunlight shone through in places.
It felt strange to feel the burning heat of it on my face again.

When we had come to this rift before, it had been
in the basement of an old barn. Now it was a pit, open
on all sides, soldiers stationed at the rim looking down
on us, weapons at the ready. This was the future of
Sirileth's gateways. Not the free travel she had hoped for.
My daughter saw it, too. The way Tor used it to invade
Yenheim. The way Lesray and the Merchant Union guarded
their gates. She tried to hide it, but I saw her wilt from the
corruption of her vision.

The guards were expecting us and let us pass. A
carriage was pulled around. I let Lesray and Sirileth enter,

promised to meet them later, then leapt into the sky with a beat of my shadowy wings.

I flew on to Lanfall, swept low over fields with new autumn growth, farmers tending to crops they could harvest when winter rolled in. My shadow passed over the people and they looked up. I drank in their fear. It was not enough. Rumours had spread, of course. Tor and their allies might have taken Yenheim, but I made enough of a scene that word of my return had spread across Isha. For too long, the Corpse Queen had become a cautionary tale, one told to scare children into obedience. It wasn't enough.

I soared over Lanfall to find the city reinvigorated since the last time. Trade had opened back up and the streets were alive once more. I picked the busiest of them and landed heavily, using a Geomantic pulse to crack cobblestones and overturn nearby carts. All eyes turned to me. The whispers started immediately, the fear growing with them.

The Corpse Queen comes.

I let my storm rage, bolts arcing off to strike the stone, to scorch buildings. Horses and trei birds bucked and reared at my passing. Citizens of Lanfall parted before me like ice before a flame. My shadow draped along the ground like a cloak, and Ssserakis used it to slither into the minds of those nearby. My horror dragged out hidden fears, wove illusions of light and sound, planted seeds of terror. We fed well. I made sure not to outstay my welcome, flaring my wings and leaping back into the sky before some fool could master their fear and turn the crowd to anger.

I flew up to the rooftop of the tallest tower of Fort Vernan and perched there, staring down at the city of Lanfall. I sat, dangled my legs over the ledge, just like I had

as a girl waiting for the final battle of the Orran-Terrelan war.
Fear spread like a plague. Whispers, rumours, tales of dark
omens and monstrous shadows. Within the hour, word had
infected every part of the city. The Corpse Queen had come
and death rode with her. A baker had taken ill suddenly, that
was the Corpse Queen's ill touch. An alleyway filled with
dead rats, Eskara's shadow had passed overhead. New crops
in the Dander's field had become diseased, best burn them
all before the evil taint spread.

The Corpse Queen comes.

Ssserakis and I drank deep, and my horror funnelled
as much power as it could into the Necromancy Source I
carried.

I heard the soldiers marching up the steps behind me
but did not respond. Ten of them, with spears and swords
and enchanted armour as if that would save them from me
if I wanted them dead. The leader was brave enough to step
forward and wise enough he didn't approach with a weapon
drawn. He told me my presence was requested and was very
polite about it. I stood slowly, swept a flashing gaze at them
all, then pulled up my shadowy hood and let them lead me
away. Ssserakis crept into their minds as we walked and
every one of those soldiers was a trembling wreck by the
time they delivered me to the summit.

The Corpse Queen comes.

I played my part in that council of jesters, as Lesray
desired. I stood by her side, silent, and weathered the
barrage of insults and threats thrown my way. I ignored the
curious glances Kento aimed at me, and the knowing smile
on Jamis' smug fucking face. I ground my teeth, swallowed
my pride, watched Sirileth doing the same. Last time she
had been here, it was as a queen, a fellow ruler. Now, she

was a pauper, a prisoner in all but name. Her voice no longer carried any weight, and well over half the summit bayed for her blood as if we hadn't been the ones to inspire the Djinn to fix the world. As if she hadn't provided them all with a revolutionary form of travel. Oh yes, I played my part and kept my silence, but I wanted to burn that council to the ground. Even with Lesray speaking for us, assuring them the threat was real, they argued for hours.

I saw Jamis smiling again, the glances he traded with his fellows of the Merchant Union, the nods they returned. Suddenly I knew the truth of it. Silva would have loved this. They were no longer actually arguing against what needed to be done. They had accepted Lesray's command over the situation. This was haggling. Defining terms. Divvying out rights to the spoils.

They seek to take my world for their own once they have won. They do not understand.

"Let them," I whispered to my horror. "Nothing but idiots arguing over who gets to drink from the poisoned well."

I would love to see them try to conquer my world. It will tear them to pieces. There was an odd finality to Ssserakis' words. I didn't have time to reason it out.

Again and again, the topic came back to blame. It was most often driven by Qadira, still angry that so much of her country had been devastated by the moon's impact. I couldn't understand why we were still talking about it. It was done. The moon had fallen, pulled out of the sky by Sirileth. The world was calming, the Djinn doing their damned jobs. The current threat was greater and had nothing to do with blame. I have never had much of a head for politics. That is probably why I saw the trap too late.

"Someone must be held accountable," Lesray said calmly. She was always calm, speaking softly in her gravelly voice and forcing others to quiet to hear her. "We are all agreed on that. Let us be done with it and then move on together."

Lesray turned slightly, gestured to Sirileth and waved her forward.

What is happening, Eska? I do not understand this bickering.

Sirileth stepped up next to Lesray, swept her darklight gaze across the gathered rulers and envoys.

"Sirileth Helsene," Lesray said. "You have already admitted to causing the moon to fall and you accepted responsibility for all that it caused."

Sirileth stared at Lesray for a long, hard moment, then nodded.

It all fell into place. We were nothing but pieces to trade for concessions. Silva had told me long ago that the best way to trade with someone is to know them. Know who they are and what they want. Give them something for free, something they need, and make them more amendable to a less favourable deal.

"I propose we pass judgement," Lesray said, curtailing the rising murmur of noise. "Sirileth Helsene has admitted her guilt. Let us give sentence and move on to more pressing concerns."

Yes, Lesray was giving Qadira and the pahht and garn and all those bastards from Tor what they wanted. But what they wanted was my daughter's head on a spike.

"*UNACCEPTABLE!*" My shadow flared out above and behind me, rising to fill half the assembly chamber. I let my storm out and it crackled around me, arced from my arms and legs and left sizzling patches in the carpet.

The Corpse Queen comes.

Lesray turned suddenly, spinning on her heel, and taking a single step towards me. Brave of her to step within reach of my shadow and storm. She leaned in close enough to whisper to me alone.

"You are to remain silent unless spoken to," she hissed at me. "That was the deal, Eskara. If I cannot show that you are under control, this summit will fall apart just like the last one."

"You think you have me under control?" I asked, trembling with my rage. My storm flashed around us. A bolt struck Lesray's leg, burning her fancy white dress and the skin beneath. She didn't even flinch as she patted out the little flame.

"I think you need to calm down before you destroy any chance of the alliance you are so desperate to secure."

"My daughter's life is not some prize to get you idle fuckers to do the right thing."

Noise filled the assembly chamber. Lesray's hold over everyone was broken. I had broken it. Everything was falling apart and I didn't know how to stop it. Luckily, my stupid, brilliant daughter had a better grasp of the situation.

Sirileth strode into the centre of the chamber, back straight, head high. "I accept," she shouted loudly enough to be heard over everyone.

We quieted. Ssserakis retreated inside my shadow and I let my storm settle. Lesray turned away from me and it took a lot of will to not form a Sourceblade and plant it in her back just as she had done to us.

Sirileth swept her darklight gaze over the gathering once again. "I accept responsibility. And I accept trial and judgement for my crimes." She closed her eyes and took a breath. I could see her trembling. "I accept the terms on one condition."

Qadira shot to her feet, leathery face snarling. "You are in no place to set conditions."

Sirileth met the queen of Polasia with a burning stare. "I am still a queen. This is a summit of rulers. Conditions are my right."

The representative from Tor, a broad man in a colourful robe, stood. "You are no queen anymore. You have no lands."

Sirileth turned her stare on the idiot. "Neither, currently, does Qadira al Rahal, yet you recognise her as queen still. Tor may occupy my lands, but Yenheim still belongs to me. The only reason I have not taken my queendom back already is by the request of Queen Alderson for peace."

Lesray stepped into the argument smoothly. "Name your condition, Queen Helsene."

"I accept trial and judgement with the sole condition of a delay. The threat from the Underworld is real. Queen Alderson has confirmed that. Once it is dealt with, I will submit to whatever judgement this council sees fit."

It was masterful and it was terrible and I could do nothing to stop it. The summit agreed to Sirileth's condition. We all knew the final outcome. Everyone was overwhelmingly in favour of execution, most of them had called for it openly. But Sirileth had given herself a way out. If she died in Sevorai, she would never have to stand trial. I hated it. Hated them. Hated everything that had brought us to this point.

I am sorry, Eska.

The summit set to arguing again and I turned aside, found a moment of privacy with my horror. "You're not going to suggest we wait until Norvet Meruun is dealt with, then kill them all?"

Ssserakis was silent for a few seconds. *No.* There was more to that statement than I understood.

Lesray pulled the summit back under control. With the matter of Sirileth and blame decided, they called for a short recess. Most of the attendees retreated to their individual chambers or coalesced into groups of minor allies.

I sank down onto a step inside the assembly chamber and brooded. I could not think of a way to stop what had just been started without losing the thing we had secured, the thing we had been fighting for. We needed this alliance, but the cost was my daughter's life. It was too fucking high.

Sirileth sat beside me, leaned her shoulder against mine. "Sorry, Mother. I didn't have time... I mean, I couldn't see any other way. It's fine. I..." She drew in a ragged breath.

My poor daughter. She'd just agreed to be executed in order to secure the alliance that might save both our worlds, and here I was sulking about not being able to stop it. What she needed now was comfort, not more guilt. I put my arm around her, hugged her. A hundred different things to say raced through my head. I could tell her we'd figure out a way to change their minds, or maybe we'd all die anyway, or Lesray could secure enough votes to save her. All meaningless words. Lies. What she needed now was the truth.

"That was brave," I said. "Stupid. Brave. A second helping of stupid." She laughed, sniffed. "I'm proud of you, Sirileth. No matter what happens now, know that I am proud of you. You've done the right thing."

She nodded and wiped her eyes. "They're really going to kill me, aren't they?" Her voice shattered on the words.

I couldn't bring myself to answer, but my silence was all the confirmation she needed.

Kento found us sitting there. She approached with a stiff back and an air of formality. "Eskara," she said by way of greeting. "Queen Helsene."

Sirileth smiled up at her sister. "Aspect." She grasped the situation so easily. No one could know who Kento really was.

"How's Esem?" I asked.

A smile flickered across Kento's face. "My daughter is fine and well. The recent turmoil did not affect Ro'shan much, and her grandmother is quite doting." Such formality.

"Lucky her," I said, not quite managing to hide my bitterness.

Kento glanced about, then lowered her voice. "I'll do what I can, Sirileth. When the time comes, the Rand will vote for lenience."

Sirileth nodded. We all knew a single vote, even the vote of the Rand, would not be enough to save her. It was a nice gesture, though.

"There's something else," Kento said hesitantly. She sighed. "I'm about to return to Ro'shan. The Rand won't be sending aid in this war effort."

"What?" I took my arm from around Sirileth and stood to meet my older daughter. Kento didn't flinch away, but neither did she meet my gaze.

"I…" Kento shook her head. "They're scared, Eskara. The Rand are scared. I don't know why. I've never seen my mother scared before." She stopped herself and took a deep breath. "I've come to say goodbye and good luck. I hope…" She looked up at me, faltered in the face of my anger. "I'm sorry." She turned and strode away.

I flopped back down on the step, felt my limbs grow heavy. Why is it every victory is tempered by at least two defeats?

The rest of the summit went more smoothly. Agreements were reached, plans set in motion. They asked how we would traverse the storm to reach the great rift. I told them the Djinn had provided the answer, and that they should assemble all their forces on Do'shan in three months' time, just before the flying city crossed the Polasian desert and battered its way through the storm.

They asked how Norvet Meruun could be defeated and I told them part of the truth. We needed armies to fight the Beating Heart's minions, to cut into its flesh and show it defeat. Only then would the true heart of the monster show itself, then we needed to hit it with everything we had. It wouldn't be enough, but they didn't need to know that. All they needed to do was turn up and fight and die and fear. Ssserakis and I would do the rest.

That was the ultimate truth. Once Norvet Meruun showed herself, the rest was up to us. And for that, we needed to be stronger. We needed the world to fear us. The summit might believe that Lesray had me under control, but the people of Ovaeris did not. I had three months to drink in as much fear as I could.

The Corpse Queen comes.

CHAPTER THIRTY FOUR

AFTER THE SUMMIT, I COULDN'T STOMACH returning to Lesray's city. Her betrayal stuck like a bone in my throat. She had planned to hand my daughter over to those arseholes in charge in return for their allegiance. Had she really expected I would just sit by and let it happen? She was lucky Sirileth saw the sense in it. I will admit, I spent time every day trying to figure out a way to keep it from happening. I had no solutions. I should probably have used my time more wisely, but we focus on the things that are most important to us. I focused on Sirileth.

The Djinn had given us Do'shan, or at least they were letting us borrow it. Part of the terms I had demanded when I gave them the secret of rebirth. It would be our base of operations, our flying fortress to assault the Other World itself. In the meantime, I decided to use it for a home.

Myself, Sirileth, Tris, his warriors, anyone else who

wanted to come I invited. Before the week was out we had a sizeable force on the flying city, enough that the ruins were quickly tidied up. Well, on the north side of the city at least. It's a big fucking city and there was no way we were making it all liveable. But a few thousand soldiers can do wonders with a mission, and we gave them that.

They were mostly terrans, many from Isha, but a small number from Rolshh. There were also some pahht and I was beyond happy to find Ishtar had come to join us.

"I am not much one for fighting these days, terrible student," she said as she stepped off the flyer her people had given her. She brought two hundred pahht warriors with her and promised there were many more coming. "But training… ha! Training I can do, even with my leg. You! Move over there. Be quicker. Hit harder. Who taught you to use a sword? A tahren? They are blind and that explains much about you." She laughed. "See, I can still shout."

She joked about it, but I knew the soldiers we had could be in no better hands than my old sword tutor.

Everywhere Do'shan flew, we picked up more people. I imagined the Djinn would been horrified to see their city's population exploding, but they were both off doing god things. Usually that would mean fuck all, but in this instance they were still busy calming the world. Last I had heard, they finally stopped the seas from boiling, which the mur were quite thankful for.

Few of the soldiers listened to me. As you can imagine, that tested the limits of my patience. I do not like being ignored, but that is what they did. I was not their leader, nor was I their general. Each force picked a different part of the city and settled in, waiting and training, happy to drain our meagre resources, but little else. Only when

Do'shan flew over Rolshh and Lesray and the rest of her soldiers joined us, did the disparate forces unite under one command. Lesray Alderson's command. I gritted my teeth, swallowed my pride one more time, and surrendered myself to her command as well. It was necessary. I told myself it was necessary. And I promised myself it wouldn't be forever.

When I was present on Do'shan, I was training. I threw myself into combat with a vigour I hadn't shown since I was preparing myself to fight the Djinn. Hours every day spent on sword forms, usually once again under Ishtar's insulting tutorage. As many hours spent each day sparring with anyone willing to test themselves against me. I didn't lose. I refused to lose. And every day I found fewer people willing to challenge me. Until one day, I entered the sparring ring, and found no one stepping forth to meet me.

I sought out Tris and grinned at my son even as I challenged him to a fight. "It's time," I said. "You said you wanted to fight me at my best. Come on, then. Let's do it."

My son looked like he didn't recognise me. He glanced around at those nearby and lowered his voice. "No. I don't think I will."

"What? Now I'm back in fighting shape, and you're too scared?" Again, that measuring frown. "I'm bigger than you, Mother. I'm stronger. And I'm faster." He shook his head. "But I'd still lose. This fire in you is... I've never seen it before. It scares me."

"Maybe it's meant to."

He actually took a step back, as if I might try to hurt him. "Is that what you want, Mother? Everyone to be afraid of you. You want me to be afraid of you?"

It was one of those rare occasions when the truth would be better than the lie. When the lie hurt to tell, and yet

I had to tell it anyway. "Yes."

"Congratulations then." He turned and walked away. And damn me, I let him.

I do not like the taste of his fear.

"Neither do I."

When I wasn't training with Ishtar or sparring with anyone not too terrified to fight me, I spread my wings and left Do'shan. Whether we were passing over Isha or Rolshh or Itexia, there were cities full of people. And where there were people, there were rumours of me. Word had spread, as it always does. Everywhere I went I heard new stories springing up.

A family was found murdered in their home, stabbed and slashed, claw marks on the walls. All knew the Corpse Queen had been in the area and it was no great leap to make the connection. Eskara Helsene was seen in the local graveyard, digging up corpses and feasting on them. A plague had come to town, picking off the weak and infirm, and a dark-winged form had passed overhead just a day before.

The rumours were everywhere. Every shitty situation, every misfortune, every unexplained death, and every ill omen predicted by some useless hedge witch. All were laid at my feet. My taloned feet apparently. That was what some of the idiots started saying about me. I had shadowy wings and taloned feet and horns and six breasts. I'm not sure where that last one came from, nor why it was considered scary. I became a monster in the minds of everyone. I didn't try denying it, nor hide from it. I fuelled the rumours as much as I could. I made appearances in every city we passed within flying distance. I stood atop burning buildings and let all those fighting the fires see me. I walked through streets, my cloak dark and eyes flashing, and sent Geomantic pulses through the ground to make it tremble beneath people's feet. Ssserakis crept into the minds of folk we passed and planted nightmares in their dreams.

It was done for a purpose. A need. We drank deep, filled ourselves and filled the Necromancy Sources I carried. Power from fear. Power enough to hopefully challenge the Beating Heart of Sevorai. It was all done for a purpose. I told myself that every day. It had to be done. I had to be the Corpse Queen. The people of Ovaeris needed to fear me. And they did.

Every day I returned to Do'shan feeling stronger. Every day I felt a little less terran, and a little more something else. Every day I hated myself more.

In the final weeks before we made our assault on Sevorai, the population of Do'shan swelled to unsustainable numbers. Soldiers from Polasia, warriors from the disparate states and nations of Isha. Pahht legionaries in rigid formations even before we got anywhere near the battle. Garn battlemasters covered in overlapping plates of metal that shifted with every slithering movement. Do'shan went from a population of ten thousand to fifty thousand. It was an army the likes of which had never been seen before.

The fear was intoxicating. Every person on that flying fortress was scared. It was a thousand rivers flowing around, feeding off each other. Fear is like that. Any emotion in substantial amounts infects others, feeds on itself, grows stronger and stronger. Ssserakis gorged, fed it into the Sources, like a giant tick sitting in the centre of Do'shan sucking on blood until it was fat enough to burst.

I took to secluding myself away at the heart of the city, at the base of Aerolis' useless tower. No one else went there. There was an aura of danger about it. I didn't care. I went there for one reason: to be closer to Silva.

I set up a little tent next to the scorched ground where I had burned her body. She wasn't there, of course. Not in spirit and not her ghost either. She was gone. Returned to her mother. Everything that made Silva the woman I loved was long dead. But I felt closer to her there. And I needed that. It helped me. I was torn between the strength of fear, the heady ecstasy of drinking it all in, and the wearying exhaustion of depression. I felt so isolated. Sirileth had all but vanished into the bowels of the flying city. Tris wanted nothing to do with me. Everyone kept their distance, too afraid of me to risk their lives getting close. I was so lonely. So tired. Ssserakis' company was all I could rely on, but my horror was struggling as well. It was taking all its concentration to funnel so much power into the Necromancy Sources and feeding on such fear was making my horror more… a horror, and less whatever the two of us were turning into.

I raised a ledge of stone to sit on and stared at the scorched ground, at Silva's grave. And for the first time since I had lost her, I truly opened my heart.

"Hi. Stupid way to start. I know you can't hear me. I know you're gone. But… It's not fair. It's not fair that you're dead. You shouldn't have gone. Shouldn't have left me all alone. Fuck! I'm sorry, Silva. I'm so sorry I killed you. I… I wish… I wish I hadn't. I wish you were here, with me. There's just so much I want to tell you, to show you.

"I have children. Not just Kento. Sirileth and Tris, too. You'd have liked them. Tris is a moody arsehole, but… So was I and you always knew what to say to me. Sirileth is so smart, so fucking pragmatic. I don't know what to say to her half the time.

"I miss you. I've never stopped missing you. Never stopped loving you either. I love you. I miss you. But I'm glad you never got to see what I've become."

I cried a little then. Maybe it was more than a little. I was wallowing. So lost was I in my misery, I didn't hear anyone sneaking up on me until it was too late. I heard the clank of metal and startled just as Sirileth dumped a bunch of armour plates on the ground beside me. She was grimy, wearing a sheen of sweat across her forehead and all down her scarred arms.

"Those are for you, Mother. I mean, for you to wear. When you go into battle." She looked a bit awkward, then raised a stone chair from the ground and slumped into it. Geomancy always came so easily to her.

"I already have armour."

She glanced at me, nodded. "I know. But leather armour is useless. I mean, I've seen the things we're going to be fighting. You need more protection. And I don't trust... I mean..." She paused, closed her eyes, and breathed deep. "I know what's going to happen to me. Even if I survive. But you... you don't have to die, Mother. But I don't trust they won't try to kill you. On the battlefield, I mean."

I laughed. "They won't."

"I don't trust that. So I made you this armour. It's enchanted against Sourcery."

I narrowed my eyes at her. "You're not an Augmancer. How did you create enchanted armour?"

She shrugged, smiled at me mischievously. "I'm not many things, Mother. I've never let it stop me from doing what needs to be done. Are your ears pierced?"

"No."

"Then this is going to hurt. Hold still." She leaned forward towards me and I recoiled.

"I said to hold still, Mother." Sirileth took a small needle from a pouch and brandished it near enough to my face I felt my eye twitching. She wasn't wrong when she said it was going to hurt. She pushed that needle through my flesh five times; one in the earlobe and then four times up the outside edge. I could feel blood running down and dripping from the wounds. When she was done with the needle, she took five metal hoops from her pouch and pushed each one through one of the little holes, securing them with a clasp. I winced and gasped a couple of times, but in my life I've been burned, stabbed, slashed, electrocuted, drowned, beaten; this pain was fairly minor all things considered. Still, I was not sure I liked having metal piercing my flesh.

"They're made of the same ore alloy that staves off rejection," Sirileth said once she'd pierced my ear and sat back down. She waved at her own ear. "Now we match. It's all I have left of the metal, so I hope it helps."

"Thank you," I said, resisting the urge to poke at my throbbing ear.

We sat in companionable silence for a while. I opened the bag of armour plates and looked through. There were pauldrons, a cuirass, leg plates and knee coverings. It looked sturdy enough, but every surface was pockmarked with little holes.

"They're for your shadow," Sirileth said when she saw me poking at one of the holes. "I didn't know how it works exactly. I mean, if Ssserakis would need holes to pour your shadow through. I suppose I could have asked."

"*They will make it easier,*" Ssserakis said, my shadow rising beside me into a vague, fizzing darkness. "*I will not have to envelop the armour to form our wings."*

Sirileth glanced at Ssserakis and then back to me. She nodded and rubbed her thumb against her braided hair. "I don't blame you, Ssserakis," she said eventually. "Or you, Mother. I mean, I am jealous." She looked up then, darklight shining in her eyes. "How could I not be? Did you know Ssserakis spoke to me inside you. I mean, when you were pregnant with me."

I looked over at my shadow. *"What? You let the crazy Aspect talk to your belly. I just spoke directly to our daughter."*

Sirileth winced. "You told me things, Ssserakis. You showed me things I should never have seen."

"You needed to know about my world as well as this one. Both belong to you."

Sirileth stared at Ssserakis, her face oddly harrowed. "I was born with memories, Ssserakis. Terrans aren't supposed to be born with memories. I remembered a place I had never been, could never go." She turned her stare on me. "I grew up feeling like I was missing something, but I didn't know what it was. I remembered you, Ssserakis. I remembered feeling loved by you. And I wanted it back, that feeling, because I didn't feel it from…" She glanced at me, lowered her gaze.

What a terrible mother I am, that I let my daughter grow up thinking she wasn't loved.

Sirileth wiped a grimy hand across her eyes. "I do not blame you, Mother. I understand why Ssserakis went to you and not me."

"I told her, Eska."

"Told her what?" I asked, suddenly scared of where this was going.

"Ssserakis told me what you and it are to each other.

That you are one. In a way I could never be. So I understand it could never have been me. But I felt... I cannot help but feel you have taken something from me." She shook her head, grit her teeth. "Just like everything always becomes about you."

"I never..."

Sirileth held up a hand to stop me. "I planned the rifts. I brought down the moon, reset and re-targeted the great rift. I mean, I made it all happen, and still Ssserakis went to you. And suddenly there is a greater threat. Of course, it's one only *you* can solve."

"Momentous events do seem to swirl about me," I said, trying for light-hearted. "You, too. I worry you might have inherited it from me. I hope you haven't."

Sirileth scoffed, shook her head. "Momentous events do not happen to you, Mother. You happen to them. It is a singular skill you have to take the end of the world and somehow make yourself the centre of it."

She twisted her hands in her lap. "I am starting to think that might be what makes a great leader. I tried my best to be a good queen. To rule fairly and make the right choices. But I always felt like people were just waiting for you to come back, to be in charge again. I mean, no matter I did, your shadow was always there, hanging over me. And you did come back and suddenly you're the centre of it all over again. The only one who can save us. The great and terrible Corpse Queen. The tip of the spear."

My old mantra floated into my head. "I am the weapon."

"Exactly, Mother. But not because you are flung into it. Because you put yourself there. You make it all about you."

I was done listening to her pity herself and blame me for it. "I have to. Don't you understand, Sirileth, no one else can do what needs to be done."

"Yes, Mother, I do understand. Very well."

Of course she did. It was why she brought down the moon. The Maker needed to be stopped, and she knew no one else could do it. And she was right. I had inserted myself into that situation. I had demanded she tell me what she was doing so I could decide if it was right. I had made it all about me.

"It can't be you this time, Sirileth. And even if it could be, I wouldn't let it. Because I know how this ends."

No, you do not.

"It ends in my death, Mother," Sirileth said. "One way or another. So have you considered that there may be another way? I'm already…" Her voice broke. She coughed, wiped a hand across her eyes again and continued. "I'm already dead. So make me the tip of the spear. Let me make my death mean something. Please. It doesn't have to be you this time."

She didn't understand.

"Because you have not told her the whole truth," Ssserakis said. *"You cannot carry me, daughter. I cannot leave Eska without killing her. And even I did, you cannot hold the power we have collected."*

Sirileth looked between us, darklight eyes burning. "What power?"

I told her the rest of the truth then. I told her everything. Why I had been playing into the role of Corpse Queen, and how Ssserakis was filling the Necromancy Sources with power. I even told her why, despite the forces we had assembled, our armies would fail. And I explained her part of the plan. She looked at me aghast when I was finished. Shook her head, buried it in her hands.

"Can you do it, I asked?"

Sirileth drew in a stuttering breath, opened her eyes, and stared hard at the ground. She nodded and when she spoke it was in a voice as bitter as lemon. "Why not? I mean, what else can they do to me? Execute me twice?"

CHAPTER
THIRTY FIVE

THE GREAT POLASIAN DESERT WAS STILL
beleaguered by the raging storm. Either the Djinn hadn't
gotten around to calming it yet, or they couldn't. With no
other options, Do'shan ploughed into the storm.

The winds, even as strong as they were, could do little
to alter the course of a mountain. They did, however, pelt the
city with sand and dirt and debris. Fifty thousand terrans,
pahht, and garn huddled in the city behind stone walls and
boarded windows. We could see nothing outside through the
maelstrom and to attempt it was to lose skin to the slicing
winds and the crap they carried.

Fear flowed around me like a rising lake.

*It is not enough, Eska. As strong as I am right now, and
as much as I have filled those dead Djinn you carry, it is not
enough. This background fear is too weak, too watery. I need more
substantial fear. It is best when they fear us.*

I was huddled in a broken hovel with six other terrans. One of the boards had come loose on a window and was banging in the gale. I turned my head, let my eyes flash with violence, and pinned one of the soldiers next to me with my stare. He cowered from me, whispered for the protection of the moons. His fear was sharp and warm and tasted of onions.

Better. But one is not enough. If we could make them all fear us like that.

"Soon, Ssserakis," I said, not caring who heard me. "Soon."

We weathered that storm for a full day. The fear turned to a sullen brooding anticipation that we could not feed on. It was the calm before the storm, which is an odd way to put it considering we were passing through a literal storm, and there is nothing more maddening than that damned waiting.

Then, as suddenly as the maelstrom hit us, it was over. Bright sun shone on Do'shan, and we all emerged to see the great rift dominating the sky ahead of us. Through it, I saw a grey expanse of rocks and plains and sky.

My world. I felt the longing in my horror's voice. A desperate need to be out of this burning light. To be where it belonged. I envied it for knowing where it belonged.

Do'shan was not fast moving and the eye of this storm was massive. We had a few minutes before we would pass through. Lesray started shouting orders, taken up by her chosen generals. I still didn't like not being in charge, but it was quite nice to leave the burden of command to someone else. I didn't have to think about orders or tactics. I was free to do what had to be done. I sauntered to the edge of Do'shan to stare at the rift and waited.

I heard a loud buzzing from above and looked up to
see a flyer descending quickly. It landed on the rocky ground
a short distance behind me. Kento climbed from the deck.
My daughter spotted me, smiled, ran over. At first I thought
she was wearing armour, but as she came closer, I realised
her chest, legs, and arms were covered in living green
vines. They moved with her every step and formed a bulky,
protective layer around her. Living armour. Only the Rand
could have created such a thing.

"Eska!" Kento said as she drew close. I grinned to see
her.

"Have the Rand changed their mind?"

Kento pulled a sour face. "No. They're scared, Eska.
Of… whatever that thing we're about to fight is."

It did not bode well that even gods were frightened of
Norvet Meruun.

*It is natural for creatures to fear what they have created. Do
you not fear our daughter?*

I refused to answer that question.

"But you're here anyway?" I asked Kento.

She flashed a smile. "My mother said we would not
help you. She did not expressly forbid me from coming to
help."

I almost flung myself at Kento and pulled her into a
hug, but I was aware there were others nearby. Our armies
were assembling. I could not give anyone reason to suspect
who Kento really was.

"This is going to sound contradictory, but I'm glad
you're here, Kento, even as I wish you weren't."

Kento shuffled her feet on the spot. "I understand
what you're doing, Eska. I agree with it. My mother might
be too afraid to help because she gave me her anger, but she

gave me her anger. Well, I'm angry."

"You hide it well."

"Thank you. This thing threatens Ovaeris. That means it threatens Esem. I won't have it. So, what do you need me to do, Eska?"

"I need you to protect your sister."

Kento's face went stony. "I can fight."

I held up my hand and claw in a placating manner. "I know. Believe me, I've seen it. But I need you to protect Sirileth. She's integral to the plan. She's the only one who can do what I need her to do."

"What? What is it you need her to do?"

I smiled.

"You're not going to tell me, are you?"

"You'd try to talk me out of it."

"It's that stupid?"

I shrugged. "No. Whatever you're thinking, it's worse."

Kento gave me a sullen shake of her head, then stalked off to find her sister. I watched her go for a few moments, smiling to myself. I might not have raised Kento, but I was still proud of how she had turned out.

"You ready for this?" I said.

Are you?

I considered the question. "No."

Ssserakis chuckled. *That makes two of us.* There was an odd melancholy to my horror's voice, but I didn't have time for it. *Brakunus is below. We should meet with him before crossing through.*

I leapt from the edge of the flying city and dove towards the dusty ground so far below. It was oddly liberating. So often I had felt the call of the void. So often

I had felt like throwing myself from a great height. Now I did. I let the wind batter my face, gravity pull me ever faster towards the end. A tight coil of excitement and anticipation wound through my guts. Then I spread my shadowy wings and pulled from a dive into a speeding soar. The ground whipped past below me and I drifted closer. I realised I was flying over hundreds of ghouls all crouched in the dirt, waiting.

Brakunus was easy to spot. He was the largest of all the ghouls; a towering, festering mound of bony grey flesh and dirty rags streaming in the winds. I hit the ground at an easy walk, my wings settling around my shoulders as a cloak. Brakunus watched me and growled low in his throat. He towered over me.

"All yours, Ssserakis," I said.

Ssserakis rose above me, a fizzing patch of darkness hovering over my head. *"Coward!"* my horror roared.

Brakunus clawed at the dirt with his monstrous paws. "I am here as commanded, Ssserakis," his voice rumbled through the ground. "I have let no others through the rift. My minions have come. We stand ready."

I glanced over my shoulder to see hundreds of ghouls of all sizes, slinking towards me. Dangerous things, ghouls, especially the older ones. This was no small force.

"What about Flowne?"

Brakunus growled again, crouched low to the ground. He still towered over us, but it was a move of submission. "I could not stop her. She moves on the wind."

Ssserakis flared larger above me, let loose a scream of rage. Brakunus cowered lower, whining, his belly against the dirt. *"You will follow us through, Coward. Join your forces to ours. We have Aire and Dialos as well. It is time to make the enemy fear us."*

"Yes." Brakunus pawed at the dirt, snarled, cowered.

The shadow of Do'shan crept over us as the flying city neared the rift. It was time to go. Ssserakis retreated inside of me. I spread my wings and leapt into the air, beating hard to gain speed and cross through first.

The air was instantly cooler, the light muted and less harsh as I crossed through the rift. I swept down to land on a nearby ridge overlooking the vast canyon that spread out before me. Water gurgled and roared as the river rushed along and disappeared into the gaping hole at the bottom of one valley. Rocky cliffs thrust up on either side, one of them was crumbling into a vast swathe of scree, the other was pockmarked with caves, small brushy trees clinging to it here and there. It was empty. I had expected to see Norvet Meruun close, her flesh advancing irresistibly, her minions filling the valley. But there was nothing.

"What's happening, Ssserakis?"

I do not know. She is close. I can feel her.

"Where's Aire and Dialos?"

My horror was silent. We both knew something was wrong. It stank of a trap. But it was too late to turn back.

Above and behind me, Do'shan passed through the great rift. It cast no shadow. Sevorai was strange, it had light but no source.

I peered into the valley, strained my senses, trying desperately to see what I was missing. Do'shan passed overhead slowly. A portal opened behind me, then another, and ten more. I heard the tramp of boots on the ground as soldiers stepped from the flying city onto Sevorai. The noise grew as more and more of our army passed through the portals.

Lesray stepped up beside me. She, too, was armoured in close fitting metal plates, but hers was painted white to make her stand out. Her mask was in place and her blonde hair braided into a tight coil.

"This is a good spot. Defensible," she said in her gravelly voice. "Where is the enemy?"

I opened my mouth to reply, realised I had nothing to say.

Lesray waved one of her pahht generals forward and ordered him to send two of their Aeromancers out to scout the surrounding area and find the enemy and her troops. I've never figured out why pahht have an affinity for Aeromancy, but the most powerful of them are unmatched in aerial prowess. Two Sourcerers launched into the air, flying without wings.

Do'shan slowed to a stop above the valley, ahead of us. It took a moment for that to sink in.

"It stopped," I said stupidly, as though everyone nearby couldn't see the same damned thing.

"It no longer has the counterbalance," Sirileth said from behind. "I mean, Ro'shan and Do'shan both move by pushing on each other, orbiting each other in an endless spiral. Now Do'shan is here, it no longer has that pressure pushing on it. It has no propulsion to move it."

I wondered if that meant Ro'shan had stopped wherever it was in Ovaeris, too. One more reason for Mezula to hate me.

Our armies continued to assemble. We left a sizeable force up on Do'shan; it was a fortress, after all. The Source weaponry that had been abandoned by the ferals when they fled the city had been repurposed, moved so they could be aimed down at the ground. Artillery from the sky. We had a huge number of Sourcerers on the ground, too. They were our heavy hitters, the majority of our foot troops there to protect them. At least, that was the plan. We were just missing one thing. An enemy to fight.

"I had imagined this going differently," Lesray said.

Last time I had been here, the valley was teeming with life. Little creatures, insects, monsters all fleeing the Beating Heart and its unstoppable advance. But it was gone.

Eaten.

The Aeromancers hadn't yet returned. A scout force of a hundred soldiers was scrambling down the scree to the valley floor. Others were setting up barricades on the cliff side. Our troops were separating into three flanks. If all else failed, here was where we would make our final stand. A useless measure. If all else failed, we had already lost.

"Pull them back!" Sirileth shouted, pointing down to the valley floor where the scout force was spreading out among the rocks, weapons drawn and ready.

"What do you see?" Lesray asked.

"Nothing," Sirileth said. She shook her head savagely. "It's not anything I see. I mean, I can feel it." She turned to look at me. "It's below us, Mother."

Lesray was already giving orders to pull the scouts back. One of her generals ran off to pass the orders on. I drew on my innate Geomancy, pushed out with senses that delved into the rock. I felt a slight tremor, a pulse. A heartbeat. Sirileth was right.

It starts. Let them see.

I turned and ripped open a portal behind us, between us and our army. It led down to the valley floor and through it we could all see the scout force picking their way through the rocky ground, beside the surging river. Thousands of soldiers shuffled to get a look at the portal. The order to retreat hadn't yet reached the scout force and they stood about, staring back at us through the portal.

The first soldier to die didn't have time to scream. He stepped across a crack in the valley floor and a fleshy, hairy tentacle snaked up out of the darkness below, wrapped around his legs and chest, dragged him down. He was gone in only a second.

Another tentacle erupted from the rushing waters of the river. It flailed in the air for a second, slapped down onto the rocky shore, swept across the bank. The first soldier leapt over it with a cry of warning. The second soldier wasn't quick enough and stabbed at the tentacle with their sword. The blade bit into flesh, spilling oozing yellow-pink gore. The tentacle convulsed, coiled around the man's legs, whipped him off his feet. He hit the ground hard and the tentacle dragged him screaming below the rushing waters.

A Polasian woman in fancy armour and a feathery headdress ran to our side of the portal and screamed into it, ordering the scouts back through so they could join us in safety. The fool had no idea of the world she had stepped into. There was no safety here. She'd learn that soon enough, they all would.

The soldiers down in the valley started running for my portal. More tentacles burst through the rocky ground, flailing blindly as they searched for prey. Two more of the soldiers were grabbed, pulled down into the ground. One woman was snatched, managed to stab the tentacle even as it coiled around a foot. Two of her comrades joined her, hacking at the tentacle until it fell away, still wriggling. They pulled her to her feet, and all three of them ran on. The severed tentacle squirmed about until it dropped back down the hole it had come from.

The first of the scouts barrelled through my portal at a dead sprint. He'd already lost his spear along the way. He collapsed to the ground, breathing hard, his fear richly sweet. Another scout was almost there when the ground beneath him shook, cracked open. A pair of jaws snapped shut around him like a vise, slicing and crushing him. The beast that had him lumbered out of the broken ground. It was the size of an abban and was more mouth than anything else. It staggered about on four hairy legs and shook the dying man in its giant beak. It bit down and the scout stopped screaming.

Fear was spreading through the armies now. It felt wonderful. A sharp, present fear. A thousand different flavours mingling into a meal that had my mouth watering as if I could actually taste it. People were going to die here. A lot of people. I couldn't stop it. I needed it to happen.

More of the scouts made it through my portal.

Close it. Let them see you for what we are.

I held the portal open.

A cry went up, one of Lesray's generals screaming a warning. Over on the pockmarked valley wall there was movement. Great, spidery things of clustered legs and oddly pahht faces were scuttling out of the caves in the rock. They stuck to the sheer cliff side and ran towards us. Some of the trees clinging to the cliff started moving too and I squinted to see they were actually creakers, each one infested with those little wriggling worms that burrowed into their skin.

"In the sky!" one of the nearby pahht shouted, pointing.

The horizon beyond Do'shan was filled with dark shapes growing steadily closer, blotting out the sky. One of the pahht Aeromancers Lesray had sent off to scout was flying back across the valley, harried by hellions flapping about them on leathery wings. The Aeromancer, banked and dived just as a hellion snapped at him, barely missing. He flew in an erratic pattern, ducking and diving, lurching to the side as if pulled by vicious winds. The hellions came at him again and again.

The last of the surviving scouts reached my portal and I snapped it shut behind them before any of Norvet Meruun's tentacles could think to come through. The Aeromancer reached us, landing on the rocky cliffside at dangerous speed, the hellions still close on his tail. Lesray stepped forward towards the cliff edge and swept out a hand, releasing a cloud of glittering ice dust. The hellions swooped in toward her and for a just a moment I thought they would grab her, put her out of my misery. But Lesray clenched her hand into a fist and the ice dust exploded into piercing icicles that skewered the two hellions in a dozen places each. They both fell to the valley floor, already too dead to cry out.

Lesray turned on the pahht Aeromancer. "What did you see?"

"They got Polach," the man cried. "Dragged her down and…"

Lesray stepped close to him, grabbed his furry jaw in her hand. "What did you see?" she asked again.

"Monsters," the pahht man said. "An army of monsters. And… and… flesh… just flesh as far as I could see."

Lesray released the Aeromancer and turned to me, her one eyebrow raised as though she expected an *I told you so*. I almost obliged.

Monsters crept out of holes in the valley floor, raced along the cliffside towards us, flew in on dark wings. And just beyond the horizon, Norvet Meruun pulsed, grew, pulsed again. The Beating Heart of Sevorai was coming.

CHAPTER
THIRTY SIX

ONE OF THE GIANT SPIDERY THINGS WITH A
pahht face was the first to reach us. It scuttled up over the
edge of the cliff. Lesray moved to meet it. She threw a kinetic
blast at the monster, staggering it, then swept her other
hand, trailing ice. Six glistening icicles thrust up out of the
ground, skewering the monster. It stabbed at the icy rocks
beneath it feebly, then fell still, dark ichor leaking.

Another of the spidery monsters gained the cliff edge
and leapt over us, speeding towards our gathering army. A
unit of pahht spearmen rushed to meet it. The front line held
shields as tall as a horse, while the back lines stabbed over
them. The monster reared, slamming segmented legs down
among the shield bearers. Three pahht died before they dealt
the monster grievous enough wounds to fell it. Both of the
spidery things had strange worms wriggling all over them,
piercing their skin.

Lesray began barking orders even as another three of the monsters gained the cliff edge. Two charged straight at the armies, the third stabbed at the ground a few times, then reared up, screaming. I was about to throw my storm into its creepy pahht face, when Tris and his painted warriors ran past me, whooping. Tris had a giant scythe in hand and swung, taking off a segmented leg at the knee. The monster turned towards him, but one of his warriors took the opportunity to leap up, grab its leg, launch herself onto its back. The pahht face snapped and the monster bucked, but the woman held on and thrust a dagger into its body again and again until it stopped moving.

A pack of khark hounds a hundred strong were scrabbling up the scree side of the nearest valley. Above, the dark wings of the hellions had reached Do'shan. I felt a familiar crackle even from so far away, and a moment later an Arcbiter released a blast of lightning. Dozens of sizzling shapes fell from the sky.

Lesray ordered everyone to retreat to the army's lines. A unified front.

People feed off each other's courage just as they do fear. This army would serve us better split.

The battle was just beginning and we couldn't have our forces slaughtered too quickly. My horror was guzzling down the fear that flowed from them, filling itself and the Necromancy Sources in my stomach.

The spidery monsters were lurching up over the cliffside in numbers now, scuttling straight towards the army, throwing themselves onto spears and into blasts of Sourcery.

"Mindless," I said. "Just ploughing into us."

"Mother?" Sirileth asked. She stood her ground as

a creaker clawed up the side of the cliff and leapt at her.
She planted her feet, extended her hand, clenched her first.
The creaker lurched to a halt in mid-air, caught in Sirileth's
kinetic grasp. My daughter clenched her hand tighter, the
creaker screamed, its legs snapped. She crushed the monster
into a bleeding pulp and released it to fall to the ground. The
infestation worms wriggled free of the creaker's broken skin,
slithering towards the cliffside.

Another creaker gained the edge and came for me.
I formed a Sourceblade in my hand and leapt to meet
it. Tough things, creakers; as big as a tree and all stabby,
spindly legs like a disembodied hand. I parried a thrusting
leg, grabbed hold of another with my claw, snapped the limb
in two, surprised by my own strength. Before the monster
could back away I darted forwards underneath it and
thrust my Sourceblade up into its body, then drew on my
Pyromancy Source, poured fire into the blade. The creaker
writhed, flames spewing into it, cooking it from the inside.
I got a good look at the worms infesting it then. Each one
was as thick as a finger and as long as a hand. They half
burrowed into the skin of the creatures they infested, their
tales waving in the air, but their heads were all rasping teeth
and strange, wispy white filaments. As the creaker writhed
above me, burning, the worms began to crawl out of its skin
and rained down around me.

Do not let them touch you.

I heaved the creaker, releasing my Sourceblade in a
puff of kinetic energy that sent it flying. It curled up like a
dying spider, its gnarly flesh still on fire and cooking, the
worms crawling free of it.

Some of the worms were still wriggling around me.
I raised my foot and crushed one beneath my heel. It burst

apart in yellowish pink blood. Not so hard to kill, but each enslaved creature was infested with hundreds of them.

"Mother," Sirileth said as she reached me. Monsters streamed past us, ignoring us as they raced for the armies. Closer to the cliff edge, Tris and his warriors had stacked up a number of kills, piling the bodies high. But I saw at least two of his people were already down. "Is this the plan?"

I nodded to my daughter. "Get back to the army. Find Kento. Stay safe."

Sirileth stared at me for a few seconds, darklight eyes burning. Then she nodded, turned, and ran. I turned the other way and raced to help Tris as a dozen khark hounds ploughed into his warriors.

A creaker barrelled into me, knocking me aside, legs scraping across my metal armour. I rolled with the momentum, came up forming a kinetic shield. The creaker leapt on me, legs stabbing. I braced my feet, held my shield, pushed the monster back. I released the shield in a rush of energy that staggered the creaker. Then hit the gnarly thing with my storm. It flew backwards, burning over the edge of the cliff.

I reached my son's group just in time to pull one of his warriors out of the way of a khark hound. I grabbed the beast by its snout with my claw, dug my talons in, pushed lightning through my shadow. The khark hound bucked, spasmed, cooked. Eventually it fell still, a smoking ruin of flesh. More of the infestation worms slithered free of it.

I found my son in the thick of the battle, his back to a dead monster, two khark hounds snapping at him. I joined one of Tris warriors, and we both stabbed spears into the beast's flank, braced, pushed the skewered khark hound into the other. We kept pushing, and Tris joined us, forming his

own spear. We heaved and threw both beasts over the edge
of the cliff to break on the drop below.

Tris grinned; skull-painted face spattered with blood.
I dragged him back from the edge, my eyes flashing with
anger. "Get back to the army. You can't fight the whole of
Sevorai alone."

My son towered over me, chest heaving. His grin
didn't falter even in the face of my chastisement. "As you
wish, Mother." He called to his remaining warriors, and they
all started running for the front lines as monsters streaked
past them.

A khark hound leapt for me and I spread my wings,
climbing into the sky. It snapped at my feet for a few
seconds, then decided I wasn't easy enough prey. It turned
and raced towards the army.

We were holding. Our lines had been drawn, forty
thousand strong, the other ten thousand still up on Do'shan.
Our Sourcerers cooked the monsters with fire, staggered
them with kinetic blasts, raised spears of rock into headlong
charges. Our soldiers crowded together, protecting each
other, poking the larger monsters to death like a hundred
ants biting and stinging a predator. We were holding.
Something was wrong.

"You said Norvet Meruun was intelligent," I mused
as I beat my wings to float above our armies.

I said she was devious, cunning.

"This ambush was clearly planned. She knew we
were coming. Why then does she throw her minions at
us so haphazardly. We're winning because there is no
organisation."

*You think this is winning, Eska? Do you truly believe this
is the enemy's full force? It is a distraction, to keep us occupied*

*while the rest of her minions arrive. These beasts throw themselves
at us like this because Norvet Meruun is too far away. She
cannot control them well at such a distance so they follow the one
command she has given them. Attack.*

Look. Down in the canyon.

I turned in the air, squinting down into the sprawling
canyon. It was filling with monsters, beasts of Sevorai.
Yurthammers lumbered out of caves, geolids swarmed out
of cracks in the ground. At the far side of the canyon I saw
swarms of imps in their thousands throwing themselves off
the cliffside, their bodies breaking as they tumbled down.
It made no sense until I saw the pile of bodies gathering at
the bottom. A minute later, a vast pack of horned abban-like
monsters stampeded over the cliffside, hooves tearing up
the rocks as they slid, hitting the mass of imp corpses and
tumbling down it to reach the canyon floor. Above, the wind
thrashers and hellions were assaulting Do'shan. Our Source
weaponry was cutting so many apart but there were more,
always more. Enough dark wings to turn the grey sky black.

Hundreds of monsters, many of which I had never
even seen before, swarmed into the canyon. Thousands, tens
of thousands. It didn't take long for me to realise the truth.
We were so very outnumbered. I felt my own fear, and it
tasted sickly sweet on my tongue.

I turned and flew back to our armies, looked for
Lesray. Our forces were vast and sprawling, but she wasn't
too hard to spot. All I had to do was look for the stupid bitch
dressed in white at the centre of it all. Lesray stood shoulder
to shoulder with a Sourcerer throwing lightning at khark
hounds. They missed one, it shouldered through the bodies
of its slain brethren and leapt at the Arcmancer. I dove,
formed a spear in my hands, slammed down into the khark

hound with enough force I cracked the stone beneath it. I pushed fire into the spear and set the hound's body alight, then leapt off it even as the infestation worms started to flee the corpse.

"Burn the worms," I shouted, not caring who heard me. "Don't let them touch you. Kill them all as they leave the bodies."

Better to let your people see they can be taken. Make them fear.

"Infested people cannot fear anything, Ssserakis."

My horror gave sullen agreement.

"I assume you have bad news," Lesray said. Her armour was not so white anymore. Spattered with blood both red and black and had a couple of dents I could swear weren't there before. The bodies were piled high before her, and the air was icy close by.

"This is just a vanguard," I said, waving vaguely at the monsters still throwing themselves against our line. "The real force is assembling in the canyon below. Tens of thousands strong."

"Can they climb the canyon?"

I shrugged. "I have no fucking idea, but I would assume so. We can't let the yurthammers get in range."

She frowned at me.

"Living artillery," I said. "All our Pyromancers combined are nothing but embers compared to what those things can throw at us."

"Deal with them," Lesray ordered.

"How…" But she had already turned away, pushing back between the lines of soldiers and calling for her generals. "Fuck!" I lingered for a few more seconds, basking in the fear. It was so strong, so filling, so close. And soon it would be gone if someone didn't figure out a way to kill a hundred yurthammers.

I could do it.

"No," I growled at my horror. "That would defeat the point. You need to conserve all the strength you can." Ssserakis was holding back everything except for my wings and claw. I needed those.

I took to the sky again, gaining height, then swooping down over the edge of the cliff. The monsters were already pouring up the scree, tearing loose avalanches of stones, some bodies crashing back down among them. But they didn't care. They were mindless, driven by Norvet Meruun's infestation. I pulled up at the canyon floor, beat my wings to gain speed, sweeping across the surging army of monsters. Some cried out, tried to reach me, but I banked away from their clumsy grabs.

The yurthammers were near the back, lumbering along, crushing anything underfoot not quick enough to get out of the way. Massive things, yurthammers, the size of a house and not a small one. They have a bulbous rear end, a frog-like head with rubbery, near translucent skin. As I closed in on one pack of a dozen of the beasts, the lead yurthammer's throat swelled up, then it belched a roiling ball of noxious green fumes at me. I twisted, banked away from the fumes. The ball hit the ground behind me, burst open. Fumes spread everywhere, choking khark hounds, melting flesh from bone. If these monsters were allowed to open fire on our forces, forty thousand people would not last long.

I twisted in the air, hit the yurthammer feet first just behind its head. My feet skidded on the beast's rubbery skin. I slipped, slammed my claw down on its back to drag bloody gouges in its flesh, slowing myself. The yurthammer howled, shook, tried to dislodge me. A ripple passed along its flesh, its skin forming stabbing spikes in a wave. I leapt over the spikes as they passed below me, formed a spear in my hands and stabbed down into the monster's back. It howled again and green fumes started seeping out of the wound around my spear. I leapt into the air, letting the spear go in a puff of kinetic energy that ripped the wound open further. Blood and fumes shot from the wound and I formed a ball of fire in my hand and threw it at the yurthammer. The flames hit the monster, ignited the fumes. The beast gave one last howl, then exploded in a gout of blood and flesh and bone.

I flapped my wings to get some distance and stared down at the mess I had created. "That seemed to work."

Congratulations. You have successfully killed a creature I used to order to move rocks. Only a hundred more to go.

The good thing about yurthammers was they were slow, lumbering brutes. I killed three more in the same fashion, igniting the gases they produced, before the wind thrashers above me took notice. A swarm of the beasts closed from above, claws snapping and rocky spears stabbing. I turned tail and fled, chased by the little buzzing arseholes. I was faster than them, but they didn't need to catch me, just pull me away from my real target.

I led the wind thrashers on a merry chase, banking left and right, skimming the ground, swooping in between monsters clamouring to get out of the valley up to our armies. Some thrashers were torn out of the air by other monsters taking swipes at me, others fell behind, gave up.

When I reached the valley wall that led up to the cliffside a few hundred feet above, I turned, beat my wings, hit the wall slowly enough it didn't crush me. I tore a chunk of stone from the wall with my claw and launched it at the oncoming wind thrashers, mixing Geomancy and Kinemancy to speed the shards of rock faster than any arrow. The debris tore through my attackers, shredding flesh, pulping bones, tearing wings. A dozen of the little bastards fell. I leapt from the wall to meet the rest of them in battle.

I will say this: if you ever somehow find yourself with wings, do not fight in mid-air. It's a shit show. I hit the first thrasher hard, knocked its spear away with my claw, planted my Sourceblade in its fuzzy body. I leapt off it only for another thrasher to smash into me. Its spear clanged against my armour and for a few seconds we were both twisting in the air, the world a spinning blur around me as we fought each other. I let my storm out to strike all around me and the little shit burst into flames. Not great considering it was clinging to me still. I threw the monster away before my clothes could catch fire. Before I could recover, the valley floor slammed into me hard enough all the air was driven from my lungs and my vision flared white.

MOVE!

I rolled away, not thinking, only obeying. A spear slammed into the ground where my head had been. I kicked out at the thrasher and it dodged away, insectile wings buzzing. Twenty of the little shits rushed forward, not attacking, just herding me back against the valley wall. They buzzed up and down, side to side, so fucking nimble. It was a problem. I was faster with my wings, soaring about like a bird of prey, but these things were more agile, able to easily dodge.

My back hit the cliff wall. Hard stone. I felt a rumble through it, the deafening beat of Norvet Meruun's heart, every pulse a growth. The devouring coastline of her flesh was close, but her core was still too far away. We needed to convince her to take control of her minions directly. We needed to prove to her she could still hurt, could still lose.

A shout from above and I glanced up to see a cadre of three pahht Aeromancers flying in. They pulled up in tight formation and released a combined blast of wind that smashed into the thrashers and flattened them against the rocky ground. It was all the opening I needed. The beasts were not agile on the ground, they didn't even have legs. I whipped my hand forward and released a wave of fire that swept over the little fuckers, setting them all ablaze. They popped and screamed and sizzled, with a smell like cooking bacon.

Minions should be afraid while they burn. These creatures were so infested they felt nothing even as they died.

The three Aeromancers hovered above. The lead Sourcerer, a male pahht with a streak of grey fur running up his face had an imperious look. "Queen Alderson sent us to help you," he said in a mocking tone I did not like.

"The one on the left sweats fear. The one on the right does not. Kill him." Suddenly all three of them were terrified.

"Stop gawking and go help someone who actually needs it." I pointed up towards the vast bulk of Do'shan where a mass of hellions were swooping in to peck at the troops we had stationed above.

The lead Aeromancer gave me a calculating look, then all three turned and zipped away as if they weighed nothing. I envied them that form of flight.

Our wings are more impressive, Eska. Your people fear dark wings.

I flew again. I had an idea of how to deal with the

yurthammers, but I needed help from Do'shan to do it. As
I climbed past the cliff face, I looked down, searching our
forces, trying to find the people I cared about. I caught a
glimpse of Sirileth and Kento, standing back-to-back with
Lesray. They were beleaguered on all sides by shaggy,
horned monsters with three heads. Lesray fought with ice,
defending with walls, attacking with icicles. Kento blurred
as she moved, her sword all but invisible as she sped herself
up with Chronomancy. Sirileth was a brutal battering ram of
kinetic force, slamming monsters four times her size about as
though they weighed nothing. I felt a strange jealousy then.
It should be me down there with my daughters, back-to-
back, our lives on the line, protecting each other.

Pay attention!

I snapped out of my reverie just in time to bank away
from a wind thrasher as it launched itself at me with spear
held between its claws. I waved a hand, released a kinetic
pulse that swatted it from the sky.

Do'shan was beset by a swarm of hellions tens of
thousands strong. We had intended it to be a flying fortress,
our own artillery to decimate the enemy forces before they
reached us. We had sorely underestimated the number of
hellions Norvet Meruun would throw our way. They flitted
about like bats, diving in, grabbing people, pulling them into
the sky and dropping them screaming to die in the valley far
below. A blast of Arcmancy from an arcbiter lanced through
a section of the swarm, roasting many of the monsters, but it
was barely denting their numbers.

As I flew level with Do'shan, I could see the soldiers
we had stationed there were struggling to fight back, with no
real idea how to fight an aerial foe. The Aeromancers I had
sent to help were picking at the edges of the swarm, tearing

the odd monster from the sky, but they could do that for hours and still be outnumbered hundreds to one.

You cannot fight this entire battle yourself, Eska. The fear from our ten thousand stationed on Do'shan was flooding me. Even with Ssserakis funnelling most of the power into the Necromancy Sources, I felt so damned strong.

I flew into the swarm, formed a sword in my hand, cut the wings from two hellions. I slammed into another, buried my blade in its back, leapt off. Another hellion spat at me, a thick grey globule of goo that hit my wings, solidifying as hard as stone in moments. I let my wings fade, dropped, the world spinning. I grabbed hold of a passing hellion with my claw, dug talons into its back, ripped one of its wings free, then leapt up away from the falling body. Ssserakis fed new energy into my shadow and fresh wings burst out of my back.

I don't know how long I fought like that. A minute? An hour? A week? Time tunnelled into the single point of fight, move, stay alive. I killed tens of hellions, enough I didn't bother keeping count. Despite my efforts, I could not get close to Do'shan's edge, so thick was the swarm.

I saw the flash of an arcbiter powering up, released my own lightning at the same time. The two blasts of electricity veered towards each other, collided, exploded in a storm of bolts that seared hundreds of hellions from the sky. I dove into the space created by the blast.

I hit the ground hard, rolling, stones pinging off my armour. Soldiers rushed in to defend me as hellions swept in my wake. I heard one soldier scream as they were grabbed, carried off, but I was suddenly surrounded and the hellions couldn't get past the thicket of spears.

"Do we have orders?" a terran woman shouted at me.

She grabbed my arm and helped me to my feet. Her terror tasted of ripe berries.

"Hold," I growled, pushed her away with my claw. I didn't have time to try to organise the forces up on the flying city. Lesray had taken command away from me for a reason, I had a more important job to do. The most important job..

I stalked through the thronging soldiers, letting them deal with the hellions for now. I ran along the edge of Do'shan, searching until I found the right weapon. A massive ringan perched on the edge so it could shoot down at the ground. Ringans were horrible things that used a Kinemancy Source to spin discs of metal up to truly terrible speeds, then released them. They could chew through stone and metal as if it was paper. This particular ringan had three separate spinning wheels each with a good thirty discs.

I climbed up onto the war machine and scooted past the soldiers protecting it with spears and bows. The operator was a swarthy pahht with a scarred lip that made him look like he was snarling. His assistants were busy reloading the metal discs, each one as large as my head.

"Can you shoot this thing at the ground?" I shouted over the noise of the swarm and the soldiers yelling at each other.

The operator looked me up and down, then nodded. "Cannot see shit past these fuckin' monsters though." His accent was so thick I barely understood.

I shuffled over to the edge, staring down at the ground so far below. It was tough to see anything but glimpses of the canyon below through the swarm of hellions flitting about.

One of the soldiers screamed as a hellion got past the spears, slammed into him with claws shredding his

metal breastplate. I flung out a hand, threw a fireball at the
monster. It burst into flames, flapping frantically, fell over
the edge to plummet away. The soldier got back to his feet
unsteadily, bleeding from the chest wounds. I looked at the
flames still clinging to my fingers and had an idea.

"Can you aim for me?" I asked the operator. "If I give
you a big flaming target?"

The man bared his teeth, a pahht version of a smile.
"Yes. But can you move fast enough to outrun?" He placed a
proud hand on the top spinning wheel.

"I hope so."

If you cannot, you will not have time to regret it. If one of
the discs hit me, it would cleave me in two.

"Get this thing loaded and be ready," I shouted as
I ran towards the edge and leapt from the ringan into the
drop.

The wind whipped at me. Hellions snapped at me.
I plummeted through it all, twisting this way and that,
slashing with a Sourceblade to catch any monsters I could.
Then I was through the swarm, free falling towards the
canyon filled with monsters. So many I could barely see
the river winding through it. There were strange beaked
serpents, lumbering bipeds with scaly skin, khark hounds,
creakers, imps, a hundred other types of nightmare, all
crowded together, pushing and eager to get to the invaders
from Ovaeris.

*Nothing but puppets. Norvet Meruun controls them
all.* I realised the truth of it then, falling towards a horde
hundreds of thousands strong. Norvet Meruun had already
won. Sevorai was hers. Half of it devoured, the other half
subjugated. Even if we could somehow vanquish the Beating
Heart, she would leave behind a desolate world.

Pity and despair serve no purpose, Eska!

I spread my wings, banked and soared towards the yurthammers. They were halfway across the canyon now and if they got much closer they could start launching their gaseous balls of death up at our armies. They needed to die.

A pack of wind thrashers noticed me, buzzed after me. I was too fast for them, my wings beating, the air stealing my breath. I passed over the first of the yurthammers, raised my hand and released a massive plume of orange flame.

I was past the first yurthammer in a second, already flying over the next.

How do we know if it —

I heard the percussive thump and crash as a couple of spinning discs smashed into the yurthammer, piercing flesh, crushing bone. I didn't have time to look back. I beat my wings harder, desperately trying to gain more speed. At the same time I kept up the fires streaming from my hand. I passed over another yurthammer and another, each time hearing the *whumps* as the ringan discs smashed into the monster just behind me.

I banked, turned in a wide arc, flying over more of the yurthammers. *Whump. Whump. Whump* Each disc sounded closer than the last. The air pulled at me as they passed.

When finally the discs stopped hitting, I extinguished my flames and pulled up, flapping hard to bring myself to a stop. I was panting from fear and panic, sweating. Ssserakis was revelling in my terror. I looked out over the carnage to see close to forty dead yurthammers, their bodies crushed and mangled.

How long did the ringan take to reload? I didn't know, but we still had twenty yurthammers lumbering

forward, wading through the corpses of their brethren. I
flew between the survivors and dove towards the ground. I
hit the rocky floor and released a Geomantic pulse infused
with Kinemancy. The earth bucked, stone cracked, holes
opened up. Some of the yurthammers stumbled, falling to
giant scaly knees, others simply fell over. It was a delay and
nothing more.

A tremor raced along the ground. I felt it through my
Geomancy, had no time to question it.

I drew on my Pyromancy and pushed out a ring of
flames that spread like a ripple through still water. They
caught on the yurthammers, burning hair and searing scales.
It was not enough to hurt them, certainly not enough to
make their fumes detonate, but I hoped it was enough to
provide a set of targets. I leapt up and away, trying to gain
distance.

A shimmer like a heat haze streaked from above and
one of the yurthammers imploded as a series of ringan discs
tore into it. More shimmers and more of the yurthammers
died, each one venting noxious fumes that choked any
smaller monsters nearby. One of the yurthammers exploded
as the flames I had set caught the fumes that escaped its
body. A gout of fire roared into the air, and more shimmers
slammed into it as the operator thought the fire a new target.
One by one, the yurthammers fell.

"Bet the bitch didn't expect me to succeed," I said
between breaths, congratulating myself.

Eska, the canyon wall.

I looked beyond the smoking corpses of the
yurthammers to the far wall of the great canyon. It took me
a moment to see what Ssserakis had meant. Above the lip of
the canyon, I could see ten great tentacles of flesh writhing

in the air. Each one must have been twenty feet across and reaching hundreds of feet into the air.

The outer tide of the enemy is here, Eska. She worms below us, before us, all around.

I gained altitude to get a better view. I could see the throbbing mass of Norvet Meruun's bulbous flesh above the lip of the canyon now. Every few seconds, a pulse of light ran through her, and she grew, expanding outwards, devouring everything.

The canyon wall shook, rocks tumbling from the edge. Monsters skittered before it, running from the little avalanches. Norvet Meruun pulsed again, and the entire canyon wall exploded outwards.

CHAPTER THIRTY SEVEN

ROCKS AS LARGE AS HOUSES TUMBLED DOWN from the broken canyon wall, squashing everything below. As the dust settled I watched in horror. The entire canyon wall, leagues of it, was gone. It was all the Beating Heart now. A pulsing, growing, devouring tide of flesh.

A wind thrasher buzzed at me, rocky spear stabbing. I lurched to the side, grabbed the spear, pulled the monster closer, shocked it with a bolt of Arcmancy. It fell spasming from the sky. I looked about for more, but I was ignored.

"They're still acting like mindless beasts."

The enemy is not close enough to take direct control. That is only the edge of her flesh. She will not bring her core near unless we show her she can lose.

Everything we'd done so far. All the hellions and thrashers dead, the yurthammers, the khark hounds, the creakers. The battlefield was already thick with blood and it

meant nothing to Norvet Meruun. We had to show her that
her minions could not beat us alone. We had to prove she
could not just roll over us with her flabby bulk. I looked up
at Do'shan, still the greatest weapon we had.

I took to the skies again and sped towards our armies.
Lesray needed to know what was happening down in the
canyon and up on Do'shan.

The cliff edge was thick with blood and bodies. Our
forces had spread out, thousands of troops moving out to
split the focus of the enemy. It was working. Most of the
khark hounds were dead. Now there were slower, hulking
monstrosities, many of which were smart enough to carry
weapons of their own. Our Sourcerers blasted them with
magics, our soldiers stabbed with spears, feathered them
with arrows, blocked with shields. From up here, it actually
looked like we were winning.

Lesray commanded from the central part of force,
surrounded by troops. I swept down on dark wings and a
poorly aimed arrow flew my way. I guess someone thought I
was one of the monsters they were fighting.

There is little difference.

"Sure there is, I'm not infested with worms."

Yet.

That was an unsettling thought, but then that was the
point. I landed behind the front lines, shoving soldiers out of
my way. They soon parted before me, fear strong and tasting
bitter like over-stewed tea. Lesray was consulting with a
burly Polasian woman, a pahht man with mostly grey fur,
and a hulking garn. From what I had seen, the garn had yet
to join the fight. It made sense, saving our strongest warriors
for the toughest fighting yet to come.

"Eskara," Lesray said by way of greeting. She looked

weary, splashed with blood. Some of her hair had pulled free of the tight braid, and the icy air around her was so cold even I felt a chill.

"The yurthammers are mostly dead," I reported like a good little soldier.

You are no minion, Eska. We are a queen!

"Mostly?" the old pahht man said in a thick accent.

"Well, there might be a few stragglers, but I did kill about a hundred of them, so yay for me." I glared him down and he didn't argue.

"How does the canyon look?" Lesray said, all icy pragmatism.

"Swarming still. But the majority of the enemy forces are struggling to find a way up to us. They're attacking mindlessly. Do'shan is beset by hellions, so if you have any more Aeromancers, send them up to help."

Lesray ignored my suggestion. She glanced at the burly Polasian woman. "Move the northern flank closer to block off those scrambling up the scree. The Southern flank can stay where they are, they're to provide us with protection. We're going to approach the cliff edge. From there, we can use our Sourcerers to rain down artillery on the monsters trapped in the canyon."

Her generals hurried away to carry out her orders and Lesray finally turned to me. She opened her mouth to speak, but I cut her off.

"Where's my daughter?"

Lesray looked me up and down. My armour was black where hers was white. My hair dark where hers was blonde. My skin dusky where hers was milky. We were opposites in so many ways, and yet we were both splashed with the blood of our mutual enemies and fighting for the survival of our world. We'd never like each other, but in that moment, I think a thread of respect was strung between us.

"Queen Helsene is fighting with the northern flank. She's a powerful Sourcerer, Eskara."

I grunted. "And my son."

Lesray sighed. "I have no idea. He refuses to follow orders."

"You have no idea," I agreed.

"You promised an army, Eskara. Monsters from this world fighting with us. Where is it?"

She meant Aire and Dialos. "Ssserakis?"

My shadow bubbled up beside me. *The Twins should be here. They swore it.*

Lesray's eye flicked from me to Ssserakis and back again. "Go find them. Bring them here."

"What about the battle?"

Lesray stalked past me. "We can survive without the great Eskara Helsene for a while."

We were never going to be friends even if we both somehow survived this shit.

"We should kill her, Eska. Think of the terror such disarray would cause."

Lesray stopped, glanced over her shoulder at me. There was iron in that gaze. Frost poured from her, pooling as chilling mist on the ground, ice creeping along the stones towards me. Then she turned her back on me, and strode away, shouting orders.

"I don't think she liked your suggestion."

Ssserakis just laughed and retreated inside. We leapt into the air, wings buffeting the soldiers below, and gained some altitude.

"Where are they, Ssserakis? Where are Aire and

Dialos?" Below us, Lesray's central force started moving, closing in on the cliff's edge. It was a good vantage point. If they could hold back the tide of monsters streaming up the cliffside, our Sourcerers could devastate the beasts gathering in the canyon below.

They should be here. My horror sounded strained. It was busy drinking in as much fear as it could, funnelling it into the three Necromancy Sources in my stomach. Yet, there was a note of panic to Ssserakis' words. *South.*

We flew south. It wasn't easy leaving the battle behind. My children were down there, fighting for their lives. The fear pouring from our armies would go to waste. But we needed to show Norvet Meruun she could lose, and we wouldn't manage that without the Twins. They would turn the tide of the battle.

We were almost out of sight when I heard the crack. It was a terrible sound like the end of the world given voice. I pulled to a halt, slowing my beating wings to a steady pulse to hover in the air. We'd forgotten about the geolids, their ability to tunnel through rock, chewing at the foundations of the earth. Weakening it. Even as I watched, the cliffside cracked, broke apart, gave way. Ten thousand of our soldiers fell with it, tumbling down the canyon wall to break upon the ground far below. The terror hit me even so far away like a wave of dread anticipation. That feeling of your foot missing a step, the surge of adrenaline, but amplified ten thousand-fold. Ssserakis sucked it all in.

"We have to go back," I said, tried to go. My wings didn't respond, just kept their steady beating to keep us in place.

And do what? If any of them survived that fall, there is nothing you can do for them, Eska. You cannot save everyone.

They are not here to be saved. The white queen was right, we need to find Aire and Dialos and bring them here. At least we know our daughters were not with those that fell.

My horror was right. And besides, if I was lucky, the fall had killed Lesray. Oddly, that thought brought me no comfort. We turned and dove, picking up speed to fly to the Twins as swiftly as possible.

We passed over a forest I remembered as expansive and bristling with life. Now it was a sparsity of defiant trees clinging to life. I saw no movement through the canopy. At the edges of the forest imps sawed at the trunks with crude tools, dragging fallen trees away.

The enemy's constant expansion comes with a price. She must consume to grow. It is her will and her purpose.

An endless existence of devouring life, spreading across the world, infecting everything she came in contact with. In some ways, I pitied her. Norvet Meruun knew no other way. She was created to do this, brought into existence by childish gods who didn't know any better. Fools with more power than sense.

"Whose nightmare was she, do you think?" I asked Ssserakis as we flew on. "Terran? Pahht? Garn?"

The nightmare of gods, maybe?

"What?"

She bears a striking resemblance to the Maker, does she not? Perhaps Norvet Meruun is what the Rand and Djinn dream of in nightmares.

"That would be a bit stupid, wouldn't it?" We crested a mountainous rise to find a vast lake before us. The surface was crystal clear and I saw mammoth crab-like things scuttling about under the waters. "Why would they make their own nightmares real?"

Ssserakis chuckled. *I know more of fear than you, do, Eska. There is a reason I have no tangible form. There is no better way to face your fear than to make it flesh and blood.*

"You might be right. Do you think Mezula or Aerolis would tell us the truth if we asked?"

Do you really think we will have chance to ask?

Past the lake was a bulbous hill, brown grass swaying in the breeze. And beyond that a vast swampland littered with bodies. We soared down to land atop the hill, my feet finding the ground spongy rather than firm.

Aire and Dialos were everywhere. Or bits of them were everywhere. Thousands of bodies torn apart, limbs discarded, skulls smashed in, serpents torn in two, eyes gouged, faces torn, bones broken. Tens of thousands of dead bodies all in one place. And standing in the centre of all that carnage was a single figure. He had seven legs, dozens of arms sticking out all over his torso, a single cracked horn on his head. Formed from the bodies of those he had killed and grafted onto himself, stood Kekran. Alone. He had killed Aire and Dialos by himself.

"How?" I whispered the word. "How is that possible?"

Ssserakis was silent.

A single serpent, among all the bodies, was still moving. It wriggled, undulated, one wing torn away to a blood stump, the other trembling. The pudgy, childish face of Dialos cried out as the serpent coiled, pushed forward, coiled again. Desperately trying to flee. Dialos saw us, even from a distance, and drew in a deep breath.

"Ssserakis," the serpent cried in a shrill voice tight with pain. "Help me."

A hoofed foot smashed the serpent's skull, crushing it.

Dialos gave a violent spasm and was gone. No other moved
down below. Aire and Dialos, the Twins, one of the lords of
Sevorai was dead. Kekran stood above the crushed serpent
and stared up at us.

Run, Eska. Fly. Ssserakis unfurled my wings before I
could argue.

Below, Kekran reached down and tore the last
remaining wing from the serpent, attached it to his back, the
flesh melding to accept it. He tore away excess legs and arms
from his own body and searched about for more wings. I
stood, watching in horrified fascination.

*Eskara, we cannot fight him. Not here. We should flee.
Return to our forces.*

Kekran found a second wing, attached it to his back,
then a third, and a fourth. He flapped them experimentally,
then started into a loping run, leapt into the air. And flew.
Four wings beat against each other like a dragonfly.

Eska!

I turned, jumped, launched a kinetic blast into the
spongy ground to give myself a push. We fled, speeding
away as fast as we could. Kekran gave chase.

We passed over the lake, over the forest, wings
beating as hard as I could. Kekran kept up, even gained on
us, his four larger, overlapping wings giving him greater
speed. Ssserakis brooded in silent panic. I wasn't far behind
my horror.

"How is that possible?" I asked, the wind whipping
away my words. "He killed all of Aire and Dialos."

My horror said nothing.

"Ssserakis," I snapped.

*He is Kekran. I always believed him capable of more than
he claimed. Typical that it takes his corruption to bring that true*

strength out of him.

I glanced over my shoulder. Behind my flapping wings, I could see Kekran gaining on us. I banked, dipped to pick up some extra speed. If we gained any distance on the fucker, I couldn't tell.

"Can he be killed?"

I do not know. He never has been before.

"But is he immortal, like you and Norvet Meruun?"

No. I am not immortal, Eska. I cannot be killed, but I can starve to death. Only Norvet Meruun and Lodoss are truly immortal.

Do'shan was in sight now, its enormous bulk a beacon. There were regular flashes at its top where Source weaponry was being fired, occasional streaks of lightning searing out across the grey sky. I climbed a little higher and saw Norvet Meruun dominating the horizon. The pinkish pulses rippling along flesh were so regular now, every three seconds, and I knew each one was accompanied by her putrid flesh gobbling up the land and everything in front of her.

It wasn't long before we flew close enough to the battle that I could see the shit we were in. The central bulk of Lesray's army, ten thousand people, had been caught in the collapsing cliffside. Not all were dead. There was a desperate struggle at the base of the cliff. Lesray, her white armour stained with dust and dirt and blood. Her left arm hung limp by her side, but she defended her surviving troops with a skill in Pyromancy I had never witnessed before. Ice formed beneath her feet and she slid along it, frosty crystals poured from her hand, freezing monsters in blocks of ice as they reached for her. Icicles rose around her, piercing beasts, pinning them in place. She pulled a wall of solid ice from the ground high enough it left a pack of khark hounds scrabbling at it in vain.

Behind Lesray was a rescue operation in progress. A small host of soldiers and Sourcerers had survived, they were busy trying to dig others out of the collapsed cliffside. Geomancers crushed stone, flung dust aside, held up sections of collapsing rock. Soldiers pulled their injured comrades from the mess. Biomancers poured energy into the wounded, not enough to fully heal them, but enough to stabilise, to get them back on their feet and shove a weapon in their hands. It was a valiant effort. It was doomed to fail.

Up on the cliffside, the northern flank, where Sirileth should be, was beset on all sides. I could make out little of the actual fighting, but I saw flashes of Sourcery and hoped it meant my daughters were still alive.

The southern flank was dealing with its own problems. Geolids were tunnelling up, erupting from the rocky ground, snatching soldiers, destabilising the earth so it opened into deadly fissures. The soldiers looked to be trying to find a way down to the canyon floor, to help the remnants of the central force.

Above, Do'shan was still dealing with the hellion swarm. Only, it wasn't just hellions anymore. I saw winged serpents that looked like flashes of green or blue, so nimble no Source weaponry could target them. The fight did not appear to be going well.

Below, Lesray staggered as a massive horned beast smashed through one of her ice walls. She shoved out at it, pushing herself back in time to stop being trampled, but it roared and rampaged, breaking down the ice for smaller monsters to swarm around its stamping legs. The garn surged forwards to meet it. A hundred battle masters. Giant slugs coated in metal armour, each wielding twenty different weapons in flailing, fleshy limbs. We'd been holding the garn in reserve for when things got bad. Well, now they were shit with a side helping of fucked.

The garn hacked the behemoth to pieces in moments, crushed the smaller monsters, poured out of the hole in the ice wall and carved a path through the canyon, creating space everywhere they went. Each one beat back its own personal circle of death with spinning blades, smashing hammers, stabbing spears. They screamed as they went and it was an undulating cry that put a chill in even my blood. Behind them, Tris and his remaining warriors followed into the canyon, holding the breach in Lesray's ice wall.

We were losing. Any way I looked at it, the battle was slipping from us. We were outnumbered, our forces were dwindling while the enemy kept getting reinforcements, pouring in from everywhere. And Norvet Meruun still hadn't bothered to show up to the fight. Her tide of flesh crept ever onward, but her core was elsewhere. Safe and secure somewhere in her ocean of a body.

"We need to prove she can still lose," I said as I slowed myself to a stop above the canyon. I turned to face Kekran as he soared towards me.

What are you doing, Eska?

"What better way to show her she can lose than to take away her favourite toys?" Kekran was the most powerful minion she had. And I was going to kill him.

Yes. YES. Ssserakis stopped funnelling power into the Sources in my stomach. It still fed on the fear flowing from our armies, but my horror gorged itself on the strength. My shadow flared, my wings spread wider, my armour grew inky spikes.

"You're supposed to be conserving all your strength, Ssserakis."

Kekran was my friend, Eska. I WILL help you fight him. I wonder if Ssserakis even had the concept of friendship before our union corrupted it.

Kekran sped towards me, stolen wings rasping against each other.

"*Kekran,*" Ssserakis screamed from my shadow. "*I will release you from this tortuous slavery.*"

I threw a forking blast of Arcmancy at Kekran as he closed on me. The lightning hit him, seared his skin, burned away one of his wings. Kekran dipped, tore one of his other wings away, recovered. He slammed into me and we spun about in the air. I stabbed a Sourceblade into his gut, dragged it around, spilling his guts. One of Kekran's arms grabbed my hand with the Sourceblade, pulled it to a stop. Two more of his arms grabbed my shoulders. Ssserakis' shadowy spikes tore into the flesh. Kekran squeezed the metal pauldrons and I heard them squeal as the metal started to bend. More of his stolen arms reached over his shoulders, clutching for my neck.

I pushed out with a wave of kinetic force, tearing free of Kekran's grip and pushing us apart. I reached up with my claw and tore my dented pauldron away.

Kekran flew towards me again and I rushed to meet him. We met in a clash of flailing fists and slicing shadow. Ssserakis cleaved two of his arms away as we spun about in the air, untethered. Kekran reached for my arms, my legs. One of his stolen hands was huge, grabbed me by the waist, squeezed hard enough I felt my armour bending, pressing in on my body. I screamed in pain. Dragged my claw over his back. Tore away one of his remaining wings. Shoved a

Sourceblade into his face.

We dropped, spinning, plummeting. The world was a dizzying blur, the wind whipped away my breath, bile rose in my throat. Kekran kept grabbing for me, but he was running out of arms. I thrust my Sourceblade down into the arm that was crushing my waist, released the blade in a rush of kinetic force that burst apart the wrist. The limb and the hand grabbing me fell away. I twisted in Kekran's reaching arms, placed my feet against his chest, kicked out with as much strength as I could, pushing us apart.

I had no idea which way was up or down, no idea how close we were to the ground, but I gained my freedom. A hand wrapped around my thigh, squeezed so tight I screamed, and suddenly I was plummeting again. Taloned fingers shredded metal, pierced flesh, tearing my leg. Ssserakis flared my shadow into a thousand inky needles, pierced every bit of Kekran's remaining arm, but the monster held on. I beat my wings and slowed us a little, but I couldn't keep us both up. The ground rushed towards us so fast. I could see it below Kekran as the monster crushed my leg.

I slammed down with fist and claw, releasing a blast of kinetic force that pulverised flesh, pulping Kekran's face and shoulders. His taloned arm tore down my leg, shredding my armour and my skin. He fell, plummeting the rest of the distance and hit the ground with a wet smack. His skin burst like a tomato crushed in a fist.

Ssserakis flared my shadow into a black blanket above me, slowing our descent. Still too fast. I hit the ground hard, felt something snap, screamed. Everything went black.

CHAPTER THIRTY EIGHT

I WAS BACK IN THE EMPEROR'S RED CELLS again. Searing needles poked into my thigh, paper thin knives wedged under my toenails, that damned hooked knife slicing away at my skin flaying my calf.

There was such noise. A cacophony of screams, rumbles, crunches. Light burned through my closed eyelids. I wanted to fall back into nothing, escape the pain in unconsciousness or even death. It was all too much. Too fucking much.

Eska!

I groaned. It was either that or scream.

Brace yourself.

Something snapped. Fresh agony exploded in my leg like someone had taken a hammer to my knee. I screamed and everything went dark again.

Eska...

Go away.

Eskara, wake up.

No.

I am sorry to do this.

I spasmed. Cold talons dug into my flesh, twisted my limbs until they almost snapped. Icy thorns spiked through my head. A tight cage crushed my heart. I gasped, opened my eyes to a battle raging around me.

Hellions winged overhead, chased by Aeromancers throwing blasts of slicing wind. The ground trembled. A garn pushed back some great, shaggy monster of muscle that beat an axe head into the slug again and again, each crushing stroke spurting blood. An imp with worms infesting its skull loped up to me, raised a spear to stab down. I rolled away from the strike, my leg screaming in agony with the movement. I thrust my claw into the imps abdomen, threw a kinetic blast that blew its spine out of its back and flung the little shit away.

My shadow crawled across my face like insects and I felt sharp slices of pain as Ssserakis sutured my wounds closed. I looked down at my torn leg to find my greave torn way and my leg coated in black shadow.

I cannot heal such damage, Eska. I have closed what wounds I can and reset your bone, but the flesh is shredded.

I grunted, felt sick from the pain, had to swallow down bile. I couldn't afford to vomit. I needed my Sources. By Lursa's fucking Tears everything hurt. I rolled onto my good leg; my bad leg splayed out to the side. I screamed in pain as I pushed back to standing. My bad leg ached down to the bone, hurt like knives cutting away the flesh, but it just about held my weight. Ssserakis was keeping it together, keeping me upright. My shadow bound my leg together and acted as a crutch all at once.

A dozen paces away, the garn finally died as the shaggy-haired monster buried its axe in the slug's face. Ichor oozed away from the sagging thing and the stink of it reached me even over the stench of the battlefield. The towering brute of muscle wrenched its axe free, turned my way. Worms wriggled all along its skin, hiding within its hair.

The monster lumbered towards me, raised the axe still dripping with garn blood. I stamped on the ground with my bad leg, the pain making my vision dim, and released a Geomantic pulse that shattered the rock at the monster's feet. It stumbled, fell up to its waist in the hole I created. Then I punched out and released a kinetic blast so strong it knocked me back, snapped the monster's neck, blasted away half its skull. The beast slumped.

I'd had enough. Enough of this battle. Enough of being slapped around. Enough of Norvet Meruun. And most fucking certainly, I'd had enough of Kekran.

Then I have some bad news for you.

I limped about, turning to see Kekran slowly rising on new hands he had torn from the host of dead around us.

"What?" I shouted at the monster. "You were fucking pulp!"

Kekran didn't respond, of course. He was infested and beyond words. He no longer resembled a terran. His body was a dark mass of rippling, discoloured muscle. His face was crushed on one side, the other half a swirling ripple of pitted flesh and one malevolent eye. He had no legs. Instead, he had twenty arms reaching out of every part of his body, like some sort of monstrous fucking starfish formed out of imp arms. Even as I watched, he reached down, ripped a dead imp's head away and pressed it against his own skull. The imp's flesh sagged, flowed, bones cracked and reformed. Kekran's head healed itself of injury. He threw the wasted body away, plucked a spear and hefted an axe from the ground and focused on me again.

"Fuck!" I sagged, suddenly certain I had no way to kill this thing. He'd just healed from being reduced to mush. I, on the other hand, was being held together by shadow and flagging willpower.

Kekran launched towards me at a scuttling run, hands acting as feet. I limped backwards, formed a shield in my claw, and a Sourceblade in my hand. I blocked, staggered away, dodged, slashed out. Every time I severed an arm, Kekran scooped another from the body strewn battlefield and grafted the limb to himself. I gave ground over and over, moving past fighting garn and slaughtered monsters. Kekran was growing all the while, grafting new limbs onto himself. He snatched a tail from a beast and attached it to his back, and suddenly I had a whip-like stinger to defend against as well as all his arms. Before long, he was wielding ten weapons at once, and had a horn sticking out of his head that threatened to gore me if I ever let him get close.

"Wings, Ssserakis." My horror obeyed instantly, unfurling my shadowy wings and blocking a stabbing spear. I leapt back, beating my wings to give me some space. Kekran immediately looked about, then tore the wings from a nearby hellion corpse.

You cannot defeat Kekran alone, Eska. We have to work together.

An idea came to me. I needed an ally. I turned and flew away, already knowing the bastard would give chase. I didn't know how much control Norvet Meruun had over him from so far away, but Kekran seemed fixated on me. Or more likely, fixated on Ssserakis.

I banked, twisted, flew, turned, searched the battlefield, flying past skirmishes and slaughters. I had to find him. And suddenly there he was. Tris was alone, all his warriors either dead or fled. He was covered in blood and I hoped none of it was his own. His painted face had run, somehow making it even more horrific. Bodies were strewn around him, monsters he had slain, friends he had lost.

"Tris!" I shouted as I flew past.

He turned, saw me zip past, spotted the fiend chasing me. He formed his scythe in hand, spun, slashed as Kekran soared past him. I pulled up, flaring my wings to slow my speed, turned and flew back to Tris. Kekran landed below me in two pieces. Tris' strike had cleaved his body cleanly. Too cleanly.

My leg buckled as I landed to next to Tris. I staggered, grit my teeth, cried out despite myself. My son steadied me with a single hand on my arm.

"Mother," he said in a growl. "You look a little banged up." I know we hadn't left things congenially, but I also knew I could rely on my son in a pinch.

"That fucker won't stop chasing me," I said between sharp breaths.

"Well, it's dealt with now, isn't... Oh, what the fuck?" I followed Tris' gaze to see Kekran had fused his two halves back together. His stolen wings fell away and the monster hauled a terran body up, probably one of Tris' friends, and ripped it apart, grafting the legs to his hips and scooping out an eyeball to replace one of his own that had popped when he crashed.

I leaned against Tris, struggling to catch my breath.

"I have an idea how to kill him, but I can't fight him alone. He's too strong."

"He must be to have put you in such a state." Tris shrugged me away and took a step forward toward Kekran. "Hey, you overgrown earwig-looking fuck! Stop eating my friends."

I grabbed hold of Tris' arm to stop him and pulled him back. He had a face as thunderous as a storm at sea.

"We split his attention, hit him from multiple sides at once. Push away all the bodies, don't let him graft any more limbs onto himself."

Tris nodded and turned. I pulled him back one last time.

"Tris, do not let him grab you. He's strong."

Again, Tris shrugged me away. "Then I suppose we just have to be stronger, Mother." He launched into a skipping run, scythe held out to the side.

I limped after my son, throwing kinetic blasts at bodies, shoving them away from us. There were a lot of bodies.

Tris loped around beside Kekran, slashed out with his scythe. Kekran didn't even block and the blade sliced through two of his arms. He lurched forward, stabbing a spear at Tris. Tris leapt back, still moving at his skipping jog, circling the monster.

Kekran reached down for the arms Tris had severed and I threw a kinetic blast, pushing them away. The monster turned to glare at me and Tris darted in again. His scythe cut through a trailing arm and Tris blasted it away with his own kinetic push. Kekran turned to my son. I rushed in, stabbed my sword through one of the monster's arm's attached to his back, let the blade go in a rush of energy that

blasted skin and bone apart. I snatched the arm out of the
air, limped backwards and threw the limb away as far as I
could. Kekran turned again and Tris slipped in and brought
his scythe around in a punishing arc.

Tris and I fought like we never had before. We circled
Kekran, savaging him like wolves taking bites then leaping
away from retribution. We wore the fucker down, slicing
off limbs, blasting body parts away, never outstaying our
welcome or letting the monster get close to us. One of his
limb fell, then another, then ten, then twenty. Kekran roared
in frustration as Tris danced in, spinning his scythe around,
lopping the last of his arms away. I snatched it out of the air
with my claw, threw it to the ground and hit it with a kinetic
blast hard enough that I pulverised flesh and bone and left
nothing but a greasy smear on the rocky ground.

I like to think there was panic in Kekran's eyes at the
end. As he finally realised he had no more limbs to steal. But
maybe he was beyond panic. I think he was too far gone.

"Well, Mother," Tris said as he moved in for the kill. "I
thought you said he was strong?"

Kekran still had his legs and launched himself at Tris.
My son cried out in surprise, tripped over his own feet and
fell back on his arse. He shouted, threw forward both hands
and hit Kekran with a blast of kinetic force that would have
cracked stone. It only staggered Kekran.

I rushed in, my own leg tearing apart at the strain,
buried my sword in one of Kekran's legs. I twisted the blade,
released it. The rush of energy blasted the leg apart at the
hip and I threw the severed limb away with another blast of
Kinemancy.

Tris recovered and snarled at Kekran. "Piece of shit!"
He spun around, twirling his scythe, buried it in Kekran's

stomach. Then, just as I had, he released the blade. Kekran exploded into two halves, his groin and remaining leg thrown one way, his chest and head the other.

We closed in on Kekran's body together. Even in pieces, blood and guts leaking everywhere, he was still struggling. He wriggled, writhed, stared at a fallen arm five paces away that both Tris and I had missed. But he couldn't reach it.

"I'm no expert," Tris said, "but don't people usually die when you cut this many bits off them?"

"Kekran is not a person," Ssserakis said from my shadow. It hovered above Kekran, staring at him as if saying goodbye. *"He was a lord of Sevorai."* My shadow turned toward me. *"Free him."*

"One more time, is it?" Tris said. He formed an axe in his hand, swung it up and then brought it down hard, cleaving Kekran's head in two. The body still wriggled. "Fuck. What is with this thing?"

I extended my hand and released an inferno that devoured the body. Flesh melted, blood boiled, bones blackened. Kekran kept wriggling all the while. Eventually the worms slithered free of his melting flesh. I burned them, too. I think Kekran died in the end. Or at least, there wasn't enough left of him to even wriggle anymore. I hoped he was dead, though I saw no ghost rise to join the others throning the battlefield. Perhaps Norvet Meruun had devoured even that and left him nothing but a shell of flesh and bone.

Tris walked away, holding his nose and blowing out his nostrils, trying to remove the stench of burning flesh. "We make quite a team, but don't think that means…"

The earth split beneath Tris and a fleshy tentacle as wide as my arm slithered out, wrapping around his legs. My son looked at me, his eyes wide. "Mother—"

I lurched into a limping run, already forming a Sourceblade. Too late. Too fucking slow. The tentacle whipped Tris up in the air, then shot back down into the earth, dragging my son down through the crack with a sickening crunch.

I screamed. No words. Just anguish, fury, hate, pain, hope, despair. I slid to my knees, shoved my hand and claw into the crack, pulled on my innate Geomancy and tore the rocks apart, flinging them away with a cry. Beneath me was nothing but Norvet Meruun. Her pulsing, throbbing flesh pink and rippling. Her heart beat and her flesh expanded, the earth cracking apart at my feet. I staggered back, staring, not believing.

"No." I said the word as if I could make it reality through sheer force of will. "NO!" I screamed at the rocks. At the smear of blood that was all that was left of my son. At the monster who had taken him. At the whole fucking world. I screamed at it! "Give him back, you fucking scab!"

It was too late. I am forever too fucking late to save those I love. Forever doomed to watch them die. Doomed to grieve. To mourn. To make my vengeance manifest as if that will make up for anything.

Norvet Meruun pulsed again, the rock shaking beneath me. Tentacles writhed up out of the hole. I felt the urge to dive into it, to follow Tris as if I could pull him out.

Eskara. It is too late. He is gone.

I knew that. I knew it. Too late to save him. Not too late to make the monster pay. You may have noticed, I do not deal well with grief. I hide it with fury, and I was furious. Beyond reason. Beyond doubt. Beyond sanity. This creature, this monster, this overgrown pimple had taken my son from me. I was going to make it pay. Make it suffer. She was going to *burn,* and I would strike the match. She would *bleed,* and I would stab the knife. She would *fear me* if I had to crack the world in two and bring down the fucking sky.

CHAPTER THIRTY NINE

I GROWLED AND THREW A BOLT OF LIGHTNING at the pulsating flesh below me. It seared the skin, tracing a dark line of fire, but nothing more. I threw another bolt, and another, and then a chain of lightning writhing down my arm, streamed from my fingers. Norvet Meruun's flesh quivered below me, blackened, melted. But it was nothing to her. I barely tickled the bitch. A tiny pin prick to be felt and then ignored.

Eskara, stop. You cannot brute force this. Stick to the plan.

The plan. Fuck the plan. The plan had just cost Tris his life. The plan was too abstract. I wanted to make Norvet Meruun hurt and I wanted to do it now. I just didn't have enough power. What I did have, was a good idea where I could get it.

I threw a kinetic blast at the ground, launching myself into the air and took flight. Hellions and wind thrashers and

Aeromancers flew past me on all sides. Below, the dwindling garn continued to battle against monsters that could have crushed a dozen terrans without noticing. Do'shan hung above us, the persistent crackle of Source weaponry lancing out to spear enemies from the sky. And, of course, Norvet Meruun was everywhere. *Thump. Thump. Thump.* Every three seconds her heart beat, the pulse of colour raced along her flesh, and she expanded, devouring her way across the canyon.

I flew down to Lesray's harried forces. My landing was not graceful. I stumbled, careened into an unfortunate soldier, threw the man aside to regain my balance. My leg was agony, bone deep aches and stabbing pain all at once.

Lesray turned to me. Her hair had pulled free of the braid, her armour was dented and stained by blood and mud, and her porcelain mask was cracked. The ground beneath her was frozen she was pulling on so much Pyromancy. "Report." Brusque and to the point, I might have appreciated that but I was holding on to my sanity by a fucking hair.

"How many Arcmancers do you have left?" I asked.

Lesray paused, glanced at one of her wounded generals. "Seventeen," she said. "Why?"

I winced as I limped closer to her. Frost crept up my wounded leg, numbing the pain a little. "Tell them to hit me with everything they have."

"What?"

I didn't have time to explain. Shouldn't have to explain. Life would be so much easier if people just did as they were fucking told. "I'll be up there," I pointed to the canyon, above the line of Norvet Meruun's creeping flesh. "Tell your Arcmancers to hit me with every bit of lightning they can muster. All of it, Lesray."

"Eskara..."

"Just fucking do it." I turned and launched myself back into the air.

Eska, this is madness. You cannot control that much energy.

I ignored my horror. I didn't care. Ssserakis was right. I fucking knew it was right, but I couldn't listen to it. I couldn't allow myself to stop and consider what I was doing. The madness that had gripped me demanded action. I had to trust in my raging storm, in my battered body.

Below me was all Norvet Meruun, her growing flesh expanding every few seconds. I hung in the air, wings beating steadily, tore the last of my dented armour away and let it fall. Sirileth had enchanted it and I couldn't have it absorbing the Sourcery that was meant for me. I waited, hoping Lesray wouldn't disobey me. I wanted to do this, even if it killed me. It would it a glorious fucking end. An end worthy of my son.

The first stream of lightning seared across the sky towards me and I sparked my fingers. The lightning slammed into me setting every nerve on fire. My storm gobbled up the energy greedily, flaring inside of me into a raging maelstrom. Another of Lesray's Arcmancers joined their lightning to the first, and another, until seventeen streams of Arcmancy were lighting up the sky, all striking me. It was an attack that should have charred me to a crisp in seconds, but I was not like others. I was the storm and the storm was inside of me. I screamed as I forced the energy into the Arcmancy Source in my stomach. The energy sparked inside, electricity suddenly feeding into both the Source and my storm, racing between them faster and faster and faster.

Somewhere inside I heard Ssserakis scream in pain, but my horror's voice was only a shadow of my own cry. Not since I first absorbed my Arcstorm had I felt such agony tearing at every part of my body. It felt like my skin was on fire, my insides cooked, my blood boiled. Still, lightning streaked across the sky and struck me. With it came memories, not mine.

A terran woman sitting on a blanket, grass all around, but she only had eyes for the man sitting across from her. A child running, fleeing, caught, pushed down to the ground. A pahht man in a tavern, drinking with old friends. A Djinn streaking across the sky, eager to join his brothers. A woman in the throes of passion, her body alight with sensation. A terran man staring down at his son. The memories flashed through me so quickly I couldn't sort them.

Another blast of lightning joined the others. From the sky, from Do'shan. Someone had fired an Arcbiter at me. The magic crashed into me.

The Nameless joined his power with his brothers and slowly a new world formed in the shadow of the old. They created the space, a pocket realm within the world, then filled it grain by grain, drop by drop. Everything was built by design. Every bit of dirt, every molecule of water, every stone, and every cave.

The sky came last, even as most of the Djinn were exhausted from the effort. They realised the world was darkness but could not create a sun. This realm had no celestial bodies, it existed within the other. So instead they created light. Not as brilliant or as passing as sunlight, but a constant luminescence that encompassed the world they had created.

When they were done, all the Djinn looked upon their

creation with a pride that resonated with all of them. Their great work, their masterpiece. A creation not even the Maker could match. They had built a world from nothing. But it was not quite complete. It needed one more thing.

All the others turned to the Nameless then. His was the final part of the puzzle. While the Guiding Light led them all, and the Chronicler remembered all their pasts, and the Glory sung their praises for eternity; it was up to the Nameless to give creations their names.

A world within the shadow of a world. A place so like its counterpart but also not. The Nameless needed only a moment to consider.

"Sevorai."

In that instant when the Arcbiter struck me, I witnessed the creation of Sevorai. I felt the pride of the Djinn made manifest. A work unrivalled in any history. At any other time, I would have taken a few moments to truly appreciate that, but I was being torn apart by energies I could not control.

It was too much for me, too much for my storm, too much to feed into the Arcmancy Source inside of me. The Source and the storm sparked against each other, two charges too close, trading lightning back and forth, growing hotter and more violent by the second. I was screaming. Ssserakis was screaming. But I couldn't hear anything past the thunder in my ears.

And then it was over. The last bolt of lightning streaked from the Sourcerers below, hit my claw and surged into me. I held it inside, all that power, that energy, that lightning raging, sparking, burning. I glowed with it, a new star forming in the sky. My eyes no longer flashed but blazed white hot and blinding to anyone foolish enough to meet my gaze. I held it all for as long as I could, the Source and my storm trading energy back and forth until it built to a searing crescendo.

Finally, when I could take it no more, I pointed down at Norvet Meruun with my claw and unleashed my super storm. A hundred searing bolts of lightning streamed from me, a thousand bolts, ten thousand, a hundred thousand. I lit Sevorai up like the sun it had never seen and threw every bit of Arcmancy I had down into the Beating Heart. Flesh sizzled, melted, burned away. Tentacles writhed, ignited, immolated. Norvet Meruun screamed in pain and the earth shook with her cries.

Through it all I roared at the bitch, my voice and Ssserakis' mixed into one. "You will fear me!"

And she did.

When the last of my storm lanced out of me, I looked down at the carnage I had wrought. Blackened, twisted flesh smoked and burned. Fatty pools popped and boiled. Below me was a ruin of flesh. It was such a small part of the Beating Heart, little more than a fingernail or a toe, but I had done such damage to that fucking toe.

My lightning had been indiscriminate in its burning slaughter. I hadn't really been able to aim it. Norvet Meruun had taken the brunt, but I had struck the canyon all over. There were dead hellions, khark hounds, yurthammers. A few of the garn had been caught in the madness, too. All dead. Nothing could had survived the violence I had unleashed. Nothing except the enemy.

Norvet Meruun pulsed, the same pinkish light racing from some far-away spot across her flesh like a ripple. She expanded again. Blood spurted, rubbery flesh flaked away, and new bulk spread, devouring the old.

She feared me, yes. Feared the pain I could cause her. I felt that new power streaming up into me. Ssserakis was gobbling it up and directing it into the Necromancy Sources. A new fear, fatty like barely cooked steak, making my mouth water. So fucking filling. But it wasn't enough. Norvet Meruun did not bring her core closer to the battle, did not reveal herself. She was scared of the pain, but still she knew she couldn't lose.

"It's not enough," I said, my voice trembling with my limbs. I had emptied myself of my storm and bereft of it I felt weak.

We cannot do that again, Eska. It burned. My horror trembled, too. Even feeding on so much fear coming from both our armies and from Norvet Meruun, Ssserakis was struggling through the pain I was causing it.

"We have to." I tried to draw on my Arcmancy Source to reignite my storm but found nothing. That little spark of energy was gone. My Arcmancy Source was gone, disintegrated inside me. How had I not broken down in rejection? I reached up and touched my ear, the same one Sirileth had pierced. The earrings were gone, melted to slag that had fused to a fleshy, angry stump, all that was left of my ear. Well, one more disfigurement. What did it matter in the long run? I was already covered in scars, missing an arm, and I didn't want to see the mess of my left leg.

Eska, we have to find our daughter. Only she can do enough damage to the enemy to shock the Beating Heart into revealing itself.

I shook my head, trying to clear away the fuzzy edges. I needed more power. From my vantage point up high, I could see Norvet Meruun pulsing, claiming more of the canyon with each beating ripple. On the south side, three yurthammers lumbered out of a cave, thick chains dragging from around their necks. The massive metal platform they were pulling rumbled out behind them, and the creature nestled on that platform began to stir. Norvet Meruun hadn't thrown everything at us, not yet. She had one more monster to unleash. Lodoss, one of the final lords of Sevorai. A true immortal. Worms wriggled all over his skin, in between his armoured plates. Segmented legs trembled, shivered, stirred to life.

Tucking my wings back, I dove towards our central force. The remnants of it were busy being reinforced by our southern flank as they used Geomancers to carve steps into the canyon wall. I swept down, passed over Lesray as she held the frontline with spearing icicles. I landed close to the bank of Arcmancers, those who had so recently poured everything they had into me. Seventeen of them, all that was left of the sixty who had arrived with us.

Most were down, vomiting up Sources, recovering from rejection. One terran woman was panicking, blood pouring from her nose and eyes, electricity sparking from her fingers. She was about to break down in an Arcstorm amidst the middle of our troops.

"Help me," she gurgled, spitting blood.

I grabbed her throat in my claw, tore it out in a single rip. She collapsed, her life flowing out of her in seconds, the burgeoning Arcstorm dying before it could form. A brief thought occurred to me; which one had she been? Which of the new memories rolling about in my mind were hers? I didn't have time to stop and consider it.

I fell upon her body and ripped into her chest with my claw, tearing a great gash out of her, digging through spilling guts and seeping gore until my claw closed around a small stone the size of a pea. I pulled it out of her steaming corpse. No time to hesitate. I slammed it into my mouth, swallowed hard past the blood. I almost gagged, but I've always been good at holding onto power.

My storm reignited, drawing energy from the new Source in my stomach. My eyes flashed and lightning arced from my skin to score lines across the rocks nearby.

As I stood, I found soldiers and Sourcerers gathered around, staring at me in horror, the fear flowing thick around them tasting syrupy. Or maybe that was the blood that was smeared across my face.

"She's feeding on the dead," one soldier said.

"She just killed that woman."

"Tore her open and started eating her."

"Corpse eater."

"Corpse Queen."

I swept my flashing gaze across them all, daring any of them to come and challenge me. None of the cowards did. Good! Let them fear me. Let them feed us that power. We needed it.

It is still not enough.

"What the hell are you doing, Eskara?" Lesray's voice behind me. I glanced over my shoulder at her and she slowed her approach. Still no fear from her. She had far too tight a grip on her emotions, but she kept her distance.

I licked my lips, tasted blood, felt sick but held it down. "Lodoss is coming," I snarled at her.

"Who?"

"The last lord of Sevorai. A giant insectile monster." If centipedes had nightmares, Lodoss was it.

Lesray deflated a little. She looked exhausted and the

ground beneath her was no longer frosting over. I didn't think she had much left to give this fight. "Our numbers are failing. I can't reach the northern flank or Do'shan. We lost over half of our troops when the cliff collapsed and…" She stopped herself, glanced about at those gathering around us. I think she realised then the soldiers didn't need to see her despairing. She was wrong about that. Their fear only grew when they watched the woman leading them crushed by the weight pressing down on her. That new fear spread like a fire as soldiers began whispering.

"We should retreat, regroup back in Ovaeris," Lesray said.

"No," I growled the word. "We don't get another shot at this, Lesray. I don't give a fuck if our soldiers are dying, they can still fight!"

I grabbed a nearby ghost in my claw. The moment I touched it, it burst into ethereal incandescence. By the shocked gasps, I guessed no one else could see the ghosts. I shoved the spectre into the body of the Sourcerer I had just killed. It was not the woman I had killed, but another ghost suddenly inhabiting a foreign body. The corpse's eyes snapped open and it sat up, glanced down at itself, screamed even through its ripped out throat.

"Shh!" I hissed at it. The corpse immediately stopped screaming and shut its mouth, eyes wide and staring at me in horror. "Better. Now get out there and fight."

The corpse stood in silence, marched through our ranks of terrified soldiers and out into the midst of battle. It probably died within moments, but that was good. The poor ghost did not deserve what I had done to it, sheathing it in a foreign body like that.

Lesray advanced on me, fists clenched. I thought she was going to take a swing, knock me down like she had in sparring so many times when we were at the academy. But she had too much control for that these days.

Screams of panic shouted from the front lines. We just

had time to turn before Lesray's wall of ice exploded inwards, flattening the front ranks and showering the rest of us in chilly shards and ice cubes the size of horses.

Lodoss reared up above, his centipede-like body twisting into the sky. Then he came crashing down, flattening hundreds of soldiers beneath his armoured bulk. As if that wasn't enough, he started thrashing about, rampaging, throwing dirt and ice and broken bodies into the air. His legs, all two hundred of them, were scythes. His segmented body was coated in armour tougher than steel and rough enough to scrape away skin if it brushed against a person. He had no face, no head at all. There was no wonder Lodoss wanted to die. His existence was nothing but a torment, and now he was infested by the enemy he was inflicting that torment on us.

The fear of our army spiked to a new high as Lodoss crashed and thrashed amongst us. Ssserakis struggled to contain it, bloated up inside of my soul like a tick swollen to bursting.

The Sources are almost full, Eska. This is as strong as I will ever be. It is time. We need our daughter.

I spread my wings and leapt into the air. Lesray and the army would have to deal with Lodoss alone. That was the lie I told myself because I knew they couldn't. A giant, immortal centipede that was also mad as a boot full of crabs. They were all going to die.

That is their purpose. Not to save, not to fight. They are here to feed us, Eska.

I knew it. Of course I fucking knew it. It was my plan. Didn't make condemning them all to death any easier. But needs must. I didn't need their love or loyalty, their awe or respect. All I needed was their fear.

I stared down as I flew, watching Lesray's last stand against Lodoss. Part of me rejoiced at it. I still hated her. Yes, it was mostly leftover bitterness at something I now knew she hadn't even done, but she had also plotted to take my daughter from me. I would not forgive her for that. As for the rest of the soldiers... well, I couldn't save them anyway. If I made it through the fight, I promised I would find their ghosts and give them peace. It was the least I could do, and also the most.

Soldiers stabbed at Lodoss with spears that skittered off his armour. Sourcerers pelted him with rocks, threw kinetic blasts at his legs, he didn't even seem to feel it. Lesray skated around his thrashing bulk on a patch of ice, freezing his legs to the rocky ground, shooting icicles to burst apart against his armoured skin. Lodoss flipped, his massive body undulating as it rolled, crushing soldiers, throwing up dirt. He tried to coil around Lesray, but she shot up above him on a pillar of ice. Lodoss crushed the pillar and Lesray fell, threw out a slide of ice and slid down it. A flailing leg caught her, gashed open her side and sent her sprawling. She hit the dirt hard, took a few seconds to move.

Lesray had told me what the Iron Legion had done, but I hadn't really understood it. I should have. He put death in me, and with it I wielded Necromancy in a way no one else thought possible, a way I still barely understood. He put life in Josef and accidentally made my best friend immortal. And in Lesray, he had put fire, and she spent every moment of every day holding it back. As I watched from above, Lesray stopped holding back the flames.

The Queen of Ice and Fire discarded her ice along with her mask. Her eye blazed and that fire spread, consuming her. She became the flames. Her spilled blood smoked, boiled, burned holes in the ground. Her armour incinerated to nothing in moments. She stalked towards Lodoss, hands held in front of her, and unleashed the fires she had been holding back for most of her life. Soldiers scrambled away, their armour melting, clothes igniting, skin burning. Bodies nearby burst into little flaming pyres. Lodoss burned, suddenly caught in an impossible inferno. His armour cracked, his legs crumbled, his skin burst and oozed out of his wounds. He tried to crush Lesray, but his body seared away before he could reach her. He tried to flee, but his legs melted before her fires. Lesray Alderson became the avatar of the sun, and Lodoss, the immortal lord of Sevorai burned away before her.

Eska. We... should go. We need to find Sirileth. There was awe in my horror's voice. I understood it. I had never even considered that Lesray might hold such power. I wondered if she would manage to rein in her flames, or if they would consume her, too? *No time to wait around and find out. She has taken away Norvet Meruun's strongest minion. The Beating Heart will never be more vulnerable than now. It is time to strike.*

I left Lesray and the battle behind, soared towards the flagging remnants of our northern flank. In truth, I had hoped to spare Sirileth what I was about to make her do. I doubted she would ever forgive me. I knew Ovaeris would never forgive her.

CHAPTER FORTY

OUR NORTHERN FLANK HAD NOT BEEN
faring well after the cliff was brought down. Isolated and
facing attacks from monsters scrambling up the scree, as
well as those skirting the canyon lip, and wind thrashers
attacking from the air. They had been pushed and pulled
about; their lines stretched thin on all sides. The once ten
thousand strong army had left a trail of bodies both monster
and person in its wake. As I soared in to join them, I guessed
they had suffered casualties roughly half their original
number. Five thousand soldiers dead. I think they would
have broken, if they'd had anywhere to run.

I landed awkwardly as I formed a spear and skewed
a khark hound from above. The attack threw me off balance
and I hit the ground at a stumble, my bad leg spiking in
savage pain, collapsing beneath me. Ssserakis took control of
my wings, dug the tips into the ground to steady me.

The soldiers I was facing, a mixture of terran and pahht, recoiled at the sight of me. I could imagine how I probably looked. What was left of my armour half melted and ripped away by the fury of the storm, my leathers underneath torn and stained. Blood smeared across my mouth, and in my hair. My ear a mangled stump of melted flesh and metal. My wings were massive shadowy taloned things, and my eyes flashed with the violence I was holding inside.

There was a commotion within the ranks, soldiers pushing aside, bowing.

"Mother?" Sirileth's voice, shouted over the racket. The soldiers moved apart for her, bowed heads in respect. They were not Yenheim soldiers, not our people, but they treated her like a queen. I had clearly missed some great ordeal, and my daughter had emerged from it as commander of the northern flank. Pride tightened my chest. "Mother. You look…"

Sirileth had not escaped the battle unharmed. She had suffered cuts to her face, a plate of her own armour had been torn away at her hip and she was wrapped in thick, bloody bandages. Her hair was a mess, the braid gone, burned away, the singed tips still smoking slightly.

I closed the distance between us, fell in my daughter's arms, sagged against her. She stiffened, not to pull away but to support me, hold me up. We held onto each other, and for just a moment I could forget the battle and all that was still left to do.

"Are you… I mean… Mother, are you hurt?"

I drew in a breath and it caught in my throat, turned into a sob that I buried in Sirileth's shoulder. Was I hurt? Yes. I was hurt, I was exhausted. But none of that mattered

because my son was gone. Because Tris was dead and…
I swallowed down the grief, pushed it into a tight ball
and locked it away deep inside. I didn't have time for it. I
couldn't afford to let it drag me into a melancholy attack. I
clutched to my daughter for a few seconds more, gripping
her so tightly we both gasped in pain, then I let go and
pushed her away a little.

"Mother, your ear." Sirileth reached up to my face. I
winced, expecting pain, but she didn't touch the mangled,
melted flesh, just held her hand near it. "I'm sorry. I didn't
think… I mean, I didn't expect you to need it. Are you
alright?"

I tried to reply, couldn't force any words past my
constricted throat. I nodded. Was I, though? The earrings
had kept me from rejection, yes, but I had absorbed an
entire Arcmancy Source. It was different to absorbing the
Arcstorm. It was more. So much more. Another thing I didn't
have time to explore just then.

I glanced past Sirileth, noticed Kento standing there. I
almost flung myself at her. We were surrounded by soldiers
and no one could know who Kento really was. I settled for
a nod, smiling at my oldest daughter. She stepped forward,
next to Sirileth. I stared at them both. Sisters yet they looked
nothing alike. Sirileth looked so much like me, but Kento
had so much of Isen in her.

Now is not the time, Eska.

Not the time, yet also the only time we'd ever have.

"How fares the battle?" Kento asked. "The other
flanks."

"Badly," I forced the word past the tightness in my
throat. "The central force is all but gone, the southern flank
is reinforcing them. Lesray… might be dead. Do'shan has

been beset from the start and can't bring the hellion swarm
under control to help out below." I paused, winced at the
agony of my leg, and tried to catch my breath. "We've dealt
a lot of damage to the enemy, killed so many of her minions.
We've taken away her strongest, but…" I shook my head,
locked my flashing gaze with Sirileth's darklight. "We're out
of options."

Sirileth reached for her braid with her hand, but the
hair was gone. She clenched it into a fist instead.

"So what do we do?" Kento asked.

I didn't take my gaze from Sirileth. "Can you do it?"

Sirileth stared at me, her darklight a fire waiting to
explode. She nodded.

A cry went up from the ranks of soldiers. The shouts
were carried through the masses. A new pack of khark
hounds had hit the southern flank. Kento turned, shouting
orders.

I reached out, took Sirileth's hand, gave it a squeeze.
She stared up at Do'shan hovering above us all. It was not a
matter of power; I knew she had that and more. It was about
the guilt, the blame. The cost to her conscience.

A blast of Arcmancy tore through the sky from up on
Do'shan, scorching dark shapes to plummet to the canyon
floor below

"There's still people up there," Sirileth said. There
were thousands of people up on Do'shan.

I nodded.

"Can't we evacuate them? I mean…"

I pulled her a few steps closer to the cliff edge.
"There's no time, Sirileth."

She grit her teeth, nodded. "Thousands of lives
given to save millions." Yes, my daughter had made that

justification once before, on her own. Now she made it on my orders. Part of me hoped she wouldn't blame me.

Better to blame us, than to blame herself.

Sirileth let out a slow, calming breath, then reached up a hand towards Do'shan.

"What's happening?" Kento asked. Her sword was drawn and she glanced over her shoulder back towards the soldiers.

Sirileth fumbled for her Source pouch with her spare hand, pulled out two small crystals and swallowed them. Then she grunted and strained against an invisible force. Up above us all, Do'shan shook.

"Eska?" Kento asked.

I glanced at my daughter. "Protect your sister." I unfurled my wings and leapt into the sky one last time. I had to be ready because we would not have long.

Below, I watched Kento reach Sirileth's side, shake her. Sirileth strained, pulling, wrenching. Even as they shrunk below me, I saw her earrings start to glow as my daughter used a power I could never hope to match. As she tore Do'shan out of the sky.

It all happened so slowly, and yet so terribly fast as well. Once it was started, there was no stopping it. Sirileth broke whatever power held the flying mountain aloft, and after that gravity did the rest.

Up on Do'shan, people panicked. Some Portamancers were quick to realise what was happening, tore open portals to the ground below, ferried as many as they could to safety. It was not many. A new type of fear flooded me, so sharp and spicy, and Ssserakis gorged on it. I hung there with lazy flaps of my wings and watched the mountain tilt and fall. Bits of it cracked away, chunks as large as villages breaking apart.

"COWARD!" Ssserakis roared across the battlefield, its voice somehow drowning out the mountain falling.

A terrible dread coiled in my stomach. Below, Brakunus and his ghouls had finally entered the battle. On the other fucking side. They appeared amidst our southern flank, leaping, tearing, slaughtering soldiers who had no idea what was happening. I watched Brakunus charge towards Sirileth, raise a massive paw. Kento blurred, darted in, stabbed her sword into the giant ghoul's gut. Too late. Brakunus slammed his hand down on my daughter and crushed Sirileth.

I screamed, tried to dive towards them, but Ssserakis wouldn't let me. My horror wrenched control of my wings away from me.

We do not have time, Eska. Look!

"Let me go, Ssserakis!"

NO! Look, Eska.

My chest hurt with a pain that had nothing to do with anything physical. It felt like my heart had simply stopped. But my horror was right again. We had a task, and if I didn't accomplish it, Sirileth's sacrifice would mean nothing. Still, I hated Ssserakis for that. I hated myself even more. And most of all, I hated Brakunus. He would die screaming!

Do'shan crashed to the ground in an explosion of rock and dust and flesh and lives. The canyon collapsed, was crushed. Do'shan fell apart, its own weight cracking itself so it impacted again and again, each time the ground visibly shook. Canyon walls crumbled; the earth was torn asunder. And over it all, Norvet Meruun screamed.

Dust erupted into the air, blown away by the shockwave, replaced, blown away again. It was a cataclysm just like Lursa falling from the sky. I formed a kinetic bubble around myself to block the dust and debris. It lasted for hours and it lasted only seconds, and when the last of Do'shan crumbled away, I frantically searched the canyon, already knowing it was fruitless. The southern flank was gone. The cliffside fallen away entirely. I could see nothing else past the dust and debris. Even if Kento was down there, still alive, I had no way to find her. It was all such chaos.

I clutched at my chest as though trying to claw out my own heart, screamed in frustration, in anguish, in grief, in sheer fucking emotion I couldn't begin to sort out. I had ordered it, pressed Sirileth to do it. I had known it needed to be done, but I hadn't thought it through. I hadn't thought...

We must be ready. Ssserakis' voice was tight in my head, thick with worry. *Our moment will come soon.*

Our moment. Our fucking moment. What did it matter anymore? All my children were dead. Tris, Sirileth, Kento. This battle... this war had already cost me everything. What did it matter anymore?

I hung there, letting Ssserakis beat my wings, and I hated. I hated Norvet Meruun. I hated Lesray. I hated Ovaeris and our gods. Sevorai and the impotent fucks who called themselves lords. And, of course, I hated myself. Because I had done this. I. Had. Done. This. And yet, I survived it. When everyone I cared about was dying, I fucking survived. The one person who didn't want to live, was the only one who didn't die. Fitting, in a fucked-up kind of way.

I saw movement far below. People had survived, were clawing their way out of the debris. Terrans, pahht, garn, monsters. It was a mess down there, but not everyone had died. The fear was diminished, so many dead, but it still reached me. I had no taste for it, but Ssserakis devoured it without relish. I saw ghosts rising, too. Thousands of them, old and new, standing amidst the chaos and slaughter, confused and lost.

Tears streamed down my cheeks. I didn't bother to wipe them away. They ran down my chin, tracking lines through the grime and blood, rained upon the canyon.

Eska, squash this melancholy. It is not over yet. Not for us.

Again my horror was right. Because I hadn't lost everything. Not quite. There was one thing I hadn't lost. I still had Ssserakis.

Eska, you have to stop lying to yourself.

"Shut up."

The ground trembled below us.

"It's happening."

The rocky ground rippled like a whipped blanket, burst apart. Norvet Meruun's crushed flesh surged, popped, bulged. Tentacles as wide as buildings shot out of the ruptured flesh, flailing about in the air, latching onto whatever they could and dragging it down to feed the monster. A bright light raced underneath the surface of her flesh, coming from the horizon, stopping at the canyon. Then, the next beat of Norvet Meruun's heart originated below us. The pulsing light spread out in an ever-expanding ring from the Beating Heart's core.

We had done it. We had hurt the bitch enough that she thought she might actually lose.

CHAPTER
FORTY ONE

I WAS THERE.

A pahht Aeromancer streaked past me, chased by hellions. I ignored them and they ignored me.

Eska, she is here.

"I see it." Norvet Meruun's beating heart lay below us. Her core. She had taken control of her own flesh directly. Her minions, those that were left started banding together, working together. Her tentacles moved faster, with more precision. I saw terrans whipped from their feet, pulled into the air, dragged down into the pulsating mass of flesh.

It is time, Eska. We must do this before she hides herself away again.

"I'm ready," I lied. I tore my eyes from the Beating Heart, searched the ruin of a battlefield for any sign of my daughters. Hoping. Hoping. Fuck hope! It was useless. They were gone.

You are delaying, Eska. We do not have time.

"I know!" I snapped.

I drew in one last deep breath of cool Sevorai air. Yes, it was time. Time to make this piece of shit ruinous fucking scab pay for everything I had lost.

I tucked my wings and dove towards the Beating Heart. I let my storm rage, drew on my Arcmancy Source to fuel it, formed a crackling shield of lightning around me. I fused Kinemancy and Pyromancy together into an arrowhead of purple fire. I became the tip of the spear driving down towards our enemy's heart. I am the fucking weapon! And at the last moment, I braced myself and plunged deep into the monster's putrid flesh.

Norvet Meruun screamed in panic. Her beating became a rapid drumbeat, each thundering pulse growing her mass. I pushed out with all the strength I had, fusing my storm with kinetic force. I carved into her flesh and it blackened around me, melting away and sizzling before my onslaught. Lightning speared out from me in every direction. The kinetic bubble I created around me held back the throbbing flesh. Blood ran like rivers down the purple haze.

There!

Norvet Meruun's core was indeed a heart. A twisted, pink organ like so many ropes tied into a haphazard knot. Vibrant colours rippled along each cord, and the heart beat faster. Her flesh pressed in on my shield, crushing it. Cracks formed along the hazy barrier. I threw out my hand, formed a second barrier inside the first just as that first barrier exploded in a puff of energy. The enemy's flesh immediately surged into the free space, pressing in.

"You have to do it now, Ssserakis," I growled.

"Quickly."

My horror was silent for a few moments. Then, *Brace yourself, Eska.*

My stomach exploded in agony. Knives shoved outwards, gutting me from the inside, fire blazed, melting my spine. I staggered from the pain, fell to my knees, screamed. Ssserakis screamed with me, but in anger and fury. My horror drew on all the power it had been collecting into the Necromancy Sources, emptying them in moments and for a short time it became a void of infinite darkness greater than the space between stars.

My claw expanded, slicing away flesh, tearing and shredding, it snapped shut around the Beating Heart's core, clutching at it. Severing sinew as quickly as it regenerated, trying to isolate the enemy. Norvet Meruun struggled, thrashed, pulsed. The flesh pressed in on my shield. I threw up another barrier just as the last one exploded. My storm crackled around the shield, burning her, blackening flesh, and boiling blood, but Norvet Meruun pressed in harder. The pressure so great my shield exploded again. I created another in the same instant, shrinking in on myself. I had so little space left. I couldn't form another shield. I pushed every bit of strength I had into this last one and hoped it would hold.

I prayed then. Not to the Rand or Djinn, not to the Maker, not the moons. I prayed to my friends, those I had left behind in Ovaeris. To Hardt and Tamura and Esem. To Josef. I prayed to the dead who had gone before me. To Silva and Imiko, Tris and Sirileth and Kento. I prayed to them all to give me the strength to hold. Not for myself. I didn't care about myself, I never had. Not for Ovaeris and its people who hated me. Not for Sevorai, a nightmarish land I had never known. I needed the strength to hold because this fight was all I had left. Everything else was gone. Everyone I cared about was dead. I would not lose. I refused to fail. Fuck Norvet Meruun. Fuck the Beating Heart. I was Eskara Helsene and I was so fucking sick of losing. This time. This time that mattered more than any other had before, I would win.

I pushed out with my shield, breathed fire, lashed out with bolts of lightning. I became Sourcery incarnate, not caring if I rejected, not caring if I broke down. It still wasn't enough. I could feel myself weakening.

A ghost drifted past me, passing through the enemy's flesh like it was nothing, drifting through my shield as though it wasn't there. I grabbed the spectre and it became whole in my grip. A terran soldier, her expression shocked as though she hadn't realised she was dead until that instant. I unravelled her and devoured what energy remained. Josef was right. Just like he could take energy from the living with his Biomancy, I could take it from the dead with my Necromancy. And I was fucking surrounded by the dead.

I called to them, drew them to me. Ghosts floated around me and I grabbed hold of them one after another, unravelling them, consuming their energy. New memories sparked to life in me. A pahht man fishing with his son. A terran woman kneading bread. A garn locked in battle with his brother. I pushed the energy I took from the ghosts, passed it through the Kinemancy Source, strengthened the shield holding back Norvet Meruun's crushing flesh.

Ssserakis fought its own battle. My horror gripped the Beating Heart's core in an icy claw of shadow, held her in place, refusing to let her flee. It burned through the energy we had hoarded at a reckless rate, cutting, slicing, forming a hardened shell of shadow around the heart, desperately trying to sever her connection to her body.

She is too strong. My horror's voice was a strained whisper in my mind.

I devoured another ghost. The memory of a terran man watching his wife sleep. I gave the power to Ssserakis. Gave it all to Ssserakis. I stopped strengthening my shield and funnelled every bit of energy I had left into my horror.

My shield cracked, spidery veins racing along it as the pressure of Norvet Meruun's expanding flesh crushed in on me. I had nothing left. No strength. No tricks. No revelations. We had thrown everything we had at the Beating Heart, and still we lost.

My shield buckled.

My shield held.

The pressure eased. Norvet Meruun's frantic pulsing stopped. I grabbed another ghost, unravelled it. A garn rolling in a patch of new mud, squealing with joy. I used the energy to shore up my shield and slowly stood. I was surrounded by quivering, pallid flesh, the pinkish light within it fading. Even as I watched, I saw it splitting apart as though it had always been formed of millions of Abominations and now they were shaking apart, becoming individual again.

"Ssserakis?" My voice echoed strangely in that little pocket cavern.

My claw was a warped, distended thing that ended in a bulging sphere the size of a cart. It rippled as if something inside was trying to pierce it and burst its way out.

She is. My horror's voice was quiet, weary, small. *That took everything, Eska. And the enemy struggles to escape. I cannot hold her long.*

I consumed another ghost. A pahht child crying while his mother walked out the door. I fed the energy to Ssserakis. My horror accepted the new strength, but it was not enough to hold Norvet Meruun for long.

"We did it?" I asked.

An Abomination slid away above me, and the grey light of Sevorai reached down into my bubble.

I told you long ago, Eska. Norvet Meruun cannot be killed. All I have done is contain her. It will not last. She will break free and when she does, all this flesh will become her again. She has grown too much from the tumour she once was. Too powerful. Too energetic.

A memory tugged at me, not one I had taken from a ghost, but not one of mine either. The Iron Legion capturing Ssserakis in a bottle.

Eska, we do not have long.

I consumed another ghost. A terran man on his hands and knees, begging for something from a king. I fed the energy to Ssserakis.

It takes so much just to hold her.

"So what do we do?"

Silence.

Eska! Stop blocking me. Listen to me. I had been taking Ssserakis' odd silences for sullen moods, but that was wrong. I saw it now. I understood it. They weren't my horror's doing at all, but times I had blocked it out because I didn't want to hear the truth. The last part of the plan that I had refused from the very beginning.

Once before, you opened up a portal to nowhere. It was true. I had torn open a portal, a hole in reality that led nowhere. The Maker had taken control of it, diverted it. *Do it again now.*

"No."

It is the only way, Eska. Open a portal and take us through. Norvet Meruun cannot die, but we can trap her in nothing for eternity.

"You'll die," I whispered.

We will die together.

I had once sacrificed myself, took my own life, to send my horror home to Sevorai so it could fight this monster we now contained. Now, I had to sacrifice us both to stop it once and for all. But Ssserakis would die. My horror would die. I had already lost so much. I couldn't do it. I couldn't lose the one family member I had left. I refused to sacrifice Ssserakis to this thing. There had to be another way.

Ssserakis' memory tickled at me again. The Iron Legion, smug fucker that he was, grinning, lecturing. He said energy can be compressed almost infinitely. Well, everything was energy, even flesh.

I consumed another ghost. A pahht man juggling five colourful balls. I fed the energy to Ssserakis. "Smaller," I growled.

What?

"Smaller, Ssserakis." I fed it the energy of another ghost. My horror did as I asked, constricting its shadow, crushing the Beating Heart smaller.

"Smaller." Another ghost fed to my horror. Ssserakis growled in my head, struggling to compress Norvet Meruun into a smaller and smaller sphere.

"Smaller!" Ssserakis crushed the Beating Heart into the size of a child, the size of a melon, the size of a head, the size of an apple. And then I was holding Norvet Meruun in my claw, a ball of shadow no larger than a Source.

What are you planning?

I slammed the Beating Heart's shadowy prison into my mouth and swallowed hard, felt it pass down my throat. It was spiky, wriggling, tasted like carrion. It rested in my stomach like fiery indigestion.

All around me, the Abominations were splitting apart, slithering against each other. Hairy tentacles slapped against my kinetic shield.

"We can't just take the Beating Heart away with us, Ssserakis. I won't let you die for it, but it's more than that. She's already breaking apart into millions of Abominations. They'll devour everything, it's what they do. We'll die, she'll be lost. But so will both our worlds."

Even inside of you she is too strong, Eska. I cannot hold her forever.

"You can. We can. Your fear. My Necromancy. We can hold her for eternity."

But you will die. You are not immortal.

And there was the worst of it. I was not immortal. I had never wanted to be immortal. Some days, I didn't even want to live. All my life I have wanted to die. To embrace that quiet, peaceful oblivion. To listen one final time to the call of the void and let it pull me under. I have stood on that edge, dancing with the call so many times. It's the escape of it, you see. I yearn to be free of it all. All the noise and the pain, the guilt and the hate, the fear and the grief. To be free of people and their demands. Most of all, I want to be free of myself. Of the voice in my head constantly reminding me of all the things I have done, the mistakes I've made, the people I've killed. The friends I've lost. I want to be free of it all, and I've always known the only way is death. The final end. Silence. Forever.

And now, in order to protect a world that hated me

almost as much as I hate myself. To save the people who
condemn me and my family as monsters. To defend the few
friends I have left. To safeguard them all, I had to embrace
immortality. It is torture. The ultimate torture. It is fucking
hell. I had to sacrifice my one chance at having peace and
live for eternity in the hell of my own mind.

It is a joke. A bad fucking joke fate has played. And I
am the punchline.

Josef had showed me how. Maybe he had seen this
coming, or maybe it had just been his form of penitence for
putting the call of the void in me in the first place.

I devoured a ghost, the memory of a terran man
eating abban stake flaring in my mind for a moment. Then
I used the energy I harvested from it to fuel my own innate
Chronomancy. The magic that had once sped my ageing
unnaturally, now stopped it. Josef was right, it took a lot of
energy, but I could freeze myself in time and live forever. An
eternal prison for a monster who would devour worlds.

Which still left us with one problem: the unleashed
Abominations. They were almost as dangerous as Norvet
Meruun herself. They would consume, grow, perhaps even
merge together and become a new Beating Heart. If allowed
to spread, they would destroy what was left of Sevorai,
maybe Ovaeris, too. But for now, they were still linked to
Norvet Meruun, and the Beating Heart was now mine.
Through Ssserakis, I could control shadow and nightmares,
feed on fear. And through Norvet Meruun, I would control
her Abominations.

I drew on her like I did my Sources, energy with
power but no purpose. My will provided that purpose and
I shaped a command just like I had the day I had created
my curse. Through Norvet Meruun, I reached to all her

Abominations and gave them a single command.
    I ordered them to rot!

CHAPTER FORTY TWO

I LIMPED THROUGH A SEA OF DECAYING
Abominations. They floundered all around me, squealing,
flailing, dying. Rotting. The order I gave them reverberated
out from me like an unending cry echoing around the whole
world, and every one of the monsters that heard it obeyed.
They didn't feel pain. Their bodies were not capable of
hurting that way. But they did recognise that they were
dying, and every single one of them was scared. A base,
animal fear; dull and tasteless. They died, and I lived.

Ssserakis withdrew its support. My horror focused
all its strength and attention inwards, containing Norvet
Meruun. The Beating Heart was inside me now, and it
wanted to escape, to devour me from the inside and begin its
eternal consumption all over again. My horror wouldn't let
it, but it took so much to keep Norvet Meruun locked inside
its shadowy cage.

I had no wings so could not fly. No claw, my arm ending in a wasted stump again. No shadow brace around my mangled leg. I formed a crutch from Kinemancy and leaned on it heavily.

That's something the stories about me like to play up. *If you hear the* tap tap tap *of a cane on your rooftop, beware, for the Corpse Queen has come for your children.* Such bullshit the bards like to tell. I can limp just fine without my cane... most days. But it is true that my leg was a ruin of torn flesh and broken bone and it has never healed quite right.

Norvet Meruun's surviving minions dispersed; hellions winging away and khark hounds loping past me. The worms were gone from their skin. They had been a part of her just like her Abominations, and they, too, had heeded my command. Free of their infestations, many of the creatures of Sevorai went back to how they had been before. Just as many did not. For some, the infestations had been inside of them too long, had eaten away too much of what they had been. When the worms died, some monsters just stopped. They did not die, but there was nothing left of them to live. Eventually they became food for others.

I crossed the canyon floor at a slow limp, picking my way over broken rock, between patches of flame, around rivers of blood, through mounds of dead. Ghosts swarmed around me, drawn to me. Many were soldiers I had brought with me to Sevorai, those who had died in this grand battle. Others were just people of Ovaeris, pulled to the great rift for a reason they couldn't fathom. I stopped occasionally to devour a ghost or two, ignoring the new memories flaring to life in my mind. I fed most of the strength I consumed to Ssserakis, to help my horror in its new eternal struggle.

I wondered if anyone else had survived, or if they had

all perished in my insane plan. Do'shan's crashing had been devastating and the canyon floor was littered with rocks the size of villages. It would be both horrifying and oddly fitting if I was the only survivor.

My thoughts led me to Sirileth and Kento. I staggered, almost collapsed, struggled to breathe past my constricting throat. I screamed then. No words. No words could match how I felt. I screamed in pain and grief and anguish and because fuck it, sometimes you cannot deal with the turmoil inside and the only thing you can do is scream. My children were dead. They were dead. And I would live forever knowing that they had died because of me. Screaming was insufficient, but it was all I had.

Ssserakis was silent, concentrating on its own struggles, but my horror extended a thread of what it was feeling towards me. We both grieved for my children.

I made my way back to the central front, or what was left of it, where Lesray and her soldiers had made their last stand. I limped past a giant, coiled corpse. Lodoss, his armoured plates twisted, blackened, smoking. His flesh burned away. A tiny, headless centipede scuttled past me, snaking along the ground, looking for safety. I let the little lord of Sevorai go.

Lord no longer. He is weak and pitiful now. He will bow.

Lesray had survived. Of course she fucking had. I found her sitting near the head of Lodoss' corpse, on a small rock. She was naked save for a heavy cloak draped around her shoulders. Her skin was smudged with ash and her mask was long gone. The right side of her face was twisted with burn scars and her eye was a roaring flame. She clutched at her side, where Lodoss had hit her, slashed her open, but no blood leaked between her fingers. I saw a fierce orange glow of fire beneath her hand.

She looked up at me, winced at some pain, eyed my stump and my leg. "Is it over?" The melted side of her face barely twitched as she spoke.

I nodded at her. A part of me whispered that now was the time to take my revenge, that she would never be more vulnerable. I ignored it. I was too exhausted to care and no longer sure Lesray was truly worthy of my vengeance. In truth, I don't think she ever was. How much of my hatred of her was truly earned? I had made Lesray the villain of my childhood and attributed so much pain to her, but I think most of that hate should have been aimed at the tutors and at the Iron Legion. And at Josef.

Lesray coughed and flames danced in her throat, licked at her lips. "Did we win?" she asked in a tight voice.

I sagged, leaning heavily on my Source crutch. "After a fashion."

"What does that mean?"

I could have lied, hidden the truth of what I had become. But honestly, I was so fucking tired of lying. Tired of hiding who I was. Tired of everything. So I found my own rock to sit on and I told her the truth. Norvet Meruun couldn't be killed, so we had isolated it, and I swallowed it. I was now the prison for the Beating Heart of Sevorai and would be for all eternity.

Fuck! When I laid it all out before someone else, it seemed like such a monumental task. All time spread out before me in an instant and I knew I would suffer through every damned moment of it.

A Biomancer found us as I explained. The pahht man looked over Lesray's injuries and despaired. He had no idea how to close wounds that gushed fire instead of blood.

She waved him away with a sigh. He looked at my leg next and growled at the back of his throat, which is the pahht way of saying *It's fucked.* He tried to fix it, but the moment he poured his Biomancy into me, something went wrong. He screamed in pain and fell away, his hand withering to a mummified claw. Yes, Biomancy no longer works on me. Too much Necromancy in my blood. Too much death inside of me.

We measured the survivors in the hundreds rather than thousands. So few of us left after everything that had happened. After everything I had done. Everyone was wounded, some worse than others. I watched men and women die, writhing on the rocky ground in agony from their injuries. I saw their ghosts rise, confused and alarmed. I unravelled them before they could get used to their new half-existence, consumed their energy and fed it to my horror. It was pleasing to see the alarm on survivor's faces when I reached out and a ghost became visible and tangible in my grip.

How long did we spend digging survivors out of the rubble? Hours, at least. I helped where I could, using Geomancy to shift earth and rocks, but we found the dead far more often than the living.

Eventually Lesray called me over and asked the question I had been considering for a while.

"How do we get out of here, Eskara?" She shook her head. "I assumed we would fly Do'shan out the way we had come, but…"

But Do'shan lay scattered all about the canyon floor. Whatever magic had held it aloft was gone, and no one but the Djinn had ever understood it anyway.

"How many Portamancers do we have left?" I asked

her.

"Four," Lesray said immediately. "Six including us."
It felt like a strange sort of victory that she remembered my
attunements.

"I've made this trek before," I said. "There is a minor
rift in Dharna, to the north. If we cross Sevorai to its relative
position we can…"

"Mother?"

My heart lurched in my chest. I spun about, desperate
to see her and dreading it at the same time. Sirileth and
Kento both stood before me. Alive! Kento was holding her
sister up, Sirileth's arm over her shoulders. They were both
battered, bruised, dirty, and bleeding. But they were both
alive.

I limped to them then. Sirileth staggered free of Kento
and we met, clutching at each other. With my wounded leg
and whatever injuries Sirileth was suffering, neither of us
could hold up the other and we both sank to the ground. I
didn't care. I sobbed into my daughter's shoulder, tried to
ask her how she had survived. My words came out a gargled
mess and I realised I didn't care how she had survived. Only
that she had. Only that they both had. Sirileth dug fingers
into my back, cried silent tears I felt on my cheek.

I looked up at Kento. I wanted to hug her too, to pull
her down into the embrace. But I couldn't. She wouldn't. She
glanced at me, smiled past her tears, nodded. It was all we
would share. It was unfathomably deficient, and somehow it
was also enough.

Ssserakis stirred within me. It cost my horror a lot to
manifest in my shadow, it was so weak, so drained from the
constant struggle against the Beating Heart. Yet it draped my
shadow over both Sirileth and myself, as close to joining our

embrace as could be. As close to a family as Sirileth had ever had.

"Did we do it?" Sirileth asked. "I mean, did you? I saw the Abominations dying."

I nodded into her shoulder, still not quite able to find my voice. It took me a while to tell her the full story. Sirileth understood, of course. I wonder how much of it she had already guessed. A new Biomancer came and saw to my daughters. They had suffered superficial wounds for the most part and while he tended to any he deemed more serious, Sirileth told me what had happened.

She had formed a kinetic shield around her just as Brakunus hit her. He'd broken two of her ribs according to the Biomancer, but it had saved her life. So, too, had the cliffside collapsing when Do'shan crashed down. Brakunus had been about to hit her again, but he'd lost his balance and Sirileth had managed to use Geomancy to create a rocky sphere around herself that protected her from the worst of the tumbling drop.

Kento, on the other hand, had been so enraged by Brakunus' attack, she'd fought him even as the cliffside fell around them. Her Chronomancy leant her speed the ghoul hadn't been able to match and she leapt over, around, and on top of him as they fell.

What happened to the coward?

I repeated Ssserakis' question. Kento grimaced. "I cut his head from his neck. It wasn't easy. He was very big."

It took a full day to rescue as many survivors as we could. Lesray held the count at just three and a half thousand. Of fifty thousand who had come to the fight. Most were terran, with a thousand pahht survivors, too. Only five of the garn had survived, but then they had been in the

canyon fighting when Do'shan dropped. We spent another
day gathering what supplies we could, then set out.

I acted as guide. I remembered the way we had
travelled from the last time we had made the trip, and if
I closed my eyes and focused on my innate Portamancy,
I could peer between the worlds. We had just six
Portamancers and a lot of people to transport. The trip
to Dharna took us five days of stuttered portal jumps.
Everywhere we went in Sevorai, we saw evidence of our
victory. Rotting Abominations littered the landscape that
had recently been all Norvet Meruun. I imagined it would
take many years for Sevorai to truly recover. Perhaps it never
would.

We flooded the streets of Dharna. Thousands of
wounded soldiers startling the citizens into thinking they
were under attack. It was much changed since my last visit.
The storm had quieted some and though sand was still flung
about in wild flurries, it was no longer so violent to strip the
flesh from bone. I could even see the great bulbous domed
rooftops the city was famous for, though I didn't have long
to study them.

The Dharna militia, a few hundred Polasians, came
to *greet* us, for what it was worth. Lesray met with them,
explained the situation. I'm not sure they really believed her.
Dharna had been all but cut off from the rest of civilisation
thanks to the storm and hadn't even heard of a combined
army of Ovaeris marching to face the demons of the
Underworld. Regardless, they helped with our wounded,
provided food and water, a place to sleep for a night.

I spent that night with my daughters. We drank.
Well, Sirileth and I drank. Kento kept watch and some
distance. She would not betray our true relationship. As

far as everyone else was concerned, the Aspect was simply
keeping a watchful eye. We talked about Tris mostly, that
night. Sirileth and I both cried, grief loosened by alcohol.
We shared stories about him and she told me a few I had
not known, like the time Tris had hidden a dead mouse,
reanimated by Necromancy in Tamura's rooms. He'd
ordered the mouse to wait until Tamura had fallen asleep
and then tickle his feet. Sirileth smiled as she remembered,
but the smile quickly faded. Their relationship had never
been easy, but she had loved her brother. I think that would
be a sentiment many of us would share. Tris had always
made being close to him hard work, always pushing people
away, but I knew he would be missed by many. I missed
him. I will always miss him.

The next day I opened a portal at the minor rift to
take us back to Lanfall. From there, we would report our
victory, and… I realised at that moment, I had no idea what
was next. Yenheim was gone, we still had friends there,
family, but I doubted we would be welcome. Neither would
I be welcome up on Ro'shan. I had nowhere to go.

*That is not true. You have an entire world. We are the last
lord of Sevorai. It belongs to us.*

We went through the portal to Lanfall, just two
hundred of us, and found ourselves surrounded by soldiers
and Source weaponry. I don't think they were expecting us
but fuck them. Surprising people is one of the great joys in
life. No sooner were we through, than Lesray stalked off
to talk to the guards. I saw heated words exchanged, then
fingers pointed my way. When Lesray approached next, it
was with soldiers at her back, and a dark look in her fiery
eye. I fucking knew I should have killed her when I had the
chance.

"Sirileth Helsene," Lesray said officiously. "We're taking you into custody now."

CHAPTER FORTY THREE

A MONTH PASSED. A MONTH OF WAITING FOR the axe to fall. Jamis and Othelia per Suano put us up. Well, they provided me with quite luxurious rooms within Fort Vernan. Sirileth, however, was not so well treated. She was kept under lock and key, stripped of her Sources, thrown in the dungeon, denied visits from everyone, even me. Of course, that didn't stop me.

The first day she was held prisoner, the guards tried to deny me. That first guard collapsed, screaming about spiders crawling under his skin. Apparently he had nightmares about it for weeks. They didn't even question my visits after that and I made sure to visit my daughter once a day.

Sirileth was bored. They gave her nothing to do, and my daughter did not do well with idleness. I brought her books to read, a couple of puzzles I found in the shops of

Lanfall. And I sat and talked to her. I realised, it was the only
time we had just sat and talked without any sort of world-
ending threat dominating the conversation. When she was
young, I was running my queendom and she was a difficult
child to talk to. When I returned after running away, there
was always too much happening, too much to do. So I used
that time to get to know my daughter properly for the first
time. Strange, that it took her looming execution for us to
finally get to know one another.

Kento returned to Ro'shan. It was somewhat easier
now given that the flying city no longer moved. It had been
somewhere over the Lonesome Ocean, between Isha and
Polasia, when Do'shan entered the great rift. Bereft of its
counterweight pushing on it, Ro'shan simply stopped. I
doubted Mezula would be pleased but fuck her and the rest
of our gods. Not like they rallied to help us fight the Beating
Heart.

I met with Othelia per Suano many times over that
month. Jamis wasn't brave enough to come before me, and
I considered that a good idea on his part. Every time I saw
the shit-eating bastard I wanted to both kiss him and cut his
throat. The former desire was not mine and I knew it well
enough to ignore it. The latter, however, was all me. So he
sent his wife to meet with me instead. We got to know each
other quite well. She liked my storm and the way it sparked
between her thighs.

Ssserakis was subdued, still struggling to contain
Norvet Meruun. It got a little easier for my horror every day,
but still took so much of its strength and concentration. It
gorged on the background fear of the city, and I devoured
every ghost that found me. Together, we were enough
to keep the Beating Heart at bay. It took a few days, but

Ssserakis gave me back my claw and began manifesting as a shadowy cloak again. It would take longer before we were strong enough for my wings.

Towards the end of that month, a new summit was called. Qadira and her vast entourage were first to arrive. I'm told their demonships moored a ways up the river by not-so-subtle request. I watched the queen of Polasia arrive from atop the tallest tower of Fort Vernan, where I had once waited for an army to attack. I made sure they all saw me, too, with an impressive display of lightning. It was probably a good job I didn't have my wings because I really wanted to swoop down and knock the dusty bitch from her horse.

Lesray was next to arrive. She came in on a flyer and I purposefully didn't go to meet her. Yes, I'm still petty when it comes down to it. We had fought together, bled together, snatched victory together. But she had also been the one who contrived this whole stupid trial. I would not forget that. She looked well, all things considered. She wore white, always white with her. Her porcelain mask was back in place, covering her flaming eye, and she wore a strange girdle that was rigid and the colour of bleached bone. I guessed it was there to hold in her flames. The air went chill around her, and the ground froze beneath every step. It is not for nothing that the world has come to know her as the Elemental.

Last to arrive was Kento, and she wasn't alone. Much to everyone's surprise, Mezula came with her. It was the first time in over a thousand years that the Rand had left her flying city, so I guess it deserved the importance Lanfall put on it. I caught Kento's eye as she stepped from the flyer and she gave me a sharp shake of her head. Then Mezula slivered forth and everyone was gasping and pointing like they had never seen a god before. Which is fair, I suppose.

It was all such an overblown affair, after that. There was kneeling and praying and idiotic worship. The Merchant Union threw a ball in Mezula's honour, as if the bitch had any. Citizens of Lanfall crowded around Fort Vernan just hoping to get a glance of the Rand. It was infuriating. Suffice to say, I did not attend the ball. I had no wish to pander to Mezula's bloated ego. I spent the time down in the dungeons instead, keeping my daughter company.

Finally, they set the date of the trial, these people who thought they had the right to judge my daughter. It was a formality, really, but they needed to have a trial to make it *official*. You can't just go around executing people in civilised society, especially not dispossessed queens. Sirileth was given time to bathe, and clean clothes before they stood her before her judges. They gave her that much dignity at least. I wore a black dress to match Sirileth's suit, a show of unity from the hated Helsenes.

I tried to assure her it was alright, that we would find a way to prove her innocence, but Sirileth only looked at me quizzically, her darklight eyes burning, and said, "But I'm not, Mother. I mean, innocent. I'm not innocent. I'm guilty of everything they say I am." She shook her head, oddly calm with the decision.

I limped into the council chambers at my daughter's side, leaning heavily on my Source cane because my leg had chosen to ache like someone had taken a hammer to it. The gathered rulers of Ovaeris went quiet at our entrance. I counted a lot of hostile stares, and very few friendly ones. Even the pahht envoy was glaring at me, probably because I'd gotten Ishtar killed. I deserved that. Kento wouldn't meet my eyes. She was stood behind her mother, staring resolutely at the floor. I knew we'd get no help there. She was going to watch as her sister was sentenced to death and do nothing.

Jamis per Suano cleared his throat. He'd recently secured the last few Merchant Union votes he needed and was king in everything but the crown. As we were all in Lanfall, it was his place to be the voice of the council.

"We're gathered here," he said in a dramatic tone, "now that the demons of the Underworld have been defeated, to hold to account Queen Sirileth Helsene."

"She is no queen," said one of the colourfully robed representatives from Tor. "She has no land, no crown, no throne, no people."

A murmur of agreement rippled through the idiots. Jamis waved his hands in the air for quiet, but it took them a while to settle back down. "It was agreed that there would be a trial," he eventually shouted over them. "We all agreed on that. And who better to judge than we who represent those who have been most wronged."

I flicked my gaze to Othelia sitting beside her husband. She met my eyes but gave nothing away. Yes, I'd find no help there, either. It didn't matter how many nights she spent in my bed instead of her husband's, she would vote with him. And he would vote with the union. I wondered if Sirileth would get even a single call for mercy.

"Queen Helsene," Jamis said again, loudly over the rising tumult. "You are..."

Sirileth stepped forward past me and raised her voice. "I did it," she said sharply. She swept her gaze around them all, making everyone in the room stare into her darklight. "Everything you accuse me of is true. I did it all. I killed people, forced them to reject Sources in order to create rifts. I pulled down the moon on Polasia, killed everyone in

Irad. And I tore down Do'shan, too. Killed thousands more who couldn't get away in time. You do not need to debate whether I'm guilty. I am." She shrugged, nodded her head, then smiled briefly. "I'm sorry, you probably wanted to make a grand spectacle of my trial, but there really is no need. Judge away."

Her honesty caught them by surprise, I think. They had been expecting her to argue her case, claim she had done only what was needed. That her actions were justified. They didn't know my daughter at all. She accepted responsibility and took that power away from them. They could still execute her, but now it was only because she let them. I was so proud. But I was still going to wrench that victory from her.

Jamis just about recovered. "Well, yes. Then we will move..."

Qadira poked one of her daughters and the young woman shot to her feet. "I call for a public execution. All of Ovaeris must see that we do not take crimes like this lightly and that Sourcerers can be held to account for their crimes. Especially as their crimes have the potential to be so much more devastating.

"We have all lost due to the actions of this woman. We have lost people, land, money. Polasia knows this better than any because we have lost more than any other." The princess glanced down at her wrinkly mother who gave her a sharp nod. "Sirileth Helsene must be executed so Ovaeris can begin to heal the wounds dealt to it."

The representative from Tor stood next, his colourful robe flapping. "We, the people of Tor, do not typically believe in execution as a form of punishment."

"Funny, that," I said loudly enough my voice echoed

into the council chamber, "because you're not above the odd assassination."

The man raised his hand, pointed at me. "You will hold your tongue, woman."

I let a slow smile spread across my face, shook my head. "No. But if you try to silence me again, I will be holding your tongue."

The chamber burst into noise. I stood by Sirileth in the centre of it, locked my flashing gaze on the man from Tor and didn't let him squirm away.

"Typical, Mother," Sirileth said, smiling. "It's my execution and you still find a way to make it about you."

One of the Merchant Union members got up from their seat, sauntered over to a table with fruit and jugs of wine sitting upon it. Yes, they had provided refreshments this time around. Because it's important, when sentencing a young woman to death, to stay fucking hydrated.

I noticed Mezula stayed silent through the rising clamour. She towered over us, even the garn representative, and her hands were always moving, the eyes in her palms watching us all. Kento stood by her side, her head lowered.

Jamis eventually managed to simmer the gathering down to a low boil so he could speak over them again. It involved lots of hand waving and shouting, and I bet he wished he had a shadow he could flare to startle them all into silence.

"We will not tolerate threats here, Eskara," he said, staring right at me.

I shrugged. "That idiot started it."

"Mother." Sirileth placed a hand on my shoulder, shook her head.

"Just exposing it for the farce it is."

She gave me a sorry smile, then turned her burning gaze back to Jamis. "You can continue." I wondered if anyone noticed that she had so easily, through me, taken control of the proceedings. Claimed an authority over them all. Did she have a plan? Had my genius daughter come up with a plan during her month of incarceration?

It took a minute for the representatives from Tor to remember where they were in their justification of murder. "The people of Tor do not usually believe in execution. But in this instance we are willing to make an exception."

"How magnanimous of you," I snarled.

"In fact, we insist upon it."

They put it to a vote then. A vote. They reduced a woman's life to a bureaucratic charade. The Merchant Union voted in favour of execution. Jamis wouldn't meet my gaze, but Othelia shot me a brief and sorry frown. The garn seemed bored by the whole affair but voted in favour. All three of the pahht envoys added their voices to the call. It became largely symbolic after that, there were still some of the most powerful yet to vote, but we could all see where it was going. Lesray gave a stirring speech about accountability in peace versus in war, then she abstained like the contrary bitch that she is. It was not a vote against, but I could see it was as far as she was willing to stretch.

That left just one voice in the assembly. Probably the most important of them all, I suppose. Mezula. Her vote could shift things. On its own, it did not count for more than any other, but votes could change. She was Rand, one of our gods. Her voice carried more influence than any other. She slithered forward to tower over us, claiming the centre of attention. Her hands darted this way and that, eyes unblinking as they looked upon us all. When she spoke, everyone went silent as the grave.

"There are crimes here far more grievous than the loss of life," she said haughtily, her voice silky smooth. "Sirileth Helsene has done irreparable damage to Ovaeris. She has becalmed Ro'shan in the middle of the Lonesome Ocean. A vital trade hub that has kept nations wealthy and supplied with needed goods for millennia. It will never move again." Two of her hands twisted my way, stared past me at Sirileth. "She has done this by destroying Do'shan. It is a crime far greater than any loss of life. I add my vote to her execution."

I would not let it happen like this. Could not let them kill Sirileth on the altar of public approval. They needed a scapegoat for all the shit the people of Ovaeris had gone through, well they could look fucking elsewhere.

"I ordered her to bring down Do'shan," I shouted into the assembly.

Qadira poked her daughter again. "And by all rights, we should be executing you right next to your daughter. It's convenient that you have put yourself out of reach of that fate."

I turned my flashing stare on the Polasian queen, advanced a few steps towards her. "Convenient? You have no idea what I have sacrificed to keep you all safe from Norvet Meruun." They had been told, of course, of how I had defeated the Beating Heart. I still wasn't sure any of them truly understood. What they did understand, is that they couldn't kill me. I was a prison for a much greater threat, and the moment I died, that threat would be unleashed upon them once more.

Qadira pushed her daughter away and stood on shaking legs to meet me face to face. "You have no voice here, Corpse Queen. This is an assembly for those with land, rule, and power. You have nothing and so you have no say."

The summit was devolving into manic noise again. Put a bunch of kings and queens in a room and they will do nothing but argue about whose crown is shiniest. Well, it was time to silence them all.

I stamped my foot and released a geomantic pulse that cracked the stone beneath me. It wasn't much, really, but it was enough to let them know I could collapse the floor and kill them all. It was enough to silence all the fools.

Do it. We will show them all.

"Queen Qadira raised a good point," I shouted, turning away from the woman to address the entire assembly. "You have to have land to be considered a queen. Well, I have more than any of you. I rule over an entire world."

My shadow bubbled beside me, and Ssserakis and I spoke in one voice. "I am the last lord of Sevorai."

"The Underworld?" one of the pahht envoys asked.

I stared lightning at the man. "If that's what you wish to call it. It belongs to me. Its lands are mine. Its people and its beasts are mine." I sent a pointed glance at Jamis. "Its resources are mine. So, I do have a voice at this assembly. And I *will* speak."

I looked at Sirileth. My daughter met my flashing gaze with her burning eyes and smiled at me. I realised then, she didn't have a plan at all. She was terrified, but was also willing to accept responsibility, even if it meant her death.

So I turned back to the assembly and made my own case.

"Judgement. You seek to judge Sirileth for her crimes as if they are new. As if none of you have done worse. What are her crimes? She has killed people with Sources? So have you, Qadira al Rahal. Would you like to remind us about your Penitent Garden, where you turned people to stone so you could freeze them in their final moments of agony. Such a petty fucking way to remind yourself that you held the power of life and death over them. Without any purpose save your own vainglorious need to dominate others.

"Those who died by Sirileth's hands were criminals and volunteers, and they gave their lives for a purpose. Through their sacrifices, she learned how to reset the great rift.

"The great rift. That was your doing, Mezula. You and the Djinn ripped open a hole in our world and gave the Maker, *your* Maker, a window into Ovaeris, then spent your lives hiding from it like children cowering in a wardrobe from an angry parent. Sirileth saved you from it. Saved us all from a danger our gods created and then hid from.

"And do not forget that Sirileth has also given you the gateways. Using the rifts, she has created a revolutionary form of travel between nations, between continents. Ro'shan may be becalmed, but it also obsolete. Thanks to Sirileth. We no longer need to rely on a flying city for speedy trade. I imagine many of you have already started profiting from the system of gateways."

"She destroyed Irad," Qadira's daughter shouted.

"Yes. She did. A city destroyed. Tens of thousands of lives lost. How many of you here can claim to be innocent of equal crimes? You, the garn, fight endlessly, slaughtering each other in the thousands. How often do traders get caught up in your brutal struggles?

"And let us not forget Polasia. For years you sent mercenaries to Terrelan, to Kadatt, to a dozen other nations to help fight their wars, to destabilise entire continents. How

many cities did your mercenaries sack? How many people
were slaughtered? I have seen the ruins of Picarr, Qadira,
and I know the force that reduced that city to ruin was
mostly Polasian. Hundreds of battles, dozens of wars, do
you really think your hands are cleaner than my daughter's?

"And then there's you again, Mezula. The Rand. Our
gods. How many people have you killed? How many lives
has your eternal war claimed over the millennia? Sirileth
could bring ruin to a hundred cities and still her crimes
would be a drop in the ocean compared to yours'."

It was a weak argument really. One crime does not
excuse another. But I was not trying to get them to excuse
Sirileth's crimes. I knew they wouldn't. Couldn't. It was the
punishment I was looking to change.

"But you are all correct," I shouted into the rising
noise. "What Sirileth has done demands accountability. But
rather than execution. I suggest exile."

The garn scoffed, a blast of oozing spittle flying from
his maw. "Exile? To where?"

Jamis stepped smoothly into the question. "The only
place we could possibly exile her to. The Underworld."

Predictably, the mess of fools started arguing again.
Some were for it as long as it got Sirileth away from their
people. Others, those bastards from Tor loudest of all, kept
pushing for execution. That was how far their vaunted love
of corporal punishment went; even when presented with
another option they still wanted to kill Sirileth. It was fear. I
could taste it. They were scared she would violate any exile
they imposed upon her.

Mezula was the one to bring a sense of order to
the rabble this time. I think she could see the tide turning.
"Unacceptable," she roared, silencing everyone. When a god

shouts, you listen. Of course, when a god shouts, it proves they are anything but. "She is too much of a danger."

And there it was. *Such a sweet taste. Sharper and more real than even yours.*

Mezula was afraid. Scared of Sirileth. I could use that. I stepped towards her. It felt a lot like placing my head in the khark hound's jaws, but I refused to back down. "Scared, Mezula?"

The Rand turned on me so sharply I almost flinched. All six of her hands surrounded me, eyes glaring from their palms.

"I understand. Sirileth brought down Do'shan. What's to stop her doing it to Ro'shan as well? Nothing. Nothing but her morality. Her conscience. But, of course, you wouldn't understand that, would you?"

Mezula slithered forwards slowly. I was forced to limp back a step, lest she crush me. "Do you think yourself above retribution, Terran? Remember who made you. I can still change what I have made."

"Now who's using threats? Go ahead, Mezula, if you think you can. I am not scared of you. Even broken, what's left of me is stronger than you have ever been." I stared at her a few seconds longer, then turned away.

Lursa's Tears but turning my back on a seething god was enough to turn my guts to water. Ssserakis feasted on my fear, plagued me with images of the Rand descending upon me while my back was turned. But I was used to my horror's little visions of terror and knew them for what they were. Nothing but illusions.

"Exile," I said loudly. "To Sevorai. Or the Underworld, if that's really what you insist on calling it. I suggest you all agree. Don't forget, there is a whole new world beyond the great rift, with countless resources and opportunities. If you execute my daughter, I will make sure no one from Ovaeris ever steps foot in Sevorai while I live. And in case some of you haven't heard it yet, I will live a very long time."

Mezula drew herself up on her tail, but Kento was suddenly there beside her, whispering to her. The rest of the assembly started up similar conversations. The possibility of profit from Sevorai piquing their interest. Nothing reveals the false altruism of public service quite like the clink of coins.

Lesray stood slowly, icy calm spreading from her as implacably as the frost creeping around her feet. Quiet fell over the chamber. The bitch enjoyed being able to do that. No one else could silence a whole room simply by standing.

"I wish to change my vote," she rasped in a quiet voice. "I vote in favour of exile." And with that, she sat.

It spread from there. The Merchant Union was next to alter their vote, of course. I was under no illusions it was out of any loyalty to me, or morality over the case I had presented. The union wanted whatever riches Sevorai could give them.

Mezula did not change her vote. Neither did Tor or Qadira. But it didn't matter. The majority voted leniency. Exile to the Underworld, never to return.

In truth, I am not sure I did Sirileth that much of a favour. Her life was spared, yes, but it was a life in a strange, unkind world. Sevorai is a place of muted light, nightmares and dangers. But it is home. My home, as it has always been in some way, and now hers, too.

CHAPTER FORTY FOUR

IT'S DIFFICULT TO JUDGE THE PASSAGE OF time in Sevorai. I often find myself peering through my strange portal sight into the other world, into Ovaeris, and wondering how many days it has been since I was last there. It seems week after week, I find fewer excuses to make the trip.

Othelia tells me a year has passed since our defeat of Norvet Meruun. A year. They pass so quickly when you're an adult, and yet each and every one seems to stretch on forever to a child. In my mind, my childhood lasted decades. Though I sometimes struggle to separate my own memories from those I have absorbed from ghosts and Djinn.

Sevorai continues to recover from the ravaging of the Beating Heart. It is slow. So much of its populations were lost, consumed by Norvet Meruun. Even now, it is a sparsely populated world. The ecosystem struggles to support the larger creatures, or so Sirileth tells me. It's a matter of food chains and biology. Grasses and trees and insects and the like need to recover first, in order for there to be enough food. It makes sense when she explains it. We import a lot of what we need. For now.

Trade has opened up between the two worlds. It is heavily policed on both ends. Sevorai has many resources that cannot be found in Ovaeris. That makes them valuable. Conversely, Sevorai has many things it simply cannot grow or produce. Abban stakes for one. Yes, they remain a favourite of mine, and for the life of me I cannot seem to get a good cacophony of abbans to stay in my world. They mill about endlessly, refusing to eat, slowly wither away and die. It's frustrating. So I import abban steaks. It's a luxury, true, but I am lord of an entire world now. I figure I can take a few liberties.

It is not without its trials. Ssserakis and I fight a daily struggle against Norvet Meruun. She sits inside of me, sulking, brooding, biding her time. She is immortal and can wait for as long as it takes. And all it will take is a single day where either my horror or I lose vigilance. We will not. We cannot.

Some wars never end. Can't end. Some shouldn't ever end. Like the wars we fight with ourselves. To be more, to be stronger, be better. Or the war we fight to survive each and every day. By beating back the hordes snapping at us, tearing us to pieces. Screaming at us to end it. I have fought this war every single day of my life. There is no truce, no reprieve. No end. Every day I strap on my armour to ward away my own hateful thoughts. I pick up my weapons to fight off the depression and anxiety trying to consume me. And I fight. Every day, I fight. I have to. For my friends. For my family. For the people of Ovaeris and of Sevorai. And for myself.

Eternity is a long time.

I have built my new city, my seat of power, close to Yenheim. The approximate location of Yenheim across worlds. It allows me to peer through and keep an eye on Hardt and his children, Tamura and his school. Yes, the crazy old Aspect set up a school. He teaches stories, history. He seems happy. So is Hardt. The big man teaches his sons, looks after his family, looks after others, too. His wife may be the mayor of Yenheim, but it's Hardt people go to when they have problems. I don't get to see them in person as much as I'd like. Yenheim is part of Tor now and I'm not exactly welcome there.

Kento visits when she can. Now Ro'shan is locked in place above the Lonesome Ocean, she is often away from the city, and occasionally finds time to come to Sevorai. She brings Esem with her, too. I've come to accept that Kento will never name me mother, and nor will she reveal to Esem I am her grandmother. I've also come to accept that it's for the best. The world cannot know for they would not treat either of them kindly. It's enough that I get to spend time with my oldest daughter, and enough that I am getting to know my granddaughter. She's a curious little thing, always questioning everything, telling people off when they treat her like a child with their answers. She gets on very well with her aunt.

Othelia visits regularly. More regularly than she strictly needs to. She is technically the ambassador of relations between the Merchant Union and Sevorai, and so needs to come here to maintain and negotiate trade deals. We rarely leave my bed chambers and our negotiations are vigorous. I think Jamis knows. I hope he cares. I hope it burns him inside that she prefers to spend her time with me.

Ishtar is alive. I should have known the wily old cat was too stubborn to die. I have no idea how she survived Do'shan crashing to the earth. I found her wandering Sevorai wearing a khark hound pelt over her shoulders, a blade of chipped bone in her paw. I asked how she had survived. She simply laughed at me, called me a terrible student, and declared I was not the only immortal one. She lives here now, calls herself my advisor though I did not ask her to that position. I do appreciate her council, even if it does always come at the end of an insult.

There are people living in Sevorai. Terrans and pahht, even a few garn. They live close to the great rift, have built a town or two. It takes a special kind of bravery to willingly live in a world of nightmares, but the people of Ovaeris are nothing if not courageous.

Josef finished his pilgrimage at some ruined temple on western Isha. He's taken it over and his following continues to grow, as does his power. They call him the Paragon, the Lifegiver, the Light. Fools worship him like some sort of new god. Worse, his followers occasionally make their pilgrimages into Sevorai. It is some sort of holy journey to them to worship at the home of the Pariah, the Deathbringer, the Darkness. Yes, that's me, apparently. It's all very fucking dramatic. Most of those that come here are idiots though and get themselves killed by the nightmares of my world. Serves them right. Those who do make it to my doors treat me with reverence. They stay until I touch them, as though I'm giving them some sort of blessing, then leave as happy as can be, not a drop of fear on them. Mythology, religion, faith. Diseases, all three. I have no idea what Josef is up to, encouraging such madness. Maybe I'll make a trip to his temple one day, face him down and demand he explain himself. Maybe. The truth there, is that I'm scared to. After all he's done to me over the years, I'm scared to get close to him again.

Speaking of gods, the Djinn finally finished *fixing* Ovaeris. At least, as much as they were willing to. The world is changed. Still ravaged by occasional but violent storms the size of continents. Still broken and more savage than ever before. But liveable. Lazy fuckers, they did the bare minimum to satisfy the terms of our agreement. Worse, they have begun to bring themselves back. It is not a swift process, but they are using the knowledge I gave them, the methods the Iron Legion slaughtered thousands to discover. When I was born, there was just one Rand and one Djinn left in the world, the last of our gods. Now, there are four of each, and more being given rebirth every year. No, I did not end the War Eternal. I gave it new life.

Ghosts continue to flock to Sevorai. They seem to be drawn to the great rift, and once they pass through, they are then drawn to me. I unravel them, consume their memories and their power. It's needed, both to keep Ssserakis strong enough to hold Norvet Meruun at bay, and also to fuel my innate Chronomancy, to keep me from ageing. To keep me immortal. But there's more to it than that.

Necromancy has always been a poorly understood school of Sourcery. As far as I'm aware, I am the only one who has ever been able to unravel ghosts, to give them a final and lasting end. I suppose I see it a duty of sorts. Poor things don't deserve the eternal half-life that death inflicts upon them. So I devour them, take their power, give them peace. It makes me feel… like I have a purpose.

It can get confusing, though. I have so many memories inside of me now. So many that aren't mine. Sometimes, I'll remember a toy I had as a child, or a lover I once bedded, only to realise that it wasn't me at all. I fear I'll lose myself in the memories of others one day.

Bah! Dramatic tripe, I know. I do fear the day one of my friend's ghosts finds their way to me. I know it will happen. I hope it is not soon.

Ssserakis and I grow closer every day. Though, that's not quite right. At times, I feel like the barrier between us is breaking down. We are not one person, not truly, but neither are we two separate people anymore. It's more complex than that. I am Eska, and my horror is Ssserakis, but together we are something else. Together, we are the Corpse Queen.

And that leaves Sirileth. Sirileth is… bored. There is not enough for her to do here in Sevorai. Not enough puzzles for her to solve, not enough trouble for her to cause. And there is something else. Sevorai is mine. And Sirileth does not want to live in my shadow, she never did. She wants her own life, her own adventures. Her own legacy. She does not realise what she asks for but knows that she won't find it here.

And so Sirileth plays with portals. The Maker showed her that other realms exist, and I don't think my daughter will ever be happy until she figures out how to inflict her darklight upon them.

Belmorose said that history is made by unsung heroes but is written by braggarts. I used to laugh at that, but now I see the truth behind it. The people of Ovaeris call the battle we fought *The Corpse Queen's War*. The war is only a year behind us and already they have shaped a fiction around it to suit their desires.

The stories tell of the mighty Queen of Ice and Fire who slew a serpent as large as a continent. Of Oporo, the garn battle master who faced down a falling mountain and survived. Half a dozen others, too, most of whom I couldn't pick out of a crowd. None of the stories mention Tris Helsene, who gave his life fighting against a monster who had slain an army.

And none of the stories, at least not those spoken of fondly, mention me. The Corpse Queen is never hailed as a hero. Her sacrifices are only told as greedy snatches of power away from more deserving hands. Her battles depicted as struggles against much greater heroes who she had to trick to defeat. The Devourer of Souls. The Bogeywoman. The Darkness Come Calling. Yes, that is how the world I was born to remembers me. Not as a hero. Only ever the villain.

...

I am the fire and the flood. The earthquake and the hurricane.
I am pestilence and war. Famine and ill omen.
I am the shadow come in the night to steal your children from their beds.
I am Eskara Helsene. The Corpse Queen. Mother of nightmares and Lord of the Underworld.
I am Death.

Books by Rob J. Hayes

The War Eternal
Along the Razor's Edge
The Lessons Never Learned
From Cold Ashes Risen
Sins of the Mother
Death's Beating Heart

The Mortal Techniques novels
Never Die
Pawn's Gambit
Spirits of Vengeance

The First Earth Saga
The Heresy Within (The Ties that Bind #1)
The Colour of Vengeance (The Ties that Bind #2)
The Price of Faith (The Ties that Bind #3)
Where Loyalties Lie (Best Laid Plans #1)
The Fifth Empire of Man (Best Laid Plans #2)
City of Kings

It Takes a Thief...
It Takes a Thief to Catch a Sunrise
It Takes a Thief to Start a Fire

Science Fantasy
Titan Hoppers

Science Fiction
Drones

Lightning Source UK Ltd.
Milton Keynes UK
UKHW012305130123
415317UK00006B/98/J

9 781915 440075